STARDUST

★

STARDUST

★

A NOVEL BY

NAN RYAN

DONALD I. FINE, INC.
NEW YORK

Library of Congress Cataloging-in-Publication Data

Ryan, Nan.
    Stardust.

        I. Title.   II. Title: Star dust.
    PS3568.Y392S74   1988   813'.54   88-45422
    ISBN 1-55611-106-1

    Manufactured in the United States of America

        10 9 8 7 6 5 4 3 2 1

For all the old Dallas gang,
"Those were the days my friends . . ."

OUTSIDE, the pre-dawn February temperature hovered at a chilly twenty-five degrees in Dallas, Texas, but inside the black Rolls-Royce Corniche, automatic dual-level, year-round air conditioning kept the roomy interior a comfortable seventy.

Laura, lids low over dark, dark eyes, head resting against the hand-tailored upholstery of carefully matched Connolly hides, uncrossed her long, slender legs as the big, powerful car turned off Preston Road and swung onto Beverly Drive. Unconsciously nipping at the fleshy inside of her cheek with sharp, punishing teeth, Laura planted both booted feet on the carpeted footrest, took a deep, slow breath and tightly clutched the lone, long-stemmed red rose.

Fifty yards ahead, before a vast gateway of grilled iron, a crowd had already gathered, though it was not yet seven and Musicland would not open to the public until straight-up noon. They had been there for hours, some since the night before. Newspaper reporters and magazine correspondents and the Japanese television camera crew. And hundreds and hundreds of ever-faithful fans clamoring to be among the first inside the hallowed grounds on this cold winter day.

Screams filled the quiet morning as the shiny Rolls was spotted by the shivering, patient throng. The big car crawled to a cautious stop directly before the locked Music Gates.

"This House Was Built on Rock and Roll," proclaimed a large brass plaque stretching across the tall iron bars.

Laura steeled herself against the loud, excited shouts of, "It's her! It's Laura Kay! Laura Kay! Can you see her? What's she wearing? Is she crying? Is Caroline in there? Laura Kay, Laura Kay, open the window! Get out and say hello."

Laura automatically hunched slender shoulders upward, thrusting the lush, wide collars of the dark Russian sable more closely about her face in a turtlelike gesture. A policeman's whistle sounded shrilly and a loud, authoritative voice called, "Move back. Watch the car. Step aside and let 'em through."

The Music Gates clanged open. The limo rolled through and onto the long pebbled drive toward the big white mansion, while mounted police, wielding nightsticks and megaphones, kept the crowd at bay. The Music Gates closed electronically behind the Rolls and Laura let out a small sigh of relief.

In seconds the big chauffeur had stopped the car before the lighted mansion and had swung open the heavy rear door. Laura stepped out into the funereal cold morning, the blood-red rose still clasped securely in her hand. From out of nowhere two tall, muscular men flanked her. The mute trio did not go up the steep marble steps of the imposing white Georgian house. Instead, Laura and the two bodyguards walked toward the carefully manicured oval of grassy ground between the mansion and the iron fence.

There at the very center, upon a slightly raised berm, a huge, fifty-ton, hand-chiseled monument of shimmering, gold-flecked, white marble shown pale pink in the rapidly rising sun. A giant guitar; the mammoth monolith had for its strings heavy chains of twenty-two carat gold, a bridge of platinum, and tuning pegs set with diamonds. The rosette was banded in rubies, while from the depths of the round sound hole an eternal flame flickered in the cold winds.

Laura stepped alone to the shiny marble monument. Her companions— eyes ever alert, ears attuned—took up positions at a respectable distance, hands crossed before them, powerful .357 Magnum revolvers resting in smooth, oiled-leather holsters beneath their topcoats.

Laura, heels of her suede boots ringing resoundingly on the cold marble, walked across the huge stone sounding board and knelt to the eternal flame. Soft sable coat pooling about her, she laid a gloved hand upon the deep grooves of the carved letter C. She traced the graceful curve with a forefinger.

THE CHIEF

Written on the huge monument: The Chief. Nothing more. No birth date, no date of death, no survivors. It wasn't necessary. The whole world knew that the Chief was C.C. McCarty and that he was born on February 16, 1936, and died tragically at age thirty-nine on September 21, 1975.

"Only a couple more years," Laura softly promised the man entombed beneath tons and tons of white marble. "Two more years and they will never set foot inside the walls again. You will rest in peace, Chief."

PART ONE

★

CHAPTER ONE

HE BURST upon the music world with the sudden energy and heat of a shooting comet. Overnight, adoring fans screamed his name in a frenzy while the handful of powerful heavyweights controlling the multibillion-dollar record business cynically predicted young C.C. McCarty's flaming talent would burn itself out as rapidly as a doomed meteor. The kid wouldn't be the first to streak across the heavens, commanding every eye, lighting up the firmament in a blaze of glory, only to crash to earth, spent and blackened.

And promptly forgotten.

Eighteen-year-old Texan C.C. McCarty skipped his high school graduation exercises from Crozier Tech in West Dallas. It wasn't that C.C. didn't pass; he made straight A's. He couldn't afford the five-dollar rental fee on the required cap and gown.

At twenty C.C. had a local hit record, a brand new '56 Chevy convertible, and mobs of teenage Dallas fans, mostly female.

At twenty-one he had a shrewd, deal-making, New Orleans-based manager, a high six-figure record contract, a new mansion in the prestigious old Highland Park section of Dallas, and millions of fans across the entire United States who, because of his dark, Comanche, good looks, dubbed him "The Chief."

At twenty-two the young, smooth-voiced, multimillionaire heartthrob had a half-dozen gold records, a fleet of expensive automobiles, a Montenegrin villa, and worldwide recognition. And he became a husband, much to the chagrin of his fans.

At twenty-three he was a movie star, dividing his time between his beloved Musicland Mansion in Highland Park and RKO studios in Holly-

3

wood, the frequent travel made easier by the acquisition of his first jet airplane, complete with two pilots on call twenty-four hours of the day. That summer, C.C. became a father.

When he turned thirty, his clever, strategy-minded manager abruptly cut his boy off from personal appearances, withholding from a frantic, panting public, their handsome, worshipped idol.

At thirty-five he made a triumphant appearance at a desert pleasure palace and the C.C.-starved world was once again at his feet. Never had the Chief sounded or looked better. Sold-out crowds streamed into Circus Maximus, the big, ornate showroom of Caesar's Palace, two hours before the dinner show curtain, flashing C notes at the tuxedoed maître d' for choice seats.

Backstage in his flower-choked dressing room, an anxious C.C. McCarty paced restlessly, lifting his wrist every few seconds to look at his watch. Beefy Buddy Hester, C.C.'s right-hand man, grinned and shook his sandy head.

"C.C., you're going to wear out the carpet."

C.C. paused. "Bud, it's been a long time since I stood before an audience." Plucking at the sharp creases of his elegantly tailored tux, he dropped down into a chair. Absently stroking the star birthmark on his dark left cheek, he said, "It's like I'm still a scared kid from the West Dallas projects."

The time in Commerce, Texas, was five minutes past 2:00 A.M. on Sunday, February 16, 1936, when a baby boy was born to Ernest and Gracie McCarty. The mother—seventeen years old, pretty, dark-haired, one-quarter Comanche Indian on her father's side—had lost a child at birth a year earlier. The father—twenty-two, tall, light-haired, soft-spoken and shy—earned only a meager salary doing janitorial chores at East Texas State Teachers College and he blamed himself for his young wife losing their first child. He'd not had the money that would have allowed the slim, fragile girl the complete rest and doctor's care she had needed during pregnancy.

Gracie had kept her job in a laundry; standing over hot, steaming ironing boards through ten-hour workdays. It had been too much for her. The baby, a girl, had come prematurely and lived but a few short hours. When, not three months later, Gracie found herself pregnant again, Ernest McCarty insisted she do nothing but guard her health and wait for the birth of their child.

He landed a second job—taking tickets at the town square's movie theater each night—and the extra money he earned made it possible for young Gracie to quit the laundry.

Gracie, groggy, exhausted, but very, very happy, looked now on the face of her newly born son. He was beautiful; lots of jet black hair, round pretty face, button nose, and Cupid's bow lips. And on his left cheek a tiny dark birthmark; a perfectly shaped, five-pointed star.

Ernest McCarty, ever attuned to his wife's feelings, misread her interest in the small imperfection. "Now, Gracie, that don't amount to nothing. Just a birthmark; likely it'll get lighter as the years go by." He smiled reassuringly and patted her gowned shoulder.

Gracie's eyes never left her baby. A radiant smile curved her mouth as she put a slim forefinger to the infant's soft cheek. "Clifford Clyde McCarty," she addressed her sleeping son, "the angels kissed you, honey. Kissed you right on the cheek because you're a special little boy. I know you are. Your Daddy knows you are. You're very, very special."

There was never any doubt in Gracie McCarty's mind that her only son was indeed special. A prettier, sweeter child never lived than Clifford Clyde, and he was a constant source of joy to his poor but proud young parents. One of the few sources of joy in their hard lives. Ernest McCarty's modest salary provided only the necessities of life; none of the luxuries.

The family lived in a small, aging clapboard house below the railroad tracks in one of Commerce's poorest sections, known as "The Hollows." Low-lying, with inadequate drainage and few improvements, the Hollows was a breeding ground for mosquitos and vermin in the hot, muggy summertime and a loblolly of mud and standing rancid water after a rain. In winter, winds whistled across the barren dirt yards and streets and in through the wide cracks of crumbling walls and broken windowpanes.

Gracie, far too sweet-tempered and kind to complain to her husband about the dismal place where blacks and poor whites lived, grew to hate the Hollows after the birth of Clifford Clyde. Her beautiful son was a special child. He deserved a better home.

As even-tempered as his pretty mother, agreeable young Clifford Clyde had no idea he should be anywhere else. He was a healthy little boy who lived in a house filled with love and laughter. A bright child, he liked to listen to the radio and by the time he was three was singing along with Bing Crosby, much to his mother's amazed delight.

Little more than two months short of Clifford Clyde's sixth birthday, the Japanese bombed Pearl Harbor and Gracie was terrified that her husband would be called away to war. Ernest didn't wait to be called; he rushed down to volunteer, feeling a strange sense of excitement. Here was a chance to change his life, to be somebody. Maybe he could get into the Air Force, train to be a fighter pilot, see the world, and send money home to his pretty wife to buy all the things he had never been able to give her.

Ernest McCarty was 4-F.

It was the janitor's job for him while the rest of the nation's virile young men marched away to glamour and excitement and hero worship. He hid his disappointment and smiled when Gracie tearfully threw herself into his arms and told him she was glad, glad, glad he wasn't leaving her and Clifford Clyde.

The first day of school was a challenge for Clifford Clyde, a heartbreak for Gracie. It was the very first time, since he had been born, that her son was parted from her. The short hours seemed agonizingly long to her. Every day she walked Clifford Clyde to and from the schoolhouse across town, reluctantly leaving him there with other boys and girls on the playground, all dressed noticeably better than her boy.

She fought the frustration that threatened to consume her. All her life she had had to make do, pinch pennies, and "wait 'til next year," and she didn't mind that. But she resented miserably that her special son, the idol of her life, should be denied the good things. The beautiful things. The expensive things. It wouldn't always be that way; it couldn't. Clifford Clyde would have better. He had to.

Perceptive, Clifford Clyde knew his mother. Though she was sunny and sweet, and often laughing, he sensed a sadness in her. Time and again he would give her a big hug, point to the star birthmark on his left cheek, and repeat what he'd heard her say over the years. "Mama, the angels kissed me because I'm special, and I'm going to be rich someday and buy you a new house and pretty dresses and everything you want."

When Clifford Clyde was nine, the war had ended, the United States the victor, and the nation was headed for prosperity. Gracie thought surely fortune had finally smiled on her own little family when Ernest was offered a better-paying job over in Dallas, sixty-five miles to the west. A cousin who had worked at the Trailways Bus Company for more than ten years told of an opening there. The position was cleaning out the buses, but the pay was half again as much as Ernest made at the college. Would Ernest be interested?

Not a week later the McCartys boxed up their few possessions, said good-bye to relatives and neighbors, and boarded a Trailways to Dallas. The three of them stayed in the small home of Cousin Billy McCarty, the Trailways employee, until they could locate a place of their own. They found a house a little larger than the one they'd left in Commerce—a room of his own for

Clifford Clyde—with big shade trees lining the narrow street. Gracie McCarty was ecstatic.

Ernest's new job was dismal and thankless. Careless travelers threw orange peelings on the floor of the buses, left sacks of chicken bones, and dropped peanut shells between the seats. And Ernest had to clean it all up. He hated the work.

But he had been on the job only a few months when he found a smooth, black leather wallet under a seat in the back of one of the buses he was cleaning. An honest man, Ernest looked inside for identification. There was none. But there were three crisp twenty-dollar bills. It was nearing Christmas. Sixty dollars could make it a very merry one. Ernest pocketed the cash and tossed the wallet into the trash.

The McCartys had a Christmas tree that year with icicles and shiny red balls and angel's hair. And presents. Ernest told Gracie that the company had given him a bonus. She never questioned it. She clasped her hands together and exclaimed, "We'll order Clifford Clyde a guitar from the Sears catalog!"

It was the best Christmas the three had ever had. Young Clifford Clyde was picking out tunes on the new Sears guitar within weeks and singing along in a clear baritone voice that his mother recognized as "special." Life could not have been better.

It didn't last.

The winter of '47 was a bitter one in Dallas and Ernest McCarty caught a cold he couldn't shake. It worsened into pneumonia and Ernest wound up in the hospital, a very sick man. He spent three weeks there before he was well enough to go home. The doctor ordered another month of bed rest and Gracie McCarty was forced to take in ironing to put food on the table. Clifford Clyde helped out too. He washed dishes in a bar-b-que place after school and dutifully laid out his money on the kitchen table when he got paid. But the two of them together, Gracie and Clifford Clyde, did not make as much as Ernest had made at the bus terminal. Times were hard. Food was scarce. The McCartys fell behind with the rent.

They left the little house on the tree-shaded street and moved to west Dallas and the barren, treeless quadrangle lined with barracklike buildings known as "the projects." They were still there when C.C.—he'd announced on his twelfth birthday that he would no longer answer to Clifford Clyde—entered high school. Money was still short. Ernest was still a beaten man. Gracie was still hoping for a better life for her rapidly growing son. C.C. was still a sweet, obedient boy who loved his Mama, went to church every Sunday, and listened attentively when Gracie

McCarty explained that he was growing into a young man and that he would soon catch the eyes of the young girls.

She indicated, with her husband silently nodding his agreement, that C.C. would encounter two very different kinds of females. Those who were ladies and those who were not. Ladies were to be treated with the same kind of respect he always showed his Mama. The other kind were to be avoided. It was a lesson repeated many, many times through his formative years.

C.C. was certain he had it all clear in his mind. For the time being all he was interested in was playing his guitar and singing. He lived in the ideal place for that. When the weather was warm, the neighborhood folks sat out on their porches in the evenings and sang. C.C. always joined in. The McCartys were one of the few white families living in the projects and often as not C.C.'s young face was the only white one in a sea of blacks. He learned their music; their intonation, their inflection, their soul.

It would one day make him rich.

A true son of old Mother Texas, C.C. stood an impressive six foot three inches tall by the time he was sixteen. The slim young giant was the idol of his proud, adoring parents, and many were the moments that both Ernest and Gracie would listen in astonished wonder while their appealingly shy, towering young son strummed his beat-up guitar and sang, solely for their benefit, in a uniquely rich and pleasing baritone.

C.C. was yet to possess a man's body to go with his man's voice, but he was strikingly handsome to his mama. Thick, rich hair as raven-black as his Comanche ancestors, eyes a deep, sultry brown, his smooth, suntanned skin had just a hint of copper. The star birthmark had grown as his face had grown and had not dimmed in color. It was a deep, almost black, discoloration that only added to his good looks and was, C.C. would find out later, an intriguing mark to women. And his smile? Why, it was blinding, brilliant . . . sunshine itself and it warmed his mother's heart each time he flashed it on her. And he flashed it on her often.

Never would Gracie have let anyone know, especially not her tall, spare son, that she felt decidedly younger than her thirty-three years and somehow embarrassingly giddy when C.C. would tap the star birthmark with a lean forefinger, wink at her, and say in that low, drawling voice, "Mama, the angels kissed your baby boy and I'm gonna be a star. And no matter how famous and rich I become, you'll always be my only girl."

The statement was not entirely true. There were presently, in his junior year at Crozier Tech High, three females who played major roles in his young life. His mother, of course, was the most important of the trio.

Connie Rae Hopkins, a fifteen-year-old sophomore, had long honey-blond hair worn in a bouncing ponytail, big blue eyes that sparkled unceasingly, an outgoing, cheerful personality, and a giant-sized crush on dark, good-looking C.C. McCarty. Adorably cute, but studious and intelligent, Connie was—C.C. was certain—a "nice" girl. He brought her to his home to meet his mama. Gracie McCarty was enchanted with the sweet child and reminded her son, after Connie had gone, that he was to be a gentleman at all times with the pretty blonde. He assured her she need not worry.

Gail Bradford, the music teacher at Crozier Tech, had been at the school only one year. A divorcée from Fort Worth, Gail, twenty-seven, slender, dark-haired, slightly aloof, had a master's in music from respected North Texas State, an ear for talent, and a genius for drawing out her students' abilities.

The first time she heard C.C. McCarty sing, Gail Bradford felt a flutter of excitement tighten her chest. Never had she heard a male voice with quite the same sensual richness as was coming from the dark youth seated at a scarred desk in the back of the room. With her skilled ear Gail was able to shut out the other forty-seven young voices and hear only C.C. And she was quick to ask that he remain behind after the others had rushed out into the hallway when the bell rang.

"You're a very talented young man, C.C." She smiled up at him.

"Thank you, ma'am," said an embarrassed, but pleased, C.C.

"I'd like to help you, if I can. Do you play an instrument?"

Proudly, shoulders lifting; "Yes, ma'am, I play the guitar."

That very afternoon Gail Bradford drove C.C. home in her white Ford convertible. Gracie McCarty smilingly welcomed the teacher into their spartan, spotless apartment, and C.C., after introducing the two women, went immediately to his after-school job at Bailey's Hardware on Wheeler, two blocks away.

Serving Gail Bradford coffee and beaming with unabashed pleasure, Gracie listened attentively while the teacher, slim legs crossed, eyes magnified slightly behind her wire-rimmed glasses, sat on the worn davenport and softly exclaimed that the McCartys had a very talented son and that his talent must be nurtured at all costs.

The word "costs" made Gracie's bright smile slip. "Mrs. Bradford," said Gracie, despairingly, "I'm afraid we haven't . . . There's no money for . . ."

"No, no, you misunderstand," assured the cultured teacher. "It will cost nothing. Nothing. I know a great deal about music, Mrs. McCarty. Your son has a gift and I wish to help him realize his full potential. I'll give him

private lessons every day after classes . . . free lessons. It's the least I can do."
Gail Bradford smiled engagingly.

Gracie's brow knit. "C.C. works at the hardware store, but I suppose . . ."
her voice trailed away. Gail Bradford sipped her coffee. Gracie McCarty
smiled suddenly. "He'll just have to quit that job. His music is the important thing."

"I wholeheartedly agree," replied a calm Gail Bradford. Gail stayed for
another half hour, drank more coffee, and talked quietly with Gracie on
Gracie's favorite subject in all the world. C.C. McCarty.

At supper that night Gracie announced that C.C. must quit the hardware
store. C.C., knowing how badly the family needed money, quickly protested, but Ernest McCarty sided with his wife.

"We'll get by, son." He clasped C.C.'s shoulder. "You learn all you can
from that teacher, you hear?"

"Alright, Daddy."

"Such a fine lady," added Gracie McCarty. "Now you pay attention and
do exactly what she tells you to do, C.C." She shook her finger in his face.

"I will, Mama."

Life fell into a very pleasant pattern for C.C. Each day after the other
students had gone, he stayed an extra hour at the school, singing and
playing his guitar in the music room for Gail Bradford, while she listened
and instructed and suggested and praised. When the hour was up, he'd dash
home, ravenously eat a quick supper—chicken fried steak, mashed
potatoes with gravy, and buttermilk biscuits, his favorites—then sprint the
eight blocks to Connie Rae Hopkins's house. The pair would sit on the
porch in the autumn moonlight and impatiently wait for the living room
lights to go out so that they could share kisses in the night shadows.

Long, sweet kisses that left C.C. burning and disturbed his sleep.

The private music lessons had been going on for more than a month. On
a muggy October day Gail Bradford stopped C.C. in the crowded school
hallway and told him, her high brow creasing slightly, that the school piano
was badly out of tune. Would he mind having their daily session at her
home? She had a fine grand piano, perfectly tuned, little used. She wanted
to teach him some new chords.

"Sure, Mrs. Bradford," said C.C., always decisive. "How far is it?"

Gail Bradford smiled. "You'll ride with me. After last bell."

"Yes, ma'am."

CHAPTER TWO

C. WAS waiting in the passenger's seat of Gail Bradford's shiny white Ford when she came down the cracked cement steps of the aging brick schoolhouse. He watched the tall, slender teacher approach, a sheaf of sheet music in one hand, purse in the other. She was clad, as usual, in severely tailored clothes and her hair, an unremarkable shade of brown, was tightly wound into a French twist at the back of her head. The wire-rimmed glasses sat firmly on her small, straight nose, magnifying wide-set hazel eyes.

Studying her, C.C. thought that the only attractive part of her face was her large mouth. Wide and full-lipped, it didn't fit the teacher's cool, sedate demeanor. But, then, neither did the high, bouncing breasts she could not entirely conceal beneath her somber clothes.

Gail Bradford reached the car, abruptly looked up, saw C.C., and as though she'd forgotten she had invited him to wait, shook her head, stepped from the curb, circled the Ford's gleaming hood and slid in under the wheel.

"C.C.," she said apologetically, "I'm sorry, I completely forgot."

"If you've got something to do, Ma'am, I sure wouldn't want . . ."

"No, no. I haven't. Truly." And Gail Bradford smiled at him. "Shall we put the convertible top down?" Her myopic eyes were on his face.

"That would be nice," said the dirt-poor kid who had never in his life ridden in a convertible automobile. In moments the white canvas top was folded into itself behind the back seat and bright October sunshine flooded the Ford's supple, red leather interior. Gail started the car and they drove away.

Eyes on the street, she said, "Get us some music, C.C."

11

C.C. leaned up, flipped on the radio, and with one dextrous finger spun the dial to 1190, fifty-thousand-watt KLIF. ". . . Must I forever be a beggar, whose golden dreams will not come true . . ." Tony Bennett's clear, resonant voice torched out his latest hit.

"Sing along," urged Gail Bradford, eyes never leaving the road.

". . . Or will I go from rags to riches, my fate is up to you," crooned C.C. and Tony.

"It just might be," murmured Gail, turning to look directly at C.C., green eyes behind her glasses twinkling ever so slightly. Before he could respond, she, too, began to sing and C.C. joined her.

Before the record had completely finished, KLIF's afternoon deejay's deep, deep voice rose up as the music faded. " 'Rags to Riches' by Tony Bennett. Tony's got a great big hit here in Big D this perfect autumn of '53. Keep that dial set on the 'mighty 1190' where we play all the hits . . ."

Another record quickly filled the airwaves and C.C. McCarty leaned back his dark head and accompanied Clyde McPhatter and the Drifters as they wailed "Money Honey." Gail Bradford nodded approvingly and cast appreciative glances at the smooth-voiced boy whose bent knees were wide apart, long arm resting on the back of her seat, lean fingers drumming out the beat on red leather, dark eyes closed with feeling.

C.C. was surprised when, the tune ending, he opened his eyes and saw that they were turning into the projects. Coolly, Gail Bradford explained. "I thought perhaps your mother might like to join us."

C.C. moved his arm from the seat. "Sure. A good idea."

Gracie McCarty was all eyes when Gail Bradford stopped the Ford before a charming green-shuttered white cottage at the end of a heavily wooded lane in Oak Cliff. Inside, she tried to mask her curiosity, but Gracie had never been in a home quite so fine. Small but elegant, Gail Bradford's leased house was much like the woman herself, immaculate, orderly, private.

The white front door opened directly into the living room where hardwood floors gleamed with mirror-brightness. Before a high-manteled fireplace a formal, blue-and-white-striped, silk-covered sofa faced two, high-backed wing chairs of blue velvet across a low oak cocktail table resting on an area rug of palest blue wool. Oak bookshelves lined the wall beneath framed watercolors, and sandwiched between two of the book-filled cases, a television set, its cabinet doors folded back revealing the thirteen-inch screen, caused Gracie to murmur, wonderingly, "Oh, my goodness."

The room's back wall was entirely of glass. An imposing black walnut grand piano sat at an angle to the room. From the long bench, the artist could look upon the room's seated guests or outdoors at the big redwood-fenced backyard. Beyond the sparkling clean glass, a white porch swing was shaded from the sun and farther out, on the rapidly browning grass, sat padded lawn furniture of pale blue.

"Have a seat, Mrs. McCarty," Gail Bradford invited and Gracie gingerly sat down on the striped silk sofa, unconsciously running an inquiring hand over the shimmering fabric. C.C. noted the wistful expression on his mama's face and his heart hurt. How she would love to have a home like this one with fine things and even a television. One day she would have a place just as grand or grander. Somehow he would see to it.

The teacher disappeared into the kitchen. Presently she returned carrying a small round silver tray with three tall, frosted glasses of ice tea. She placed the tray on the low cocktail table and urged the McCartys to help themselves. Gracie sipped the tea slowly. C.C. drank his down in two long pulls. Gail never touched her glass.

All business, Gail strode to the piano, took a seat on the bench, uncovered the ivory keys, and motioned C.C. to pick up his guitar. Eyes squinting thoughtfully behind her glasses, Gail struck a chord, identified it for C.C., and ordered him to play it on his guitar. Again she struck the chord. Again he echoed it.

Two hours later, Gracie McCarty sat squirming on the sofa, eyes darting again and again to the glass-domed clock on the mantel. She was tired and her head ached and she wanted to go home. She had thought listening to the pair practice would be enjoyable, but the serious-minded music teacher had not allowed C.C. to sing so much as one song the whole afternoon.

Instead Gail Bradford had drilled him mercilessly on complicated chords, insisting he repeat them over and over. The only singing he had been allowed was the running up and down the chromatic scale. The exercises, Gracie was sure, were beneficial to C.C., but repetitive and boring to listen to.

She could hardly hide her relief when Gail Bradford abruptly ceased playing, stood up, and announced authoritatively, "That's enough for today, C.C. Tomorrow we'll go over these same exercises again. It will take two or three days, perhaps a week, before we're ready to move on." She rubbed her stiff neck.

"Yeah," C.C. agreed, almost apologetically, "I haven't quite got the hang of it yet."

"You will," assured Gail Bradford. Then to Gracie "Mrs. McCarty, I think he's doing fine, don't you?" She ushered the shorter woman to the front door and out into the gathering dusk.

"Real fine," murmured Gracie, smiling politely.

"Mama said she's not coming with us today," C.C. informed Gail Bradford when they met at her parked Ford the next afternoon. "Said she was just in the way."

Gail Bradford didn't seem surprised. "Then it's straight to my place?"

"I guess so."

It was hot on the ride to the cottage. The convertible's top was down. A glaring Texas sun beat on the unprotected pair. C.C. felt the back of his cotton shirt sticking to the red leather upholstery. He glanced at the prim teacher. Her face was shiny and wisps of wilted hair, escaping from the drooping French twist, were clinging damply to her slender neck.

Heat was coming up from the brick pavement, thermals rising in shimmering, shape-distorting waves as the white Ford crawled down traffic-clogged Jefferson Avenue past the Texas theater. *Houdini* held over for an extra week. Next door at Taylor's Drug, the after-school crowd, hot and thirsty, rushed in for Cokes and ice-cream sodas, sweaters, pulled on in the cool morning, long since shed.

Gail braked the Ford at a red light. She glanced at C.C. His tanned throat and long arms were gleaming with sweat, the white cotton shirt sticking to his chest and shoulders.

"Hot, C.C.?"

C.C. gave a low whistle. "Sure am. You too?"

"You have no idea." She smiled at him in a way that made the muscles in his stomach contract sharply.

Inside the cottage it was a few degrees cooler, but still uncomfortably warm. Gail Bradford saw C.C. casting hopeful glances at the window air conditioner.

"We can't have the air while you sing. It's not good for your throat." She tossed her handbag and sheet music atop the grand piano. "There are other ways to cool down. Get yourself a Coke and I'll change." C.C. looked puzzled. Mrs. Bradford had never changed her clothes before.

Gail started toward the bedroom and, almost as an afterthought, said, "Take off your shirt, C.C. See if that won't help."

C.C. hesitated, shrugged his shoulders, and unbuttoned the shirt. Bare-chested, feeling a little foolish, he went into the small, cheerful kitchen. He jerked open the Frigidaire and helped himself to an ice-cold Coke. In one long swallow, he emptied the bottle and ambled back into the quiet, warm living room.

Hands shoved down into his Levi's pockets, he was standing, his back to the room, looking out at the fenced rear yard, when he heard Gail say softly, "Ready to begin?"

Slowly he pivoted. And blinked. And blinked once more.

Mrs. Gail Bradford, his music teacher, a lady he had never seen in anything but sensible skirts and blouses and suits, was wearing a tight white T-shirt and a pair of skin-tight white short shorts. Barefooted, she stood smiling at him, that wide, soft mouth stretched appealingly upward.

Methodically, she removed the pins from her upswept hair. The brown tresses came tumbling down and Gail shook her head around and combed her fingers through the light locks. Smiling, she sat down on the piano bench.

Speechless, C.C. took up his guitar and raised the strap over his head. Gail began to play. And as she gently stroked the black and white keys, she spoke in a low, soft voice, a hint of a mysterious smile still touching her lips, "Know what I do when it's hot and I'm here alone, C.C.?"

"No Ma'am."

Gail continued to play softly, eyes closed, leaning forward, shoulders lifting with feeling. The song ended. She rose and, holding his gaze, peeled the tight T-shirt up over her head and off, dropping it carelessly to the gleaming hardwood floor.

"I take off my clothes when I play the piano," she stated calmly and unzipped the tight white shorts. Thunderstruck, C.C. stared, unbelieving, while she wiggled out of her shorts. They slipped to the floor; she stepped free of them.

Totally nude, Gail sat back down and began playing. In a voice as tutorial as ever, she instructed, "Alright, now A sharp should follow . . ."

C.C. tried his best to pay attention. To listen. It was impossible. A naked woman was sitting not six feet from him in this over-warm room and he could hear nothing but the pounding of the blood in his ears.

Gail Bradford continued to play and to instruct. She never looked at C.C. She gave the healthy young man plenty of time to leisurely ogle her. She issued commands for him to play. He did not obey.

Presently she rose and went to him. Wordlessly, she lifted the guitar strap over his head and carefully placed the instrument on the piano bench, taking her time, her movements slow and sensual. C.C. stood, hands at his sides, staring at her, his dark eyes wide.

"I play better naked, don't you think, C.C.?" He said nothing. He didn't know what to say, what to do. She did. She lifted her hands to the low-riding waistband of his Levi's. Speaking softly, seductively, she said, "Don't you want to be naked with me, C.C.? It feels so good. So free."

"I . . . I don't need to be that free," mumbled the frightened young man, but he put forth no effort to stop her from undressing him.

"Yes, you do," said Gail. Smiling, she urged the fly of his worn Levi's apart, slipped the very tips of her fingers inside the elastic waistband of his white jockey shorts and, looking directly into his dazed, dark eyes, pulled the underwear away from his hot, flushed skin. Slowly she lowered the shorts down his flat brown belly until the head of his rapidly swelling masculinity burst out.

C.C. groaned aloud.

Gail smiled and lifted a hand to her mouth. While C.C. held his breath, she put out her tongue and licked her forefinger. He felt light-headed and weak. She popped the finger into her mouth and sucked it and C.C. felt his knees start to buckle. Wet and gleaming, the slim finger came out of her mouth and moved down, down, while his dark, startled eyes and her hazel, knowing ones followed its languid descent.

Gail placed the moist finger on C.C.'s naked pulsating cock and a strangled breath broke from his tight throat. She toyed with him, drawing wet, warm patterns upon the head of the jerking, rigid rod and then slowly, teasingly she slid the finger down its center . . . all the way to the base. And she smiled triumphantly as stunned confusion gave way to total arousal in the dark, hooded eyes looking down at her.

She gave him a playful little squeeze, took her hand out of his shorts, and said sweetly, "Want to take off your pants and come to the bedroom with me?"

Naked and perspiring, he was inside the blue-and-white bedroom by the time she got the sheets turned down. He pulled her to him, snatched off her wire-rimmed glasses, bent and kissed her hotly, hungrily, feeling as though he was literally on fire. His heart speeded out of control when he felt her bare breasts, belly, and thighs pressing insistently against his inflamed body. Roughly, he shoved her down to the bed, pushing her forcefully onto her back. Gail Bradford obligingly spread her legs wide apart and flung her slender arms up over her head.

"Take it, C.C.," she invited and he did.

He fell upon her with a pent-up hunger that nearly frightened—and thoroughly excited—the sophisticated woman. She gasped in awe when he thrust deeply into her, stretching her with his hot, eager fullness.

He was youth and beauty and purity.

He was violent and greedy and artless.

After no more than half a dozen deep plowing pumps, he exploded in a wrenching, shuddering climax and collapsed atop her, panting and gasping for breath. She lay beneath his slick, hot young body and smiled; unsated, but fulfilled. She knew there would be many afternoons when this sexy young stallion would satisfy her hunger. She had only to teach him how.

Gail kissed C.C.'s sweat-dampened right shoulder and gently urged him over onto his back. Laughing softly, she took the eyeglasses he still clutched in his hand, put them on, and said, "Jump in the shower, C.C., we've work to do."

"I can't move," was all he could manage, but at her insistence, he agilely rolled up from the soft bed and followed her into the bathroom.

"No, lovey," said Gail when C.C., freshly showered, came back into the living room and picked up his discarded Levi's. "Don't put on your clothes. We'll practice naked. You'll be surprised how much it will improve your playing. And your singing."

"You got to be kidding," C.C. objected.

"I'm not joking. Trust me, lovey," and, unashamedly nude and completely at ease, she sat down at the piano. Never again did the pair wear clothes for their music sessions.

"Yes, that's it, C.C." Gail would encourage as he stood naked in the sun-splashed room, eyes half-closed, singing with provocative, raw emotion. "Your voice has a new sensuality, a new excitement. You're vulnerable and responsive and it comes through in your phrasing; a caressing of the words, the added sensitivity."

C.C. would grin and admit to her, "It's just that when we take off our clothes I want to make love."

"I know, lovey, and it makes you sing better. It always will. Whenever you perform, you'll feel like you're as bare as we are now." She smiled and rose from the piano. "And because you feel sexual, you'll make the audience feel sexual. What a success you'll be; the females in the audience will feel like you're making love to them."

He never doubted her. "Won't their boyfriends and husbands get mad?"

"No. They'll reap the benefits and thank you for it." She touched his birthmarked cheek. "Let's go to bed. I'll teach you to be a polished performer there, as well as on the stage."

Lying on his back, an arm folded under his head, C.C. listened while Gail Bradford ran her fingers through his crew-cut dark hair, over his smooth, hairless chest, along his rib cage and well-muscled belly, and told him of how she would make him an expert lover.

"You have expressive eyes, C.C.," she murmured. "They're the first thing I noticed about you. The dark, beautiful eyes and that interesting birthmark." She leaned down and kissed the dark star, teasing at it with her tongue. "And your voice, of course. The first time I heard you sing, I knew I had to go to bed with you."

"You serious?"

"Very. You'll have the same effect on hundreds of women and we don't want them to be disappointed, do we?"

He looked hurt. "You're disappointed in . . ."

Her mouth stopped his words. She kissed him into silence, then went on, as though he had not spoken. Placing a caressing hand on his groin, she toyed with the warm, soft flesh, the crisp, raven hair. "This, my love," she cupped him possessively, "is as important as your voice and you must learn how to use it with the same controlled expertise. I can show you how and I will. For instance . . ."

And Gail's voice would be low, breathless, ". . . and this is the tickle spot on me, C.C. No, no, up a little, lovey, and . . . yes, yes, . . . oh, that's it . . . caress me gently . . . easy, easy . . ." Other times it would be C.C. pleading, rasping ". . . let me put it in now . . . aaaah, don't, Gail, I can't stand it . . . Jesus, Jesus . . . with your mouth . . . ummm . . . my, God . . . what are you doing to me . . ."

Rapidly C.C. learned how to please a woman and he took great pleasure in his accomplishments. So did his teacher. Within weeks Gail Bradford hardly recognized her lover as the young, inexperienced boy that had jumped on her that first afternoon and promptly spilled himself in her. Ever conscious of her feelings, the ardent young man now took his solicitous time arousing her to a fever pitch.

There were sex-hot afternoons when Gail was afraid he had learned his lesson too well, days when she felt herself becoming more and more excited, felt as though she would surely go crazy and tear him to pieces if he didn't stop toying with her and bring her to climax immediately.

After the uninhibited loving sessions, the spent pair would lie on Gail's rumpled bed and talk quietly. Gail knew how to draw him out and within weeks C.C. McCarty was telling her things he'd never told anyone else. She said she knew he had to take a lot of razzing from the boys at school because he didn't go out for sports. Why didn't he tell them his reason? That he was afraid of injuring his hands and not being able to play the guitar.

He said he didn't figure he owed them an explanation and she kissed him affectionately because she liked his answer. Liked his courage in handling obstacles in a casual manner. Liked him for never feeling sorry for himself when he might have. Liked him because he vowed he would get out of the projects one way or the other.

And he liked her. Liked her immensely, although he was positive she was exactly the kind of woman his mama had warned him about, had told him to avoid. He didn't care. Gail Bradford was a lot more exciting than any "lady" he'd ever known.

And more honest. She told him she decided to seduce him the first time she heard him sing. Said, yes she had slept with several men, but he was the youngest, the only schoolboy. Said she loved his dark, strong body and would always love him in a special way. Told him she had been married twice. Widowed once—he had left her a little money. Divorced the second time—he was boring and stingy. No, she would never marry again. She wanted to do as she pleased, when she pleased, and what pleased her most right now was to spend her days with him.

C.C. told her his fondest dream was to make lots and lots of money and buy a big Cadillac, load his parents in it, and head right up onto the Houston street viaduct, speed across the Trinity River, and pull up before one of those fine mansions in Highland Park and say, "Mama, Daddy, this is our new home."

"You'll do it one day, lovey. Wait and see."

After a time, Gail told C.C. that women didn't always want to make love in the same room, the same bed. They enjoyed the wildness, the spontaneity of a man loving them in different locations as well as different positions.

In answer, he quickly undressed her and urged her out the back door. He took her in the porch swing . . . with it swinging to and fro. The next day they copulated on the blue padded lawn furniture. Later on the lawn.

The weather turned and they made love on the blue wool rug before a crackling fire. And in the hot, steamy shower. Atop the kitchen table. Upon the piano bench. And back in the bed.

In a matter of months, C.C. McCarty changed from a rather backward boy to a self-assured young man who could charm attractive women with a minimum of effort.

Gail persuaded him to perform at a school assembly one cold February day just after he had turned seventeen.

C.C. played his guitar and sang Johnny Ace's "Help Me Somebody," and every female wanted desperately to help him. He cast a powerful spell over his audience. The young kids didn't understand what was happening to them. They were stimulated and nervous and excited. C.C. did nothing but sing the song. The unleashed fire was in his deep, resonant voice and dark, humid eyes. He stood perfectly still, never once moving his lithe, sensual body.

Gail Bradford was in the audience that day. She knew exactly what was happening. C.C. had let his thoughts float free; he was gloriously naked, making love to his audience. The strong, sexual message transferred itself to the kids.

It was a power that would remain with him throughout his career.

CHAPTER THREE

L ET me loan you the money." She stroked the bare, brown back of the lean young male stretched out naked on his stomach.

C.C. never opened his dark eyes. "No, Gail."

"But lovey, it's only five dollars. There'd be no hurry to pay me back and . . ."

C.C. abruptly flipped over and reached for her, pulling her down onto his smooth chest. "Graduation exercises mean nothing to me, Gail. Honest. I need no cap and gown to know I've completed my high school studies."

She gently scolded. "You've too much pride, C.C. I want to do this and . . ."

"I said no." He was adamant.

Gail sighed. C.C. had grown up in the year and a half she had known him. The realization filled her with possessive pride, and at the same time made her melancholy. At eighteen he was a man and soon, she knew, she would lose him completely. Already she was sharing him with young, pretty girls who screamed and sighed and threw themselves at him when they heard him sing.

Far too wise to mention it to him, Gail found herself trying harder to please, to excite, to hold him. And she knew, even as she lay locked in his strong arms, that the bliss she had found with her beautiful young Comanche was too dear to last.

"Sorry, lovey," she whispered. She took a shallow breath and couldn't stop herself from saying, "You're graduating from high school. Do you want your diploma from me as well?" She felt her throat constrict. She was asking if it was over between them. If he was finished with her as well as with school.

21

C.C. kissed her. Against her mouth he said, "No, I want you to go right on teaching me forever." He bit her bottom lip and murmured, "Give me a lesson, teacher. Show me. Show me, Gail."

Grateful, relieved, Gail Bradford smiled and slid down to kiss his throat. She knew he was sincere; he honestly believed that he would never want to leave her. She knew it was only a matter of time. She'd make the most of it. For him. And for herself.

Against his warm, clean-smelling chest she murmured, "I've nothing new to show you, C.C." She licked a wet, hot line down over his ridged belly. His reaction was immediate and involuntary. Gail Bradford sighed happily and slid lower. She lifted her head. Playfully she blew a warm breath on his pulsing erection. Then, looking into his eyes, she put out her tongue, licked her lips wetly and let her gaze drop to his straining masculinity.

And she asked permission. "May I?"

"You may," Valentina Trent coolly gave permission. The muscular black giant nodded his closely cropped head, peeled the covering white sheet from her bare prone body, and placed both huge dark hands on her pale back. Thumbs at the base of her neck, he rotated them in slow, pressing circles.

"Mmmmm, Davy, that's delicious," purred Valentina, eyes closed, head turned to one side, cheek resting on the sheet-draped table.

It was very warm in this large upstairs exercise studio. Valentina purposely kept it that way. She had chosen this particular room at the back side of the mansion for its eastern exposure. There'd been only a half-dozen small windows before she had remodeled. Now floor-to-ceiling glass, wrapping around two sides of the large corner room, allowed bright, morning sunlight to penetrate even the far reaches of the all-white sanctuary.

Valentina called it her gym. She never actually exercised, but she told herself that if she perspired, exertion was unnecessary. So she covered the floor with deep white carpet, painted the walls the same colorless ivory and left the gleaming glass undraped. She had a huge square tub of white Italian marble installed, moved in a couple of white velvet chaise lounges for catnaps and relaxation, and had a long flat massaging table built to specifications—tall enough so that the six foot six Davy Thomas did not have to stoop over to reach her with his magic, soothing hands.

When the studio was still in the planning stages, she had summoned Davy to the mansion, called him into the spacious living room downstairs, and ordered him to stand before the builder she had engaged for the project.

Facing Davy, Valentina unceremoniously placed a hand on the tall black man's taut abdomen and brashly searched beneath his belt buckle for his navel.

Locating it, she pushed a forefinger into the small indentation, smiled and issued instructions to the baffled builder. "Get out your measure, Mr. Anderson. I want the table to reach exactly to Davy's belly button."

And it did.

The rectangular table, fashioned of fine polished pecan and cushioned with smooth, vanilla leather, measured six feet in length, three feet in width, and stood four feet six inches high—to Davy Thomas's navel. Stairs were required for Valentina to mount her custom table, which she did each morning at precisely 8:00 A.M. Handing her white terry robe to Della, her maid, Valentina, totally naked, climbed the steps and stretched out on her stomach. Della draped a fresh white sheet over her, meticulously folding it so that it covered the plump white body from shoulder blades to the backs of her knees. Satisfied her mistress's modesty would be preserved, Della quietly retreated.

At exactly 8:05, Davy Thomas, his gigantic frame swathed in spotless white—clean white T-shirt stretching across his muscular chest and powerful arms, white cotton slacks molded over slim hips and huge, sinewy thighs—silently entered the room, his white rubber-soled shoes making no sound on the deep white carpet. He crossed to the custom-built massage table, paused three feet from it, and stood, unspeaking, huge hands clasped behind him, until Valentina acknowledged his presence by saying, "You may."

Only then did the massive twenty-eight-year-old black masseur step forward to peel away the covering sheet. Valentina enjoyed the morning ritual immensely. Some of her most satisfying moments were spent lying naked in this warm white room while Davy's big black hands masterfully kneaded the stiffness and fatigue from her bare white body.

It was a wonderful way to begin each new day. While he rubbed and stroked and kneaded, she often began work, issuing commands to her office staff downtown via the white telephone at her elbow. On more than one occasion she had, from her studio, finalized an all-important record deal with a coveted recording artist that Bluebonnet had been religiously courting. She liked to jokingly boast that she had signed up some of her biggest stars while she lay wonderfully naked beneath a handsome black Goliath.

Valentina was in no mood to mix business with her massage on this particular May morning. She felt lazy, delightfully so, and wished only to lie and relax and enjoy to the fullest this good life she was privileged to lead.

While Davy's firm hands moved down to her waist, Valentina sighed happily, rose to her elbows, and rested her chin in her hands.

Beyond the sparkling wall of glass before her, a lush green carpet of grass sloped gently down to a willow-hung brook, the back boundary of her ten-acre estate. It was a vista that never failed to please her.

Purposely she had had all fruit trees removed from the grounds. She forbade her gardener to plant any kind of shrub, tree, or vine that bore any kind of bounty. It was not that she didn't like to eat both fruits and vegetables, she most assuredly did. But she never wanted to see a limb hanging heavy with peaches or pears or plums. She bridled at the notion of row upon row of watermelons or cantaloupes or onions.

Or oranges.

If she desired fresh pineapple or mangos or red bell peppers, she had them within the hour. They came from the same place as the porterhouse steaks and Chambord preserves and Montrachet. Simon David's. The specialty food shop on Inwood Road took the order on the phone, promptly filled it, then sped through the traffic across town to her White Rock mansion.

No, there would be no fruit trees or vegetable vines on her beloved estate. But lying naked now in the spring sunlight, watching the tiny beads of diamond dew evaporate from the emerald blades of grass, she reflected, as she had so many times, on other mornings much like this one, when she was a child and all that she could see, in any direction, was row upon row of watermelons or cantaloupes or onions. Or cabbages or lettuces or tomatoes.

Or oranges.

CHAPTER FOUR

W ANT an orange?" The pretty fourteen-year-old girl swept sleep-tangled blond hair back off her face and looked remorsefully at the frail boy standing quietly in the kitchen doorway. There had been nothing in the house to eat but oranges for the past forty-eight hours. Now there was only one of those left and it was beginning to shrivel.

"No, Linda," the child shook his dark head and smiled at his older half-sister. "I'm not hungry. You eat it." His large, gray eyes were those of a boy far older than his nine years. He inclined his head toward the room beyond the tiny kitchen where they stood in the warm May sunlight. "She not home yet?"

Linda shook her head, frowning. Seeing the deep sadness in the big eyes fastened on her, she brightened at once. "She'll be back. Don't you worry."

"I hope she never comes back," said the boy resolutely, shoving small pale hands down into the deep pockets of his worn jeans and biting his bottom lip.

Linda hurried to him. Cupping his dark head in her hands, she pulled the pale little face against her chest and felt a pair of small, strong arms grip her tenaciously. And she soothed this sad half-brother who was still too young to fully understand how the mother they shared cared so little for them that she thought nothing of leaving them alone for days at a time with no food in the house and no money.

Linda had faced it long ago. Their mother did not love them. At least not enough to properly care for them. For as long as she could remember, Linda had played the role of parent to the troubled dark-haired half-brother whose father had left when the boy was three months old, never to be heard from again. It had been much the same with her own father. Riley Shaw had stayed a few months past Linda's third birthday and Linda could recall little about him.

There had been too many men in between and years ago male faces and voices and bodies had ceased being distinctive. Every type man imaginable had spent nights under their south Dallas roof and Linda had seen and heard things no impressionable fourteen-year-old soon could forget. She was no longer shocked by any of it, but she was saddened that the big-eyed boy clinging to her was now old enough to realize what their mother was.

"Mama will be back, hon." She rocked him back and forth. "When you get home from school this afternoon, she'll likely be here waiting for us."

The boy lifted his dark head, nodded forcefully, and gave his big sister a bright, forced smile. "I know she will." He pulled from her embrace. "You better get dressed; we'll be late for school."

Linda beamed down at the boy. "Wait and walk with me?"

"Sure."

"Good, I'll hurry." She dashed from the room, calling over her shoulder, "Eat it, hon. Eat the orange."

He picked up the orange. Holding it loosely in his right hand, the child opened the door off the kitchen. His mother's bedroom. Empty now in the May sunlight, the bed was unmade. Nylons were draped across a stool before the vanity. On the cluttered dresser stood bottles of bright red nail polish and Tabu perfume and a jar of Pond's cold cream and an open box of dusting powder, the big white puff left outside the square gold-and-white box. Movie magazines lay scattered on the floor next to an ashtray filled with stale cigarette butts and a half-empty package of Chesterfields.

The boy gritted his teeth. His mother did not smoke.

He laid aside the orange and took from his wallet a cracked black-and-white snapshot. Fondly, he stared at it.

A young man with sandy hair, a wide, infectious grin, and aviator's goggles swinging from his sunburned neck looked up at him. His daddy. Mitchell F. Rawley. Mitch, they called him, his mother had said.

He would have to take her word for it; he couldn't remember his daddy. His daddy had left them. And he didn't blame him one bit. It was his mother's fault, all her fault.

The child carefully placed the cherished photograph back into his wallet, jerked up the orange, and whirled about, retreating. He rushed through the narrow shotgun house and out onto the sloping wooden front porch. He hated his mother. Hated her!

He knew what she did back there in that room behind the kitchen. He had awakened too many nights, in the room he shared with his sister, to the sound of masculine voices carrying through the thin walls, men saying dirty things in the darkness. Had heard his mother's giddy laughter and her sighs and moans.

His mother was no good. His beautiful, sweet-smelling, black-haired mother was no good. She was a . . .

"Ready, Ryker?" Linda's voice shook him from his painful reveries.

He squinted up at her. Linda was tall and slim and cheerful and pretty. And good. Her long, honey-blond hair haloed her small face in the brilliant sunshine. Her faded dress was clean and ironed and smelled of fresh air. She helped him with his lessons, cooked his meals when there was food in the house, washed his clothes, played games with him, and never, ever, left him alone.

The skinny boy grinned at this sister who called him Ryker. She had given him the nickname. Only to her was he Ryker. Everyone else called him Charles. Charles was his name, but he hated it. He liked Ryker. Liked it because she had given it to him.

Ryker loved Linda. She was all he needed. His world was alright as long as Linda was in it.

The pair swung down off the porch. He held out his hand to her. It bore the orange. "Don't you want it, Linda?"

"No. No, I don't."

"Me neither. I hate oranges."

She laughed and it was music to his ears. A soft, lilting, wonderful sound that warmed his boy's heart.

"Give it me," ordered Linda and Ryker complied. She took it, wound up her arm like a major league baseball player, and threw the shriveling orange as far as she could while her adoring brother clapped and laughed delightedly and jumped up and down.

Winking down at him, she dusted her hands together dismissively and said, "I shall never eat another orange for as long as I live."

"Me neither!"

The room was hot and noisy and full of rock and roll and people were sweating and drunk.

Sitting next to C.C. in the cavernous nightclub was Buddy Hester, a brawny, ruddy-faced boy from the neighborhood. C.C.'s best friend from high school, Buddy was a tender-hearted, good-natured boy whose only personal taste of glory had occurred on the gridiron at Crozier Tech High. At twenty—Buddy had failed a couple of times back in grammar school— he stood an even six feet and weighed an impressive two hundred and fifty pounds. Sandy-haired and "so ugly he was cute," Buddy had fists the size of small hams, a deep, massive chest, an enormous neck, twinkling hazel eyes, and a nose many-times broken. And he wore an habitual smile that made him appear to be missing the jack, queen, king, and ace.

Buddy's sentences were frequently punctuated with deep chuckles, and his reaction to most things, good or bad, was to shake his sandy head, grin widely, and exclaim loudly, "Shitfire!" He loved hamburgers from Civil's drive-in, girls with big breasts, and telling corny jokes.

An uncomplicated, big, happy youth. Buddy was happy that he had managed to graduate from high school. Happy he had found a job on the loading docks at Central Freight Lines. And happy that C.C. McCarty was his best friend. In the six months since they had graduated, C.C. had become a Dallas celebrity. To Buddy's delight, the limelight hadn't changed C.C.

Buddy lifted his foamy glass of beer, took a long, deep pull and glanced over at his friend. C.C. was nervous. Buddy could tell. C.C. was always nervous when it was almost time to perform. Buddy understood; C.C. had explained that it was a lot like when he, Buddy, was playing football and time came for the big game. That made sense to Buddy, so he kept real quiet at moments like this. There'd be time for fun and girls and raising hell after the show.

". . . and this will be his fifth performance. Welcome him back to Lou Anne's Club," boomed an amplified voice. "A big round of applause for C.C. McCarty!"

The bright spotlight left the announcer, swung swiftly to a table below left-center stage, catching C.C. as he rose agilely from his chair. Screams and whistles filled the big nightclub as he made his loose-limbed way up to the stage, spotlight moving with him.

"Chief, chief," came excited chants from young girls who had heard their new teen heartthrob was part Comanche. "Let me be your squaw, chief," they screamed while he stood silently before them, every teenybopper's dream in a pair of charcoal gray slacks with pegged legs, a soft, pastel pink, long-sleeved shirt making his bronzed skin appear darker than ever, and the lone, hothouse red rose Gail Bradford had sent tucked into the buttonhole of his breast pocket, adding a sensuous splash of scarlet. Raven hair carefully clipped in a stylish crew cut, dark, liquid eyes slowly sweeping about the vast room, full beestung lips fixed in an appealingly arrogant pout, C.C. mentally prepared himself for the performance.

While the small combo behind him vamped, he let heavy eyelids slide closed and allowed his thoughts to drift back to Gail Bradford's Oak Cliff living room. He was standing there, naked, bare feet apart, chest and belly and legs warmed by the sun spilling through the plate glass. He could feel a slow, pleasing heat envelop him.

C.C. lifted a long, pink-sleeved arm, opened his sultry eyes, and gave the band a downbeat. "I'm your lover man," he sang seductively and the crowd burst into hysterics.

Ponytailed girls screamed and cried and dug long pink-painted nails into their flushed cheeks. They stomped and clapped and murmured his name. And some broke free from boyfriends and hurled themselves toward the stage. They were stopped by off-duty policemen hired especially for C.C. McCarty's engagement.

Buddy Hester shook his sandy head and muttered a barely audible "Shitfire!" He never failed to be amazed at the crowd's reaction to his friend. All C.C. did was stand there perfectly still and sing, yet the girls were acting like somebody had put Spanish fly in their Cokes. And after the show there would be dozens of pretty girls fighting to be C.C.'s for the night.

Buddy was not a very intelligent young man, but even he could see that C.C. McCarty wielded a potent power over his audience. Buddy squinted up at the tall, handsome singer, puzzling over it. But not for long. Buddy never pondered on anything for long. It never occurred to him that C.C. McCarty, with his talent and power, might become a hugely successful show business star and leave him behind.

His thoughts did not go beyond midnight. At midnight the show would end and C.C. would need him to run interference while they dashed for the safety of Buddy's old blue '49 Chevy. Buddy was glad to do it for him: C.C. was his best pal.

C.C., long, bronze fingers clutching the microphone, crooned slumberously, ". . . and then we'll have good lovin' all night . . ."

Before him a sea of young female faces wore an ever-changing kaleidoscope of expressions. Awe. Worship. Adoration. Shock. Fear. Happiness. Pain.

And hunger.

C.C. took it in stride as much as any eighteen-year-old kid from the projects could. He was thrilled, naturally, that he could hold and sway his audience so easily, just as Gail had told him he would. From that first night last summer when he'd jumped up on stage and sang a couple of songs over at Jimmy's Club on Mockingbird, he had received this kind of reception. And it hadn't been long before he had started getting paid. The Toro Club in Oak Cliff. Dewey Groom's Longhorn Ballroom down off Industrial. Fitzgerald's on Maple. The Penguin over in Fort Worth. And Jack's out off the Mansfield Highway. Dottie's Chatterbox.

He was in demand and it was sweet, so sweet. For the first time in his life he had a little money in his pocket. The clothes he wore were brand new and he had moved the family out of the projects to a pleasant little white house on a quiet street off Kessler Parkway. Green shutters, a backyard, a room of his own, flowerbeds for his mother—a real home. He almost had the down payment on a car and if things kept going the way they were, he could soon quit the daytime job at Bailey's Hardware and devote himself full time to his music.

". . . and you'll get all I got, baby," he suggestively concluded, voice rich and low and sensuous.

Thunderous applause swept the giant hall and the enamored females pulled their hair and jumped up and down, firm breasts bouncing under fuzzy lambswool sweaters, colorful crinolines flashing beneath full circular skirts of felt and corduroy. They squealed and sobbed and pleaded for more.

"Chief, I love you! Chief, please, please . . ." screamed sexually excited teenagers, longing for this youthful symbol of male virility to give to them what he had promised in his closing song.

Amidst the mayhem, at a checker-clothed table to the right of the stage, one female was not on her feet. She sat relaxed and unmoving in her chair. She did not shout. She did not scream. She calmly placed her gold cigarette case inside her black satin evening bag, snapped the bag shut, reached for her gloves and allowed her attentive companion to drape a long, silver fox stole about her shoulders.

But once she was inside the darkened back seat of her silver-gray Fleetwood Cadillac limousine, and the powerful car was speeding up Greenville Avenue toward Loop 12, she began to chuckle naughtily. And to slowly slide the black satin skirt of her tight, figure-hugging sheath up sheer stockinged legs. Laughter bubbling from her parted lips, the fair-skinned, auburn-haired woman peeled off a pair of black lace briefs while her startled escort stared transfixed and swallowed hard.

"Neil," said the sole stockholder and chairperson of Bluebonnet Records, dangling the wispy garment before the nose of her baffled vice president, "I've found Bluebonnet's next superstar." She lowered the window and tossed the bit of dampened black lace out into the foggy November night. "C.C. McCarty made me wet my pants."

"Valentina Trent!"

CHAPTER FIVE

WHITE Rock Lake glistened brilliantly in the fading April sunlight. A breath of wind stirred the placid water, sending lazy ripples across the calm surface to lap at the western banks. Shadows lengthened rapidly as dusk approached. The warm, humid air began to cool. Budding trees whispered softly in the gentle breeze.

The imposing white mansion on the lake's peaceful east shore blazed in the dying sun. Every wide gleaming window became a reflective mirror of orange flame and the iron lightning rod atop its tallest gable a glittering incandescent spear, lifting to ignite the very heavens above.

Everything gleamed inside as well. Freshly polished silver and sparkling clean crystal and glistening chandeliers. Waxed wooden bannisters and tabletops and doorframes. Glossy marble entry floors and sculpted statues and ornate fireplaces.

Valentina Trent's opulent White Rock mansion was all decked out for a gala spring party. Dozens of blood-red roses had been delivered from florists' hothouses and artistically arranged in cut crystal vases, their pleasing, seductive scent sweetening the air in all the spacious, high-ceilinged downstairs rooms.

At least, all the rooms save one.

The aroma of tempting foods filled the big, spotlessly white mammoth kitchen with its porcelain countertops and long worktables and tall refrigerators. Fresh baby shrimp, flown in from the Gulf earlier in the day, boiled atop the stove in a huge aluminum vat. The Maine lobsters to follow. Tender chunks of aged beef simmered in a thick wine sauce. Fillets of palice, poached gently in cider, awaited the thick mushroom sauce that would turn the European flounder into a delicacy fit for the most finicky palates.

31

Fragile pastries baked in the ovens. Thick rich cream toppings would be added at the last possible moment. Crisp vegetables and fresh fruits from the downtown farmer's market, delivered after 6:00 P.M., had been washed and scraped and sliced and arranged on porcelain serving platters. Vintage wines had been brought up out of the cellar, dusted, and chilled or left at room temperature as prescribed.

Great tins of Beluga caviar would shortly be spooned into deep silver pedestal bowls; the chopped egg, diced onions, lemon slices, and thin triangles of toast arranged on accompanying silver trays. Magnums of Dom Pérignon chilled in icy splendor deep down in silver buckets.

Messiuer Jacquez Carondelet, a noted New Orleans chef, had flown in earlier in the week to plan the party menu, place food orders, and oversee all preparations. He stood now—white chefs hat slightly askew, bushy black mustache twitching inquiringly—tasting a rich sauce made of cream, egg yolks, and cognac. He savored, smacked his lips thoughtfully, then swallowed slowly, a wide, satisfied grin spreading over his round, swarthy face.

Upstairs in the master suite, Valentina Trent also wore a satisfied smile. Reclining in her sunken tub of smooth ivory marble, body submerged in rich perfume-scented suds, head resting on a bath pillow, eyes covered with cotton squares soaked in witch hazel, Valentina sighed lazily.

And smiled.

She smiled because tonight . . . and positively by tomorrow in her downtown office suite . . . she would have the young, handsome C.C. McCarty snared securely in her trap, never to be free again. It had taken brilliant orchestration on her part, but then, wasn't she an expert strategist? Hadn't she learned early in life that people were pawns to be moved about, taken, or swept right off the board?

Or knighted, if she so saw fit.

But all, even the knighted, were to be controlled and manipulated, not the other way round. There were two kinds of people in this world. The buyers and the bought. She had been both and she far preferred being the buyer.

Valentina's lazy smile slipped a bit. She would have to be very, very cautious with C.C. McCarty. She was the buyer; he the bought. That's the way she wanted it to remain. She could not allow their roles to ever reverse the way hers had with the powerful Kirkland Trent all those years ago.

The smile returned.

She needn't worry; C.C. McCarty was not as clever as she had been. In truth she was never the bought; she was the buyer from the beginning. She had only allowed Kirkland to believe that he had bought her.

Valentina laughed aloud.

Even then, when she was an uneducated eighteen-year-old and Kirkland Trent a wealthy sixty-two-year-old tycoon, she had been the real manipulator, he merely a pawn to be moved and taken and swept right off the board.

In downtown Dallas servicemen on furlough had lined the soda fountain at H. L. Green's on that sweltering July day in 1944. Overhead, a slow-turning ceiling fan stirred the hot, muggy air while from the jukebox the Andrews sisters sang "Don't Sit Under the Apple Tree With Anyone Else But Me." Two gray-haired ladies in summer shirtwaist dresses and straw hats ate chicken salad sandwiches in a booth on the far wall. An anemic-looking young mother, crying baby in her right arm, took a large bottle of Syrup Pepsum from the shelves and made her way to the cash register.

A month past her eighteenth birthday, Valentina Jones—she had discarded the Perez her first week in Dallas—auburn hair tied up in a snood, white apron covering her skirt and blouse, placed a tall chocolate soda on the counter before a youthful sailor, favoring him with a full-lipped smile.

She felt like smiling at everyone. This was to be her final day at H. L. Green's on Elm Street. Thanks to Neil Allen, she would start her new job at Bluebonnet Records come Monday morning. And after a couple of weeks in her new position as receptionist, she could give Neil the brush and enjoy her freedom again.

It wasn't that Neil was a bad sort. Actually, he was nice enough and terribly smart and not all that ugly if one could overlook the protruding Adam's apple and the Clark Gable ears. Neil's eyes were a soft shade of brown and he had straight teeth and a good complexion. Dating him these last three months had not been all that distasteful. Except for the sex.

In bed he was as repugnant as Johnny McNeill had been back in the orange groves of the Valley, and she would never have agreed to sleep with him if he hadn't promised that he would make it worth her while. He said he could introduce her to rich record stars, that he held a lofty position at Bluebonnet Records and counted among his closest friends many of the industry's most impressive names.

He had not been entirely truthful. He did work at Bluebonnet, but only as an errand boy. He knew no stars, no recording artists, no big names. He did, however, know the president and sole owner of the privately held Bluebonnet Records. The powerful Kirkland Trent had gone to college with Neil Allen's father and had graciously offered his old acquaintance's 4-F son a job when his academic studies were completed.

A dramatic arts major, twenty-one-year-old Neil promptly accepted

Kirkland Trent's offer, assuring the aging company president that he wanted to learn the business from the ground up. Trent had waved him away, swiveling in his chair to pick up the ever-ringing telephone.

A few weeks after beginning at Bluebonnet, Neil, on his lunch hour, had sauntered across the street to Green's drugstore and seen Valentina behind the counter. It was love at first sight. He asked her out. Tired of dating lonely, amorous soldiers and sailors, she accepted and was fascinated from the beginning by the tales Neil told of the recording business.

His job sounded a lot more exciting than the one she had at H. L. Green's. She immediately started badgering him to ask his boss if there was anything she might do at Bluebonnet Records.

Neil, longing to please her, terrified she would make good her threat to stop sleeping with him if he didn't get her an interview, screwed up his courage and asked the company president if he would permit a friend to apply for a position at Bluebonnet.

"Send her over," said Kirkland Trent, without emotion. "Be glad to help you out."

So three days later, a nervous, excited Valentina Jones stepped from the elevators out into the Tower Petroleum Building fifth-floor studios of Bluebonnet Records, where she painstakingly filled out a long employment application, handed it to a smartly dressed secretary, and sat down on a camel-backed sofa to wait.

Five minutes later she was ushered into the biggest office she had ever seen. "Mr. Trent, Miss Jones," the poised secretary introduced them and left Valentina on her own.

"Come in, Miss Jones," Kirkland Trent's voice was soft and modulated.

Valentina crossed a mile of deep gray carpet to a massive mahogany desk. Behind it, Kirkland Trent stood smiling. Shorter than she and overweight, he was an unattractive man with small, close-set blue eyes, a large nose, and tight lips, above which was a black pencil-thin mustache. Almost completely bald, only a horseshoe of wispy gray hair grew around his gleaming pate.

But his gray summer suit was expensive and superbly tailored, his white shirt immaculate, his tie a natty, striped raw silk. His hands were well tended, nails buffed and trimmed. A shiny gold watch gleamed on his left wrist.

"Won't you have a seat, Miss Jones," he indicated one of a pair of high-backed wing chairs. He took his own facing her, picked up her resume, and studied it thoughtfully, a forefinger stroking the thin mustache. She waited. The small blue eyes lifted and came to rest on her.

"Miss Jones, you're in luck," he said finally. "Bluebonnet needs a receptionist. Our girl just found out she is pregnant. Suppose you could manage the position?"

"I can do anything, Mr. Trent."

He smiled. "Your feminine candor is refreshing."

The job secured, Valentina dropped Neil Allen on the spot. Stunned, heartsick, he demanded to know why. She told him they were simply not meant for each other. She spared him the true reason. He could do nothing more for her and she saw no sense in wasting her time on him. To her way of thinking, Neil had no complaints coming. The times she had allowed him to make love to her—times that had never been pleasurable for her—had been his payment in advance.

The scales were balanced.

The subtle seduction of Kirkland Trent began almost at once, though neither he nor Valentina realized it. For her part, she found the short, balding man anything but handsome, and yet, there was about him an unnamed kind of appeal, a quiet sureness, an aura of authority that clung to him like the tailored suits he wore.

The aging tycoon, old enough to be her grandfather, commanded Valentina's interest if for no other reason than he was the president of one of the most successful recording companies in the country and that his office, that bastion behind heavy closed doors, was the hallowed chamber wherein hundred-thousand-dollar deals were finalized and signed into being by his hand, and his alone.

It boggled her young mind and made her extremely curious about the man himself. Valentina began casually questioning her co-workers about their employer. She learned that Kirkland Trent's wife had left him two years ago after twenty years of marriage. Childless, he lived alone in a mansion on White Rock Lake where he led a quiet life, entertaining infrequently.

He had built the giant Bluebonnet Recording Company into a multi-million-dollar empire almost single-handedly, defying the odds, stupefying the smart money that said a recording or music publishing company could never be successful outside New York, Los Angeles, or Nashville. He was a clever finder of talent, a brilliant deal-maker, and a hard man to get to know. A cold, unfeeling man, his detractors declared.

Never had there been a breath of scandal about Kirkland Trent, although dozens of young female hopefuls, and a male or two besides, had offered themselves to him, hoping for that all-important break in the crowded music business. He had been a devoted husband who had never shown any interest in other women. Since his wife's departure, he graciously escorted widows and divorcées to important social affairs about town, but never established anything other than a brotherly alliance with any of them.

The more Valentina learned of Kirkland Trent, the more intrigued she became. From all she had heard, she was left with the distinct impression that the rich Kirkland Trent was very, very different from the men she had known. A wealthy man of ice who wielded power without emotion.

Could the ice be thawed? She intended to find out.

Kirkland Trent paid no attention to Valentina Jones. At first. He wasn't quite sure when he began to notice the young, fair-skinned redhead. Didn't realize that the plump, pretty girl had begun to smile seductively at him when he passed her reception desk. Couldn't put his finger on the exact morning when he'd first been snared by a pair of flirty brown eyes lifting to his.

He knew only that he had begun to look forward to seeing Valentina Jones at her desk each day, fresh and smiling and attractive. Even when he began to think up excuses to summon the young girl to his office, he told himself that it meant nothing.

When he commenced to gently tease and question her about Neil Allen and her other boyfriends, he silently argued that he felt protective toward her. Fatherly. She was the daughter he had never had. It was natural that he was relieved to hear her declare that she and Neil were only friends, that she had no fellow.

Little by little, day by day, his obsession grew.

Valentina missed a day of work and Kirkland Trent was beside himself. His secretary said she had called in sick. A half-dozen times he strode by her empty desk and felt a sharp stab of pain. The long workday finally ended. Tempted to go to her rooming house, he looked up the address in her personnel files. He ordered his chauffeur to drive him there. But when the big car eased up to the curb before the ramshackle building, Kirkland Trent suddenly felt foolish and commanded his driver to get him away from there in a hurry.

At home he ambled through his big, empty mansion berating himself. How could a man of his intelligence have let a naive young girl get under his skin? Alone in his study, he dropped a couple of ice cubes in a cocktail glass, poured two fingers of Chivas Regal Scotch, and faced the truth. What he felt for Valentina Jones was neither fatherly nor acceptable. The young, voluptuous redhead had become a living sexual fantasy from which he was never free.

He didn't sleep well that night. He found little consolation in telling himself that he was totally blameless, that he was simply a lonely man who had been too long without sex. After all, months before Nellie had left, they had no longer shared a bed, had not made love. And after she was gone . . . well he hadn't wanted anyone else.

Valentina Jones happened to walk into his life at a time when he was extremely vulnerable and if he were not very, very careful . . . That would never do! He was no old fool that went about seducing innocent children.

By morning Kirkland Trent had come up with a solution. His enemies did not call him ruthless for nothing. From the wall safe in his bedroom, he took five crisp one-hundred-dollar bills. He stroked his mustache and smiled.

He knew a great deal more about Valentina than she realized. Diplomatically, he had drawn out Neil Allen. Young Allen had volunteered all he knew of the red-haired girl. She was alone in Dallas, lived in a run-down boardinghouse, had come from a poor family in south Texas, and dreamed of one day having enough money to wear fine clothes, and eat at the best restaurants, and ride in taxicabs instead of buses.

Once he arrived at the office, Kirkland Trent almost discarded his plan. Valentina was at her desk, pretty as a picture, smiling sunnily up at him, her generous breasts appealingly outlined in a tight sweater of faded periwinkle blue. He drew a labored breath and hurried on into his office, exhaling heavily once he was inside.

But he stuck to his guns.

At the lunch hour when the outer office was virtually deserted, he went out to Valentina's desk, pulled open the top drawer, and placed a long, white envelope inside. Five one-hundred-dollar bills were inside the unsealed envelope. Glancing nervously about, he walked away, confident she would do exactly as he expected.

His plan was for her to see the money, tell no one she had found it, take it, and spend it. He, in turn, would confront her with the truth; she would break down and confess that she had stolen the money. Wherein he would gallantly allow her to resign. Her shameful thievery would remain a secret between the two of them and feeling certain she was sorry for her crime, he would see to it she found gainful employment someplace else.

But she would no longer work for Bluebonnet Records.

CHAPTER SIX

VALENTINA found the money that very afternoon. She was certain that Kirkland Trent had placed it there, but she was not certain why. She puzzled over it, thought about asking him, dismissed that notion, and promptly came up with a plan of her own.

She didn't hesitate to take the money. If he had not wanted her to do so, he would not have put it in her desk. So when Saturday came, Valentina did what every female loves to do. Spend. She bought clothes. A half-dozen Sloppy Joe sweaters in bright, bold colors. Pleated skirts of tweed and corduroy and gaberdine. Flashy dresses of taffeta and velvet and flannel. A winter coat of royal purple wool with gold nailheads outlining the yolk, both front and back. New saddle oxfords and ankle-strap heels of fire-engine red. Handbags and hats and gloves. Perfume and lipsticks and mascara and dusting powder.

And when she had spent all the money, save fifty dollars, Valentina marched into Neiman Marcus and told the slim clerk, whose fixed expression was one of disdain, that she wanted to look at the fine lingerie.

The clerk's cold eyes dropped from Valentina's fresh face to the many bags she carried; bags from Lerner's and Virginia Dare and Penney's. The woman gave a little dismissive toss of her head. "My dear, if you need new cotton bloomers, there's a Sears store just down . . ."

"My dear," Valentina cut in, "I've come to buy the most expensive brassiere and panties this store has. I am able to pay more than you make in a month, so move it!"

Startled, taken aback, the wide-eyed storeclerk recoiled, coughed nervously, and pivoted. "If you'll kindly follow me."

* * *

It was two weeks and four days before Kirkland Trent called Valentina Jones into his office to accuse her of stealing the money. Just past two in the afternoon, Trent's secretary stepped over to the reception area and quietly told Valentina that Mr. Trent wished to have a word with her. Valentina smiled.

And she said calmly, "I've one little errand to run, Betty. Will you kindly tell Mr. Trent that I will be in to see him in fifteen minutes?"

The secretary nodded and turned away. Valentina pulled open the bottom drawer of her desk, took out her purse and a white bag with the gold Neiman Marcus signature splashed boldly across it. Calmly she strode into the ladies room, locked the door, and patiently stripped. From her handbag she took the clean washcloth she had been carrying for over two weeks.

She wet the cloth in hot, steamy water and proceeded to give herself a refreshing sponge bath. She hummed softly, studying herself speculatively in the mirror over the basin. When she was nice and clean, Valentina opened the Neiman's bag, drew out an incredibly fragile-looking bra of sky blue lace. She slipped the satin straps over her shoulders and leaned forward to let her full, heavy breasts fall into the wispy cups. Deftly hooking it behind her, she straightened, shook out the blue lace panties and stepped into them. She tossed her old, worn underwear into the trash repository, hurriedly redressed, unlocked the restroom door, and went directly to Kirkland Trent's office.

"You wanted to see me, Mr. Trent?"

"Close the door, Miss Jones," his tone was cold, his face stern.

Valentina felt her bravado slipping away. She must have been insane to imagine that she could stir up this indifferent old man. She had misread him, underestimated him. She had been foolish to believe he wanted her; that he had left the money in her desk as a form of payment in advance.

He was not like most men, for goodness sake! He was a rich, highly intelligent, commanding company president. His only interest was his record business and she could have entered his office stark naked without arousing him.

Valentina, head bowed slightly, silently crossed to him, feeling miserably defeated, yet inexplicably attracted. The patina of power about him was more potent than ever. He was displeased, obviously, and held her very future in his well-groomed hands. That knowledge was both frightening and exciting.

She took a chair, forcing herself to look directly into his displeased blue eyes. He came right to the point.

"You stole five hundred dollars, Miss Jones. I personally placed an envelope containing the money in your desk drawer. Will you deny that you took it?" His tone was edged with anger.

Valentina swallowed hard. "I took the money, Mr. Trent."

She felt small and defenseless. She was seated across from one of the most powerful men in Dallas and she was terrified. What might he do with her? Fire her from Bluebonnet? Put her in jail? Send her back to the Rio Grande Valley? Or worse, have her deported to Mexico? She began to perspire. Her plan had been idiotic. It would never, ever work.

"I thought as much, Miss Jones." His tone was icily accusing. "You've been wearing new dresses and shoes each day. You bought them with my money."

"I could take them back and . . ."

"Clothes that have been worn are not returnable, Miss Jones." He reminded her.

Suddenly angry that he had waited so long to accuse her, she lifted her chin and questioned. "Then why, I wonder, did you wait for two weeks to ask about the money. Had you mentioned it sooner, I could have returned the merchandise."

He was thrown slightly off center by her defiance. He cleared his throat. "We're getting off the subject, Miss Jones. You, young lady, are a thief and I won't allow thieves to be employed at Bluebonnet. I shall tell my secretary to give you two weeks severance and we'll let this incident remain a secret between the two of us. I'm sure you'll be able to find employment—"

He was firing her! Damn him!

It was now or never. Valentina sucked in a quick breath, wet her lips, and said. "Would you like to see what else your five hundred bought for me?" She smiled at him.

"Why no, I would not, I . . ."

"You're going to," she said, interrupting, rising from her chair, and Kirkland Trent stared, unblinking, when Valentina slowly lifted her skirt.

With the rising of that skirt, the base of power shifted.

His small blue eyes grew round as silver dollars. His face pinkened and the stiff white collar of his shirt was suddenly too tight.

Valentina felt like laughing out loud. She did not. She kept her face purposely rigid, her eyes angry as she raised the skirt all the way to her waist. She held it there for a long moment, allowing the red-faced man to have a good look.

The fragile blue lace panties may as well have been transparent for all they concealed. Nothing more than a gossamer wisp of sensuous silk lace caressing her flesh, the seductive little garment left no question to the startled beholder that the young female raising her skirts for him was all woman, from the graceful arch of her hip, to the gently rounded curve of her stomach, to the shadowy triangle of thick auburn hair between her thighs.

Valentina had him aroused and knew it. And, for the first time in her life, she felt mildly aroused herself. She was enjoying the little game and was half-way looking forward to its outcome.

"See these panties, Mr. Trent? You bought them for me at Neiman Marcus. Aren't they lovely?"

"They're . . . you're beautiful, beautiful," choked the now-perspiring man, beads of moisture dotting his thin black mustache, his gleaming forehead.

"Well you can have them back!" She slowly rotated her generous hips, hooked her thumbs into the elastic waistband and shoved the panties down over her hips to her knees, allowing her full gray skirt to fall back into place. Stepping out of the frothy blue lace, she twirled the panties about on one forefinger and swayed directly over to the thunderstruck man behind the desk.

Laughing softly, she mischievously placed the undergarment atop his balding pate and said, "There. They're all yours, Mr. Trent. Worn only once for about ten minutes." She stood beside his chair, smiling down at him.

Kirkland Trent slowly pulled the panties from his gleaming head and dropped them to the thick carpet. "Miss Jones, I won't fire you if you'll . . . if you'll . . ."

"What, Mr. Trent?" Valentina reached out a hand to cup his full cheek.

"Let me look at you again," his tone was almost apologetic.

Never had Valentina seen a man as excited as Kirkland Trent. His bald head was pressed against the back of his high leather chair, his hands were gripping the arms so tightly his knuckles were white. She wondered just how far she could push him.

Valentina laughed softly and lithely climbed up onto his massive mahogany desk. With the swift agility of youth, she shot to her feet. Awed, mesmerized, Kirkland Trent gaped up at her, hardly able to breathe. She stood there atop his desk, smiling down at him, hands on her hips.

And then she made him wait no longer. She again lifted her skirts to her waist. While a perspiring, panting Kirkland Trent stared, open-mouthed, admiring her naked beauty, she moved her feet apart, kicking documents and papers aside, posing there, feeling heady and faint with newfound power.

"Valentina," he begged, "I'll give you another five hundred if you'll come down here and let me touch you."

Slowly, seductively, she bent her knees and lowered herself into a crouching position directly in front of him, skirts held high about her waist. Kirkland Trent leaned closer, nervously stroking at his thin black mustache, beady blue eyes riveted to the slick female flesh peeking from a tangle of curly auburn hair. He was dizzy and almost sick with desire. Fleetingly he marveled that in all the twenty years with his wife, he had never shared a moment as wonderfully dirty as this one.

"Valentina, Valentina," he rasped, as his eager hand sought the feminine warmth she was blatantly exposing.

After only a brief glance at the erection straining her boss's expensive flannel slacks, Valentina closed her eyes and thought idly that his fingers toying with her was not all that unpleasant. As a matter of fact, she was rather enjoying it.

A smile of pure pleasure played on her lips. This was unlike her other sexual experiences and Valentina felt her arousal swiftly rising. It was strange, this new sensation, this new tingling. Here she was, in the offices of Bluebonnet Records, bare-bottomed, sitting on her heels atop the desk of the aging company president, his soft, short fingers exploring her eagerly, while from behind his chair strong winter sunshine streamed in the uncurtained window.

Valentina's heavy eyelids fluttered open and her mouth rounded into a shocked O. Directly behind Trent's tall chair, a scaffolding with two men in white coveralls was slowly lowering into view. Transfixed, she watched as hips, chests, and finally faces appeared through the plate glass.

Her first inclination was to scream. But before any sound could rise from her throat, she had lost the desire. The window washers, their masculine faces rapidly becoming distorted with passion, raised the level of her desire. Her heart pounded forcefully and the gentle throbbing between her legs grew painfully intense.

Moaning softly, she impulsively clasped Kirkland Trent's balding head in her hands and turned his face up to hers. "Mr. Trent, make love to me!"

"Yes, yes," he gasped and immediately rose on watery legs, shaky hands fumbling with his zipper.

Valentina looked to her enrapt voyeurs for approval as she sat down flat on the desk, swung her parted legs over its edge, and hastily unbuttoned her blouse, showing them her lacy new bra. They nodded excitedly, urging her on. Her eyes came back to Kirkland Trent.

He had released himself from his trousers. Forcefully, he pushed her over onto her back. Standing, he entered her at once, then leaned down to kiss her. But she turned her head away and urged his mouth to her breasts, unwilling to lose eye contact with the watching workmen. Kirkland Trent's thin mustached lips eagerly closed over a throbbing, lace-covered nipple.

In seconds her climax began while she looked over Trent's shoulder straight into the hot, glazed eyes of the entranced window washers.

And she knew, as she writhed beneath a ramming, thrusting Kirkland Trent, that she had found the secret of pleasurable sex.

Power.

The presence of power made all the difference. Trent was a powerful old man and making love to him in the very office where he wielded that power was incredibly exciting.

Attaining release, Valentina smiled dreamily up at the white-coveralled workmen. They, too, had played an important role in her newfound ecstasy. And she wondered, how could she manage to have an audience present when next she engaged in sex.

Power. And an audience. An unbeatable combination.

"Valentina, Valentina," Kirkland Trent gasped when it was over and he was rezipping his pants, "I'll give you the five hundred today. I'll write you a check and you can . . ."

"No," she stopped him, rising to a sitting position, modestly lowering her skirts, "I don't want the five hundred, Mr. Trent. Truly I don't." And she didn't. She wanted a great deal more.

She wanted to be Mrs. Kirkland Trent.

She smiled sweetly at him and added, "I only want my beautiful blue lace panties I bought at Neiman Marcus. I've never had anything from Neiman Marcus before and I . . ."

"Oh, my dear child," he hastily retrieved the discarded briefs from the carpet, "certainly you may have them. You'll have lots of lovely things from Neiman's. That I promise you."

She clasped the panties to her breasts and looked into his adoring blue eyes. "You needn't buy me things."

"Humor an old man, Valentina. Allow me, please." He sank tiredly, happily back down into his chair.

"I will if . . ." she paused and lowered her head.

"If what, Valentina? Tell me, sugar."

She shyly put out her hand. He grasped it tightly. Her eyes lifted to his and she whispered, "If you'll promise to make love to me again here in your office."

"Dear God," he wheezed.

*   *   *

It took Valentina less than three months to persuade Kirkland Trent to marry her. Passion-heated afternoons in his office made his life so pleasurable that when one day, out of the blue, she refused him, he was frantic.

"But why, sugar? What have I done?" he pleaded and cajoled, "I'll give you a new fur coat. A car. How would you like that?"

Petulantly, she shook her red head. "No! You only want my body; you don't care about me. You don't."

"That's not true. Why Valentina, sugar, I'm crazy about you."

"Then marry me."

"Marry you?"

"Marry me."

"But I can't . . . I . . . I . . ." he stammered.

"Why not?"

"Because I . . . I never . . ."

"If you don't marry me," she interrupted threateningly, "I'll walk right out that door and you'll never see me again, Mr. Kirkland Trent." She spun around and stalked toward the door.

He stopped her. "Wait." She paused, and he never saw the look of triumph spread over her face, nor did Valentina see the look of fear on his. "We'll drive up to Ardmore today and get married," his voice was strained, "there's no wait for blood tests in Oklahoma."

Valentina whirled and came flying into his outstretched arms. "Oh, Mr. Trent, I'll be a good wife, truly I will."

And she was.

So enthralled was Valentina with her new role of wife to a highly respected and influential man, she coddled him and fussed over him and was at his side twenty-four hours of the day. She told him she did not want to leave her job at Bluebonnet, that she wanted him to teach her the business. He was delighted; Nellie had never expressed the slightest interest in the record industry. Immediately Kirkland Trent moved his senior vice president out of the office next to his own and called in a top Dallas decorator to fashion the space into a charmingly feminine province for his baby bride.

The new Mrs. Kirkland Trent was overjoyed.

From the beginning, Trent allowed her to sit in on important meetings with department heads. Astute, eager, Valentina listened intently to the discussions and arguments regarding the costs of cutting demos, packaging, promotion, and the like.

In no time she was offering suggestions to seasoned record company executives. Tactfully, they listened. In time they paid attention. Almost grudgingly recognizing that some of her ideas were near-brilliant, they implemented them. Uneducated, but extremely bright, Valentina Perez Jones Trent was perceptive, quick, and thrived in the thrilling atmosphere of major decision-making, hurried business lunches, and Super Chief railroad travel.

The implements of power.

Kirkland Trent taught his new, young bride more than the recording business. He told her she should dress differently. Valentina was shocked when he threw out her new purple coat with the gold nailheads and the spike-heeled red ankle-strap shoes; she had thought them beautiful and expensive looking. He assured her they were neither.

He took her to Neiman Marcus. Seated on a luxurious, plum-colored armchair, sipping Chivas Regal from a clinking cocktail glass in a private changing salon, he watched while his elated young wife enthusiastically modeled the most beautiful clothes she had ever put on her ripe body.

Kirkland Trent's taste was impeccable. Wisely, he did not choose clothes that were too old for Valentina. He picked vibrant hues and expensive fabrics and youthful designs, having no desire to make the child charmer appear older and sophisticated. There would be time enough for that, he told her. She listened and learned and became the best-dressed teenager in all Dallas.

With patient pleasure, Kirkland Trent tutored Valentina on scores of subjects. From him she learned the social graces, how to master a confusing array of cutlery at the dinner table, how to control the servants, how to make drawing room conversation with his peers, how to give successful parties.

He introduced her to fine foods and Valentina found she much preferred filet mignon to hamburgers, Belgian chocolates to Baby Ruths, and vintage wine to R C Colas. She came to enjoy long, lazy weekends of lying upon a rose velvet chaise in her upstairs bedroom suite, wearing only an exquisite nightgown of sensuous satin, while her aging, worshipful husband sat at her feet and happily ladled dollops of rich Russian caviar into her mouth and lifted sparkling flutes of French champagne to her thirsty lips.

"A pampered Cleopatra with her faithful serf," teased the indulgent Kirkland Trent.

"Who is Cleopatra and what's a serf," asked his wide-eyed wife and Trent chuckled, his round belly jerking beneath the expensive smoking jacket.

"Sugar, downstairs there's a vast library with hundreds of books. Perhaps after dinner you might wish to choose something to read."

Valentina shrugged bare shoulders and motioned for more caviar. "Trent, it's Saturday night. You know very well I always listen to 'Your Hit Parade' on the radio."

"I'll listen with you, sugar," said Kirkland Trent. "Maybe tomorrow afternoon we can go together to the library and read."

"On one condition," she told him.

"What condition, sugar?"

"You'll take me to the picture show tomorrow night. *The Lost Weekend* is playing and I adore Ray Milland."

Trent took her to the show. He took her anywhere she wished to go and he took her everywhere he had to go, assuring her that with his wealth and position people would welcome them as a couple no matter what they might say privately about the marriage.

"You'll find, my sweet red-haired Mexican wife, that money and power have a way of adding acceptance and respectability to a union such as ours."

Valentina stared at her husband. "How did you know?"

The balding bridegroom stroked his neatly clipped mustache. "You'll also find that with money you can garner just about any information you are seeking."

"How much do you know about me?"

"Everything," said Kirkland Trent. "You entered this country illegally. You left your Mexican family in the citrus belt of Texas four years ago when you were fourteen. You wrote them for a time, sent them money at first, but have not been in touch with them for over a year." He smiled and added, "Don't look so worried. Money also buys silence. Your past is dead and buried, sugar. Unless, of course, you wish to contact your family."

Valentina looked at the smug man and smiled. There were some secrets even his money could not uncover. Trent didn't know about the picture she kept in her billfold. A picture her mother had given her the day she left home.

It was of a young man with sandy hair, a wide, infectious smile, and aviator's goggles swinging from his sunburned neck. The handsome Anglo cropduster who had fathered her. Her daddy; the man whose name she had never known. Valentina had never told anyone about him. She saw no reason to tell Trent.

Her miserable existence in the Rio Grande Valley flashed through her mind and Valentina, determined that nothing and nobody would jeopardize this new, glorious life of riches and splendor, said resolutely, "You, Trent, are my only family."

"So be it," said the man with the power to make it the truth.

*   *   *

Kirkland Trent remained sexually intoxicated by his child bride and discovered, to his delight, that in the bedroom at least, his teen mate could teach him a thing or two. He loved it. Valentina did things to him that his first wife had never even heard about and would have been outraged had he suggested them. It was a whole new carnal world of joy for him. She made him feel like a virile young stud and he was insatiable, wanting her endlessly.

Valentina enjoyed their lovemaking sessions in his office . . . or in her office . . . even if the window washers were not in attendance. The essence of excitement was present. There was always the distinct danger of being caught, as indeed they had been a time or two. Valentina usually managed to leave the door unlocked and on a couple of occasions—once in her office, once in Trent's—a rude messenger had knocked briskly and barged right in before they could call out. It was wonderful. Valentina had had the same kind of wild climax as that first day on his desk.

At home it was more of a problem. She found making love to Kirkland Trent in the privacy of their bedroom tediously tiresome. But she was innovative and had little trouble arousing her husband in other rooms of the house where a silent servant might happen past. Frequently their breakfasts on the back terrace turned into lovemaking sessions while Sabacha, the young Japanese gardener, pruned the hedges not a stone's throw away.

And on their way to work, in the back of the black Lincoln limousine, Valentina luxuriated in lying spread-legged on the burgundy velour seat while her aging husband paid homage to her with his wet mustached mouth. And the young chauffeur, rearview mirror tilted strategically, paid homage with his heated hazel eyes.

All in all theirs was a satisfactory union and when—five years to the day after their wedding ceremony—Kirkland Trent died of a massive heart attack on the floor of his office while a naked Valentina sat astride him, she was genuinely grieved.

It had been such a pleasant day. They had walked, arm in arm, over to the Adolphus Hotel for a long, leisurely lunch. And at that lunch they had sipped wine and talked of the upcoming appointment with their battery of attorneys. Holding her hand and looking into her eyes, Trent had said, "I'm leaving everything to you. The attorneys are to have the will drawn in time for next week's meeting."

It was mid-afternoon when they returned to the office, full, lazy, content.

"Trent, darling, what time is it?" Valentina asked when, yawning lazily, they stepped inside his office.

He raised his arm, pushed back the French cuff and looked at the heavy gold watch with its platinum face. "Sugar, it's ten minutes til three."

"Good," she said, smiling. "The Stamps Baxter Quartet and their manager aren't due here until 3:30." She began unbuttoning her cream silk blouse.

In minutes both were fully undressed. "Where do you want it, sugar?" asked sixty-seven-year-old Kirkland Trent, accustomed to being bossed about by his twenty-three-year-old wife.

"Ummmmm," pondered Valentina, "why don't you stretch out on the floor, Trent. I'll get on top."

He did and she climbed astride him, settling herself just below his round, flabby belly. Playfully she tickled his gray hairy chest before she wrapped her fingers around his jerking shaft and guided it into her. It was exquisite. Flushed by all the wine they had consumed at lunch, Valentina felt hot and dizzy and excited. Her husband was just as flushed and dizzy and excited.

"Good, isn't it Trent?" she quizzed, hands on his shoulders. He moaned for an answer and she smiled. She sat straight up then, tossed her head back and saw, to her supreme pleasure, scaffolding slowly lowering from the floor above. Determined to stretch out the act until her audience could move into viewing position, she abruptly stopped the movements of her hips. Her husband whimpered at the loss. "Hold on, Trent, old boy, hold on," she soothed, "wait, Trent . . . wait just a . . ."

Two sun-darkened male faces appeared through the glass and Valentina saluted them with an open-mouthed smile and the burlesque bouncing of her bare, heavy breasts. And she went into action.

"Okay, Trent, old boy, I'm going to give it all to you now," she bragged and began to ride him wildly, grinding her hips, gripping him tightly, squeezing him with her strong pale thighs.

He worked too, pumping up into her, grunting with exertion, striving mightily to be the vigorous lover, while Valentina, looking unwaveringly at the pair of watching men—one furiously rubbing a powerful erection through his white coveralls, the other licking dry lips and clinging to the supporting suspension cables for dear life—felt the beginning tremors of a climax unlike any she had ever had.

Out of control she squirmed and jerked and screamed until finally she collapsed atop her prone, limp husband, murmuring breathlessly, "My God, Trent . . . Trent. Trent? Oh my God. Trent, Trent!"

CHAPTER SEVEN

LAURA carefully placed the blood-red rose on the gold-flecked marble guitar monument, directly atop the large deeply etched C. Slowly, she rose to her feet. She remained immobile for a long silent moment, a solitary figure silhouetted against the pinkening winter sky. Cold February winds whipped the raven hair about her rigid face and stung dark eyes that were misting with emotion.

Releasing an inaudible sigh, Laura turned, walked wearily across the marble tomb and stepped down onto the winter-browned grass. Never looking back, she proceeded across the dead lawn, crossed the pebbled drive, and ascended the marble steps of the gleaming white mansion. Buddy Hester and Hal Alcott, her two most trusted bodyguards, followed at a respectful distance.

Laura stood before the tall fanlighted double doors and extracted a gold key from her Gucci shoulder bag. When the big doors swung inward, she turned back to the two huge men who had taken up their posts below the marble steps.

"Buddy, it's cold. Come in and wait for me," and she disappeared inside the palatial mansion. Her footfalls echoing loudly in the quiet entry hall, Laura never glanced down at the floor of shiny marble that had been quarried in Italy, nor up at the English cut glass chandelier sparkling above her head. She didn't turn right at the arched doorway leading into the spacious, high-ceilinged living room where the hardwood floors were covered with a Directoire Aubusson carpet upon which stately Chippendale furniture rested. Nor left to the huge dining room with its English pedestal banquet table meticulously laid with fine Worcester porcelain, as though a dozen important guests were expected for dinner.

49

The ostentatious, antique-filled rooms held no interest for Laura. She purposely passed these spotlessly clean, lifeless rooms, proceeding to the very back of the house. Down three marble steps, into the huge oak-paneled library where the floor was topped with a worn nineteenth-century Kashan Persian carpet.

Laura smiled.

It was this warm, cluttered room that she most cherished. It was this room she loved to visit. It was this room where the past became the present; where the Chief had taught her to read, taught her to sing, taught her to chord a guitar.

It was here in this trophy-bedecked, highly masculine library where her first memories of the Chief took form. It was here in this sun-splashed shrine that she had seen him for the final time.

Shrugging out of her sable, Laura tossed it carelessly over the back of a well-worn leather chair. As she had done one thousand times before, she moved along the tribute-covered walls, fondly studying their contents. The gold and platinum records were there, all forty of them, framed and hung in neat, symmetric rows. And pictures, dozens and dozens of pictures.

The youthful Chief shaking hands with Ed Sullivan. With Dick Clark on American Bandstand. With Jackie Gleason. The Chief and President Eisenhower, holding up golf clubs in triumphant gestures. The Chief with a vigorous young President John Kennedy, both men in tuxes, champagne glasses in hand, celebrating the Irishman's forty-second birthday. With General Westmoreland and Alex Burton at Da Nang. Atop the rear seat of a dark Lincoln convertible, hand lifted, waving over the head of Lady Bird Johnson; President Lyndon Baines Johnson with a long, protective arm draped around the Chief's wide shoulders.

Pictures taken on movie locations with glamourous leading ladies. The beautiful young Natalie Wood. And sexy Marilyn Monroe. And angelic-looking Pier Angeli. Pictures made in Vegas with good friends. The Chief and Tom Jones, a grip on themselves, clowning for the camera, two Caesar's superstars. And with Elvis. The Chief and the King. Elvis proudly holding up the prized FBI badge President Nixon had presented to him, the shiny silver shield almost obscuring the Chief's smiling face.

Pictures of his parents. Ernest and Gracie McCarty, the boyish Chief standing between them, hugging them both and flashing that million-dollar smile. Wedding pictures; a gorgeous young couple looking happy and healthy and heart-stoppingly handsome.

Laura moved on.

There were awards. Everywhere, awards. Grammys claiming every available square inch of tabletop, bookcase, television set. And guitars. A valuable, mahogany Martin from Umanov's mounted on the wall beside the marble fireplace. A beautiful Ovation of rosewood with silver head and bridge bone, leaning against a door frame. An expensive, irreplacable 1958 Gibson Moderne, one of only seventeen ever made. All the Chief's guitars were here in this souvenir-filled room. Save one. The old Sears guitar that Ernest and Gracie McCarty had given to their nine-year-old son on Christmas morning, 1945.

It was missing.

Laura ground her teeth. If the instrument had been lost or destroyed accidentally, she would not have cared so much. What upset her was that it was not lost. It was not destroyed. It was in the possession of the one person on earth who had no right to it.

"Damn her," Laura muttered bitterly "Damn that bitch! I'll get the guitar and the company back, if it takes a lifetime!"

Angrily, she snatched her sable from the leather chair, held it over her folded arms, and made one last sweep around the room. Within hours the throngs outside the Music Gates would swarm through this dear room, looking, prying, touching.

The thought made Laura sick. She knew how the Chief would have hated it. How many times had she heard him say, "This is my home, my refuge, my sanctuary. I don't want anyone here except my friends and family. There has to be a part of me that does not belong to my fans. There has to be!"

Feeling his strong presence in the room, Laura at last lifted dark eyes to the life-sized Dimitri Vail portrait of the Chief above the marble fireplace. Wearing the only costume in which he ever appeared before an audience— superbly tailored tuxedo, white shirt, black tie, and one red rose in his satin lapel—the Chief smiled down at her, his black, snaring eyes looking squarely into hers.

Laura smiled back at him. And she repeated what she had said at his grave. "Just a couple more years, Daddy."

She turned and left the room.

"Robert," she said, stepping into the limo, "before we go to Love Field, run me out by Missy's house." Weary from the past few sleepless nights, Laura leaned her head back against the plush leather and closed her scratchy eyes.

And saw once again the horribly shocking scene at the lakehouse. A graphic, grotesque picture that kept running incessantly through her mind, like a movie being replayed over and over again no matter how hard she tried to vanquish it.

Missy DiGrassi, naked, slept peacefully between a ten-thousand-dollar set of silk crepe de chine sheets, hand-embroidered in Italy. She was alone in the climate-controlled bedroom of what she jokingly referred to as her "North Dallas Forty." A large, pink, Italian-type villa with forty rooms, the estate was admittedly so immense that Missy had not yet been inside many of the rooms.

The twenty-thousand-square-foot mansion, containing an indoor pool, guest house, and staff quarters, sat directly in the middle of forty acres of elaborately landscaped grounds with gazebos, formal gardens, lily pools, terraces, and stucco-covered stables for prized polo ponies.

The rambling villa's location had been chosen by the handsome and wealthy Venezuelan, Arto DiGrassi, as much for its proximity to the Willow Bend Polo and Hunt Club as for its vast acreage. Three years in the building, "North Dallas Forty" was exactly to Missy's hedonistic liking.

More space—all with custom-designed marble floors inlaid with rich Honduran mahogany—than she could ever use. More mohair-covered walls than she could ever fill with expensive paintings. More fine imported couches and sofas and chairs than she could ever sit upon. More Bentleys and Rolls-Royces and Mercedes in the eight-car garage than she could ever drive. More exotic foods in the freezers and refrigerators than she could ever eat. More liquor and champagne in the wine cellar than she could ever drink.

Just the right amount of everything to suit Missy DeGrassi.

Missy jerked slightly when the servant knocked on her bedroom door. "Mrs. DeGrassi, you have a visitor."

"Go away!" snarled Missy.

"Ah . . . I'm sorry to disturb you, Mrs. DiGrassi, but—"

"Well, then quit disturbing me, damn it," shouted Missy irritably. "Leave me alone!" She snatched the silk sheet up over her blond head and squeezed her eyes tightly shut.

"Ma'am," the servant persisted, "the lady says its important."

"What lady?" came the muffled, half-interested voice.

"It's Laura, Missy," came the firm answer and Missy recognized her voice.

"Laura?" Missy's sleepy eyes came open and she threw off the covers.

"Yes, it's me. Get up, I need to talk to you. I'll be waiting downstairs."

"Downstairs, hell. Come in here." But Laura had already turned away. Missy sighed heavily and got out of bed.

Yawning, she threw her long, bare legs over the bed's edge and sat, looking about on the cluttered, carpeted floor for something to throw on. Barefoot, wild mane of blond hair spilling down her back and into her eyes, she stumbled down the carpeted winding staircase, scratching her left breast, wearing nothing but a long, over-sized "I am a personal friend of Joe Bob Briggs" T-shirt.

Wincing loudly when her feet touched the cold marble of the hallway, Missy rushed into the living room, glanced first at Laura, then at the gold Deniere clock atop the marble mantel.

"Jesus Christ, Laura, it's the middle of the night."

The sight of her annoyed friend made Laura smile, despite her misery. "It's seven-thirty. Some people are already at work."

"I'm not 'some people,' and you know very well I never get up before noon." Missy flopped down on the Donghia sofa beside Laura.

"You're lazy, Missy," said Laura, still smiling.

"Good for you. Take what's behind curtain two." From a silver box atop the black laquer coffee table, she drew a cigarette, but did not light it. "I tried to get you to spend the night here, then you wouldn't have—"

"Missy, I just came from Musicland."

Missy pushed her hair out of her eyes. "Oh, God, on top of everything you've been through."

"It's his birthday," Laura's voice was flat, tired, and the smile had left her lips.

Missy shook her head, disgustedly. "You're a real glutton for punishment, aren't you? There's no unwritten law stating you must go to his grave every year. I would think that . . ."

"I have to, Missy." Laura said quietly.

"Bullshit," Missy responded, lighting her cigarette and waving it about like Bette Davis. "The man's dead, Laura. He's been dead for eight years. Haven't the past few days been hard enough on you without adding to it?"

Laura sighed. The past few days had been a living nightmare, totally draining her. She leaned her dark head back against the tall sofa. "It just seems to get worse instead of better. I keep seeing them and . . . I . . . God . . . you can't imagine, Missy," she murmured miserably. "That's why I'm here again this morning. I thought you might offer a little . . ."

" . . . more understanding?" Missy finished the sentence. "You've come to the wrong place, kiddo." She bolted up from the couch. "Call the pity hotline. Stop a wino on the street. Write Dear Abby. But don't expect me to get all teary-eyed at this hour."

"You're a hard woman, Missy."

"And you're a crybaby. Come on, let's go have some coffee. I might break out a bottle of champagne and toast the morning." She laughed huskily. "It's been so long since I've seen one."

Laura couldn't keep from smiling. Missy's sharp tongue was exactly what she needed during this painful period of her life. Missy knew it. Laura knew it. That's why she had come here this early in the morning. The rest of her friends and family had always coddled and protected her. From the moment they met all those years ago at Hockaday, and Missy had walked right up to her and said brashly, "Stop that blubbering and blow you nose, you're not a baby," their relationship had been a very special one. One in which the formidable Missy showed very little mercy. And priceless friendship.

Laura followed her barefooted hostess to the huge many-windowed kitchen. In an alcove overlooking the terraced back gardens, the two old friends sat at one end of a long cloth-draped table and drank coffee from Nymphenburg porcelain cups while Missy ordered champagne brought to the table as though she were in a restaurant.

"This is Bollinger, 1966. One hundred dollars a bottle," Missy announced as she poured the golden bubbly into gleaming tulip flutes of Orrefors crystal.

Laughing, she lifted her glass.

"Sleeping till noon!"

"Champagne for breakfast!"

"To the Forbes Four Hundred." They clicked their flutes in toast.

Missy drank greedily and sighed with satisfaction. But seeing the tentative smile already slipping from her friend's face, she snapped, "Oh, come on, Laura, get your shit together and quit moping around. It's a great, big beautiful world out there. Hold your nose and jump on in."

Laura sipped her wine. "I've done that a time or two. Look how it turned out."

"So, big deal." Missy shook her blond head. "Where's your spirit of adventure? Where's your derring-do? Your balls?" She emptied her champagne glass. "Come on, drink up. And screw Stephen Flynn and the horse he rode on!"

Laura drank. Missy refilled her glass.

Together they finished the bottle of Bollingers. And when Missy poured the last drop into Laura's raised glass, both young women were laughing foolishly at everything the other had to say.

"Know where I'm going from here?" Laura, feeling wonderfully relaxed, licked her lips, savoring the wine's rich taste.

"Back out to the lake house?"

Laura's face darkened. "I'll never go there again."

"Sorry, I forgot." Missy shrugged. "Padre? Palm Springs? Vegas?"

Laura, grinning again, wagged her dark head back and forth.

"So, I give up. Where?"

"Montenegro."

"Lord love a duck! I've wasted a perfectly good bottle of Bollingers trying to cheer you up and now you tell me you're going to that remote cliff house you own in dreary old Yugoslavia. You're really suicidal, aren't you?"

Tipsy, tired, tickled, Laura halfheartedly defended herself. "At the time I made plans to go, it seemed like a brilliant idea."

"It stinks," declared Missy. "It's the other side of the world, you don't know a soul over there, and nobody knows you, and its hard to get to and its isolated and . . ."

"Missy, you've just made me recall why I'm going there."

CHAPTER EIGHT

LAURA stood on the private balcony of her Montenegrin home in the old walled city of Budva. Perched on a tiny spit of land jutting out into the Adriatic Sea, the town itself seemed isolated from the rest of the world. And Laura's house, a comfortable six-room one-level structure that had served as the honeymoon cottage of her parents, was set apart from its neighbors, save for one identical house built directly atop it. A house whose unknown owner had never been in residence when Laura visited Yugoslavia.

Six acres of rocky terrain separated the two twin villas from the main road that curved around the peninsula. A steep narrow path wound upward from the road to the front gates of the property. Two gates were side by side; one led into Laura's walled courtyard, the other into her absent neighbor's.

When Laura had arrived two days prior, she had released a sigh of relief to see no sign of activity in the upper apartment. No parked automobiles. No lights on inside. No open drapes or blinds. She had lucked out; the owners were not there.

Insisting she would be perfectly safe in this secluded cliffside house, Laura had exiled her pilots and bodyguards to the Plaza Hotel in town, longing for the healing balm of seclusion. No, she assured them, she needed nothing, would need nothing for the length of her stay. The efficient caretakers had put the place in order, laid in food and drink, and had seen to it that there was plenty of firewood for the fireplace.

She wanted nothing but to be alone.

Laura, her slender body draped in a long, comfortable caftan of soft amber wool, tried desperately to find peace and contentment in the spectacular scenery surrounding her on this springlike February afternoon. Behind her towering mountains rose to meet the cobalt-blue skies and below, far below, the sea churned restlessly at her feet. The surf crashing against the rocky cliffs was a familiar, seductive sound.

Laura drew a slow, weary breath. On every other occasion that she had stood on this stone balcony, she had thrilled to the rhythmic, constant pounding of the waters below. Always before the wild and rugged beauty of this isolated paradise had brought a special pleasure. She had spent happy hours here on this secluded deck, watching the boats bobbing in the tiny harbor, eating figs and peaches and melons from the nearby Lake Shadra orchids, sunning herself nude in the hot Montenegrin sun.

This time, it held no joy for her.

It mattered little that the island was already a-blossom with the first signs of spring and that the mid-February weather was as warm as May in Dallas, so warm she was barefoot. And was bare beneath her caftan.

Nothing much mattered. Nothing at all.

Laura felt the tears slipping down her cheeks before she realized she was crying. She didn't bother to brush them away. She stood, hands clinging to the black wrought iron railing, and quietly cried. The past few days had been a purgatory of pain and humiliation. How blind she had been. How incredibly stupid not to have guessed that Stephen was . . . that he was . . . Since that night . . . that horrible night . . . she had gone about in a daze of agony and embarrassment and resentment that was making her physically ill. She couldn't sleep, she couldn't eat. Her appetite for food gone. Her appetite for life was gone.

There was nowhere to turn, no one who could comprehend the depth of her pain. Not even Missy. How could Missy fully understand when nothing so terrible, so degrading, had ever happened to her. And she had told no one else what had happened. Only Missy knew of her shame.

Laura was alone with her misery, half a world away from anyone she knew, searching for a solace she could not find. If anything, she felt worse, more betrayed, more lost. Duped. Unwanted. Unloved.

In her despair Laura never realized when the sun set across the sea or when the twinkling lights came on in the Bay of Kotor or when the warm air cooled with night's approach.

As a full Montenegrin moon sailed high in the sky, she still stood on the cold stone balcony, her senses dulled by heartache, her thoughts tortured and muddled, her will to fight on waning.

Tears drying on her cheeks, Laura leaned way out over the iron railing and looked straight down at the deep, dark waters of the bay. Mesmerized by the surging, foamy currents, she stared, unblinking, at the murky waters swirling and rushing and relentlessly pounding the cliffs.

She felt as though they were pulling her toward them, as though the crashing breakers were rhythmically calling to her, "C-o-m-e L-a-u-r-a . . . c-o-m-e L-a-u-r-a . . . c-o-m-e L-a-u-r-a." Her breath grew short and she felt lightheaded and dizzy. But she continued to lean a little farther out . . . a little farther out . . .

Laura screamed and jerked upright as something huge and solid fell directly before her face and plummeted into the dark, deep waters. She heard a loud splash as the object hit the water. With eyes wide and frightened, she searched frantically below.

"Help!" The voice was faint, the sound almost carried away in the wind and the surf. "Help." She heard it again and followed it to its source, heart hammering in her chest.

A human being bobbed about in the frigid waters, arms flailing frantically in the air, faint cries snapping Laura into action. Without a thought to her safety, she climbed swiftly atop the iron railing, drew a deep breath, arched her tall, slender body, and dove into the churning sea.

Momentum carried her several feet beneath the dark surface. An excellent swimmer, Laura turned an agile somersault in the depths and shot to the top, parting the waters less than fifty feet from the thrashing drowning victim. Swimming with long, determined strokes, Laura arrived in time to fill both her hands with wet, thick hair and jerk a submerging head up above the crest.

"Don't fight me," she shouted into the moonlit features of a man. Quickly sliding her hands beneath his armspits, fear engulfed her. He was huge; a solidly built man who weighed, she was certain, twice what she did. If he struggled, they would both be lost. "Don't fight, don't fight," she repeated, shouting, feet furiously treading the water. "I can get you back if you do as I tell you!"

Sputtering, spitting water, the man nodded silent acquiescence, hands coming up to her shoulders, large body bumping against hers, eyes flashing in the moonlight.

"I'm going to turn you onto your back," Laura warned and, relieved that he was not panicky, eased him over in the water, stretching a slender arm across his wide, bare chest.

Immediately, she began swimming, using her free arm expertly and kicking her feet in rhythmic, scissoring movements. And she dismissed the notion, as soon as it came, of heading straight for the nearest cliffs. It would do little good to reach rock that soared fifty feet in the air, straight up.

She felt a moment of terror. They were at least two hundred yards from the nearest point where sloping rock, protruding out into the water, gave access to the land. Could she swim that far in the cold, choppy sea? Could she make it all the way with her burden?

Doggedly she swam through the swift current, tiring right arm slicing through the icy waters, left clinging tenaciously to a solid male chest. Night winds swirled her dark wet hair into her stinging eyes and the soggy wool caftan clung heavily to her body, weighing her down, impeding movement.

Muscles aching, breath short and labored, Laura made her sure way through the deep, chill waters of the bay, goal firmly in mind, though not yet in sight. Around the island's perimeter she swam, barely skirting the towering, steep granite bluffs.

The wind grew stronger. The water, colder. Laura felt herself being tugged under by a high wave. She closed her mouth and tried with waning strength to push the man upward, to keep him from going under. She was submerged. Her arm slipped from his chest. She couldn't see him; she couldn't feel him. A scream was gathering in her aching throat. She had let him drown. My God, he was gone, he was gone!

A pair of strong male hands gripped her waist and pushed her up. Her head broke the water. Gasping for air, she watched gratefully as his wet head come up out of the depths.

"You okay?" he shouted against the wind.

"I'm fine," she returned as they both bobbed about in the dangerous, battering current. "Assume your position."

He did so, turning onto his back, allowing her to drape her arm across him once more. Off she swam, legs kicking violently, heart pounding, a silent prayer rising from her wet lips.

Progress was agonizingly slow. They were not going to make it, Laura thought miserably. It was too far; she was too tired. Total exhaustion draining her strength so that she could no longer move her arms and legs, Laura gave a defeated little sob.

But a strange thing happened.

They continued to slice through the water, she and the stranger, though her limbs were limp and useless, trailing along in the water. They were not sinking. Their positions were the same; he on his back, she on her stomach at his side. And they were moving nearer and nearer to the rocky beach and twinkling lights beyond.

Laura could feel the muscles of his chest pulling and moving beneath her arm; and then his long, powerful legs kicking at the water. Too tired to do otherwise, she relaxed against him, realizing that it was he, not she, that was swimming, keeping them afloat, propelling them to safety. In moments she was being lifted high in his arms as he walked out of the sea and deftly climbed the rocks.

Grateful to be alive, Laura wrapped tired arms around the strong column of his neck and collapsed against him, face pressed against his gleaming broad chest. Beneath her ear, his heart beat a slow, steady rhythm as though the last few terrifying, strenuous moments in the water had not occurred.

The man said nothing as he agilely picked his way up the boulder-strewn path toward the cliffs. Laura was too tired to speak. She closed her eyes against the bright moonlight and rested, laboring for breath. Her eyes came open and the silence was broken when he stepped through the squeaking courtyard gate of his house.

"No," she said, struggling against him, "put me down. I want to get out of these wet clothes."

He immediately halted but did not put her down. "I've a fire going and I'll lend you a robe." It was not an order, it was an invitation. And his voice was deep, soft, its gentle resonance strangely at odds with his enormous size.

Wet and exhausted, Laura agreed. She felt no fear of this man who both looked and sounded American. She had just saved his life; would he dare harm her?

Upstairs, he released her in the small entry hall. She stood dripping water on the black slate floor, the long, saturated caftan sticking to her chilled body. He stood before her, rivulets running down his massive chest, slacks plastered to his muscular body, hair pressed to his head.

"Take the master bath," he said. "There's a robe hanging behind the door."

There was no mistaking that accent. She was half a world away from Texas. And in the room with a Texan. A big, clumsy Texan who had fallen into the sea and almost gotten them both drowned.

"Promise you'll stay off the balcony?" she gently teased.

"I'll be in the guest shower," he said, unsmiling, and lifted big sunburned hands up to smooth the wet, brown hair off his face. "Sure you'll be okay?"

Puzzled, she frowned up at him. "Of course," she stepped past him into the living room where the tall French doors stood open to the balcony and the night air. Shivering, she hurried through the chilled room and into the master bedroom.

Ten minutes later, wearing a black terry robe that reached almost to the floor, damp hair smoothed back behind her ears, Laura reentered the living room. The doors had been closed against the night. The fire had been built up and now burned brightly in the fireplace. Two brandy snifters, a brandy warmer—its tiny flame ablaze—and a silver bowl filled with blue muscatel grapes rested on the slate hearth near the fire. And her tall Texas companion, showered and dressed in faded Levi's and a white polo shirt stretching across wide shoulders, was jabbing at the flaming logs with an iron poker.

Her bare feet made no sound on the deep carpet and the man whose shower she had used remained unaware of her presence. Quietly Laura observed him for a long, thoughtful moment.

A giant of a man, his was a great, leonine head, with strong chiseled features, high, flat cheekbones and a heavilycut chin. Light-haired, bronzed, he had a deep, powerful chest and huge, muscular arms. He looked to be about thirty-five, a vigorous, good-looking Texan. He turned fully to the fire, stoking, punching, his broad, shoulders lifting, muscles bunching and working back and forth.

Laura cleared her throat. He turned slowly and smiled at her. "Come warm yourself by the fire." His voice was commanding.

Clutching the lapels of the black terry robe, she cautiously crossed to him, nervously feeling that the entire room was completely filled with his strong masculinity.

Releasing the poker he put out a huge hand. "Griff. Griff Deaton," he introduced himself.

"Hello," she said, placing her hand in his, feeling her fingers swallowed up in his sure, warm grip.

"And you?" he waited, still holding her hand.

"Laura Flynn." She looked straight up into his light eyes, waiting for some flicker of recognition. There was none. "You don't know who I am?"

He looked thoughtful. He studied her, still holding her hand in his. He shook his great head. "Should I?"

She studied his ruggedly handsome face. She saw only honesty. "No, no reason. No reason at all."

He squeezed her hand tightly and released it. "Well, Laura Flynn, what we need is some warmed Napoleon brandy. How about it?"

"The very thing," she responded, feeling decidedly less lonely, almost lighthearted.

They sat cross-legged on the floor before the fire and sipped their heated brandy, saying little, studying one another with great interest. Laura was the first to look away. Circling her glass's top with an index finger, she finally said, smiling, "Aren't you going to thank me for saving your life?"

"You have it backwards."

Her head snapped up and she stared at him. "What are you talking about?"

Griff Deaton grinned engagingly. "I saved you."

"You saved me?" Her dark eyes grew stormy. "What a ridiculous thing to say. You fell off your balcony and I . . ."

"Jumped."

"Yes, I jumped in and . . ."

"No. I mean, *I* jumped."

"You jumped?" Her brows knitted. "But I thought . . . you surely . . . Why? Why would anyone . . ."

"To save you."

"Save me? I wasn't in the water."

"You would have been, if I hadn't jumped."

Laura shook her head incredulously. "Your jumping is what put me into the water! I certainly would not have—"

"Ever see *It's A Wonderful Life?*" Griff Deaton interrupted.

"I beg your pardon."

"*It's A Wonderful Life.* The movie. Jimmy Stewart, Donna Reed. Surely you've seen it. They show it at least a dozen times on television each Christmas season."

Laura stared at him. "Certainly I've seen it, but I don't . . . What has . . ."

"The guardian angel jumped off the bridge because he knew Jimmy Stewart was going to leap and kill himself." Griff looked straight into Laura's eyes. "The angel saved Jimmy. He jumped so that Jimmy had to fish him out."

Laura felt her cheeks grow hot. Nervously, she laughed. "You actually think that I intended to leap to my death?"

"You considered it." His eyes held hers. "A beautiful, modern-day Queen Teuta," he added softly.

"I have no idea what you're talking about."

"Back in 228 B.C., Illyrian Queen Teuta jumped from these very cliffs to her death in the bay."

"Why?" asked Laura, anxious to turn the conversation away from herself.

"She drowned herself rather than submit to the Romans." He took a drink of brandy and balanced the glass on a bent knee. "Are the Romans after you, Laura Flynn?"

"Don't be silly," Laura responded.

"Then why were . . ."

Laura sprang to her feet. "Thanks for the shower and the brandy. I'll go now."

A huge male hand shot out and caught the hem of the black terry robe. "Stay, Laura. Stay for a while."

"I can't." She jerked the robe free.

"I'm lonely," said Griff Deaton, truthfully. "I hate being alone. Please stay." Looking down into his blue, blue eyes Laura read a hint of melancholy in their depths, despite his wide smile.

"If I stay, no questions." She meant it; she was not up to sharing her troubles with a stranger thousands of miles from home, even if he was a fellow Texan. "I don't pry into others' lives; I expect the same deference."

"You got it, sweetheart," he raised his hand, palm open. She put hers into it and allowed him to gently urge her back to the floor. "I won't ask another question. We'll talk about any subject you choose."

"Tell me more about the history of this place," she said, taking up her brandy glass and curling her long, slender legs beneath her.

Griff Deaton winked at her. "Let's see . . ." he absently rubbed his chin, "the tragic and beautiful Teuta was a pirate queen, the godmother of two millennia of Adriatic pirates who . . ."

Laura listened to his smooth, male voice as he told her more of the ancient, beautiful land of mountains and water and grottoes and coves and waterfalls and olive groves and frescoed churches and island convents and monasteries. She had no idea if what he said was true or if he were making it up as he went, and it really didn't matter. She liked hearing him speak and watching him gesture with his big, bronzed hands.

Deaton's sure, deep voice and the flickering fire and the smooth brandy warmed her. Pleasantly tired from her unscheduled swim in the cold bay, Laura felt herself relaxing for the first time in days, felt a sweet lassitude possessing her body. A body that had been tense for so long. She yawned, stretched her legs out beside her, and leaned on an outstretched arm.

Thoughtfully, lazily, she studied the huge brown-haired man whose soothing voice and rugged looks were decidedly pleasing to the eye and ear. She tried to imagine what his occupation might be. Long-haul truck driver? Wild bronc rider with the rodeo? Physical education teacher at some state college? Roughneck in the North Texas oil fields?

One thing for certain, he was as different as night and day from . . . from . . .

Laura continued to sip the smooth brandy and to closely watch the powerful muscles ripple beneath his white polo shirt as her companion gestured with his huge hands, embellishing a story for her delight. And she noted the way his thick brown hair fell casually over his high, wide forehead, the way his blue eyes gleamed in the firelight, the way his mouth—that firm, full-lipped mouth—stretched into an appealingly boyish grin with little effort.

Had he mentioned his last name? She was sure he had, but for the life of her she couldn't recall what it was. Griff, that's all she remembered. Griff. It fit him. Griff. She liked it. She liked Griff. Griff, with his heavy-lidded blue eyes, reminded her of a young Robert Mitchum; he looked like a big, sleepy lion.

Griff was strong and virile-looking. He was a strapping, vigorous, lusty man, and being in his presence made Laura feel small and feminine. And good, very good.

Did this big blue-eyed giant find her the least bit appealing, Laura wondered suddenly. With the events of the past few shocking days, she had good reason to doubt her allure, her desirability.

"Griff," Laura abruptly interrupted his monologue, "do you think I'm attractive?"

"You're a very desirable woman," said Griff without hesitation. The very words she so needed to hear.

"Griff."

"Ummmm?"

"Make love to me."

Griff Deaton's sleepy blue eyes widened. He stared at her with a riveting intensity that was almost frightening. Laura wished immediately she had never made such a shameless and foolish request. He was sure to reject her.

After all, this big, rugged man had no idea who she was, so why on earth would he want her? He wouldn't. She was not C.C.'s daughter here in his firelit living room, so of course he wouldn't want her. Had any man ever wanted her for herself?

Griff Deaton said nothing.

Slowly, lazily he drained his brandy glass and set it aside. His eyes—those beautiful blue eyes—had not left her and Laura could hear her heart pounding in her ears. His left hand, that huge, warm hand, slowly lifted to the terry lapel of her robe. He took the fabric between thumb and forefinger and slid them slowly up and down the lapel. Laura held her breath.

"You sure? You know nothing about me, sweetheart," his voice was warm, caressing, fingers toying teasingly with the black terry lapel.

Laura drew a shallow breath. "I need only to know that you want me," she answered honestly.

A hint of a smile touched his wide lips as his large hand slipped deftly inside the black robe to cup and lift a bare, firm breast. Laura trembled at his touch. Calloused thumb brushing across the taut nipple, Griff Deaton said gently, "I want you, Good Queen Teuta." His voice lowered, "God yes, darlin', I want you."

And then his mouth was on hers, hot and open and commanding. The black terry robe was swept away and she was naked in his big arms, thrilling to ardent, anxious lovemaking that was like the man himself. Rugged yet sensitive. Aggressive yet restrained. Rough yet tender. The sight of his big bronzed hands on her bare trembling body was almost as exciting as his practiced touch on the tingling flesh.

He caressed her with an urgent patience that made her breasts swell, her belly contract, her legs part, while he kissed her hungrily, hotly, as though he was starving for the taste of her.

Soon he was as bare as she, the firelight playing on his wide, bronzed shoulders, his thick hair. He was above her, a gentle giant of extraordinary male beauty, a naked stranger who wanted her just for herself.

Laura came almost immediately.

And then he really made love to her. He slowly, expertly aroused her again, his masterful mouth traveling leisurely, lovingly over her flushed body, nibbling on dewy skin, plucking at hardening nipples, nipping at quivering flesh, lapping at throbbing femininity.

And after another earth-shaking climax, a sated, limp Laura, her hands slipping from the rich brown hair of his leonine head down to his massive, muscular shoulders, laughed deep in her throat and said, "Griff, before you take it out, I have just one question."

Griff Deaton smiled down at her. "I'm never going to take it out, darlin'. I'll just leave it in forever."

"Mmmmm," she sighed happily. Then: "Griff, are you married?"

She felt the muscles beneath her fingertips tense. Looking straight into her eyes, Griff Deaton didn't hesitate. "Yes, sweetheart, I am. I'm a married man." The heavy lids lowered slightly over melancholy blue eyes. "And you, Laura?"

"Yes," she answered, "I, too, am married."

CHAPTER NINE

IT WAS his very first automobile. A brand new 1956 Bel Air Chevrolet convertible. A smooth-looking machine; custom navy blue paint job, white walls, leather interior, hi-fi radio, air conditioning, power windows. All the extras that money could buy.

C.C. McCarty, behind the wheel, was alone in the shiny new car. He was smiling; pleased with himself and his world. Swiftly he drove the flashy convertible across the Trinity River in the fading April dusk, the balmy winds stinging his face, ruffling his hair, and causing his eyes to burn.

He felt as free as the wind and as wild. An instrumental blared out from the radio and C.C. supplied the words, keeping time with lean fingers drumming out the beat on the steering wheel. His right foot, shod in a new, soft, black loafer, tromped the accelerator and the powerful car shot forward. C.C. jammed the heel of his hand to the horn and passed a carload of pretty young girls in a yellow Plymouth, favoring them with a teeth-flashing smile and a shouted invitation to "catch up if you can."

"Chief, Chief," they screamed, recognizing him, and tried to overtake him. But the hot Bel Air sucked them up its shiny chrome tailpipe and after a lifting of his long arm high in the air to wave a teasing good-bye, C.C. again gunned the powerful engine and streaked into the glittering, lighted skyline of a spectacular nighttime Dallas.

Passing below the famous Flying Red Horse, C.C. inhaled deeply of the heavy spring air and figured he was the luckiest twenty-year-old alive. It was all ahead of him; a world full of goodies just waiting for him to reach out and grab hold of.

C.C. braked to a stop at a traffic light on Commerce, sighing with satisfaction. He was on the way to Valentina Trent's party, thrown to honor

66

his winning last night's talent contest at Moody Coliseum. Tomorrow he would go to her Republic Towers office and collect the prize. A recording contract with her company, Bluebonnet. And then . . . rock on. Look out world. The sky's the limit.

Valentina Trent shook off the past with the last of her bath bubbles. Rising, she stepped out onto the velvety rose-hued carpet and studied herself in the mirror.

She didn't like what she saw. At eighteen she had been voluptuous; now at twenty-eight she was almost pudgy. Frowning, she lifted the pendulous breasts. Hands filled with the soft mounds of flesh, she sighed unhappily.

Eyes lowering to her hips, she whined, "Too broad, damn it. And that stomach. I look like I'm three months gone."

Her palms closed over her rounded belly, pushing impotently on the soft white flesh, willing it to flatten. Lastly, she peered over her shoulder into the mirror behind her. A string of curse words erupted from her mouth.

"It's your fault, Kirkland Trent, you old bastard. Always poking food at me, saying how cute I looked in my baby fat."

Her hands slipped around her thighs to the cheeks of her spreading derriere. Gripping them, she masochistically shook the heavy flesh up and down, watching in disgusted frustration their Jello dance.

"That black son of a bitch Davy is not earning his money!" she addressed the rippling buttocks. "A massage every damned day and still he hasn't worked off any pounds."

With one last groan of despair, she released the jiggling cheeks and shouted irritably, a vein standing out on her pale forehead, "Della, where are you? Get in here this minute and dry me off!"

Valentina's mood had sweetened considerably when, humming softly, she descended the wide marble staircase an hour later. Overly ripe curves reined in beneath a boned merry-widow and firm girdle, she felt sure she was stunning in an obscenely expensive evening gown of breezy black-and-white dotted swiss.

Heavy breasts pushed up and spilling from the frilly ruffles dipping low around her shoulders, waist nipped in, hips and full bottom concealed in the gown's flowing skirts, Valentina Trent would catch some male eyes this night, she had no doubt.

There was one pair of eyes she wished fervently to capture. The dark, humid eyes of young C.C. McCarty.

Valentina reached the bottom of the stairs, swept grandly across the black-and-white scored entry and paused at the great arched doorway to the living room. She stood and looked with gratified pleasure, as she often did, upon this elegant room.

The walls were painted a soft grape. An imported marble Italian-style fireplace burned low, casting soft, mellow light over the fine furnishings. Embroidered sofa pillows of shimmering grape-and-gold silk adorned couches of Wedgewood blue velvet. Armless chairs of patterned brocade added a pleasing play of different textures to the ensemble. An abundance of crystal candlesticks and vases and porcelains shimmered in the gentle firelight. Original works of art—Cézanne, Dufey, and El Greco—dotted the walls in heavy gold-gilt frames. A massive gold-framed mirror reached from the eighteen-foot ceiling to the marble mantelpiece, adding dimension to the already gigantic room.

It was a beautiful room, she thought proudly. A luxurious, expensively appointed room. A sensual, romantic room. A room where a darkly handsome young singer would soon be spending all his evenings.

Valentina gave her grand palace's main court one last admiring glance, strode inside, flipping a gold wall switch that caused the huge suspended chandelier at the room's center to blaze with shimmering light. She smiled at the tall slender man standing before the fireplace, a cocktail in his hand.

"Neil, darling," she strode forward, "you're early." She turned a powdered cheek up for him to kiss.

"I'm always early, Valentina, you know that." Dutifully, Neil Allen pressed closed lips to her cheek and smiled at her. "You look marvelous."

"Do I?" Her eyes lit briefly, hopefully. Then she scowled, pouting. "You always say that."

"I always mean it," he countered and took a drink of his Scotch.

She straightened his black tie. "You're sweet, Neil. I don't know what I would do without you."

"You always say that," Neil Allen good-naturedly mocked her.

"And I mean it. Now . . ." she whirled away from him, "let me see . . ." She hurried across the room and out the open French doors to the side terrace. Chairs and square tables, draped with crisp white linen, were set up beneath gently swaying Japanese lanterns. The centerpiece on each was a white porcelain vase in the shape of a guitar, holding one long-stemmed red rose. Beyond the terrace the swimming pool shimmered invitingly, lantern light reflected on its smooth mirror surface. At the pool's far edge, a tuxedoed, eight-piece orchestra was tuning.

Valentina gave the area no more than one long assessing glance before returning to the living room and Neil Allen. "Fix me a drink, will you, Neil. We've a few minutes before the guests arrive and I'm nervous as a cat."

Neil chuckled scornfully. "Valentina, I don't believe you've ever been nervous in your entire life." He stepped over to the drink trolley, lifted the stopper from a cut crystal decanter, and poured generously of the gin. Adding a dash of tonic and a little ice, he said, "Was all this necessary, Val?"

Valentina took her drink from him. "All what?"

Neil, picking up his scotch, returned to the fireplace. His back to her, he said, "It's been six months since that night we first saw the kid perform at Lou Anne's." He turned to face her, his brown eyes accusing. "You could have signed him to a contract that night, had him in your . . ."

"That's your problem, Neil. You have no idea how to work people, nor to get what you want from them. I do." Her chin lifted. She came to stand directly before him. "Sure, I could have signed C.C. McCarty as soon as I saw him, but that would have been stupid." She smiled wickedly and licked her red, painted lips. "These past six months the handsome Comanche has come to appreciate my position, my power. He knows now just how much I've done for him, how much more I can do."

She took a deep, long breath. "I've introduced him to some of our biggest recording stars, allowed him to get an idea of the kind of money they make." Abruptly, she flung out a bejeweled hand in an encompassing gesture. "Tonight he'll be in my home, meet lots of interesting people, drink vintage champagne, eat caviar, and dance with beautiful women. See how the other half lives, so to speak."

Neil Allen downed the last of his scotch. "You're an amazing woman, Valentina. And a lucky one. Did it ever occur to you that in waiting, you ran the risk of losing McCarty to some other recording company?"

"I thought about that," she smiled, catlike. "C.C. is not as clever as I was at his age, Neil." She gave a dismissive toss of her auburn head. "No, he's a beautiful, irresistible man-boy and remarkably naive. You know what he came from. You met his folks last night; salt of the earth, ignorant, never been anywhere or done anything. Bless C.C., he has no earthly idea that he could go out to the Coast or up to Nashville and quickly become a star."

She sighed triumphantly. "Believe me, Neil, old friend, when that boy comes to my office tomorrow to sign the contract, he will be so grateful, I'll own him, body and soul. He'll do anything I tell him to do."

Neil couldn't help himself. "And I've a pretty good idea what you'll tell him to do."

Unruffled, Valentina laughed. "I'm sure you do, dear. Wanna' watch?" She reached up and smoothed back a loose lock of his thinning brown hair.

Neil Allen fought the distaste rising up to choke him, wondering, as he had the past decade, why he stayed. He had stood by all those years she was married to Kirkland Trent. When Trent had died, he dared hope she would turn to him. After all he had had her first. Perhaps in her loss she would need him once more. She did not.

Six weeks after she buried Trent, Valentina had taken her first lover, a country singer Neil himself had spotted at Ma Brand's. She had signed the performer to a Bluebonnet contract, promptly made love to him on her office couch, then marched straight into Neil's office to boast about it, sparing no details.

Since then he had lost count of her industry love affairs, but not his desire for her. Neil slumped tiredly. He had the most disagreeable feeling that the dark, Indian-looking McCarty boy would monopolize her attentions. And for a long time.

"Valentina," he tried one last time, "McCarty's just a kid and . . ."

"Get this straight, Neil Allen. I do as I please, when I please, to whom I please. If you don't approve, feel free to leave me and Bluebonnet Records. Is that clear?"

"Crystal. I'm sorry."

"You should be. Now, be a good boy and help me show C.C. and my guests a good time tonight." She stepped closer, so close her pushed-up breasts were touching his white shirtfront. Laying a hand on his lapel, she whispered sweetly, "You're very important in my life, Neil. Promise me you'll always be here for me."

Despising himself for his weakness, he said resignedly, "You can count on me, Val."

"Yes, I can," said Valentina, turned, and flounced away.

C.C. wheeled the navy convertible to a stop in the pebbled drive before Valentina's White Rock mansion. The outdoor staff was lined up to park the arriving cars. A smiling uniformed black youth dashed forward to jerk the Chevrolet door open. C.C. stepped out into the April night.

"Be careful with it, man, I just bought . . ." The carpark, already under the wheel, smiling broadly, gunned the engine and sped away, tossing gravel up beneath the spinning white walls. ". . . the car this week."

C.C. shook his head, pivoted, and looked up at the palatial dwelling. Lights blazing from every window of the two-and-a-half-story home, it was

an imposing sight. Music and laughter drifted across the sloping manicured lawn.

C.C. swallowed nervously, hitched up his suit pants, checked the red
rose in his lapel, and made his way toward the party, his demeanor one of
casual nonchalance, belying his awe and apprehension.

CHAPTER TEN

H E'LL never work again in this business!" Valentina declared acidly. It was late the next afternoon. She was in Neil Allen's office, pacing back and forth before his desk, her brown eyes snapping with anger.

"Now, Val, that's going a little too far. The boy—"

"The boy is an ignorant, arrogant little bastard and I'm telling you, Neil Allen, the only singing he'll ever do will be in the shower!" She picked up a bronze paperweight and threw it across the room. The heavy object hit the panelled walls with a resounding thump.

Neil Allen never blinked. "Dear, it's not the end of the world. Come sit down. I'll fix you a drink and we'll talk."

"I don't want a drink," she shouted angrily, "and I don't want to talk. I want C.C. McCarty." And Neil Allen could hardly believe his eyes. Valentina Trent was crying.

"Val, darling," he rose hurriedly and circled the desk.

"Don't touch me," she warned angrily, "and don't you dare feel sorry for me!" With that she stormed from his office, went into her own, violently slamming the door behind her.

Valentina, tears streaming down her hot cheeks, sank wearily down into her high-backed chair, a feeling of hopelessness and confusion claiming her. She couldn't believe it. She could not believe it.

The day had begun so perfectly. She had breakfasted alone on the terrace, taking time to appreciate the beauty of the blossoming spring settling over her vast estate. It had seemed so fitting that in this season of new beginnings, new hope, new beauty, she would be starting a new and beautiful relationship.

Valentina groaned mournfully. And the disappointing day replayed itself in her mind as sharp and as clear as a film shot in old-time Technicolor.

* * *

C.C. and his parents arrived at her Republic Towers office at ten minutes before noon.

"Mrs. Trent is in the conference room," said Viola, Valentina's secretary.

The trio followed the tall, slender woman across a vast sunny office of cypress panelled walls, floor-to-ceiling glass, and plush, deep carpeting to a door at the room's east end.

Valentina Trent, every inch the successful, no-nonsense lady business executive in a Chanel suit of black-and-white houndstooth, white silk blouse, and alligator highheels, materialized from within—confident, cordial, commanding.

"Mr. and Mrs. McCarty," she extended her hand to Gracie, "delighted you could come. So nice to see you both again." Her smile was full-lipped and winning and the two McCartys found themselves charmed by this powerful woman.

"I've taken the liberty of ordering a light lunch for us," she thrust an outstretched hand to Ernest McCarty. "We'll take our time, become better acquainted."

"Sounds mighty fine," said Ernest, stiffly.

Valentina's brown eyes lifted to C.C. He winked at her and she felt a great rush of adrenaline flood her body.

At one end of the long, oval conference table where the finest napery had been draped and gleaming brass lamps cast diffused light on Christoff silver and Spanish hand-blown stemware, they sat down to eat. Without a single signal given, a white-coated waiter appeared to fill water and iced tea glasses. Quietly he disappeared, then returned carrying a huge tray loaded with silver-domed serving dishes.

Over poached salmon, asparagus spears, and hot Parkerhouse rolls with creamery butter, Valentina Trent explained to her wide-eyed luncheon guests that their son was on the brink of becoming one of the country's major recording stars. With her, Valentina, and the acclaimed Bluebonnet label behind him, there were no limits to how far he could go.

"Today is the beginning," said Valentina, directing her attention to Gracie McCarty. "We'll get him signed, then have him cut a couple of demos early next week. Only our best musicians will work with C.C." She smiled suddenly and confided, "Just last week I managed to steal one of the best bass guitarists in the business away from Chess in Chicago. I already have the most talented keyboard man and . . . we'll make certain the sound is perfect before we cut a master."

Valentina took a sip of iced tea. "We get a good master, then our promotion men will go to work. Soon we'll have our salesmen pushing it to the radio stations all across the country. When the record charts," she smiled warmly at C.C., "he'll open acts for club headliners, be booked to appear on national television and . . ."

Ernest and Gracie hung on to every word. So did C.C. All three envisioned a bright future, with the expert guiding help of this very capable lady. When the last of the lemon mousse and English coffee had been consumed, they were all three glowing with happiness.

"Gracie, Ernest," Valentina, rising, said, "I wonder if you would mind terribly waiting in the reception lobby for a few minutes." She took their arms, walked between them, guiding them through her office. "C.C. and I need to have a short conference."

"Mrs. Trent," said Gracie gayly, "you two just take all the time you need."

"They're good folks," said Valentina when she had closed her office door behind them.

"The best," C.C. replied proudly, displaying a sensitivity which was endearing. He lounged carelessly, arms folded, half-sitting, half-leaning atop her gleaming cherry wood desk. He was smiling.

Valentina came to stand directly before him. She too was smiling. "I'm sure you long to do nice things for them."

"I intend to."

"Good." She stepped closer. "Would you like to do nice things for me as well?" She put out the tip of her tongue and wet her lips.

C.C.'s arms came unfolded. "Like what?"

Valentina lifted short fingers with brightly painted nails up to his open collar. Toying with the starched cotton, she came directly to the point. "C.C., I want the two of us to be close." Her lashes lowered, then fluttered open. "I want you to be my lover."

For a long uncertain moment, C.C. stared at her. His lean hand came up to cover hers. "Valentina," he said, voice low and soft, "I'm flattered, really I am, but I don't think so."

The warmth in Valentina's brown eyes swiftly turned to surprised anger. She snatched her hand from his. "You don't think so?" She shook her auburn head, disbelievingly. "Just like that? You don't think so!"

"Valentina, listen, I . . ."

"No, sonny boy, you listen." Her hands went to her hips, her chin lifted defiantly. "Correct me if I'm wrong. I was under the impression you want to be a star." C.C. looked straight into her eyes, but said nothing. "Well? Don't you? Answer me."

"I want to sing," said C.C., evenly.

"I know," she replied, her voice softening. "I know you do, C.C. And you want to be a star as well. Imagine playing to packed auditoriums where ten, twenty thousand glassy-eyed fans scream and worship you and cling to every note that falls from your lips. Envision having record albums with your name and your face on the cover displayed in stores all across America." She moved closer, catching a distinct flicker of interest in his dark eyes. "The best hotel suites and stretch Cadillac limousines and trips on ocean-liners. Champagne and thick steaks. Fancy clothes and a beautiful home." She zeroed in, knowing full well where his vulnerability lay. "Your sweet mother deserves a fine home, doesn't she? Don't you want it for her? Don't you want all these things for yourself?" She paused, her eyes holding his.

"Sure you do. And you're looking at the lady who can give it all to you." She reached around him, picked up the recording contract from her desk and dangled it between thumb and forefinger. "It's a generous contract, C.C. A contract any beginner would give his eyeteeth for." She waited, holding his gaze.

C.C. felt the perspiration start in his hairline. He wanted that contract as badly as he had ever wanted anything in his life. And while Valentina Trent was by no means beautiful, she was certainly not ugly. Too short and plump for his taste, but taking her to bed a couple of times wouldn't be that bad.

Inwardly C.C. sighed. "Valentina, I want the contract, but—"

Exasperated, Valentina tossed the contract back atop the desk, her brown eyes flashing with a mixture of indignation and desire. She took a step backward and deftly whisked the side zipper of her tailored, black-and-white, houndstooth skirt down, shoved the skirt to the floor, stepped out of it, and kicked it aside. She threw her head back then and waited, confident, in charge, out of patience.

C.C. McCarty blinked in disbelief and stared at her. She wore nothing beneath the discarded skirt but a black lace garter belt and black sheer stockings. No slip. No panties. No nothing. She stood there in the afternoon sunlight, feet slightly apart, hands on ample hips, a look of heat and hunger filling her brown eyes.

"I want your prick," she stated brashly, "and I want it now. Right now. As soon as I've had it, we'll sign the contract." Again she wet her lips with the tip of her tongue and moved red-nailed fingers down over her naked belly to play in the auburn triangle of curls between her fleshy white thighs. "Will you give it to me?"

C.C.'s shock gave way to disgust. Then to regret. Finally to cold anger.

She was going to withhold the contract he had won unless he gave her what she demanded. He looked at the less than appealing femininity she was brazenly displaying. He heard her quickening breath in the quiet, sun-filled room. His gaze lifted to meet hers as he rose to his full imposing height.

"No," said C.C., calmly, "I don't think I will."

He stepped past her and leisurely headed for the door. Valentina, stunned, outraged, stood rooted to the spot for only a second before she flew into action. Beating him to the door, she threw herself up against it and hissed, "You smug, stupid bastard, you'll pay for this insult, you hear me?"

C.C. just smiled. "Everybody in Dallas can hear you, Valentina."

"I don't care!" she said through anger-thinned lips "I don't care!" She grabbed his upper arms and shook him violently. "You can't say no to me, C.C. McCarty! I won't let you. I'm offering you a fortune for—"

"My voice is for sale, not my body," he calmly removed her hands.

Those hands came right back to clutch anxiously at his white shirtfront. "Everybody in this world is for sale, including you, you just don't know it yet."

"I'm not going to argue, Valentina, I'm just going to leave. I thought you were looking for a singer, but you're hunting for a stud to service you. Well, we both lose, so if you'll kindly step aside." He put strong hands to her waist and easily lifted her—kicking and clawing at him though she was—out of his way.

Sobbing now, out of anger and frustration, she cried, "Think I'm too old for you? Is that it? Well, I'm not, damn you, I'm twenty-eight, not as old as that skinny schoolteacher you've been banging for the past four years." C.C.'s eyes narrowed and his jaw tightened. "That's right," she went on, "I've had you followed. I know all about you, C.C. McCarty!"

"You're sick, Valentina," he said.

"I am not!" she grabbed at him again. "No, please don't go. I can be so good to you. You'll never need any woman but me. I'll see you get to the top, I can do it, darling."

His reply was, "See you around, Valentina."

Bested, furious, she slapped his dark face and shouted, "You'll never make it, you hear me! I'll see you back in the projects where you belong, you low-rent son of a bitch!"

But she said it to his disappearing back because C.C. had turned, quietly opened the door, and left her there, screaming insults and sobbing.

Valentina stormed across her office, kicking at the discarded skirt as she went. Livid, she plopped her bare bottom down into her burgundy leather chair and buzzed her secretary, Viola.

"Yes, Mrs. Trent?"

"Viola," Valentina sniffed, "who was that blond guy that took second place in the talent contest?"

"He's Sammy Deanne, Valentina."

"Do we know how to get in touch with Deanne?"

"Why yes, he works at the Baker Hotel as a—"

"Call him up and tell him to come over. I want him here in fifteen minutes at the latest." As an afterthought, she ordered, "Ring up the Cinders Club, I want to talk to Nick Taylor."

Nick Taylor's gruff voice came on the line. Valentina, cradling the receiver between wet cheek and shoulder, said sweetly, "How's it going, Nick, baby?"

"Valentina, sweetheart," rasped Nick Taylor, signaling the slender blond standing in his office door to step inside. "The kid filled the house last week." He laughed deep in his throat, "My God, the women all a hollern' and shoutin' 'Chief, Chief.' It's the damndest thing I've ever seen. In all the years I've owned clubs I can't remember ever—"

"Fire C.C. McCarty, Nick."

"Fire him? What the hell do you mean? He's packing the place and I've got him for a week's run so why—"

"Nick, you still sleeping with that blond cigarette girl you have working at the club?" There was a silence on the line. "I saw your wife at Neiman's style show last week at the Statler." Valentina laughed and continued, "Marge is such a dear. So trusting and . . ."

"Alright, goddammit, Valentina, I'll ace the kid. But you keep your big mouth shut around my wife!"

"Sure thing, Nick. Later," and she hung up. She had time for a couple more similar calls. To Joey Black, manager over at the Vapor's. Was he still holding out club receipts on old William Hennessy, the Vapor's connected owner? And to Doug Barker. Was the illegal blackjack game still going on every night after hours?

Viola buzzed to announce Mr. Sammy Deanne's arrival.

"Send him in," Valentina swiveled her chair, discreetly placing her knees beneath the desk.

The door opened. A wide-shouldered, muscular blond man entered. He wore his brown bellman's uniform. Sammy Deanne smilingly crossed to her. "Mrs. Trent, you wanted to see me?"

Valentina let her eyes slowly move down his body. Shorter than C.C. McCarty, Deanne was stocky, bronzed, and not half as good-looking as C.C. Nor half as talented.

"Take off your jacket and shirt, Mr. Deanne," ordered Valentina.

He didn't hesitate. He shrugged out of his jacket, anxiously flipped open shirt buttons and jerked the long tails out of his tight trousers. He stood before her, awaiting further instruction.

"Want to be an entertainer, Deanne?" Eagerly he nodded. Smiling, Valentina rolled her chair back and motioned him around the desk. Quickly, he obeyed, his eyes widening when he saw that she was naked from the waist down. Valentina laughed, slowly raised a stocking-clad leg, hooking a knee over the chair's arm.

"Entertain me."

C.C. found the nightclub doors of Dallas solidly slammed in his face. Nobody would hire him. There was no doubt in his mind who was responsible.

Summer came and C.C., edgy and restless, agreed to go out on the road with Gail Bradford's old college friend, Donny Lucas. Lucas, a former trumpet player with the acclaimed North Texas Lab band, was putting a group together. He needed a singer. C.C. needed to sing.

It was a hard way of life. Playing small towns throughout Texas in some of the roughest joints C.C. had ever been inside. Pinky's in Lubbock. The Stompede in Big Spring. The Corral in Midland.

Odessa and San Angelo and Abilene. Synder and Lamesa and Sweetwater. Rowdy honkytonks that were a far cry from the sedate, sophisticated supper clubs back in Dallas. The money wasn't bad, but the atmosphere in those dives was volcanic and C.C. never stepped onstage that he didn't feel he was standing on a powder keg.

Fearing for his life, C.C. persuaded Buddy Hester to quit his job at the freight lines and come with him on the road. Buddy, wearing his perpetual foolish grin and chewing Spearmint gum, caught up with the boys in Russellville, Arkansas. It was a good thing he did. Thirty minutes into the evening's show, trouble erupted. A big, beer-drinking cowboy started toward the stage.

"I don't like that Indian's looks," he roared, loudly, "so I'm gonna' change em' for him." And he sailed his beer bottle through the air straight at C.C.'s dark head.

Up popped the grinning Buddy Hester, miraculously catching the bottle in mid-flight. Not a drop of beer was spilled. With bottle in hand, Buddy jumped from the stage and was down to the cowboy. Still grinning, Buddy handed the beer back to the big man and invited him out of the building.

"Sorry you did that, pal?" asked Buddy once they were outdoors.

"No, I ain't." The cowboy smirked, turned up the beer bottle, drained it, and tossed away the empty. "Sure as hell ain't sorry."

With lightning speed, Buddy's right ham-fist slammed into the man's jaw with such violent force he crumpled to the ground.

"Now you are, asshole," said Buddy, grinning. Then he pivoted, like a matador turning his back on an angry bull, and walked unhurriedly away.

He felt great. He was going to like this new job. And he was going to be good at it. Anybody wanted to get C.C. McCarty, they'd have to come through him.

Summer came and went. Early autumn the group went home to Dallas. It was a disappointing visit for C.C. Gail Bradford was no longer there. The neighborhood kids said she was fired from her Crozier Tech teaching job. No one knew where she had gone. C.C. felt responsible. He knew who was behind the firing. Quickly he was learning that people who crossed Valentina seemed to have extraordinarily bad luck.

After only forty-eight hours in Dallas, C.C. and the boys went back out on the road. Donny had booked a grueling three-month swing through Mississippi, Alabama, and Louisiana.

It was cold and wet in the Southland. On the coldest, wettest day of all, a drizzling Saturday, December 8, with only a week left of the tour, the group pulled into Shreveport, Louisiana to find their show had been cancelled.

Depressed, weary, wondering if he would ever get a break, C.C. turned down the offers of the others to go out on the town. Alone, he went to the Louisiana Hayride.

And so it was that he was backstage on that cold, rainy night when the show's biggest draw, a show business veteran, a respected, much-loved country star, fell over onto his face atop the table in his dressing room. Dead drunk. Passed out. Sound asleep.

"Chief," somebody said, shoving a guitar in his hands, "how would you like to sing a couple of songs for the crowd?"

CHAPTER ELEVEN

HIS name was W. Ward Ashford and he was in Shreveport on that wet Friday night. Ashford, known to his friends and family as "Ash," a slim, small-boned man who stood barely five feet six inches tall, was one month away from his forty-third birthday. The dapper, debonair Ash, with his iron-gray hair, perpetual suntan, custom suits, and gentle southern voice, was a highly regarded gentleman in the society circles of New Orleans, where he lived in the fashionable Garden District with his pale-haired wife, Charmaine, and their ten-year-old daughter, Anne Elizabeth.

Ash Ashford was a real estate developer in the Crescent City. He had come to Shreveport to close a transaction, bringing his family along for company. An indulgent father, he had let his daughter persuade him to take her to the Hayride on that chilled, drizzling December night. She'd never been there. Couldn't they go, please, daddy, please?

Ash sighed wearily. It was cold and raining and he could tell by the look on Charmaine's face she had no intention of going along. All day he had looked forward to a hot shower, a meal from room service, and a warm bed. But Anne Elizabeth was a clever little girl. She casually mentioned that it would be fun to see the new performers appearing on the Hayride. Many stars had gotten their starts there, so she heard. That was tantamount to ringing the bell for the old firehorse.

Ash Ashford had once been a successful West Coast talent agent.

For more than fifteen years Ash Ashford's energies had gone into the search for new talent. And to negotiating lucrative contracts for his show business clients. His phenomenal deal-making success, charm, and persuasive powers had made him almost as famous as his clients.

There in the perfect California climate, he lived the good life with his pale-haired wife, Charmaine, a New Orleans girl he had met at the 1940 Mardi Gras. Ash had a rented sprawling white brick house in the Holmby Hills section of Bel Air where Betty Grable had once lived, an impressive office on Sunset strip, and a stable of important clients—mostly glamourous female movie stars whose astronomical salaries poured money into his pockets.

His business prospered. His reputation grew; his phone rang off the wall. Long lunch hours were spent in a choice banquette at the Beverly Hills Hotel's Polo Lounge. The Polo became his second office; he took calls there, scheduled appointments, hustled clients, and cajoled petulant stars, bought lunches, drank dry martinis, and smoothly charmed the powerful wheeler dealers of the entertainment industry.

He was known as a boy-genius; the hottest young agent on the West Coast. Word of his shrewd deal-making spread to the East Coast. Stage actors called, longing to break into the movies, cabaret singers hoping to make it in musicals.

He traveled to New York, taking Charmaine and the new baby, Anne Elizabeth, and the child's nurse with him. They took a suite in the Pierre on the Park and spent a whirlwind week mixing business with pleasure. Broadway sparkled and nightclubs were alive with revelers bent on the pursuit of pleasure.

The glamourous Ashfords were an instant hit with the gay crowd at the Stork Club and La Conga. Dorothy Kilgallen, the noted columnist, stopped by their table for a drink. Her next day's column was filled with accolades for "California's youthful, silver-haired super agent and his breathtaking wife, in town at the Pierre . . ." The telephone in their suite began ringing before dawn.

During those busy, exciting years, Ash rarely indulged in the only vice with the power to truly seduce him. Gambling. Ash loved to gamble, had won and lost small fortunes before he married Charmaine. But his wife didn't like him to gamble; constantly she was at him to quit. For her, he did. Almost. And his days were so full, he hardly missed the action.

His business was a constant gamble for ever-bigger stakes and Ash loved the exquisite agony of sweating out the make-or-break answers on big, important contracts. There was that constant element of chance to his profession and Ash thrived on it.

And, too, he had an adorable child and a loving wife whose regal, pristine looks—and secretly passionate nature—kept him intrigued. Charmaine was the perfect mate. Ever the sedate lady in public; the exact opposite in private.

"Do you suppose George Raft ever made love to Betty Grable in this pool?" Ash asked Charmaine one dark midnight while they swam in the secluded kidney-shaped swimming pool behind the rented mansion.

"I don't know," teased his wife, "but if you don't fuck me in it, I'm going in search of Mr. Raft."

Ash Ashford had an immediate erection. To hear his refined, aristocratic wife use such graphic language was the ultimate turn-on. She never uttered so much as an undignified "gosh" or "damn" before company.

His arms went around her. "Say it again for me, sweetheart. Say it."

She kissed his wet mouth. "Fuck me, Ash. Fuck me in Betty Grable's Hollywood pool."

Ash fucked her.

If Ash was totally happy with his life in California, Charmaine was not. She longed to return to her New Orleans home. From the beginning Charmaine began trying to persuade her dynamo husband to give up his agenting and take her back. Her sister's husband owned a prosperous real estate company; Ash could become his partner.

It wasn't only that Charmaine missed her family. She never fully approved of her husband's profession. She suspected that some of the people Ash handled were less than quality folk and told him as much. Ash, smiling, musedly thought that she would have been shocked to the roots of her pale, gleaming hair had she known the background and habits of some of his most successful clients.

Like statuesque, exotic Brenda Morgan. An orphan raised in a half-dozen foster homes before winding up on the streets of L.A. and in the bed of a top Hollywood producer. Brenda Morgan was a highly paid star with a nasty temper, an unquenchable thirst for straight bourbon, and a yen for pretty young starlets.

Or big, handsome heartthrob, Randy Oakes. Oakes with his muscular physique and hair-covered chest and sinewy legs was all male, but could not conquer his fetish for wearing women's underwear. Which wouldn't have been so bad, except for the fact that Oakes, between camera takes, insisted on lying about in his trailer-dressing room with the door widely ajar, garbed in only his lacy panties and bra. More than one Hollywood reporter had been pressured to keep Oakes's unmentionables unmentioned.

There was the French starlet, Nicole, who tried to seduce Ash every time she came to his Sunset Boulevard office, stripping to the skin the moment his door was closed. And Nicky Angleo, a handsome Italian singer who cried on Ash's shoulder because he was impotent. Hadn't had it up in five years, Nicky wept. Or breathtakingly luscious, multitalented Diane Dawson, married to a sadistic man who took all the money she earned and thanked her for it by regularly beating her up, always taking pains not to mar her face so that she couldn't work. Or poor, lovely Leigh Bartlett who could neither read nor write and had to learn all her lines by repeating them after a hired coach.

Ash never spoke of those people's problems at home, but he had a special place in his heart for all his naughty, mixed-up, spoiled, "show people," and knew he would miss them and the fast-paced action of agenting.

He would also miss the Gardena card parlors and Hollywood Park, and the trips to that small, rapidly growing desert city a few hours drive from Los Angeles. Las Vegas, Nevada. But he loved his wife and wanted her happy.

The Ashfords moved to New Orleans. Ash became partners in the prestigious real estate firm. Charmaine was content. Ash Ashford was not.

He missed California and his colorful clients. He missed the fast track and excitement of Hollywood. He was bored. He was restless. He eased that restlessness by joining some prominent real estate investors at their private clubs for afternoons of gin rummy or poker. It saved his sanity. A rather expensive form of therapy.

The gambling had started again. And the losing. Within a couple of years Ash Ashford had lost the majority of his life's savings. A worrisome fact he kept carefully hidden from his wife. He would, he told himself, find a way to replace the missing money before she was the wiser.

"Ladies and gentlemen," the Hayride's master of ceremonies lifted his hands for quiet. "I know you're all waiting to see the star of our show . . ." Whistles and foot-stomping drowned him out. His lips continued to move, he continued to gesture for silence. ". . . unfortunate . . . badly wanted to sing for you . . . far too ill . . ."

A word here and there could be heard above the din. Finally, the crowd quietened. "For those who didn't hear, Guy Odom, the reigning star of the Louisiana Hayride, has come down with a bad case of laryngitis." The speaker smiled weakly, "This cold Louisiana winter finally got to Guy." Waiting for the disappointed sighs and sporadic clapping and whistling to abate, he said, "In Guy's place a new young singer will step on this stage for the first time. He's from Dallas, Texas, and I'll bet some of you have heard

of him. Let's give a warm Hayride welcome to C.C. McCarty . . . The
Chief."

Ash Ashford, appraising the tall, handsome youth with his keen agent's
eye, leaned forward, interest piqued. And his gambler's heart pounded
beneath the tailored navy sport coat when the boy broke into the recent Guy
Mitchell hit, "Heartaches by the Number." The cavernous place fell silent
as a smooth, rich voice filled the room. Ash Ashford—like everybody
else—listened, entranced, to the tall, good-looking singer.

And Ash, with his nose for special talent, saw standing before him on
that Hayride stage the answer to all his money problems. Eight to five the
kid had no manager or agent, Ash thought happily. He smiled. After
tonight he would.

Urging his confused daughter up out of her seat mid-way through C.C.'s
first number, Ash grabbed her hand and guided her backstage. They were
there, waiting, when C.C., after numerous curtain calls, walked off the
stage, flushed with exhilaration.

"Son," said Ash, warmly, offering his hand. "I'm Ash Ashford, this is my
daughter, Anne Elizabeth."

A firm brown hand gripped Ash's. "Pleased to meet you Mr. Ashford,
Anne. I'm C.C. McCarty."

Ash wasted little time with preliminaries. "Have you found yourself a
manager yet, C.C.?" C.C. shook his head no. "Any records, any contracts,
any . . ." Ash's chest was tight.

"No, sir."

Ash could hardly conceal his wild joy. Hastily guiding C.C. into a
supply room, he told C.C. of his background, of his many successes, his
expertise, concluding with a slick pitch to represent C.C., promising to
"push you up there where you belong." C.C. was interested, but skeptical.
Valentina's contract demands were still fresh in his mind, now some silver-
haired stranger was promising to do great things for him if he'd "do what I
tell you."

Ash read the interest, and the apprehension, in C.C.'s expressive eyes.
"C.C.," Ash said, drawing Anne Elizabeth to stand directly before him,
"this girl is my only child. More precious to me than anything on
earth."

C.C. smiled down at the ten-year-old. "I'm sure she is, Mr. Ashford."

"You let me manage your career, I swear to God I'll never ask you to do
anything I wouldn't ask this innocent baby to do."

A grandstand play, but it worked. "Mr. Ashford, you just got yourself a
singer."

"Son, you just hired yourself a manager," said Ash, "we'll work out all the details at my hotel. Let's go."

By the time they exited the musty backstage storeroom, C.C. was already taking his new manager's career advice. When asked if he would sing another song for the crowd, he deferred to Ash.

The shorter, older man stepped in front of him and said gently, "Sorry, boys, my client, The Chief, no longer appears on this stage or any other without being paid."

The client-manager arrangement was worked out that very night over numerous cups of black coffee in Ashford's hotel suite. Ash did most of the talking.

"We'll form a corporation, C.C. That way we can live off of it and write a lot off in taxes. You and I will be the sole owners in the holding company." Ash paused, lit a cigarette, and added casually, "A fifty-fifty split. You'll have fifty percent, so will I." Calmly looking at C.C., Ash waited, knowing C.C. would object, hoping he could be persuaded to give up twenty-five percent.

"That doesn't seem quite fair," C.C. rubbed his chin.

"Well, then how about . . ."

"I'll keep sixty; you take forty," C.C. suggested.

Ash could hardly keep from laughing out loud. "Shake on it, son."

That settled, Ash told C.C. they would get started right away. "The first thing we'll do is cut a demo. There are some small recording studios here in Shreveport. We'll hustle up some bootleg musicians and . . ."

"Bootleg?"

"Non-union. That way the session won't cost but a few hundred dollars. We get a sound we like, we'll go ahead and cut a master. We can't afford to press thousands of records, so we'll sell the master to a company in Nashville or L. A. Once it gets on the regional charts we'll—"

"Mr. Ashford, what are the chances of me getting a hit the first time out?"

"Slim and none for most new artists, but with a lot of promotion behind you, you'll get there."

"How are we going to get any promotion?"

Ash smiled, "Let me worry about that."

They talked the night through, Ash Ashford explaining his plans to guide C.C.'s career; C.C. opening up and telling the older man of his missed chance with Bluebonnet Records and of Valentina's sexual demands.

"You don't need Valentina Trent or Bluebonnet. RCA, Capital, MGM, and all the other major labels will by bidding for you. You're going to be a star, kid, or my name's not Ash Ashford."

On a sunny Dallas morning, a long, white Cadillac de Ville, with extra chrome and a continental kit on its low-slung trunk, eased to a stop at Sonny's Texaco on Lover's Lane. A dark-haired man of medium build and swarthy complexion got out. Tony Benadetto, flashily dressed, lots of gold jewelry glittering in the winter sunshine, spoke to the uniformed service station attendant before going next door to the Toddle House.

Half an hour later, Benadetto returned for his car. The white de Ville, newly washed, gleamed to perfection. Smiling, tipping heavily, Tony Benadetto got into the sleek automobile and drove away.

In a hurry, Tony cursed under his breath when he came up on a slow-moving city bus, expelling nasty fumes. The bus braked to a stop to discharge passengers, then lumbered away. But Tony was caught by the red light.

"Damn it to hell," he muttered, then: "Jesus Christ," as his eyes went to one of the two passengers who had just gotten off the crosstown bus. An extremely pretty young girl with shiny blond hair and an appealingly curvaceous figure demanded his interest. Tony grinned appreciatively, watching the pretty girl's blond hair toss in the cold winds and the bounce of her full, firm breasts. With the pretty girl was a pallid, skinny dark-haired boy.

Tony rolled down the Caddy window. "Hey, baby, ever ride in a Cadillac De Ville?"

The pair were directly in front of the car's shiny white hood. The girl glanced at Tony, smiled, then quickly looked away. The pale boy glared at him.

Tony had caught the brief flicker of interest in the girl's eyes. It was easy to envision her in his car, settled close on the leather seat. Taking her with him to Fort Worth, buying her a few drinks at the Suite 225 Club, then cruising on out to Camp Bowie to a motel for an afternoon of fun.

Tony grinned, and tried again. "Doll, get rid of junior and we'll go grab some lunch. I'll show you a real good time."

Quickening her pace, the girl grabbed the boy's hand and pulled him along with her. Or tried to. The child broke from her and went dashing toward the car. With a look of wild fury in his gray eyes, he thrust a small hand inside the car, grabbed the soft lapel of Tony Benadetto's fine cashmere coat, twisted viciously, and said through clenched teeth, "That's my sister you're trying to pick up, mister. Stay away from her!"

"Hey, kid, don't get excited. Nobody wants to harm your sister, I want to show her a good time."

"You'll show her nothing! Get out of here and leave us alone!"

Tony, laughing, but uneasily, sped away while the skinny, angry child stood shaking his fist.

Sixteen-year-old Linda Shaw smiled tolerantly at her protective brother. "Ryker, don't you think you were a little too hard on that poor man?" She affectionately ruffled his dark hair.

"No. I'm never going to let any man treat you like . . . like . . ." He lowered his head. Raising it again and looking straight into her eyes, he declared, "Men are not going to use you the way they have our mother. I'll kill the man that tries!" The big gray eyes in the pale little face were fierce.

Ash Ashford and C.C. had watched Benadetto come and go. Ash got out of the car, hurried into the Texaco. "The man with the white Caddy come in here often?"

"Mr. Benadetto? Yeah, he's my best customer."

"Tips real good, I bet."

"Better'n anybody."

Ash pulled a crisp twenty-dollar bill from his pocket. "It's yours if you can remember which radio station the Caddy was tuned to when Benadetto drove in."

The attendant grinned happily. "That's easy. KGKO. 1480 on the dial. Mr. Benadetto never listens to any other station."

"You just made yourself twenty bucks."

"Done," said Ash to C.C., getting back into the car. "Let's get on out to KGKO."

Ash Ashford—C.C. was rapidly learning—let no moss grow beneath his well-shod feet. Only a week had passed since they had met and already C.C. had recorded "Flaming Love," his own composition, backed up on the flip side with a cover of the Laverne Baker hit, "Tweedlee Dee."

And Ash had informed C.C. that Tony Benadetto was the biggest independent record promoter in the Southwest. "Benadetto gets behind a record and school's out."

Now, as they speeded out Northwest Highway toward radio station KGKO, C.C. asked his manager how they were going to persuade the disc jockeys to play "Flaming Love."

Ash shook his silver head. "Step on it, C.C., I want Benadetto to hear the song on his way to Fort Worth."

*   *   *

"Hey, man, you come with that kind of bread, I'll personally make it a hit," bragged KGKO's mid-day jock, "Bad Boy" Satarino.

"Play the record once an hour for a couple of days, that's all I ask," said Ash. He handed over a hundred dollar bill. "Don't mention the artist's name. We'll see if anybody recognizes the voice."

The deejay grinned, stuffed the bill into his pants pocket and pulled down his microphone. "Ah, kiddies, have I got a great new hit for you," he purred, cuing the 45 on the turntable. "You'll be calling up old Bad and saying, "Oooh, Bad Boy, I like it, I like it. Give it to me again. Yeah!"

Back in the car with C.C., Ash glanced at his gold wristwatch. He said, "We have half an hour to eat lunch, then it's downtown for the appointment with the prospective publicist. Afterwards we'll get out to Mystic Productions to see about setting up a tour of the—"

"Ash," C.C. interrupted, "I'm not sure I like bribing the jocks to play my record."

"C.C. don't start with me. I'm bribing no one; I'm doing a little business, that's all."

C.C. shot him a dark look. "It doesn't seem right."

"No? Well it won't seem right when you sell a million copies of a record and only get paid on half that number, but it will likely happen all the same. Look, C.C., I told you I wouldn't ask you do to anything I wouldn't ask Anne Elizabeth to do. I meant it, but I didn't agree to be as lily-white as you, now did I?"

"No, I guess not, but . . ."

"You're going to see a lot in this business that doesn't seem right. But it's no different from any other business. That's not so, it is different. It's a hell of a lot more fun." He laughed and C.C. laughed with him.

Zooming back down Northwest Highway, they heard "Flaming Love" played for the first time on the air. Both reached for the volume control, shouting, "Up! Up! Turn it up!"

C.C. had heard his record a hundred times, but not like this. This was different. He was on the radio! It was a fabulous moment, one he would never forget. He sang along with himself, his dark eyes dancing, heart beating wildly with joy. He had arrived. He was going to be a star.

When the record faded away, C.C. turned to his manager. "You're right, Ash. This business is a hell of a lot more fun."

The older man grinned. "Wait until the record charts. Now there's a thrill for you." He looked again at his watch. "I hope that Italian is in his car."

Tony Benadetto was in his car. He was halfway between Dallas and Fort Worth when Bad Boy Satarino played "Flaming Love."

Benadetto wheeled the Lincoln into the first pay phone he could find, dialed up KGKO and said, "Put me through to Bad Boy Satarino."

"Bad here," came the jock's easy voice.

"Who was that artist singing 'Flaming Love'?"

"You like the record?"

"Who was it, damn it?"

Bad smiled into the phone and caressed the C note in his pocket. "A Dallas boy. C.C. McCarty. Better known as The Chief."

CHAPTER TWELVE

DECCA pressed "Flaming Love" two days after Nick Benadetto played the demo for Vic Hammond, an executive in the Decca specialties department. Hammond listened to the recording three times and picked up the phone to contact the artist's manager. Neither Ash Ashford nor Decca released for publication the amount of money that changed hands, but C.C. went right out and bought his folks a brand new Lincoln Continental, white with red leather interior. Ash Ashford bought his wife a new mink, his daughter a baby grand piano. And treated himself to a day-long session of high-stakes poker at a penthouse suite in the Monteleone Hotel in New Orleans' French Quarter.

Overnight "Flaming Love" became a hit in Dallas and Ash Ashford worked round the clock with Mystic Productions to get C.C. out on the road. Less than a week after the national release of "Flaming Love," C.C. was on tour.

A well-organized, month-long tour beginning in rainy Seattle on New Years Eve, 1956. Portland was the next stop. Then San Francisco, Salt Lake, Denver, Albuquerque, Oklahoma City, Little Rock, Memphis, Birmingham, Jacksonville, and winding up, on the next to the last day of an unusually warm January 1957, in Miami Beach, Florida.

Ash had planned skillfully. C.C.'s first record was breaking across the country as he traveled from city to city. Fans that saw the explosively exciting entertainer on stage walked out of the performance and heard his unmistakable rich voice on their car radios. And they descended on the record stores in droves, clamoring for and fighting over the valuable little 45 discs containing their newest idol's voice.

By tour's end, "Flaming Love" was number one across the country and The Chief was such a hot property that Buddy Hester, his old friend and muscle-bound protector, could no longer handle alone the momentous responsibility for C.C.'s safety.

Off-duty police officers were hired to escort the bright new star into and out of the auditoriums. C.C. was thrilled by his newfound celebrity; loved every minute of his dreamlike existence.

Long legs stretched out in the back of a hired limo—the first one he had ever ridden in—C.C. waved happily to the screaming mobs spilling into the street outside Miami Beach's Ocean Front Pier, where in less than an hour he would step on stage before another screaming sold-out house.

"Bud," he marveled, turning in the seat, "can you believe this? It's unreal, it makes no sense. Don't these people know I'm just like them?"

Buddy, in one of his rare flashes of insight, said, "No, C.C., you're not. You're special; a star. And you're gonna' be a star 'til the day you die. No use thinking you can ever be ordinary again, cause it ain't gonna' happen."

C.C. unconsciously fingered the star birthmark on his cheek and grinned. "Some famous people claim they hate this kind of thing. I don't believe it for a minute. I'll never get enough of it. The day will never come that I tire of it."

The New Orleans weather was near perfect. Sunshine. High wispy clouds. Soft balmy breeze off the river.

On the Commander's Palace Patio, the huge oak dripped dappled shade down on yellow-clothed tables ringing the splashing fountain.

Ash Ashford unbuttoned the middle button of his tan poplin suit, loosened his paisley tie, and lifted a glass of Pouilly-Fuissé.

"Happy twenty-first birthday, C.C. Hope every year brings you more success and happiness."

"Thanks, Ash," C.C. leaned forward and touched the stemmed glass to his manager's. "I don't see how it can get any better than this." He took a drink of the wine, then turned his attention to the shrimp remoulade.

Ash ladled a spoonful of turtle soup, did not lift it to his lips. "Ah, but it will. There's so much ahead, C.C. Gold records, international tours, television, and movies. And enough money to have all the things you've ever dreamed about."

"A house," C.C. said emphatically, as a white-coated waiter placed a plate of golden trout with pecans before him. "I want a nice house for Mama and Daddy. We've never owned a home."

Touched by C.C.'s openness, his childlike honesty, Ash smiled fondly at the boy-man who had not yet begun to comprehend his worth. "Houses, C.C. You'll own houses, not just one. Several."

"You really think I'm going to make that kind of money?"

"Kid," said the silver-haired man who was a blend of street cockiness and aristocratic charm, "you're going to be a multimillionaire."

C.C. went to the West Coast to cut another record that February. The song appeared on the Billboard chart with a bullet beside it and jumped, within three weeks, fifty-five places. C.C. did not sit idle in those three weeks.

Heeding his manager's advice to "Work hard, get out there and meet those promo guys, visit the radio stations, do some interviews, charm the press, kid, they can make you or break you," C.C. energetically put in eighteen-hour days without complaint.

And delighted everyone whose path he crossed with his easy charm and polite manners. Promotional men, too often subjected to prima donna, pain-in-the-ass stars, found the amiable young man refreshing. So did talk show hosts and newspaper columnists, who were too often stuck with uncommunicative, impossible-to-interview celebrities.

By summer C.C. had recorded four more of his own compositions. All went straight to the top of the *Billboard* and *Cashbox* charts and "Flaming Love" went gold. C.C. was again on tour, making a wide sweep of the western states. Ash Ashford, back in New Orleans, received calls from the network television variety shows.

Milton Berle's producers wanted C.C., but Ash didn't like their offer. Jackie Gleason's people were eager to have The Chief on the Great One's show. Ed Sullivan was interested. Perry Como. Jack Benny.

If ever a man enjoyed his fame and all that went with it, it was C.C. McCarty. Quickly he developed a taste for lush living. He loved the expensive clothes, sleek cars, good food, and fine hotel rooms. He liked buying presents for his mama and daddy and in the spring of '57, he presented them with the biggest gift of all.

Exactly as it had always been in his dreams, the weather in Dallas was near perfect on that late afternoon when he hustled his folks into the white Lincoln, drove them across the Trinity river, and headed for Highland Park.

So proud he was about to burst, C.C. pulled to a stop before a big, white, two-story Georgian mansion on shady Beverly Drive.

"Mama, Daddy, that's our new home."

"He won't last," scoffed Valentina Trent. "A flash in the pan. An invention of the press. A year from now everybody will have forgotten him." She snatched a cigarette from a gold case and reached for her Tanqueray and tonic.

Neil Allen, Valentina, and her latest "discovery"—dark-haired, muscular Johnny Knight—were having lunch at Benny Bicker's downtown University Club. Knight—twenty-four, flashily attractive, a singer of moderate talent and monstrous ambition—had recently replaced the blond ex-bellman, Sammy Deanne, as Valentina's plaything.

Valentina acquired and discarded male hopefuls the way she acquired and discarded her designer-original clothes. With bored indifference once she had worn them a few times.

Johnny Knight lifted a gold Dupont lighter to her cigarette. "I agree, Valentina." He smiled winningly, laid the lighter down, and put his large hand beneath the folds of the red linen tablecloth. Rough fingers pushed up an expensive cinnamon-hued silk crepe skirt and found a stockinged knee. He gave it a possessive squeeze. Valentina slanted him a quick, fleeting smile before saying, "Why so silent, Neil?" She glared at her vice president. "Do you disagree with me?"

Neil Allen's slim shoulders sagged. But he spoke what was on his mind. "I believe," he chose his words carefully, "that C.C. McCarty will be one of the biggest talents the music industry has ever seen."

Valentina bristled. She knew he was right. C.C. was unstoppable, a multitalented phenomenon that happens once in a lifetime, a natural born entertainer with the looks, voice, and sex appeal to bring the most jaded of audiences to their knees.

"You really should have signed the boy, Valentina." Neil couldn't help himself. It was so rare that Valentina squirmed. It was an amusing sight. And any mention of C.C. McCarty brought about the same reaction, even when it was she who brought up his name. Her face grew flushed, her eyes grew hard, her well-defined jaw jutted just a bit further forward.

"I know what I'm doing, Neil," she snapped. "I'll not have an artist under contract to Bluebonnet who is as unprofessional and ungrateful as that arrogant, ignorant Indian from the projects."

Johnny Knight, one hand still on Valentina's knee, stuck a small fork into his crab cocktail. "Valentina, I'm very grateful. You'll never know how much I—"

"Quiet, Johnny," she ordered, without bothering to look at him. "Neil, since you seem to be in one of your disagreeable moods, why don't you go on back to the office. Eat one of your little waxed-paper-wrapped sandwiches at your desk." She wrinkled her nose. "We're here to relax and enjoy ourselves, not to talk business."

Quietly, Neil Allen placed his napkin on the table, rose, and left.

"Screw him," Valentina said, turned to Johnny Knight, and smiled sweetly. Leaning close, she whispered, "Johnny, darling, I don't believe I've ever climaxed in the University Club. Give me a first. Slide your fingers on up and make me come before our entree is brought out of the kitchen."

Johnny Knight did as he was told.

Linda Shaw couldn't believe her good fortune. She would, she knew, be the envy of every girl in America if they could see her now. In bed with The Chief! She felt a surge of sheer joy rush through her bare body as she lay on her side, quietly studying the perfect profile of the sleeping man. Smiling dreamily, Linda relived the glorious moment of their meeting earlier in the day.

Behind a glass, scarf-filled counter at Neiman Marcus, she had looked up to see the tall, dark man filling her vision.

It was the Christmas season and Linda had landed a part-time position at the exclusive specialty store. Her first day on the job, a Saturday, and she was nervous. When she saw him, she was speechless.

C.C. winked at her, picked up a long, silk scarf from atop a neat stack, and playfully looped it around her neck. Drawing her to him with it, he said, "I'll take a dozen scarves like this in every color," he paused and slowly drew her closer, "if you'll agree to have dinner with me when you get off work."

No sooner had he walked out of the store than Linda excitedly called her younger brother. "Ryker, you'll never guess what happened. The Chief came in the store and asked me for a date!"

"You better watch out for him, Linda," came Ryker's skeptical voice. "He's a big star, he might try something funny and . . ."

"I will, don't worry. Nothing will happen. I'll be home by midnight, I promise."

Linda hung up the phone, cringing. At twelve, her brother was more fiercely protective than ever. So protective it almost frightened her.

At six sharp Linda's heart pounded when she stepped out into the cold December dusk to find a long powder blue Cadillac, the Sewell Village emblem on its trunk, parked at the curb. A muscular man was behind the wheel. C.C. climbed out of the passenger's side, took her arm, and handed her into the roomy back seat of the big sedan.

She paid little attention to where they were going, she was far too enamored of the handsome man who held her hand and teased her and made her laugh. When the big Caddy finally rolled to a stop, they were in front of the Texas Hotel in Fort Worth.

After dinner, Buddy Hester disappeared and it was just the two of them.

She and The Chief. And it was only a matter of time before they were upstairs in an opulent suite.

Linda sighed happily.

This magnificent man's lovemaking had so thrilled her, she dreamed of making love to him for a lifetime. He was not her first, but he was certainly the best. He was handsomer than her high school boyfriend, and smoother, and more experienced. And richer. Much, much richer.

Absently stroking her right breast, Linda stared at the naked star and let her imagination run wild.

The Chief, after this magical night in her arms, would be so in love, he would want her for his wife. He'd insist they marry; then she and Ryker would move into the big Highland Park mansion she had read about. She'd have furs and diamonds and servants and Ryker would go to one of those fancy private schools for rich kids. She would travel with the famous husband who was so mad about her, he couldn't bear having her out of his sight.

Longing to make the wonderful dream a reality, Linda Shaw used the only ammunition in her arsenal.

She moved closer to C.C. He lay on his back, an arm above his head. Pressing a warm hand to his flat belly, Linda began kissing his lips, gently, tenderly, licking at them, until he awakened. His eyes came open. Linda raised up, purposely allowing her full, bare breasts to swing close to his questing lips.

She secretly smiled when his hungering mouth closed over a hardening nipple and his arms came crushingly around her. He sat her astride him and they made heated love. And when at last his eyes helplessly closed and he grasped her bare buttocks and groaned loudly in his release, Linda felt triumphant and confident.

Leaning down, she playfully bit his slick throat and said breathlessly, "Was I good, Chief?"

"Ah, baby," praised C.C.

"I'm glad." She inhaled the unique scent of him. "I've never been so happy in my seventeen years."

C.C.'s eyes flew open and he pushed her up, gripping her upper arms. "Seventeen?" he repeated, surprised. She looked much older. "Honey, you're too young to be in bed with me. You're just a girl."

"I'm a woman. You should know that better than anybody."

He smiled, but looked at his watch. "I told Bud to meet us in the lobby at eleven. Put your clothes on, it's time I take you home."

Linda wrapped possessive arms around him and gripped his ribs tightly with her knees. "You'll call me first thing when you get back from California?"

"Sure, darlin'. I'll call you."

THIS HOUSE WAS BUILT ON ROCK AND ROLL

Those words graced a huge brass plaque that stretched across the tall, newly installed, wrought iron gates at the Beverly Drive entrance to the palatial white palace C.C. had christened Musicland.

The last of the Gabberts trucks had unloaded the rooms full of the new furniture Gracie McCarty had chosen. The heavy custom drapery had been hung, new lush carpets laid. Everything was ready.

The McCartys moved into Musicland in time for the holidays. A blue spruce tree, reaching almost to the fourteen-foot ceiling, was loaded with brightly wrapped, expensive gifts. All bought by C.C. for his parents.

The gifts were never to be opened.

Directly after lunch on Christmas Eve—a sumptuous spread catered by the Highland Park Cafeteria—Ernest and Gracie got into the white Lincoln. They were driving to Commerce to spend the afternoon, a visit they had planned for weeks. Baskets of fruit and shiny packages in the back seat, big smiles on their faces, they drove away, waving and promising to be back by dark.

C.C. had suggested they let Bud drive them since it was still foggy, but Ernest, his shy smile broader than usual, explained that he wanted to be the one behind the wheel of the fine automobile, the only one he had ever owned.

"You know, son, we'll be seeing a lot of old friends and, well, I guess I just kinda want to show off a little."

"I understand, Daddy," C.C. clasped his shoulder. "Make Mama wear the fur I bought her."

So Gracie in her mink and Ernest in a new Chesterfield topcoat drove the flashy Lincoln out of the pebbled drive and disappeared into the mist.

Out on the highway, Ernest never saw the slow-crawling eighteen-wheeler loaded with oil well machinery until he was upon it. He slammed on the brakes, but it was too late. The Lincoln ran right under the heavy truck, shearing off the car's gleaming white top, and instantly killing its occupants.

CHAPTER THIRTEEN

WOMEN. Women. Women.

Swarms of panting females had begun to press yearningly outside the gates of Musicland and to dog C.C.'s every move, every step. He could no longer go out in public without being mobbed. Girls and women fought to touch him. They tore his clothes, they pulled his black, wavy hair, they fainted and sobbed and begged for souvenirs.

The object of a million sexual fantasies, he was, at twenty-two, a mature man. There was about him a sizzling, barely leashed sensuality that seemed to pulse from every pore. He could step on a stage, stand there in that casual, relaxed stance, all sleek and handsome and sexy, and send an audience into spasms of joy. Just looking at him was a treat and then when he opened his mouth and sang . . .

C.C. loved the women just as they loved him. A naturally sexual animal, he had his pick of beautiful, exotic, sophisticated ladies wherever he went, and often as not, he reached out and helped himself. Insatiable, vigorous, healthy, C.C., when he was not on stage or before the cameras, could often be found in bed with a gorgeous woman. Morning, noon, or night, if he desired her, he took her. His voracious sexual appetite for the most part amused his watchful manager. Ash Ashford was a clever man. He knew that as long as his valuable client loved every woman as opposed to only one, it was better for his career.

After the tragic accident that killed Ernest and Gracie McCarty, Ash Ashford spent a lot more time with his boy. Devastated by the shocking loss, C.C. was numbed with grief. After the funeral, Ash remained in Dallas, sending his wife and daughter home to New Orleans. Leasing a luxury duplex "behind the Pink Wall" (that fashionable district of Dallas bounded

by Northwest Highway and Preston Road and surrounded by a high wall
built of bright pink brick), Ash told C.C. he was there for him. "Need me,
son, just call." And he meant it.

Ash had a battery of phones installed in the apartment. And he promptly
went to work securing for C.C. the entourage needed for a superstar.
Within days there was a full-time staff in residence at Musicland: a cook,
housekeeper, chauffeur, gardener, and a twenty-four-hour guard on the
gate.

In mid-January, he sent C.C. to the West Coast to begin shooting his first
motion picture at RKO. Howard Hughes had seen C.C. perform on Ed
Sullivan's "Toast of the Town," and liked what he saw. And he paid C.C. the
unheard-of price of one million dollars to star in the musical, *Hearts On
Fire*.

Ash told C.C., "Kid, here's how hot you are. I made the same deal with
RKO that I get on your records. Five years after the movie's release, all rights
revert back to the Big Chief Corporation. We'll own it."

"That's pretty good, huh?"

Ash laughed heartily. "Not bad, C.C. Not bad."

C.C. was a natural born actor, though his role required very little of that.
He played his guitar and sang and made love to a beautiful young starlet for
the cameras and finished the shooting in less than six weeks. By the time he
returned to Dallas, Ash had hired a secretary, a road manager, and another
bodyguard.

"I have Buddy," C.C. protested, flopping tiredly down into an easy chair
in the panelled library of the mansion. "Can't he handle it here in Dallas
and then we can hire off-duty cops out on the road?"

"You're a target for every skitzo nut case in the country," reasoned Ash
Ashford. "I want at least two men with you at all times. I've ordered
electronic surveillance equipment installed this week." He scratched his
tanned jaw. "There are fans down at the gates most of time, trying to slip
past the guard. The phone rings off the wall; I don't want you answering it
anymore, C.C."

As he spoke the phone rang and C.C. automatically reached for it.
"They'll pick it up," Ash stopped him. "Now, as I was saying, I've found a
man who—"

"Excuse me, Ash, C.C.," Sheila Rice, C.C.'s new secretary, stood in the
doorway. "There's a Linda Shaw on the line, says it's urgent, that she must
speak to you, C.C."

"Linda Shaw?" C.C. repeated thoughtfully. He shook his dark head.
"The name doesn't ring a bell."

"She's been calling five and six times a day for a month. She says she's your girlfriend and that . . ."

"Sheila, Sheila," Ash lifted a hand to silence her. "They all think they're C.C.'s girlfriend. Just tell her he's not available."

"Sure thing, Mr. Ashford."

Within a week C.C. was on tour, crisscrossing the country in a grueling schedule that left little time to reflect on the loss of his family or the emptiness their passing had left in his heart. There was time for women, however, and at the conclusion of each night's performance, C.C. would choose an eager beauty from the screaming crowd before he was hustled to a waiting limo flanked by Buddy Hester and the new bodyguard, Michael Shephard. And as if by magic, not half an hour after arriving back at his hotel, the chosen beauty would be delivered to his suite.

Any red-blooded male alive would have enjoyed his lofty position, and C.C. McCarty was no exception to the rule. He was living a fantasy. "Some people dream it, other people live it," his agent liked to remind him. And C.C. was quick to agree.

He was cutting records that zoomed right to the top of the charts, making movies that were instant box office hits, and appearing in auditoriums and coliseums where the tickets—at $5.00 a head—were gone within hours of going on sale. His fan mail already numbered in the thousands of letters per week and was growing steadily.

He had custom-tailored tuxes and Cadillacs and the Musicland Mansion. And women. Lots and lots of women.

"Mr. Ashford," Sheila the secretary rang him one afternoon when he'd just arrived from New Orleans. Tossing the keys on the bar in his Pink Wall apartment, Ash loosened his tie.

"Yes, Sheila, what is it?"

"I hate to disturb you but I think we've got a bit of a problem," she gave a high, nervous little laugh.

Ash clutched the receiver. "What kind of problem?"

"Well, if you recall, I've told you about a girl named Linda Shaw who keeps calling here for C.C. and . . ."

"Honey, I told you to blow her off, C.C. doesn't have time for—"

"Hear me through, Mr. Ashford," Sheila cut in on him. "Miss Shaw insists that she's pregnant and that C.C. is the father of her unborn child."

"I see," Ash answered calmly. "Tell you what, Sheila, you give me Miss Shaw's phone number and I'll handle it."

"Oh, good, she's near hysterics and I . . ."

"Sheila, give me the number and just forget about Linda Shaw. Do you know what I'm mean?"

There was a long pause. "You don't want me to say anything about this."

"Have you told anyone?"

"No, sir. Not a soul. I was just waiting until you got back in town."

"Good girl. You did the right thing. Don't even bother C.C. with it when he comes in tonight. He'll be tired, no use giving him anything to worry about. After all, the poor boy hasn't gotten over losing his folks."

"That's so true, Mr. Ashford."

"Miss Shaw, there is one thousand dollars cash and an address inside," the messenger handed her an envelope.

Eyes red and puffy, shoulders slumped with rejection, Linda Shaw silently took the proffered money and closed the door in the man's face. Like a sleepwalker she crossed to the worn couch and sat down, the sealed envelope clutched tightly in her hand.

Frightened, heartsick, the young pregnant girl knew she was left with no choice. She had been a fool to believe that a man like C.C. McCarty would marry her simply because she was carrying his child.

In the beginning, Linda had kept telling herself—kept telling Ryker— that C.C. truly cared about her, that she was his girlfriend and he would call and take her out again, that he was just terribly busy. And then when she had discovered she was pregnant, she was sure that would make the difference. She was elated; glad she had gotten pregnant. She would tell C.C., he would marry her and she and Ryker would move into the Musicland mansion in Highland Park where she would give birth to a beautiful, perfect child.

Linda gripped the envelope. The Chief didn't care. He wouldn't even come on the telephone and talk with her. He had had a stranger call to tell her there would be no marriage, no home in Highland Park. She would be given the money and an appointment for an abortion. A car would be sent at sundown on this very day. She would be driven across town to have her problem "taken care of."

Linda cringed at the thought. And cringed yet again when the front door opened and Ryker came hurrying in.

"Heard anything? Has he called you?" his hands went to slim hips and he stood, feet wide apart, gray eyes fixed on her. He did not know that his adored sister, the sister he was sure was as pure as the Virgin Mary, was pregnant. She had not told him. She planned never to tell him.

"Ryker, C.C. McCarty is not going to call me. I've been foolish to think that he would." She forced a smile. "I just consider myself a very lucky girl to have dated him once."

"Aw, to hell with McCarty," said Ryker. "You don't need him. We don't need anybody, do we, Linda?"

Linda's smile widened and she took his hand. "Mama's been gone for months and we've made it okay so far."

"Sure. I don't miss her one bit. Long as I've got you, that's all I need."

"Same here. Ry, I've got an appointment tonight . . . won't take long."

"What kind of appointment. Can I go?"

"No, no . . . I'll go alone. It's . . . it's a business appointment. I'm going to interview for a job."

"At night?" he quizzed. "How you gonna get there?"

"The company is sending a car. Isn't that nice?"

It was not the baby blue Cadillac which Linda so well remembered that came at dusk to collect her. It was a long, black Packard sedan and the driver was a stranger; a balding, stern-faced man who remained totally silent throughout the ride.

Linda, alone and afraid in the plush back seat, was just as silent. She had no idea where she was going. But she knew all too well why she was going. Her cold hands went protectively to her flat stomach. The child growing inside would no longer be there on the return trip. A wave of sudden nausea sent hot water flooding into her mouth. She swallowed and leaned forward to lower the window. Cold night air hit her hot face and she inhaled anxiously, convulsively.

And when she leaned back, she realized they were traveling on Preston not too far from . . . A car, coming from the opposite direction, turned directly in front of the black sedan. A shiny, baby blue Cadillac. Two men were in the back seat and they were laughing. One had gleaming silver hair. The other, raven black. Linda's eyes flew up to the corner street sign.

Beverly Drive.

Bitterly she envisioned C.C. McCarty relaxing at the mansion, having a fine dinner with his friends, while she was being carted to a dirty, abandoned building somewhere out in the country to let an alcoholic old quack plunge a knife into her body! She ground her teeth in anger and fear while her imagination continued to conjure up horrid scenes of herself lying naked on a cold table in a filthy room, while a bleary-eyed butcher scraped away the new life from within her.

She was shaken from her dreadful reveries when the Packard rolled to a stop before a large, brightly lit sprawling ranch-style house of yellow brick.

The solemn driver opened Linda's car door and ushered her up the front walk.

"There must be some mistake," Linda foolishly protested, "this surely can't be the . . ."

"No mistake, Miss. This is the address."

He rang the doorbell, turned, and went back to the car, leaving her standing there alone, shivering.

The front door swung open and a smiling black maid stood before her. "I . . . I'm Linda Shaw," Linda told her.

"Come on in, honey," invited the mountainous black woman and Linda followed her through the tastefully decorated house into a big, cheerful kitchen where a family was seated around a circular table eating the evening meal.

A light-haired, slender man rose, smiled, and introduced himself. "Miss Shaw, I'm Doctor Allison. This is my wife, Betty, and my children, Zeke, Philip, and Janet. Kids, say hello to Miss Shaw." Three handsome children all grinned and said hi before turning their attention back to their rare roast beef and mashed potatoes.

Linda stood stiffly near the table, confused, unbelieving. Dr. Allison, standing, bent and took a couple more bites of food, wiped his mouth on a napkin and said to the black maid, "Bessie, put the coffee on. I'll be back in time for dessert." And he took Linda's arm, "Right this way, Miss Shaw."

He showed her to a door at the very back of the house, stopping to take a set of keys from his pocket. When they were inside, he threw the bolt and Linda shivered. She looked about. The room was exactly like a physician's office. There was a white cabinet along one side of the windowless room where Dr. Allison went to the sink and began meticulously washing his hands. On the counter beside him, a chrome-and-glass sterilizer was hissing, steam circulating inside. At the room's center, a long, narrow table was draped with an immaculate white sheet. Linda saw no tray filled with long, sharp knives, but she was sure they were there somewhere.

"Linda," the doctor's voice broke in and she whirled to look at him. He held a syringe in his right hand. "First thing we'll do," he said, "is give you some penicillin to prevent any infection." He smiled at her. "Take off your panties and lean over the table."

"Yes sir," she said, and turning from him, stepped out of the cotton underpants. Dutifully, she leaned over the table, lifted her skirts and was given a shot.

"There," he said, "now climb up there on the table. We'll take care of you right now."

Linda felt her heart pounding against her ribs as she got onto the table. And it doubled its furious beating when the slim, pleasant doctor instructed, "Pull your skirt up out of the way and let your knees fall apart. Wider, wider. That's it, now slide down toward me a little. Further, come on, Linda, come to me."

He turned and walked away, and from her side vision Linda saw him open a drawer, take out a pair of rubber gloves and slide his hands inside, then move on. Linda closed her eyes and bit her jaw until it bled. He is getting out the knives. Oh, dear God, let me out of here!

Smiling still, Dr. Allison returned with a long rubber tube in his gloved right hand. "This won't hurt a bit, Linda. I'll put this sterile tube up into your womb, that's all there is to it. Once the air hits the fetus, well . . ." Softly whistling, he calmly threaded the still warm rubber tube up into her tight vagina and beyond. When it was in place, he put both hands flat on the table on either side of her, grinned and questioned, "Now, was that bad? Bet you were expecting knives and blood and unpleasantness." He gave her a fake cuff to her quivering chin. "That's not the way I do it. This is just as effective."

"Yes sir."

"You'll leave here, go home, and . . . hmmmm . . . I'd say by early morning you'll start getting results."

"Results, doctor?"

He nodded. "You'll start bleeding and before you know it, your troubles will all be behind you."

"But what if . . . what if something goes wrong. Should I call you?"

For the first time, the doctor quit smiling. "No. Under no circumstance are you to call me. You have any trouble, get to a hospital and say nothing about me."

Within five minutes Linda had her pants back on and was preceding the slender doctor down the hall. They stepped into the kitchen and Dr. Allison, smiling sunnily once more, said, "Bessie, cut me a big slice of that pie and pour my coffee."

Linda left the happy Allison family eating cherry pie topped with ice cream in a big, attractive house in an upper-class neighborhood. A neighborhood of wealthy, upright people whom, Linda was certain, admired and respected the successful, dedicated physician, Dr. James Allison, a fine pillar of the community.

At 4:30 the next morning, the alarm went off by his bed and a very sleepy Ryker Rawley reached out to punch it in. Hunching into his jeans and buttoning his shirt, the boy picked up his jacket, ready for his paper route.

He started through the house. And he heard a low, keening sound, like that of an injured animal. He stopped, listened, and burst into his sister's bedroom.

Ashen-faced, her eyes glazed, Linda lay upon her bed, writhing, her hands clutching, clawing at her stomach.

"What is it?" Ryker fell to his knees beside her. "Linda, what's wrong?"

She gave no answer, she continued to moan and toss wildly about. Tears and perspiration rolled down her pale cheeks and glistened on her tautened throat. Her sweat-soaked nightgown clung to her damp flesh.

"Oh, God," shouted Ryker, panicky, "what is it? My sweet Linda, what's happening?"

"No, no, no," cried Linda as a new wave of tearing, ripping pain sent her slender legs into thrashing kicks and the bedcovers flew to the floor.

And then Ryker knew.

"Jesus God," he wailed, seeing the pool of blood in which she lay. He shot to his feet. "You're miscarrying . . . Linda, you're . . ." He fell back to his knees again. "What can I do? I don't know what to do. Doctor, that's it . . . you need a doctor."

"No, Ryker," she clutched at his sleeve, her agonized eyes pleading with him. "You can't. It's . . . it's against the law to have an abortion. I could go to jail."

"You could die," screamed her brother, pulling from her grasp. "I'm calling an ambulance." And he turned and fled the room, crying and cursing under his breath. "That bastard. That no good bastard. I'll kill the son of a bitch. I'll blow C.C. McCarty's head off!"

The phone call made, he was back at Linda's bedside, fighting the fear and the nausea enveloping him. The scent of blood hung heavy in the air and the bed on which his sister lay was soaked crimson. Her face, that beautiful face, was growing whiter by the minute and her lips were turning blue.

"Don't worry Linda," he soothed, tears streaming down his cheeks, "they'll fix you right up at the hospital. You'll be okay, you'll be okay."

The horrible pain stopped. Linda felt as though she were floating off the bed. She smiled at the pale, frightened face above her.

"Yes," she managed weakly, feeling a sweet lassitude claiming her tired body. "Fine . . . I'll be fine . . ."

After what seemed an eternity to Ryker, he heard the high, distinctive whine of the ambulance's siren in the distance. Linda didn't hear it.

Linda would never hear anything again.

Later that morning, C.C., asleep at Musicland, was awakened by a disturbance beyond the front gates. Rousing, he threw back the covers, stepped into a pair of Levis, and wandered downstairs. The house was silent. No Buddy. No Michael. He opened the front door and saw police cars, three of them, parked at the estate's entrance.

"What's happening?" he rubbed his eyes and questioned Buddy coming across the yard, reholstering his gun.

Grinning as usual, Buddy told him. "Nothing to worry about. Some crackpot kid broke into a pawnshop, stole a gun, and showed up here at daybreak trying to climb the fence." He put a beefy hand to C.C.'s bare shoulder and urged him back indoors.

"What did he want?"

Buddy cleared his throat. "Said he was going to kill you for what you did to his sister."

C.C. frowned. "What's the kid's name?"

"The little bastard refuses to say. The cops are taking him downtown, guess they'll find some kind of I.D. on him. He can't be more than twelve or thirteen. Just some freaked-out nut."

C.C. nodded. Then yawned and scratched his stomach. "Had breakfast yet?"

By summer C.C. had recorded four more records. Beginning to realize his worth, he had courteously suggested that Snuff Garrett be his producer and Delbert McClinton be his arranger, and that, whenever possible, the recording sessions be held in Ed Burnet's Dallas studios. Preferably at night. Everyone was more than happy to accommodate him.

C.C. had another RKO musical in the can. *Banjo Man* was released in July and movie houses across the country did landslide business. His picture made the covers of *Life, Look, Time, Newsweek,* and all the movie magazines. The Chief's popularity grew daily. So did his wealth.

An automobile lover, he bought himself a gray gull-winged Mercedes coupe and spent one whole morning polishing it in the pebbled drive at Musicland. But when he drove it out the gates, his fans, eager to touch anything that belonged to their idol, pressed anxious hands to the shiny finish and ran along beside the slow-moving Mercedes. Waving, smiling, C.C. soon gave up the notion of going for a ride. Turning back for the mansion, he said to Buddy, "Jesus, they're going to love me to death one of these days, Bud."

"Yeah," grinned Buddy, "especially the women."

"Especially the women," C.C. laughingly echoed, and wondered if he'd ever find "the" woman out of all the women who loved him. There were times when he longed for the girl of his dreams to come into his life. He'd know her in an instant, he was sure. She'd be sweet and beautiful and pure.

C.C. wanted an innocent girl to be his wife, the mother of his children. He wanted to know that he was the only man in her life, the only man who would ever be in her life. He wanted to be the one to teach her about love. He wanted a woman who would be faithful to him, just as his beloved mother had been to his daddy.

Inwardly, C.C. sighed. He'd had dozens . . . hundreds of women . . . in the past few years. Not one had truly captured his heart.

And then he met Caroline.

CHAPTER FOURTEEN

CAROLINE Louise Mansfield was—if there ever was one—the quintessential Highland Park girl. A highborn beauty of keen intelligence and abundant charm, Caroline had, from her christening in the First Presbyterian Church swathed in an ancestral Irish lace baptismal gown, to her coming-out ball at the Dallas Country Club gowned in white silk organdy and white rosebuds, been the center of attention wherever she went.

A fifth generation Dallasite, Caroline Mansfield had known from babyhood exactly who she was and what she was about. Her father, the distinguished, gray-haired Commodore Thomas F. Mansfield, retired Navy man and insurance executive, had met and married the refined Lenore Jesse Leigh, when she was only eighteen, he a seasoned thirty.

Lenore Jesse Mansfield reigned over the stately Mansfield mansion on Armstrong Parkway as a queen in her castle. No royal heir came until Lenore Jesse reached middle age. Forty when Caroline was born, Lenore Jesse was that same year chosen to head up the Texas Chapter of the Magna Charta Dames, that exclusive organization whose members had to prove kinship to one of the twenty-five barons who forced King John to approve the Magna Charta in 1215. Lenore Jesse felt she was the natural choice; after all she could prove kinship to no less than three of the famous barons.

The Mansfields of Texas were unquestionably a part of the ruling, envied upper crust.

"Dazzling" was the word most applied to the beautiful eighteen-year-old Caroline Mansfield. She was, everybody wholeheartedly agreed, the most dazzling deb of 1958, stunning in a decade of delectable debutantes. Gleaming emerald eyes held a teasing challenge, and perfectly curved lips of cherry red caused many a male's heartbeat to accelerate.

Dazzling Caroline had been in love with True Youngblood for as long as she, or anyone else, could remember. The third son of a wealthy oil tycoon, True Youngblood, a graduate of Southern Methodist University, was blond, good-looking, and devoted to Caroline. The perfect match for her, friends said.

Both were well-adjusted, happy young people. Caroline was in many ways very much like her aging, ailing father. Loyal, kind, easy-going, even-tempered, eager to please those whom she loved. She was also like her regal, unbending, still attractive mother. She enjoyed to the fullest the privileged life she led. The constant parties and balls and luncheons and concerts and operas. Expensive clothes, her stately old home in Highland Park, and all the attention, she took as her due.

And, in one regard at least, she was like every other teenager in the country. She was simply wild for "The Chief." Pictures, dozens of pictures, of C.C. McCarty decorated the walls of her bedroom. His discs played continuously on her record player. She had seen both of his movies a half-dozen times each. She was also guilty, though Lenore Jesse never knew and would not have approved, of loitering at the Music Gates with her girl-friends, hoping to catch a glimpse of the Dark God.

"Caroline."

"Hmmmm?"

"Would you rather have the Chief sing to you or make love to you?" Diane Harrelson asked thoughtfully. The two young girls were stretched out across Caroline's white-and-yellow, chintz-hung bed on that hot August afternoon, listening to their idol's rich voice throbbing loudly from the record player.

Caroline turned onto her stomach, rested her chin in one hand, and smiled. "I think," she purred lazily, "I'd like for the Chief to sing to me while he made love to me." She cut her big green eyes to her friend. "What better way to keep time to the music?" They screamed with laughter.

When they'd calmed, Diane said dreamily, "Can you believe we're finally going to see him in the flesh this very night?"

Caroline and True Youngblood were to double-date with Diane and Justin Beck for the evening. The foursome were to attend the one-hundred-dollar-a-ticket United Cerebral Palsy Benefit at Fair Park Coliseum. The featured and only performer, donating his valuable time for the worthwhile cause, was The Chief himself, C.C. McCarty.

The girls had been looking forward to the big night for weeks, and had made True and Justin promise to secure seats down close to the stage, their fondest hope being that they might get to touch the tall, handsome singer, to get his autograph.

Caroline had chosen for the concert a lovely dress of snowy white lace. Full billowing long skirt, tightly nipped-in waist, low cut and strapless, the frothy white dress showed off to the fullest advantage her deeply suntanned bare shoulders and back. She would be, she knew, "dazzling."

C.C. tucked the deep red rose into the satin lapel of his impeccably tailored black evening jacket, took one last, long drag off his cigarette, dropped it, crushed it out with the toe of his shiny black patent leather shoe, and strode casually on stage while the orchestra played a medley of his hits.

The black-tie and ball-gown crowd welcomed him with thunderous applause. C.C. stood there, smiling broadly, six feet three inches of lean, self-assured virility. He took up the microphone, unbuttoned his tux jacket, shoved a brown hand down into his pants pocket, and slid smoothly into his first number, while the sophisticated crowd behaved like any crowd that ever watched him perform.

Awed and electrified and out of control.

C.C. sang for a solid hour, mesmerizing the glittering gathering with the greatest of ease. Then, promising to return in exactly thirty minutes, C.C. smiled warmly while the orchestra behind him went into the intro of his last number prior to intermission.

C.C. let his musical come-in cue pass. He stepped away from the microphone, moving to the lip of the stage. Squeals and whistles filled the air when the lithe, long-legged man jumped agilely from the stage and made his way to the lucky ringsiders. Eager fingers reached for him, to touch, to squeeze, to cling.

A beautiful young woman in a frothy white lace gown took his hand and pressed a note into it. C.C., smiling brilliantly, palmed it, and shook hands with the man seated next to her before going on down the line, nodding, gripping hands, signing autographs.

When he'd shaken all the hands he could reach, he climbed back on stage and walked unhurriedly to the piano for a glass of water. His tuxedoed back temporarily turned on his adoring audience, he quickly read the message from the beautiful white lace-gowned girl.

Chief
You savage. I'll come backstage at
intermission and lick your lance.
Your eager Squaw

C.C. shoved the note into a pocket, drank the water, and turned back to the crowd. He purposely walked down center stage to get another look at the pretty young woman. He liked what he saw. He nodded, almost imperceptibly, to her before taking up the mike to sing the last song.

The number ended, he stood bowing to his audience while they cheered and whistled and the heavy velvet curtain came crashing down in front of him. Leisurely, C.C. made his way to the wings.

"Bud, a pretty young woman in a white lace dress will be coming on back. Give us ten minutes."

Grinning knowingly, Buddy Hester said, "Sure, everybody else out."

C.C. was naked when she stepped inside the dressing room. She smiled, catlike, went to him and gave his mouth a hot, wet kiss. Then her glistening red lips dropped to his chin and she bit him playfully while her hands clasped his ribs fleetingly, then skimmed down his body, coming to rest on his hair-dusted, sinewy thighs.

She kissed his throat, his shoulders, his chest. With heated lips and lambent tongue and teasing teeth, she moved steadily down his rigid body while he stood, feet apart, dark eyes clouding with passion.

"Do it, baby," he groaned, his lean fingers reaching out to tangle in her lustrous hair.

She was on her knees before him, the white lace dress billowing around her. She nuzzled her small, perfectly shaped nose in the crisp, damp hair of his groin and sprinkled kisses over his hard, flat belly.

She tilted her head back and looked up at him, her wet lips parted, her eyes gleaming. "Want to come in my mouth, Chief?"

He trembled.

She put out her tongue and touched it to his erect, throbbing penis. It jerked violently and his breath came out in a quick gasping rush. She licked him then, just as she had promised in the note, starting at the broad base and licking upward to the smooth, velvet tip, while her hands cupped and toyed and squeezed.

And just when she knew he could stand it no more, she took him in her mouth and worked him expertly.

"Buddy," Ash Ashford, dapper in evening clothes, encountered Buddy Hester standing at the dressing room door. "I need to talk to C.C."

Buddy's muscular arm shot across the portal. "Sorry, Ash, he's busy." Buddy rolled his eyes, grinned, and handed Ash the note that had dropped from C.C.'s pocket.

Hastily Ash read it, smiled, and shook his silver head. "If every woman that wanted to lick that thing were permitted, they'd wear it completely away within a week." Both men laughed. "I'm getting out of here, Buddy," Ash added, smiling, "looks like everything's under control and I've got a little poker game going over at the apartment 'behind the wall.' Tell C.C. I'll see him tomorrow."

"I'll do it, Ash." The older man walked away and Buddy, arms crossed over his massive chest, backed up against the door and heard the sighs and moans coming from within.

"Ahhhh," groaned C.C., spilling himself into her mouth. His hands gripped her head while she swallowed the thick, spurting semen he pumped into her. And when she released him, she rose before him, licked her lips greedily, and smiled.

"Who are you?" C.C. laid a hand to the side of her throat.

"Does it really matter?" she responded coolly.

Smoothing at her tangled hair and pulling up her low-cut bodice, she left him without another word while he fought for breath and sagged tiredly against the dressing table. Retracing the path that had brought her backstage, she went through a door leading outside, circled the building, dashed back up the steep front steps, and became swallowed up in the milling crowd.

She glided down the center aisle and slipped into her seat with nobody the wiser. Certainly not the man seated beside her. She had said she was going to the ladies room and he had no reason to doubt her. He smiled when she leaned close and whispered, "Miss me?"

He lowered his face to hers and gave her a quick, affectionate kiss as the lights began to dim. "Yes," he murmured, "it may be our first anniversary but I'm still not used to having such a beautiful wife."

Showered and changed, C.C. waited in the wings while the President of the Cerebral Palsy Guild stood before the microphone at center stage, reintroducing him. He idly gazed out at the crowd, hunting the pretty woman who had just serviced him so expertly. She was back in her seat, her hand tucked around the arm of the man next to her. She was smiling at him and whispering and looking for all the world as if she were the most contented, and innocent, of young ladies.

". . . my pleasure to present him to you once more . . . The Chief," said the President and hurried to the wings.

The spotlight left the stage to beacon fleetingly over the crowd as C.C. strolled out. He stopped in mid-stride and stared. The roving spotlight had captured and framed the most breathtaking young woman he had ever laid eyes on. Caught as she was in the white circle of illumination, she took on an almost ethereal beauty, as though she were not of this world, rather a heavenly angel.

Shimmering masses of gold-gilt hair falling about her bare shoulders appeared silver. Half-petulant cherry red lips turned deep purple, and sparkling emerald eyes were turquoise. Silky, golden tanned skin contrasted gloriously with delicate snow white lace.

She was dazzling.

Instantly C.C. wanted her with a passion so white-hot it made him weak and dizzy and half-hard again. He wondered how he could make it through the show. How he could wait another hour . . . another minute . . . to have her.

He continued to stare, his dark eyes locked on her, memorizing everything about her, and when he went into his first song, a ballad, he sang it just for her.

Caroline squirmed in her seat, put out her tongue to moisten her dry lips, and commanded her heart to slow it beating. It refused to obey. C.C.'s hour-long performance was one of the most exciting, enjoyable experiences of her life.

Not for C.C.

It was the worst hour of his life because he could not touch the angelic vision in white lace. At long last the opening strains of his closing number began. C.C. again went down into the audience.

Ignoring all the outstretched hands grabbing at him, he moved directly to her. He took the blood-red rose from his lapel and carefully tucked it into her glittering gold hair over her small left ear.

"Stay with me, sweetheart," he said and it was more a plea than a command.

They were at each other like two untamed animals once the heavy car door was closed. While C.C.'s driver guided the Cadillac limousine into the stream of automobiles carrying socialites out of the Fair grounds, C.C. and Caroline, ignoring the honks and shouts, kissed hotly and hugged each other tightly in the roomy back seat.

". . . really shouldn't be doing this," gasped Caroline between long, open-mouthed kisses. ". . . not fair to my boyfriend . . . was supposed to come with me this evening but he's not back from Midland . . ."

"Mmmmm," was C.C.'s only response as his lips took hers again, then slipped over her chin to her throat and moved brazenly down to the swell of her breasts atop the white lace bodice.

"Chief . . ." she breathed, and gave in to desire.

Practiced lips and tongue driving her wild, C.C.'s lean hand stole beneath the delicate white lace to caress silky limbs. Excited to a fever pitch, Caroline didn't stop him when he ran his hand over the flushed skin of her inner thighs, then slowly, deftly took from her her panties. Nor did she protest when his fingers, those smooth, brown fingers, moved to the mass of silky gold curls between her legs.

C.C. lifted his head to watch her face while he touched her. Her beautiful emerald eyes were half-closed, her lips were parted, and her breath was rapid and shallow. Gently, lovingly he caressed her until her flat belly was contracting and her back was arching. Fingers wet with her passion, he slipped them into her and Caroline stiffened and gasped.

He stopped at once and stared at her.

"My God, are you a virgin?" he asked.

"Yes, Chief," she whispered. "You'll be my first."

For a long moment C.C. said nothing. Then he kissed Caroline's open lips and said, "And your last. Put your britches back on, baby. I'm going to marry you."

CHAPTER FIFTEEN

ID she suck your brains out the head of your dick?" was Ash Ashford's reaction to C.C.'s wedding plans.

Dark eyes flashed angrily. "She's not that kind, Ash. She's a sweet, innocent young girl, and I love her."

"Love her? C.C., you don't even know her."

"I know I love her and I'm going to marry her."

Ash sighed disgustedly. "Damn it, C.C., you're just a kid yourself. You want to tie yourself down?"

C.C. lifted wide shoulders and grinned. "I have to have her."

Ash rose from his chair, walked to the bar, and brought down the Scotch. "Have her? Hell, you can have her. Have her the way you have all your other women." He smiled then and purposely made his voice calm, modulated. "Move the girl in here to Musicland for a couple of weeks; you'll tire . . ."

"Ash, I am going to marry Caroline Mansfield."

Ash Ashford felt a tightness in his chest. He poured two fingers of J & B, took a soothing swallow, and crossed the room to where C.C. lounged on the deep leather couch, long legs sprawled out before him.

Ash sat down. "C.C., why do you think I'm opposed to this marriage?"

C.C. shook a Viceroy from a pack, stuck the cork tip in his mouth, and rolled it around in his full lips. "You got me."

Ash hid his irritation. "Your career, son," he said softly. "Millions of women are in love with you. They dream about you at night, they buy your records and come to your concerts and go to your movies. As long as you stay single you . . ."

"My fans won't desert me because I get married," C.C. lit the cigarette and drew smoke deep into his lungs.

Ash tossed down the Scotch. "You're wrong, C.C. Fans are fickle. They love you now because you're their living, breathing sexual fantasy. You're handsome and masculine and virile. Most importantly, single. There's nothing exciting about a settled married man. Women want to feel like you're making love to them, that you belong to them."

"I'm sure there's some truth in what you say, Ash, but I'll take my chances."

Ash ground his even white teeth. "C.C., there's a lot of agents in this business that would have tried to turn you gay just so this kind of problem would never arise." C.C.'s eyes widened. "It's true, we've both seen it," Ash went on, "but I never did that to you, did I?"

"No, but it wouldn't have . . ."

"Okay, okay, you wouldn't have gone for it. My point is I've been straight with you in every way, have I not?"

"You have."

"Don't do it. Don't marry the girl. It's career suicide."

"So be it," said the independent, smitten C.C. McCarty.

Ash tried another tack. "What kind of life do think it will be for the girl?"

"Caroline's her name, Ash. Caroline. Caroline Mansfield. A great life, I hope. I love her and I'll give her . . ."

"How's Caroline going to like sharing you with other women?" Ash interrupted. "Do you suppose the ladies will quit throwing themselves at you just because you take a bride?" He wagged his silver head from side to side. "It's not like that, C.C. Women will try to go to bed with you— married or not. They'll still have to have you."

"Nobody is going to have me but Caroline."

Ash's lips twisted into a half-smile. "How long can a red-blooded boy like yourself resist hot, eager beauties like the one you had during intermission last night at Fair Park?"

Unmoved, C.C. replied. "Forever. As long as I have Caroline."

"Are you out of your mind?" was Lenore Jesse Mansfield's reaction to the shocking, repellent news.

"Yes!" squealed an excited, glowing Caroline, ignoring her mother's stricken face. "Yes, yes, yes! I'm out of my mind with joy!"

"Dear God, you can't mean this! You're enjoying one of your infantile jokes. You're marrying True Youngblood as soon as you get your degree from Southern Methodist!"

"No, Mother, I'm marrying the Chief and there'll be no degree. I'll be traveling with my husband, there'll be no time for college."

Lenore Jesse, her fair face flushed with high color, fragile hands shaking violently, turned to her husband for support. "Thomas, tell her it's out of the question! Tell her we forbid it!"

Commodore Mansfield was almost as upset as his wife, but a bit more diplomatic. "Won't you think it over, Caroline? You're so young and you hardly know this boy. It wouldn't be wise to rush into marriage with a stranger."

Caroline smiled at her distinguished, aging father. "Daddy, didn't you fall in love with mother the first night you met her?"

The old man mused. "Why, I don't recall . . . perhaps . . ." his face broke into a hint of a recollecting smile and he looked at Lenore Jesse. "Darling, the child's right. Remember that first evening you came to dinner here and we went . . ."

"Thomas!" Lenore Jesse's green eyes snapped fire at him. Her regal head swung back in her daughter's direction. "We simply will not have you embarrassing us this way. Marry a recording star, indeed! One hires show people to entertain at weddings. One does not marry them."

It was Caroline's eyes now that snapped with anger. "I'm very proud of the fact that the man who is to be my husband is an entertainer, a very successful one. I'm the luckiest girl alive. Millions and millions of women would give anything to be in my shoes."

Lenore Jesse refused to give up. "Your 'successful entertainer' came from the West Dallas projects, or had you forgotten that bit of biography. His people were nothing but ignorant, uneducated white trash who lived in abject poverty and—"

"Stop! Stop it, Mother! I'll not listen to another word, not one more. I am eighteen, old enough to marry without your consent. I am going to marry C.C. McCarty if I have to elope to do it." She rose and stormed from the room.

True Youngblood, the jilted fiancé, took the devastating news like the refined young gentleman he was. Conditioned from the cradle, he— adhering to the Youngblood code of showing no emotion, no matter how unfortunate the circumstances—stepped graciously aside, his wounded pride carefully concealed.

"Every happiness, Caroline. You'll always be special to me and should there ever come a time you need me, I'll be there for you."

Ushers in morning coats. Bridesmaids in mulberry velvet dresses. Orange blossoms, delicate baby's breath, and tall white candles. Friends and well-wishers arriving in a steady stream of long black limos before the majestic, gothic, Presbyterian Church on University Boulevard.

Photographers from all over the world, jostling, flashing, and shooting. Fans, hundreds of them, filling the church grounds, straining to see, hoping for a fleeting glimpse of their idol and his bride. Policemen, on foot and on horseback, directing traffic, holding back the crowds, constructing a human tunnel through which the celebrated couple could safely pass. Bodyguards and security agents, pistols riding their armpits, eyes wary and roving, escorting the nervous bridegroom into the side chapel doors.

And finally, Miss Caroline Louise Mansfield, radiant and smiling, alighting from a white stretch Mercedes, a dazzling virginal vision in an antique ivory satin wedding gown, its bodice of French alençon lace, ten-foot-train trailing behind her on the red carpeted church steps. Gold-gilt hair gleaming beneath the headdress and veil, emerald eyes dancing with excitement and happiness, she waved to the crowd and disappeared inside.

At precisely 8:00 A.M. on that Saturday morning, November 15, in the year of our Lord 1958, a nervous, handsome Clifford Clyde McCarty exchanged solemn vows with the young, beautiful Caroline Louise Mansfield before three hundred invited, well-heeled guests. Ash was there with his wife Charmaine and daughter Anne Elizabeth. Buddy Hester was the grinning best man. Caroline's closest friend, Diane Harrelson, the teary-eyed maid of honor.

Liveried servants balancing silver trays laden with sparkling glasses of French champagne passed among the guests at the wedding reception-brunch in the Dallas County Club's vast ballroom. Friends kissed the dazzling bride, congratulated the proud groom, and gravitated toward the long linen-draped tables where elaborate ice sculptures reigned over a sumptuous spread of rich breakfast delicacies.

Sliced melon, papaya, and fresh strawberries arranged artfully on beds of chipped ice. Piping hot croissants, danishes, and muffins in silver baskets. Eggs Benedict and cheese-scrambled eggs and crab omelettes in glass-and-silver chafing dishes. Apple-smoked bacon and country sausage and Virginia baked ham. Raspberry preserves, orange marmalade, and natural honey. Coffee and cocoa and hot tea. Freshly squeezed orange juice, spicy Bloody Marys, and Tuaca-laced cream.

And a three-foot-tall wedding cake.

Smiling for the photographers, the new Mrs. C.C. McCarty sliced a large piece of the rich white cake and laughingly fed it to her husband. They looped their arms, lifted their champagne glasses, and drank. And glowingly accepted the many toasts proposed to their bright future and lasting bliss.

Less than an hour later, the wedded pair had departed the club and were inside the bridal suite at the stately Melrose Hotel, the reception and their guests totally forgotten as C.C. carried a blushing, laughing Caroline straight through the suite's sitting room to the turned-down, ivory, silk-sheeted bed.

Caroline's exquisite white peignoir lay draped across an ivory-velvet vanity chair. She never put it on. Naked, she lay in the long, dark arms of her experienced husband, eager to become a woman. She thrilled to the thought that she was making love to the famous Chief; gloried in the knowledge that all women wanted him. And she had him. She felt certain he would be the best of lovers, a fantasy come true. C.C. didn't disappoint her.

They remained abed throughout the entire first day of their marriage, thrilling each other, pleasing each other, shocking each other.

The next day they left on their honeymoon.

It was C.C.'s first taste of transatlantic travel, though his young bride had lost count of the crossings she had made with the Commodore and Lenore Jesse.

The pair stood at the railing of the majestic Ile de France and watched the skyline of New York slip below the horizon and disappear. The trip took a week, and a glorious week it was for the honeymooners. C.C., a celebrity, was noticed, of course, but the maître d'hotel and the wealthy passengers were accustomed to the famous and so left the passionate pair alone.

As first-class passengers, they had the run of the elegant salons of the upper decks, the restaurant where they dined in evening clothes, the cocktail lounges where the bartender concocted exotic drinks for their delight, and the grand ballroom where they danced nightly.

Mornings they strolled the deck hand in hand, the cold ocean winds stinging their cheeks and making their eyes water. And afternoons they made love in their opulent stateroom.

When they stepped ashore at Naples, Caroline thought it was their final destination. That the honeymoon cottage her bridegroom told her of was surely on the beautiful isle of Capri. She was ecstatic.

She was also mistaken.

"Yugoslavia?" she repeated disbelievingly for the tenth time when, two days later, she stepped into the living room of a remote stucco dwelling perched high atop steep rocky cliffs in the Montenegrin village of Budva.

C.C. laughed good-naturedly and hugged her. "It's perfect, don't you agree? The day after we met, I called up Ebby Holiday Realtors. I told her to get in touch with her contacts and find a place where no one would ever think to look for us."

"You actually bought this place?"

"Yes, sweetheart," he told her proudly. "It belongs to us."

"Couldn't she have found something a little . . . a bit . . . closer to home?"

"Sure, but that's the fun of it. We're a world away from everyone we know." He took her hand, led her through the tall French doors and out onto the flat stone balcony. An afternoon storm was blowing in from Africa. High breakers crashed against the cliffs far below. Palms bordering the property bent in the strong cold winds.

C.C. fell instantly in love with the place. "I wish," he said, happily, his eyes scanning the turbulent Adriatic sea, "we could stay here forever."

Caroline, though she kept it to herself, did not share his enthusiasm. The place he found so appealingly private, wonderfully romantic, and irresistibly seductive, was to his pampered eighteen-year-old bride, rustic, remote, and lonely.

They were to spend a month. They left after a week. Caroline was homesick. The holidays were nearing. Couldn't they please be in Dallas for Christmas?

"Of course, baby, anything you say."

CHAPTER SIXTEEN

BEING married to the Chief was thrilling. Caroline traveled everywhere with her husband, living out of suitcases in lavish hotel suites and keeping odd hours and plugging into his celebrity. The fun-loving Dallas deb was quickly caught up in the whirl of sold-out concerts, and star-studded parties, and constant excitement. Wherever they went flashbulbs popped and fans gathered and sleek limos whisked them to their next stop. They were the most sought-after couple in America, pursued and warmly welcomed into the homes of the country's rich and powerful.

C.C. was tender, caring, and deeply in love with Caroline. So when, not four months after the wedding, Caroline told him she was pregnant, he was delighted, despite the fact it would mean a separation. They would again travel together after the birth of their baby, he told her happily.

Caroline returned to Dallas, while C.C. began shooting a new movie. The loneliness of Musicland without C.C. was a terrible letdown after the glitter and excitement of traveling across the country with one of the world's most famous men.

C.C. suffered too. Passionately in love, he missed his bride and flew home at every opportunity. The separations were painful, but the reunions were sweet and golden.

He was completely happy.

Valentina Trent was not.

Seated rigidly in her chauffeur-driven Cadillac, the skirt of her beige Mainbacker dress draped discreetly over her knees, she sighed wearily. On her way to the Baylor Hospital Auxiliary luncheon at the Lakewood Country Club, her thoughts were not on the luncheon. They were on C.C. McCarty.

Valentina snapped open her lizard bag and drew out a cigarette case of eighteen carat gold with diamonds set in platinum. She opened the gleaming case and withdrew an Old Gold, irritably tapping it on the back of her kid-gloved hand.

Why, she wondered miserably, had C.C., of all the recording hopefuls to pass through the doors of Bluebonnet, refused her? And why did that refusal continue to plague her? If she had played her hand differently, would he have come to her in time? If she had signed him to a contract and demanded nothing of him, would he have found her more appealing? Would they have become lovers along the way? Could she have been Mrs. C.C. McCarty today, instead of that golden-haired fifth-generation rich brat from Highland Park?

Valentina smiled ruefully. God knows she and C.C. would have been more suited as a couple. Two of a kind. Both from poor backgrounds who had risen above it to make something of themselves. She had shaken the dust of the Rio Grande Valley from her feet just as C.C. had climbed from the mire of the West Dallas projects. They belonged together, if only . . .

Valentina snuffed out her cigarette in the ashtray and immediately lit a fresh one.

To hell with C.C. McCarty! She didn't need him; she didn't want him. She was sick of hearing about him, of reading about him every time she picked up a newspaper or a magazine. Of hearing his distinctive sultry voice each time she switched on the radio.

She'd fix him if it took forever. That arrogant bastard had the world at his feet now, but it wouldn't last. And when he was back in West Dallas where he belonged, would that spoiled little debutante with the gold hair want him still?

Valentina smiled, the blood racing through her veins. She envisioned C.C. in a few short years. A has-been. Down and out. Forgotten. Broke. Then he'd come crawling to her. He would beg her for what he had so stupidly turned down in her office that day.

Would she give it to him? Never!

"Madam, we're here," Stanley, the chauffeur, snapped her from her reveries.

Taking his hand, she stepped out under the club's drive-through, smiling warmly to Pauline Douglas, committee chairman. Mrs. Douglas hurried to Valentina, took her arm, and whispered conspiratorially, "Have you heard the latest on Caroline and the Chief? They're going to have a baby."

One hundred miles southwest of Dallas, a pale-haired man in a conservative gray business suit stood at an upstairs window in the brick two-story administration building of Gatesville State Home for Boys. Hands locked behind him, he watched a skinny boy cross the windy quadrangle of the state correctional institution, coming in his direction.

Dr. Raymond Buck, the school's psychologist, smiled warmly when the boy came into the office.

"Have a seat, Charles," he indicated a straight-backed chair across the desk. "How are you this morning?"

"Exactly like I was the last time you asked me that," was Ryker Rawley's sullen reply.

Dr. Buck laced his fingers atop the desk and continued smiling. "How old are you now, Charles?"

Ryker rolled big gray eyes. "You want to know, look it up in the records."

The doctor glanced at the sheets of paper spread out before him. "Fourteen this July. That correct, Charles?" Nothing. No answer. "I recall when I was fourteen, I was attending . . ."

"Doc, I don't give a damn what you were doing when you were fourteen or fifteen or twenty-one."

Dr. Buck fought the mild annoyance and feeling of helplessness this complicated, uncommunicative youth always spurred. "Your teachers tell me you get high marks, that you are a very intelligent young man."

Ryker shrugged, shifted in his chair, crossed one leg over the other and started swinging it, a habit he knew irritated the doctor.

Dr. Buck ignored the ploy. "Tell me again, Charles, why you are such an angry boy. So angry that you attempted to kill a man. So angry that after all this time you are still not sorry."

"He's no man," spat Ryker, his swinging foot stilling, his big gray eyes glittering. "He's a murderer! And I'm sorry, alright, sorry I didn't get him! Sorry the rich, cold-hearted bastard is still alive! Sorry I'll have to wait until I get out of here to finish the job!"

Caroline, growing larger with each passing day, stayed behind in Dallas when C.C. left on the 1959 nationwide tour in early May. Feeling unattractive, lonely, and sorry for herself, she called up her mother's favorite interior decorator, Jeffrey Fox, and asked him to have a look at Musicland.

"My God, it's even worse than Lenore Jesse told me," sniffed the diminutive, impeccably dressed Fox. He swept through the rooms, eyes darting this way and that, one hand riding a prominent hipbone. "I don't know, I don't know," he lamented dramatically, "am I up to this? There's so much to be done. God give me strength; I see nothing worth saving. We'll be fortunate if a Salvation Army truck is willing to cart this . . ." his patrician nose wrinkled, "this junk away."

"I told C.C. I plan to redecorate; he said I can have whatever I want," offered Caroline, apologetically.

"Did he? How gallant," Fox's full lip curled disdainfully. ". . . Hmm, perhaps a tapestry-covered French sofa or a Duncan Phyfe here. Maybe a couple of English Chippendale chairs and an Ipswich chest over there and . . ." He glided about, talking to himself, Caroline following. Abruptly, he stopped. "I had planned on a well-deserved vacation, but I couldn't get a bit of rest knowing this monumental task awaits me." He sighed, theatrically. "I'll get up to New York next week and haunt Sotheby's; see what we can find. Meanwhile, Caroline, I'd keep my friends away from Musicland, were I you."

"You would? Why?"

"Dear girl," he chastised scornfully, "surely the most celebrated post-deb in Dallas wouldn't want the Idlewild Club to know that their lovely little pet with all her ancient credentials is living like *this*?" he lifted a fluttering hand and waved it about.

"You won't tell anyone, will you?" Caroline heard herself ask, and felt ashamed. What would C.C. think if he could hear her.

"Judas Priest, darling, I'd sooner cut my tongue out than blab. I have to be going now. Kiss, kiss," he said, puckering, and busing the air.

She walked with him down the steps of Musicland. "Thanks for coming, Jeffrey."

"Don't mention it, love," he said, his gaze going to the closed gates in the distance. "Isn't there something you can do about that, Caroline?" He was referring to the fans beyond the fence.

Caroline smiled. "They won't be there tomorrow."

"No? You plan to banish them then?" He was fully approving.

"By tomorrow they will have heard that the Chief is out of town." She brushed a wisp of gold-gilt hair from her eyes. "He's the attraction here, not I."

Ash Ashford left the '59 tour in Los Angeles. Turning the reins over to C.C.'s competent road manager, Guy Stearns, Ash checked out of the Beverly Hills Hotel and caught the next flight. Not home to New Orleans and Charmaine, but to Las Vegas.

Charmaine believed her husband was still on the tour. He saw no reason to tell her differently. Feeling somewhat like a small, naughty boy, Ash called up Charmaine from the Riviera.

"Sweetheart," he said when she picked up the phone. "Everything okay there? Anne Elizabeth behaving herself?"

"We're fine, darling. Still in L.A.?"

"That's right."

"Where to next, Ash?"

"On up to San Francisco, then Seattle."

"You'll call me every night?"

"Certainly, darling."

Ash hung up the phone, smiled, and felt his heartbeat speed. There was no real hurry to get downstairs to the tables. He would be in Vegas for several days. No reason to rush. He would unpack, take a hot shower, maybe call room service, relax a while before he did any serious gambling.

He was still telling himself that as he hurried for the elevator. The heavy chrome doors opened and he stepped out into the bustling casino. Slot machines crunched, dice clicked, cards flicked. And Ash Ashford, palms moist, belly tight, squeezed in at a crowded crap table.

Swallowed up in a euphoric world of agonizing rapture that only a true gambler can understand, Ash stood at the tables for the next twenty-four hours, vitally alive, his anxious eyes following fixedly every roll of the tumbling red dice.

C.C. came in off the road July 1, announcing he had a surprise for Caroline. He had purchased, sight-unseen, a beach house on Padre Island, that long, white sandy strip of barrier isle off the coast of South Texas in the Gulf of Mexico. Would she like to take her very pregnant self down for a couple of weeks in the sun?

She would, she said, but Dr. Donald McGuire, her esteemed obstetrician, had cautioned her against long car rides.

So C.C. told her of his second surprise. His first airplane, a gleaming six-seater, was waiting at Love Field, a seasoned ex-air force pilot, Bert McDuff, standing by to take the controls.

The short vacation at Padre was relaxing and wonderful. C.C.'s dark skin deepened to a rich nut brown while Caroline's lovely limbs turned a honey gold. It was while C.C. lay dozing on their private beach one lazy afternoon that Caroline, spreading oil on his broad, smooth back, said casually, "Darling, I've ordered new furniture for Musicland."

C.C. never opened his eyes. "Fine, sweetheart, long as it's not that kind of stuff your mother and daddy have."

Caroline's hand stopped its circular motion on his back. "You mean antiques?"

"Yes, antiques. I hate 'em. I feel the same way Elvis does. I was raised on a bunch of goddamn antiques."

"C.C. I didn't know you felt so strongly about . . . I thought sure . . ."

He rolled over onto his back. "God, don't tell me," his dark eyes flashed briefly with anger. "I'm not going to have a bunch of old ugly furniture in my . . ." He saw the stricken look on her lovely face and was immediately sorry for upsetting her. "Hey, baby, it's alright. You want antiques, it's okay with me." He pulled her into his arms. "Anything you do is okay with me," he said and meant it.

Caroline was, to him, a beautiful blond dream, his cherished angel, his only love, and even with the world at his feet, he could not believe that this golden-haired charmer actually belonged to him.

She could have told him that she wanted to dynamite Musicland and C.C. would have given the go-ahead.

The Padre days were glorious but brief. The pair returned to Dallas. The very next day C.C. flew back to the Coast and RKO to begin another movie.

In August he was in Dallas to attend the world premiere of *The Grand Passion*, the film he had made with sexy French co-star, Gabrielle DuBois.

Premiere night, C.C. and Gabrielle, glamourous in evening clothes, arrived at downtown Dallas' Majestic Theater where great search lights pierced the night skies and thousands of fans stood behind saw-horse barriers. C.C. helped his leading lady from the long white limo while the crowd screamed and surged forward, longing to touch the glittering pair.

Caroline, due to deliver at any minute, was excluded from the festivities. Fat and miserable and jealous, she remained in seclusion at Musicland.

Never in her young life had she had felt so left out. So unwanted. So alone.

So resentful.

CHAPTER SEVENTEEN

C. C.'s DAUGHTER was born on August 14, a year to the day after her parents met. C.C. was at the post-premiere party at the Statler when the call came from Musicland. He raced to Baylor University Hospital in his evening clothes.

Laura Kay McCarty came into the world as the summer dawn was breaking. Her famous daddy, haggard, unshaven, was awed by the sight of the infant in his exhausted wife's arms. Almost reverently he studied the tiny baby with her jet black hair, cute button nose, and rosebud lips.

"She looks like you, C.C." said a groggy Caroline.

"A little I suppose. I wonder if . . ." He laid a hand to the side of Laura Kay's soft pink cheek, leaning closer, dark eyes intense. After examining her little face, he insisted on unwrapping his daughter from her downy pink blankets.

"But C.C. why? You'll wake her. You'll make her cry."

"Shhh," he said, pushing the baby's soft batiste gown up over her tiny stomach, touching, looking, inspecting. He found what he was searching for on Laura Kay's left leg. There, high up on a healthy little thigh, a perfect black star birthmark. "Look, Caroline, honey. Look."

"The birthmark . . . just like the one on your cheek."

He touched the tiny imperfection on his daughter's soft flesh and said to her, "The angels kissed you, honey. Cause you're special. Real special."

The first word she said was Daddy. The first steps she took were into his outstretched arms. The first song she learned was his latest rock and roll hit. The first fit she threw was because he was leaving her.

126

Again.

"Now, hush, Laura Kay," Caroline scolded her screaming two-year-old daughter. "You know very well daddy has to go away."

"No!" squealed Laura Kay. "Daddy, Daddy."

Caroline laid her forehead to her child's. "Oh, sweetheart, Daddy will be back. Please don't cry."

"I'll take her, Ma'am," the British nanny came down the steps of Musicland.

"Thank you," Caroline said distractedly, feeling very much like crying as loudly as her unhappy daughter.

She stood on the steps in the hot September sunshine feeling lost and let down, like she always felt when C.C. left Musicland. From beyond the tall fence she could hear the squeals and shouts from the fans as his car drove through the gates.

Caroline hugged her arms to her ribs. It wasn't the way she had thought it would be, her life with C.C. She had envisioned being with him all the time, traveling with him on the tours, living with him on location while he filmed movies. Being a part of all the fun and excitement, sharing the limelight.

They were apart more than they were together.

She couldn't travel with a two-year-old and she couldn't leave her behind. Caroline turned and wearily walked up the steps of Musicland. And she wondered what she was going to do with herself all day. What she was going to do with herself until her husband came back.

C.C. hated leaving. He was due to open at Madison Square Garden in two days, the beginning of another long, arduous tour. He asked Caroline to come with him, to bring the baby and come with him. She refused, explaining their child couldn't live in strange hotel rooms for six weeks. Reluctantly, he agreed that she was right.

C.C. was lonely when he was away, but rarely alone. His entourage had grown in the past year. Besides Buddy Hester and Michael Shephard, the bodyguards, and his road manager, Guy Stearns, there was McDuff the senior pilot and Red Barton, the co-pilot.

C.C. had sold the six-seater and bought a shiny white French Caravelle, a starter jet with lots more room. Now his arranger traveled with him and his conductor, and some of his own musicians, along with a quartet of female backup singers, The Nightingales. The advance man, a driver, a packer and baggage man, and a couple of versatile, amiable, jack-of-all trade kind of guys, Benny Hamilton and Pat Murphy. And on occasion, Ash Ashford.

All were fiercely protective of the Chief, and of their position in his organization. An unassuming and sensitive man, C.C. was an undemanding boss who inspired loyalty rather than having to ask for it. These people became family to him and the easy camaraderie he shared with his crew helped to ease the tension of his stressful, and strangely, lonely profession.

Up to his sideburns in women, C.C. held them at arm's length, a fact that both baffled and amused the lusty boys in his entourage who had no such qualms about having a good time on the road. C.C. would stop in at the nightly backstage parties, have perhaps one drink, two at the most, then go to his bedroom suite alone to spend hours on the phone to his wife, greatly disappointing the ever-present bevy of beautiful women who let him know they were available anytime for his pleasure.

When C.C. was in Dallas, he tried to make up to his family for the times he had to be gone. Tired, longing only to relax, he agreed one evening to a posh dinner party at Musicland, though he hated having outsiders in his beloved retreat. Caroline invited the town's gay set, young, wealthy friends she had known all her life.

One was a gorgeous girl named Mary Beth McCallister. A close friend and fellow junior leager, Mary Beth, Caroline told C.C., prided herself on having the most beautiful breasts in Dallas. All her expensive clothes were cut to enhance these assets. Including the smokey silk crepe gown she wore on this night.

C.C. caught himself looking at the celebrated bosom.

Later in the evening, C.C., slightly bored and suffering from a mild stomach ache, slipped quietly away and hurried up the stairs.

He tiptoed into the nursery and grinning, picked up his wide-awake daughter. "Why aren't you asleep, you little scamp?"

"Stay up late like you, Daddy," Laura Kay answered, her tiny fingers toying with his mouth.

He laughed and kissed her. "Mommy catches you awake, we'll both be in big trouble." He lowered her back into her crib. "Love you, angel, now go to sleep."

"Night, Daddy."

C.C. crossed the hall to the master bedroom, walked through and into the bath. Opening the mirrored medicine cabinet, he stood before it, searching for antacids.

"Lose something?"

He pivoted to see Mary Beth McCallister standing in the doorway, one bare, creamy shoulder pressed against the doorjamb. Quickly, she pushed away, stepped inside, and closed the bathroom door. She leaned back against it, pressing in the button lock.

"Is there something I can do for you, Mary Beth?" C.C.'s dark gaze held hers.

Mary Beth McCallister smiled provocatively, lifted her hands, and slowly, seductively peeled the smoke crepe bodice down until her large, magnificent breasts spilled out. C.C. felt his belly tighten. "How would you like to lick my nipples, Chief?"

C.C. McCarty allowed his eyes to caress the beautiful bare breasts with their silver-dollar-sized nipples. He crossed the carpeted bathroom to her, lifted both hands to grip the door frame on either side of Mary Beth McCallister, trapping her inside his long arms. And he said, "Mary Beth, I can think of nothing I'd like better." Her eyes were wide with excitement. She trembled slightly. Her breath grew shallow and uneven. "Just give me a minute and I'll run down and ask my wife if she'll let me."

"Bastard!" she hissed angrily, pushing on his chest and snatching her dress back up over her heaving breasts. Calmly C.C. stepped past her, unlocked the door, and walked out of the bathroom.

The yacht *Valentine* entered the harbor at Monte Carlo as the May sun was setting. The sparkling bay was crowded with pleasure craft of all shapes and sizes, the smaller ones bobbing in the turquoise sea, the larger, more luxurious ones regally riding the waters like mighty monarchs.

The *Valentine*—her red-and-white flag proudly flying in the balmy breeze, her scarlet hull and red-and-white superstructure gleaming in the dying Mediterranean sun—slid through the channel, all one hundred thirty-two feet of her, her mate calmly issuing orders to the helmsman atop the flying bridge.

"Come left," said the mate.

"Left, sir," answered the helmsman, his strong, bronzed hands gently coaxing the wheel.

"Steady up."

"Steady up, sir."

Valentina Trent, relaxing in a deck chair on the fantail with her Texas guests, found steaming into the glittering ports along the Italian and French Rivieras on her spanking new yacht to be extremely rewarding. Dark sunglasses covering her eyes, the briefest bikini she could find covering her voluptuous body, she loved reclining on the teakwood deck where the people in other craft (most of them less large and elegant than the *Valentine*) could stare at her and speculate on who she was and where she was from.

On this particular warm May day, with her smartly uniformed captain in his starched whites and his billed cap emblazoned with gold standing on the bridge, she sighed with self-satisfaction. While the *Valentine* crept slowly forward to the point where she would drop anchor, and the crew scurried about obeying shouted orders, Valentina felt wonderfully powerful, as powerful as when seated behind her desk in the penthouse offices of Bluebonnet Records.

Feeling powerful was a sweet sensation of which she never tired. And her power was absolute here on this sleek vessel. The captain took his orders from her. If she wished to leave port in the middle of the night, Captain Colin Rath snapped off a crisp military salute and the yacht was underway immediately. If she felt hungry at 4:00 A.M., she touched a buzzer beside her bed and her chef hurried to the galley to fix a five-course meal.

And if a guest displeased her—as Cliff Hardwick, her latest lover, had done—she simply banished him from the *Valentine*.

The incident had happened in Cannes. Hardwick had wanted to go ashore to do some club-hopping. Valentina wasn't in the mood. They argued. Hardwick went ashore without her. And didn't return until after three o'clock in the morning. Furious, she threw all his clothes out of his stateroom and informed him he was no longer welcome, either on the *Valentine* or at Bluebonnet Records in Dallas.

Cliff Hardwick, with nothing but the evening clothes on his back, was rowed ashore in the dinghy and abandoned like a leper.

Valentina smiled as she thought about it. For weeks the moderately talented Hardwick had been getting too big for his britches. He had almost forgotten who called the shots, who paid the tab, who gave the orders.

Valentina breathed deeply. She hadn't missed him for a minute. After the first couple of months with him, he had begun to bore her, and the only reason she had invited him on the cruise was so she would have a dependable escort. Which he turned out not to be. No matter, she didn't need him at her elbow in these carefree resort towns. She would have more fun without him, would find someone new.

Valentina heard the mighty engines reverse and the heavy anchor splash down into the water. She lifted her eyes to the glittering fairyland principality before her, the lights of evening twinkling on in the hotels and restaurants and pastel villas nestled in greenery high up on the rocky cliffs.

She would dress and go ashore with the others, she thought pleasantly. Have dinner at the Hotel de Paris and perhaps visit the famed Monte Carlo Casino for an hour or two of baccarat. Who could tell, she might meet some interesting Frenchmen ashore.

She sighed and stretched lazily.

Too bad she couldn't go as she was. She smiled. How wonderfully civilized the French and Italians were. She was lying here wearing only the bottom half of her red bikini; a practice she had fallen into after meeting the lovely little Anna in Portofino. At first she'd been mildly shocked to see that half the women on the beaches and on the yachts were bare-breasted. Quickly she had come to approve fully of the custom upon first seeing Anna.

It was mid-afternoon. She and Cliff had breakfasted at the plush Hotel Splendido overlooking the harbor, shopped the morning away, and lunched on delicious slices of cheese focaccia at Panificio Canale. Full and lazy from the Italian wine they'd consumed, they decided a stroll through the Plaza and down to the beach would be in order.

She stood there alone, the lovely Anna, looking wistfully out to the majestic *Valentine*, lying at anchor offshore. Incredibly lovely with long, dark hair, huge black eyes, and a slender, olive body, breasts unshamedly bare, Anna turned and smiled when Valentina said, "Would you like to go on board, Miss . . . ?"

"This is your grand ship of red?"

"It is," Valentina said sweetly, her eyes sweeping over the near-naked girl.

"Anna," the girl said, beaming, "I am Anna DeMarco. I would like very much to visit your ship." Her dark eyes locked with Valentina's.

An idea rapidly formed in Valentina's mind. Sex with Clifford had become dreadfully dull. Perhaps this charming Italian girl was what they both needed. A dash of spice.

Valentina, big-brimmed hat shading her eyes against the sun-glittering water, looked toward the yacht. Her guests were ashore, shopping, eating, drinking, sunning. No one was on board but the dozing crew. It might prove to be an enjoyable afternoon.

She had never made love to a woman.

As the three were rowed toward the imposing red yacht, Anna turned to Valentina and complimented. "Your clothes are very beautiful." Her eyes swept over the expensive red silk blouse, the tailored snow-white slacks, the leather high-heeled sandals. "But, I should think you would be too warm."

Valentina giggled like a teenager. "I am getting warmer by the minute," she said, her brown eyes dropping to Anna's bare brown breasts.

Anna smiled and drew a long, deep breath.

Cliff Hardwick was mildly surprised when Valentina, after pouring champagne for him, Anna, and herself suggested the three of them go into her stateroom where it was cool and quiet. In the six months he had known her, Valentina had never allowed him inside her bedroom. Neither at the White Rock mansion in Dallas nor her stateroom on this big yacht. She only made love to him in her office or in her limo, a quirky fetish he never questioned.

But the look in her eyes on this warm afternoon was all too familiar. She was hot, real hot. She had taken the Italian girl's hand and was leading her purposefully toward the forward stateroom. Anna looked over her shoulder at him and smiled seductively. He felt his groin swell. Sick to death of screwing Valentina, he decided it might not be such a bad afternoon. Surely Valentina would allow him a turn at the pretty dark-skinned girl, although it would be just like the bitch to keep her all for herself. He quickened his pace and followed the pair.

Out of the glaring Italian sunshine, they stepped into the spacious stateroom, its interior of dark, richly varnished Burma teak. The furniture was all of gold and red. Red velvet couches. Gold silk easy chairs. Red satin sheets on the oversized bed.

"I'd like you to have something nice, Anna," Valentina went directly to her dresser where a velvet padded jewelry box rested amidst dozens of bottles of expensive French perfumes. "Here. This looks like you, I think." She took from the box a rope of fine cultured pearls, walked directly to the big-eyed Anna and stood before her, caressing the exquisite necklace. "Would you like the pearls?"

The girl's dark eyes glittered greedily. "I would."

"You'll give me an afternoon of pleasure?"

"I will," said Anna, willing to do anything that would make the pearls her own.

Valentina smiled at the taller girl, raised her hands and draped the expensive necklace over Anna's dark head. "Get undressed, Cliff," Valentina ordered over her shoulder, never taking her eyes from Anna. She lifted her fingers to cup the girl's pretty face. And she leaned forward and kissed Anna on the lips, a long, passionate kiss.

When their lips separated, Valentina allowed her hands to slip from the girl's face to the rope of pearls. She moved the pearls slowly out over the full, naked breasts, framing them. "Beautiful," she murmured, "so beautiful." She bent and kissed the left nipple.

Raising her head, Valentina released the pearls and hooked her fingers in Anna's bright blue bikini briefs. And slowly peeled them down. Anna stepped out of them and smiled at Valentina.

"Undress me," Valentina huskily commanded Anna and Anna quickly obeyed.

Valentina lay sprawled naked upon the red satin sheets while an equally naked Anna kissed her hotly, her wide, wet lips covering Valentina's, her tongue thrusting deeply into Valentina's open mouth. Valentina sighed, thinking what a strange sensation to lie naked with another woman, to have bare flesh, as soft as her own, touching hers, to feel a pair of baby soft lips sucking at her aching breasts, a hand so small and gentle pressing between her legs.

Valentina watched Cliffs face as the uninhibited girl made love to her. Fully aroused, huge and throbbing, he stood with one knee on the bed, leaning over her, aching to join them, impatiently waiting his turn. Waiting until Valentina gave him permission. It gave Valentina a wonderful sense of power to know he was suffering, so idly she thought she would lie here for hours while this lovely child kissed and caressed her heated body, allowing him only the voyeur's role.

Anna abruptly took her lips from Valentina's flesh and turned Valentina about in the bed, urging her across it, placing Valentina's bare feet upon the carpeted floor. She pushed Valentina's plump legs wide apart and knelt on the floor between them.

"Sit up," she commanded Valentina and Valentina obeyed. Then held her breath as Anna smiled catlike before lowering her face between Valentina's fleshy thighs.

"Ahhhh," Valentina cried joyfully as the girl's silky tongue began its gentle stroking. Valentina reached up to Cliff. He bent to her, kissing her mouth savagely before she pushed him away and focused entirely on the lovely dark-haired creature lapping at her. Anna was a jewel. She knew her sexual technique and performed with an expertise that pushed the overly excited Valentina to near-hysteria.

Anna would take the older woman almost to the crest, lashing her hungrily, hotly, savagely, and just when Valentina's climax was close, Anna would take her marvelous mouth away, back off and stare up at Valentina with hard, glittering eyes as if she might never go back to her work.

"Please, Anna," Valentina begged, her hands in the girl's hair, trying to force her head back down, her mouth back on its target. "I'm hurting bad, I have to come or I'll explode. My, God, don't torture me this way."

Back Anna would dip, to kiss, to lick, to bite.

When Valentina climaxed she screamed in orgasmic ecstasy and rocked her pelvis forward against the Italian girl's talented mouth. And then she fell over onto her back, spent, dazed, drained.

Anna sat back on her heels and wiped her glistening mouth. Cliff grabbed Anna roughly up and into his arms. Kissing, they fell over onto the

bed beside Valentina. Valentina turned her head and watched appreciatively as Cliff climbed atop the slender olive-skinned girl, shoving his
pulsing penis deep inside her. They rocked the big bed, and finding their
rhythm, moved together with practiced precision, Valentina forgotten
beside them.

Valentina, calming now, raising herself to her elbows, enjoyed the
beauty of the mating couple locked together in animal passion. For a time.

But the pair continued to be lost in each other, holding off their releases,
immensely enjoying the other's experienced body. Valentina became
aroused again. She wanted in on the fun.

"Cliff," she said, tapping his perspiring shoulder, "Get off her, darling. I
want your cock. It's mine, give it to me."

Cliff ignored Valentina, kept pumping away in the beautiful Italian, his
bare buttocks lifting and lowering, eyes glazed with passion.

"Anna, that's enough," Valentina cautioned the girl. "Stop before he
comes. I want him, dammit, he belongs to me."

Anna, too, ignored Valentina. She kept bucking wildly up against her
partner, her lips and teeth nibbling hungrily on a muscled shoulder.

"Did you hear me," Valentina was growing panicky, "I said for you to . . .
no . . . no . . ."

The entwined couple were attaining a violent orgasm before her angered
eyes, their cries of rapture carrying on the still afternoon air, their eyes
locked.

Blindingly furious and thoroughly stimulated, Valentina sobbed petulantly when Cliff collapsed atop Anna, completely spent, and rolled off and
onto his back.

"You little bitch," screamed Valentina at Anna, "How dare you ignore
my orders!" She reached down and took hold of the pearls lying on Anna's
breasts to yank them from her. But Anna grabbed Valentina's hand and
stopped her.

She twisted Valentina's wrist away and pushed her arm behind her. With
her free hand, Anna tangled her fingers in Valentina's wilted red hair and
drew Valentina's mouth to her own. She kissed the excited, angry Valentina, thrusting her tongue deeply into Valentina's mouth. Then she said,
"I'll make him ready again. You'll get yours, Valentina." She kissed her
again, biting playfully at Valentina's bottom lip.

Whimpering softly, Valentina turned her head to see the nimble,
naughty Anna burying her eager face in Cliff's soft groin. The dark-haired
girl only smiled when he groaned, and she slid from the bed. As she had
done with Valentina, Anna pushed his legs wide apart and knelt between

them. Cliff was hard within seconds, but Anna continued to work on him, taking him deep into her throat, sliding her wet mouth up and down, driving him half out of his mind.

Valentina, tears dried on her puffy cheeks, labored breath loud in the room, had risen from the bed. She stood directly behind Anna, her excitement rapidly becoming manic.

Abruptly Anna stopped, though Cliff moaned and begged through clenched teeth. She eluded him, and after turning to Valentina and kissing her one last long, hot time, she guided the plump, inflamed Valentina down astride Cliff's thrusting masculinity.

Frenzied, they made loud, lusty love and were so transported, they never knew when their skilled companion left the stateroom.

Both were disappointed when they found she had gone. It was the best sex either had had in years. They went looking for Anna that night and then again the next afternoon. But Anna was gone.

They chose another young woman, but the magic was missing. Valentina found herself repulsed by making love to a female and pushed the girl away, feeling nauseous and disgusted.

The afternoon with Anna had been one of those magical once-in-a-lifetime interludes. It had happened only because she was bored with Cliff and with the cruise. It was men she liked, not women.

And it was in her office where she liked to make love, not a bedroom.

Valentina lazily sighed.

Yes, she would go ashore tonight. Perhaps some handsome Frenchman might like to go to Texas and have a singing career. The idea made her tingle. A debonair Charles Aznavour-type to enjoy on hot summer afternoons in her fortieth-floor Bluebonnet office.

Sounded like fun.

CHAPTER EIGHTEEN

VALENTINA, swathed in a backless, beaded white Balenciaga, stepped into the small, ornate elevator of the Monte Carlo Casino at half-past eleven. She was alone.

She had enjoyed an outrageously fattening meal at the Hotel de Paris with five of her Texas cruise companions, but nixed their repeated urgings to return with them aboard the *Valentine* for a long evening of partying. In truth they were all beginning to bore her and she was secretly glad none chose to accompany her to the casino.

Valentina exited the elevator on the second floor of the old club and walked unhurriedly into the elegant, high-ceilinged gaming room. It was a quiet night. A few chattering, laughing Frenchmen huddled around a roulette table. A large swarthy-skinned Arab, seated between two bought beauties, played baccarat.

Valentina was debating taking a seat when a man's voice, speaking English as only Americans do, attracted her attention. She turned to see a dapper silver-haired gentleman in a crisp white dinner jacket standing alone at the one crap table. She couldn't quite make out his words, but his request was unmistakable. The man wanted casino credit.

A stone-faced pit boss was shaking his head no.

Valentina felt her pulse quicken. The American asking for credit was Ash Ashford. They had never met, but she knew who he was, just as he, she felt sure, knew who she was. And if Ash Ashford were in Monte Carlo, did that mean C.C. McCarty was as well?

Valentina casually sauntered closer to the crap table.

"I'm good for it, you know that," Ash was pleading his case. "I have all kinds of credit in Vegas and the Bahamas."

"This is Monte Carlo, sir," the hollow-cheeked, seated boxman never unlaced his long fingers, "you have no credit here."

"Just a couple of hundred," Ash entreated.

"I'm sorry, sir. The answer is no."

Ash, beaten, turned to walk away. A hand on his arm stopped him. Valentina stepped in beside him and placed her silver evening bag atop the polished wooden chip rack. From it she took two thousand dollars in French francs. She tossed the money on the table. "Hundred-franc chips, please," she said to the croupier, then turned to look up at Ash. "Your credit is good with this American."

"That's very kind, but . . ."

"Allow me," said she and pressed half the stack of shiny checks into the palm of his hand.

Valentina leaned over and placed one of the checks on the pass line and picked up the dice. Ash hurried to put down a chip. Six was her point and she bucked it. Ash Ashford smiled and let his two hundred ride.

For a brief time, they were lucky. But the dice grew cold and their stacks of chips evaporated. She pulled more money from her evening bag. They put new chips on the pass line and Valentina picked up the dice, threw, and promptly sevened out.

She laughed and took Ash's arm. "It's not our night. Buy me a drink, Mr. Ashford."

"My pleasure, Mrs. Trent."

In the bar, they sat at a tiny square table. He drank Scotch. She, gin and tonic. He was, he said, in Monte Carlo scouting the location of C.C.'s next picture.

"Really? I had no idea that sort of thing fell under the responsibility of one's manager." She fixed him with a knowing look.

He flushed beneath his tan. He had told his wife that he had to go to the South of France with a couple of the RKO front-office guys to make the necessary arrangements for C.C.'s next picture. Charmaine had believed him.

"I'll pay you back as soon as . . ."

"I'm not worried about the money, Mr. Ashford." She paused. "I don't suppose your famous client is with you, is he?" She held her breath.

"C.C.'s in Dallas, Mrs. Trent."

"I see." She sipped her gin. "Poor little Caroline McCarty," she licked her top lip. "It must be terrible being married to a man like the Chief."

Ash took a pack of French cigarettes from his jacket pocket and offered her one. She took it and leaned forward while he held a silver lighter. "A man like the Chief?" he repeated. "Mrs. Trent, C.C. is as nice a kid as I've ever known."

She inhaled. "Of course, he is, Mr. Ashford, but he's only human. Surely with all those women on the road . . ."

"There's only one woman for C.C. Caroline McCarty."

He looked her straight in the eye and it was her turn to flush. Miserably she wondered if C.C. had told Ash about that long-ago day in her office. She lifted her chin defiantly. "Hmmmm. Perhaps. Then maybe he's just very clever at hiding his transgressions. Most of us have something we feel we must hide, don't you agree?"

His eyes held hers. She was letting him know she had knocked him off for a sick gambler. He squirmed. "I suppose we do, Mrs. Trent," he replied.

She liked the flicker of guilt she saw in his eyes. And she liked him. He was a strikingly handsome man with his tanned skin and that gleaming silver hair. And his weaknesses.

The waiter brought more drinks and Valentina Trent and Ash Ashford, understanding each other all too well, continued to drink. Both were scammers and saw themselves in each other. And secretly admired one another. Ash knew what made her tick, had heard all the stories about her, and held none of it against her. He figured she was allowed. He had no idea the lady was still obsessed with C.C., that never a day passed she did not think of the star.

And dream of revenge.

Valentina learned that C.C. was a conscientious husband and entertainer who was often so weighed down with the pressure of his profession and worry over his family, he had great difficulty resting. Most nights, Ash confided, the poor boy never closed his tired eyes, so wound up was he after a performance. Sleep rarely came until after the sun was high in the sky and then C.C. slept fitfully for only a few hours at a time.

Valentina found out something even more interesting that warm May evening. Praising the generosity of his talented client, Ash unthinkingly told Valentina of the Chief's unselfish desire to share with those around him some of his good fortune.

"He intends to give small percentages of the corporation to his most loyal employees. Name another entertainer who would be so magnanimous."

"Do you mean . . . they'll own them vested? They can be bought and sold?" she blurted out, the wheels already turning in her head.

"Sure," answered Ash, smiling, "but they'll never want to sell. C.C.'s got a long, solid career ahead of him. His people will be making money from their points for many years to come."

"Hmmmm," she mused, feeling excitement building inside. "And you, Ash," she dropped the formality of calling him Mr. Ashford, "I understand you have a hefty piece yourself?" She smiled, hoping he would volunteer the information, the exact percentage.

He smiled back at her. "Enough so that I'll be able to pay back what I borrowed at the crap table."

She didn't press it. She had learned quite enough for one evening. She had found out that the unsophisticated Chief was still faithful to his little Dallas wife. That the pressures of his high-flying career were causing him to have trouble getting rest. That the stupid Comanche-looking singer was giving away pieces of himself to that hovering, ass-kissing crew of his.

And she had learned that his brilliant, deal-making manager was a degenerate gambler. Surely with all those tidbits of information, she would figure a way to use them to her advantage.

Knowledge was power, so they said.

And she liked power.

Power made her feel good. Made her feel romantic.

She sipped her gin and tonic and let her eyes rest on Ash Ashford's bronzed face. "How would you like to come out to my yacht for a nightcap, Ash?"

"Give me a raincheck, Valentina. I'm dead tired."

"If anyone asks you if you're C.C.'s daughter, what do you say?" They were in the library at Musicland, C.C. and his daughter. C.C. was crouched down in front of the four-year-old Laura Kay, lean hands encircling her tiny waist.

Laura Kay grinned at her daddy. "I say no!"

"And then what do you do?"

She twisted at the dark hairs on the back of his hand and frowned. "I say *no!*"

"That's right, darlin', but then after you say no, you run just as fast as you can. You yell and scream and kick and do anything you have to do to get away." Laura Kay pulled at the cuff of his shirt. "Look at me, Laura Kay." She lifted her eyes to her daddy's. "Tell me again, what do you do if someone asks if you are C.C.'s daughter?"

Her narrow shoulders lifted and fell. "I say no! and I run away screaming!"

"Yes, baby, that's exactly what you do." He rose, lifting her up into his arms. "And you never go down to the front gates, you hear me?" She nodded, wrapping her short arms around his neck. "You play in the back yard, never the front. You stay out of sight if someone you don't know comes to Musicland."

"And I don't have my picture taken, do I, daddy?"

C.C. smiled and kissed her cheek. "Never. I don't need any pictures of you, darlin'. I carry that pretty little face with me wherever I go."

Laura Kay was to learn that there would never be pictures taken of her, so afraid was her father of a kidnapping. She would never own a house key. Somebody would always be there to let her in, because should she lose a key, it could be dangerous. She thought nothing of it. If her daddy said that was the way it had to be, then that was the way it had to be.

"Can we read now, daddy?" asked the child when C.C., with her in his arms, settled into his favorite leather easy chair.

"You bet we can," he said and picked up the latest copy of *Variety*. He read to his tiny daughter, making a wonderful game of it, reading dramatically as though he were telling a great story, his deep voice adding tones and inflections that made his daughter clap her small hands and giggle. And when he came to the jargon the trade publication used dozens of times in each issue, he would point with a long, lean finger and quiz his daughter.

"Let's see, Laura Kay, I can't . . . I don't know what this word is. Can you help me?"

"Boffo!" she would shout happily, or, "socko . . . solid hit . . . brisk biz . . . top-grossing films . . . slim 25 G's . . ."

C.C. would roar with laughter. To see and hear this tiny dark-haired Dresden doll spouting out show business shorthand like an old pro delighted him no end.

Caroline was not that amused. She entered the library shaking her head. "Laura Kay," she interrupted her husband's theatrical reading of an article about the across-the-country opening of *Monte Carlo Magic*, his latest RKO movie, "it's time for you to get upstairs and get your leotards. Nanny's taking you out to Julian's for your lessons."

"Mommy," the child screwed up her face, "I don't want to go. I want to stay here with daddy and read the trades." She threw her arms around his neck possessively and hugged him tight. C.C. grinned.

"You are going to Julian's, Laura Kay. Now jump down and go upstairs."

The child looked hopefully to her daddy for help.

He sided with her mother. "Go on, darlin'. You want to grow up to be a graceful young lady like your mother." He lowered her to her feet and reluctantly she left the room.

"C.C.," said Caroline, after she had gone, "I wish you would read to Laura Kay from her story books instead of *Variety* and *Cashbox* and *Billboard*." She sat on the arm of his chair.

"Why? She's interested and that's what makes her learn the words."

"She's interested because you are interested. What will they think when she starts kindergarten next year at Lamplighter and goes about using expressions like 'solid B.O.'?" She wrinkled her nose.

C.C. laughed and kissed her. "You have a point." He lifted a hand to the gleaming gold hair framing her beautiful face.

"One other thing, darling, I'm having *Town and Country* in next week to do a layout on Musicland and I'll probably need to buy a few pieces—"

"*Town and Country* can take a flying fuck, Caroline," C.C. broke in heatedly.

Thunderstruck, Caroline stared at her husband as though he had hit her. "What do you mean, C.C.? I've already told them they can come and I . . ."

"You can just untell them," said C.C., his dark eyes flashing. She stood and he rose to face her. "Do you never listen to a damn thing I say?" he thundered. "This is my home, Caroline, not some goddamned museum."

"Darling, darling," she cut in, "you don't understand. It's considered an honor to have *Town and Country* come into—"

"No! That's final, Caroline. They are not coming here. There has to be some privacy for me somewhere on this earth. Some place where the world can't get to me."

Caroline was shocked by the depth of C.C.'s outrage. The fierce expression in his black eyes almost frightened her. Never had she seen him so adamant. "C.C., I . . . I'm sorry, I just didn't think you . . ." Her chin began to quiver and tears welled up in her big emerald eyes.

He softened. "Darlin', in the five years we've been together have I ever said no to anything you wanted to do?" She bit her lip and shook her head. He reached for her, pulling her into his embrace. "Listen to me, sweetheart, and try to understand. Everywhere I go people want a piece of me. I'm not complaining. I love it, I love my fans and I love my life and all the money I make, but the happiest times are when I'm here with you and Laura Kay at Musicland. Know why? Because nobody can follow me through those gates and come inside. Here, I can relax with my family like any ordinary Joe."

"I'm sorry, C.C."

"I never want anybody inside the gates of Musicland except our employees and our friends. Okay?"

"Okay," she agreed, still more than a little upset that the man who had never raised his voice to her had lashed out so angrily.

"Okay," he repeated, grinning, and tilted her face up. "I love you, baby," he told her, "I believe we just had our first fuss. Let's make it our last, what do you say?"

"Alright," she said and kissed him.

It wasn't their last. Not a month later Caroline hurried into the library one afternoon. C.C. was looking over a movie script. Buddy Hester was there. Caroline frowned when she saw the big bodyguard sprawled out on the long sofa, drinking a beer and watching a baseball game on television.

C.C. looked up when she entered. "Hi, hon, how was the luncheon?"

"Fun. I so wish you could have gone, C.C. Mary Beth McCallester showed up with the man she's to marry and he's so interesting." Caroline nodded to Buddy and leaned down to kiss her husband's cheek. "I could listen to him talk forever about his huge stable of Arabian horses." She took a seat on a footstool before C.C.'s chair. "C.C., let's buy some. Let's invest in some beautiful Arabians."

"Caroline, what exactly do Arabian horses do?" C.C. looked quizzically at her.

"They eat and they shit," interjected Buddy Hester, before she could answer. Then he hooted with laughter. That was bad enough, but C.C. laughed too.

Caroline was furious. She shot to her feet. "Damn you! Damn you both!" she shouted angrily, "You're nothing but ignorant West Dallas riffraff and I . . . I . . ." She caught herself, but it was too late. She had said too much and she knew it.

She burst into frustrated tears and fled the room, leaving the two gaping men looking after her.

"Bud, I apologize for Caroline, she was off base and . . ."

"Hey, C.C., that's okay." Buddy started grinning again. "Hell, I know what I am, how about you?" He laughed heartily, untouched by Caroline's insult.

"Sure do," said C.C. "I'm the richest piece of West Dallas riffraff that ever lived." They both howled with laughter.

It was much later when C.C. opened their bedroom door and stepped inside. He stood there, hands in his pockets, smiling at her. "Caroline, buy as many Arabian horses as you like. I suppose we had better start searching for a ranch to—"

"C.C.," she interrupted, coming to him, "I'm sorry. I'm sorry. I didn't mean it! I didn't mean it . . ." And she began to sob.

C.C. took her in his arms. "Course you didn't, honey. Forget it, baby. I have."

"Oh, C.C.," she wailed, looking up at him, "I was so afraid you'd think . . . I didn't mean . . . I'll apologize to Buddy next time I . . ."

C.C. silenced her with his lips. They kissed anxiously, as though they were in great danger of losing something. As though they had already lost something. The kisses grew hotter, deeper, and they slipped to their knees. He made love to her there on the floor.

It was the first time C.C. had ever taken his wife with anything but the greatest of tenderness. Almost savagely he took her, longing to punish her. It had the opposite effect. Caroline thrilled to the primitive loving and when she came, she didn't call him C.C. in her ecstasy or even darling or sweetheart.

She called him Chief.

It hurt him almost as much as her calling him riffraff. And he wondered, had she ever loved him? Or was his wife just another curious fan?

CHAPTER NINETEEN

"FUCK the Beatles!"

"Bunch of long-haired sissies come over here, think they can take over. We were getting 60 ratings on Ed Sullivan when they were jacking off in junior high." C.C. switched off the radio, silencing the four young Liverpool upstarts midway through "I Wanna Hold Your Hand." "Let's get to work around here!," he said, not stirring from the couch.

C.C., his lead guitarist, Al Bowie, and his piano player, Doc DuBois, were in the rehearsal studio at the back edge of Musicland, a huge, soundproof room secluded from the mansion by dense hedges and tall live oaks.

Al Bowie exchanged glances with Doc DuBois. Doc, a cadaverously thin man with a pallid complexion, watery blue eyes, a dry sense of humor, and a cigarette constantly dangling from his thin lips, grinned, took his seat on the piano bench and began playing "I Want to Hold Your Hand."

Al Bowie chuckled. C.C., lounging lazily on a long brown corduroy couch, laughed heartily, picked up a bag of Frito Lay potato chips from the side table, and sailed them at Doc's graying head. The package caught Doc on a boney right shoulder, split open, and spilled out onto the keyboard and into his lap.

One-handed, Doc continued to play the Beatles' hit, while with the other he grabbed up a bunch of the crisp potato chips, popping them into his mouth. "You still get these things free, Chief?"

"Coming out of my ears," C.C. admitted, "and I only met the head of Frito Lay one time." He helped Doc clean away the scattered chips so they could begin work.

Their project on this sweltering July morning was to produce a "scratch

144

tape." C.C., with Al on guitar and Doc at the piano, would record a very rough tape of songs for the next Chief album. The tape would be sent to RCA—he had switched to RCA at the beginning of 1964—in L. A., musicians would lay in the instrumental by listening to C.C.'s voice on earphones. Still later, C.C. and his backup singers would go to the Los Angeles and record the vocal tracks.

Making scratch tapes was boring. C.C. always worked best with an audience and liked having one present, even at recording sessions. Here at the rehearsal studio there was no one to play off of. Besides, C.C. was tired after a sleepless night and it was Friday and he was anxious to finish up and head for his Weatherford Ranch, *Cielo Vista*, for a long Fourth of July holiday weekend with his family.

It was nearing noon when they finished up, pleased with what they had done and glad it was over. C.C., rubbing his tired neck, glanced up when Doc said, "Looks like we have company."

A beautiful little girl with ebony hair and sparkling black eyes had quietly slipped into the room while the men were concentrating on their music. Her daddy grinned broadly at the cherished child coming toward him. "Hi, sweetheart. How did you like that last song?"

Laura Kay McCarty took his big hand. "I just heard a better one on the radio." She smiled up at him.

"Oh yeah. What was it?"

She nodded happily. "I Want to Hold Your Hand." She started giggling.

"Why you little . . ." he scooped her up into his arms, growling and biting her neck while she squealed with laughter.

C.C. was still in a relaxed, happy mood when Caroline called him in to lunch. He didn't have to be called twice. He was starving.

He took his place at the head of the long pedestal table and looked at the plate before him. "What's this?" he tilted the china plate and stared down at the food.

"Stuffed turkey breasts and endive salad," answered Caroline, pleasantly, "and for desert there's—"

C.C.'s fist came down on the table with such force it sounded like a pistol shot. Caroline jumped and dropped her fork. Laura Kay stared, open-mouthed, at her daddy.

"Good God, we netted four million dollars last year," thundered C.C., "isn't that enough to buy steak and potatoes! If I've told you once, I've told you a thousand times I don't like this crap. I want a steak and if I can't it get here I'll go someplace where I can." His dark eyes snapped with anger and he violently shoved the plate away.

"C.C. you're out of sorts because you've been up all night and . . ."

"I am hungry, Caroline! Damn it to hell, I'm hungry."

"Don't talk like that in front of Laura Kay!"

"I'll talk any way I please. I'm hungry! And I don't want any turkey or veal or lamb or snails or lobster. Or asparagus or spinach or carrots or cauliflower. I want a huge, well-done steak and I'm not leaving for *Cielo Vista* until I get one!"

"And I'm not leaving either!" chimed in Laura Kay, pushing her plate aside and folding short arms over her chest.

C.C. got his steak. So did C.C.'s daughter.

The air was strained between C.C. and Caroline later that afternoon as they drove westward toward Weatherford. Silent, they sat in the back seat of a newly acquired, midnight blue 1951 Rolls Royce seven-passenger enclosed limousine.

Laura Kay was between them, happily unaware of the friction. She was singing, ". . . I want to hold your ha-an-an-d, I want to hold your hand."

"I want to hold your ha-an-an-an-d," crooned the Beatles from a bedside radio in a suburban Mesquite motel room, while a perspiring naked woman whimpered and pleaded to be let go. The nude man pinning her down, a slim, fair-skinned, black-haired youth with hard, chiseled features and cruel, smokey eyes, turned a deaf ear to the Beatles and to the woman.

She was his birthday present to himself and for the past three hours they had been in this room, celebrating his nineteenth year.

The woman, a twenty-six-year-old cocktail waitress with frizzy brown hair and enormous breasts had met the birthday boy at the neighborhood bar where she worked. The bar where she was expected in less than half an hour for her regular 6:00 P.M. till closing shift.

"Honey, I got to go to work," she whined as once again the slim, pale-skinned male forced her legs apart with his knee.

"Hush, bitch," said the cold-eyed boy, his long pale fingers enclosing a mountainous breast.

"Don't you talk to me like that," sniffed the waitress, "I'm a lady!" Incensed, she beat her fists on his broad, hair-roughened chest.

Open-palmed he hit her across the face. "You're a slut, just like all the others. You're all alike."

She was crying, tears gushing, runny mascara making blackened paths down each heavily made-up cheek.

Uncaring, he moved between her legs and forcefully took her. While he ground his pelvis in the slow, erotic movements of loving, he coldly accused, "You're no good, baby. Say it. Tell me you're no good."

The cocktail waitress, still crying, finally lifted her arms around his neck and began to move with him, aroused again, burning hot for this cruel young kid with no heart who was such an expert lover. She wrapped her legs around him and kissed his shoulder, sobbing, "I'm no good. No good . . ." Her eyes were closing in ecstasy.

"That's it," praised Ryker Rawley sliding deeper into her, "take it all. Fuck me good, whore."

Valentina Trent, on that hot July evening, was at The Cipango Club on Cedar Springs, one of Dallas' toniest private clubs. Seated in a high-backed leather banquette that offered a great degree of privacy, she waited for her invited guest. The crowd at the Cipango was sparse. Most members had fled the steaming city for the lakes and country homes and holiday celebrations. Valentina sipped a Tanqueray and tonic and smoked her third Old Gold.

And plotted.

"Mrs. Trent?" She looked up to see a light-haired, slim young man in a dark suit standing before her.

She smiled warmly. "Do sit down, Mr. Hamilton."

Benny Hamilton looked about nervously and slid into the circular banquette. He felt guilty about being here, about meeting this woman whom he knew C.C. McCarty regarded as the enemy.

"I won't keep you in suspense, Mr. Hamilton," Valentina smiled winningly. "You're wondering why I wanted to see you."

"That I am," admitted Benny Hamilton, nodding to the waiter who had just placed a Scotch and water before him. "I'm sure it has something to do with the Chief. Am I right?"

Valentina softly laughed. "McCarty pay you well for being one of his flunkies?" Benny Hamilton's eyes narrowed slightly. "Oh come on, Hamilton," Valentina continued, "you know what you are. Are you well paid?"

Benny Hamilton took a swallow of Scotch. "Enough."

"I doubt that," said Valentina coolly. "How would you like to supplement your meager income?" She read the alarm in his eyes. "No, dear boy, I don't want to sleep with you. You're not my type. I want us to be partners."

"Partners? In what?"

Valentina smiled.

Within an hour she had explained. Benny Hamilton was shocked by her proposals. But interested.

She told him she knew that he had a cousin in Waco who was a struggling doctor. She wanted the young doctor to move to Dallas.

"That's impossible," said Benny, "my cousin has a very successful practice and—"

"Your cousin only barely got his degree in Bologna, Italy. No American medical school would admit him. As for his 'successful practice'—it wouldn't keep a nurse's aide busy, so let's just cut the crap, Hamilton."

"As I said, I want the doctor in Dallas," Valentina's tone was flat. "He's to become friends with the Chief."

What if the Chief doesn't like my cousin, Benny said. He will, she promised, because the Doc is going to help the Chief with his sleeping problems. You saying you want him to get the Chief hooked on downers, Benny asked. Not just downers, uppers too, she suggested. And that's not all, she said gleefully, I have been interviewing young ladies for the past six months. For what, Benny wanted to know. To seduce C.C. McCarty, she told him gladly. You're nuts, lady, he laughed at her idea. I think not, she laughed, too, and asked if he had ever seen Candy Barr over at Abe's Colony Club.

His eyes practically misted recalling the luscious blond stripper whose childlike, innocent beauty had set Dallas on its ear a decade earlier. He nodded his head and murmured soulfully, "What a honey . . ."

"I've found a young lady that looks a great deal like Candy Barr looked at seventeen."

"Nobody looks that good," said Benny skeptically.

"This girl looks better and she's bought my plan."

"What exactly is the plan?"

"She's to show up at C.C.'s next appearance, make sure he sees her. Then she plays hard to get."

Benny Hamilton lifted his hand in the air, signaling for another Scotch. "Lady, I've been around the Chief when some of the most beautiful women I've ever laid eyes on threw themselves at his head and he never gave them a tumble."

"I know," she agreed, "so imagine how appealing my client will be. She'll refuse him . . . for a while."

Hamilton was ready to get out of the restaurant and away from this dangerous woman, when she revealed what his part was in her schemes. "Get your cousin, the doctor, to Dallas. I'll finance his new practice and see you're taken care of."

"How much?"

She knew she had him. "The sums will be modest until you've achieved success, but once the doc gets C.C. hooked on pills and you get him laid, fifty thousand cash."

Hamilton's eyes widened. "Jesus, you'd pay me that kind of dough for—"

"I'm paying you 'that kind of dough' to keep your mouth shut. Talk and you get nothing."

"Hell, you think I'm crazy! I go through with this, wild horses couldn't drag it out of me."

"Good. Do you know where I live, Mr. Hamilton?"

"Sure, out by White Rock Lake."

"Sit here half an hour after I leave, then drive out to my house."

"What for?"

"The young lady I told you about is at my home. She claims to be an expert in bed, but all I have is her word. You'll stay the weekend with us. I want you to make love to her and see if she's as good as she looks. You would know a good piece of ass, wouldn't you?" She smiled at him. "We don't want the Chief to be disappointed in his first adulterous affair." Before he could answer, she rose, laughing softly, and walked away.

In New Orleans on that hot, muggy evening, a contrite Ash Ashford tiptoed into his bedroom, hoping against hope that the beautiful woman lying in the bed would be sound asleep.

She wasn't.

"How much?"

"Hi, sweetheart." Ash tried to sound casual. "I didn't mean to wake you."

"How much, Ash?" Charmaine's tone was cold.

"What makes you think I—"

"Damn you, Ash Ashford," she cut him off, lunging from the bed and coming to stand facing him. "It's two in the morning. You've been gambling again and I want to know how much money you lost?"

Ash took a deep breath. "Fifteen."

"Hundred?"

"Thousand."

"You son of a bitch!"

CHAPTER TWENTY

THEY were not the kind of little girls who attended public schools. They were the pampered daughters of Dallas' wealthy and influential citizens. Their mothers had attended Hockaday and their grandmothers had been students when the old school was located on Greenville Avenue.

For the past decade the fortunate few who were accepted—and could pay the price—greeted the stern headmistress each morning in the ultra-modern facility on Midway Road in North Dallas.

Laura Kay McCarty, six years old, reluctantly entered the doors of one of the most exclusive private schools in all Texas, clinging to Caroline's hand, her big dark eyes filled with apprehension.

Everywhere she looked were girls. Girls all sizes and all ages. Little girls crying and whining to their mothers. Big, grown-up girls, their pretty faces bare of makeup, smiling confidently. Girls all dressed alike in starched green uniforms, exactly like the one she herself wore.

Laura Kay wanted to go home. She told her mother as much, but Caroline shushed her and said she was a lucky little girl to be attending Hockaday. Laura Kay felt anything but lucky.

The first confusing day passed, but the second was far worse. Now she was on her own. Tearfully Laura Kay had hugged her understanding daddy good-bye while he crouched on the steps of Musicland. She whispered in his ear, "Don't make me go, daddy." To her shock, the man who had always allowed her anything she wanted, had hugged her extra tightly, but said, "You'll be okay, sweetheart. You'll do fine."

She didn't.

She hated the strange school with all its rules and regulations and green-uniformed girls. She was embarrassed and resentful when the older students pointed at her and whispered, "Look at her. She's the Chief's daughter. Looks just like him, doesn't she? Maybe she'll tell us about him."

Laura Kay didn't want to tell these girls about her daddy. He was her daddy, not theirs, and she would not share him with them.

At first break Laura Kay dutifully filed out of the building for the little playground with the other first-graders. It seemed to her they all had friends to play with while she had nobody. They giggled and got out their jump ropes and pushed right past her, their arms around each other. She felt desolate and lonely. She would share her famous daddy with them, if only they would ask her to play.

She stood alone at the edge of the schoolyard beneath a live oak, the tears she had tried to hold back, splashing down her cheeks. She hated it here! She wanted to go home and never, ever come back. Her hands went up to cover her unhappy face.

"Stop that blubbering and blow your nose," came a clear, young voice from right in front of her.

Laura Kay's hands came down. She sniffed and blinked. A girl exactly her height with flaxen curls and wide blue eyes was standing before her, hands on her hips.

"Who . . . who are you?" Laura Kay managed.

"Missy Graham. Here," the girl snatched the lace-trimmed handkerchief from Laura's breast pocket and thrust it at her. "Who are you?"

Laura Kay blew her nose. "I'm Laura Kay McCarty. My daddy's C.C. McCarty."

"Well my daddy's Bennett Graham."

"Who's Bennett Graham?" asked Laura Kay.

Missy Graham shook her blond curls disbelievingly. "Only one of the richest men in Texas!"

"Oh."

"Who is C.C. McCarty?"

It was Laura Kay's turn to wag her head piteously. "Only the most famous singer in the whole wide world! And I'm going to be a famous singer, too, cause I've got his birthmark." She jerked up her skirt and proudly tapped the black star on her left thigh. "Daddy says I'm special."

"Yeah, well, I don't have to sing. I'm rich," stated Missy Graham. "Come on, let's go swing." She took Laura Kay's hand and together they skipped to the playground.

Laura Kay's enrollment in Hockaday was not the only change at Musicland that year. Caroline, complaining of C.C.'s nocturnal habits, asked that he move out of their big bedroom. He was keeping her awake and she had to have her rest if she were to see their daughter off to school each morning and meet with the various committees that depended on her. She had the servants take all of his clothes and personal belongings and deposit them in a big, never-used room at the end of the hall.

C.C. let her know he wasn't too crazy about the new arrangement, but she laughed and said, "Don't be silly, darling. You can visit me anytime you choose."

"I don't like the idea of having to 'visit' my wife in my own home," said C.C.

C.C. was still smarting over the slight when Ash flew in from New Orleans to tell of the new strategy he had mapped out for C.C.'s career.

"Jesus, Ash, what's wrong with the way things are going? We made more money—"

"Nothing, nothing," assured Ash. "You're on top, C. C., and I want you to stay there."

C.C. shrugged wide shoulders. "Won't I?"

"You will if you listen to me."

Ash revealed his plans to cut off C.C.'s personal appearances. C.C. didn't like it. Ash assured him it was the wise thing to do, explaining he was to continue making movies and cutting records.

"You've toured the country too many times in the past few years, you're in danger of overexposure," Ash warned.

"Ash, we've sold out the house in every city on every tour."

"Exactly, C.C. We'll be pulling out while the fans are still wanting more. That's as it should be. I've seen great draws stay at the party too long and there's nothing sadder than a half-filled house." Ash smiled and continued, "I've scheduled one last appearance at the Hollywood Bowl in L.A. for three weeks from last Saturday night. From there you'll go right into your next movie for MGM, *West Point Cadet*.

"Ash," protested C. C., "the script is a real piece of shit. Couldn't we wait until something better—"

"We're not trying for the Academy Award, C.C. We leave for the Coast in two weeks. You report to the studio in three."

C.C. told Caroline that he would no longer be touring. He would be spending most of his time in California making movies, keeping regular hours, coming home each evening at 6:00 P.M. Since he wouldn't be on the road, they could live a normal life just like she had always wanted. Why didn't they hunt for a big house in Beverly Hills and divide their time between California and Dallas.

Caroline wouldn't consider it. She reminded C.C. that their daughter had just begun her first year at Hockaday.

"They have schools in California, darlin'," he smiled and pulled her into his arms.

"Laura Kay has to go to Hockaday, C. C.," she looked up at her husband. "It means so much to . . . to . . ."

"To Laura Kay?" His tone was flat.

"Yes."

C.C. dropped his arms away. "Come off it, Caroline. You know damned well Laura Kay couldn't care less about some fancy girls' school. You and your Momma are the 'good little Hockadaisies.' "

"Make fun if you wish, C. C., but remember that your daughter's safety is a constant concern. Bodyguards escorting her to school everyday in a limo are much less noticeable at Hockaday where many of the children are chauffeured. She's not just any little girl. She's C.C.'s daughter."

"You're right, honey," he said and again pulled her to him. "I'm sorry. It's just that I get lonely as hell when I'm away from you."

Caroline put her arms around her husband's trim waist. "You're not the only one who gets lonely. Make love to me."

"Your room or mine?"

He had been in Los Angeles for three days and already he was lonely and restless. It was Thursday. The show at the Bowl was Saturday night. C.C. felt caged and edgy. And bored.

Benny Hamilton told him about a new restaurant; Maetos's in Westwood. The locals were raving about the place. Why not get some of the guys together and go there for dinner? C.C. at first said no, then changed his mind.

"Yes, Ben. Make reservations for nine. Hell, if I don't get out of this hotel, I'll go nuts." He grinned, went to his bedroom, and slept the afternoon away.

Rested and hungry, he got up around eight, showered, shaved, and left the Beverly Wilshire Hotel for the restaurant with five members of his entourage, including the likeable Benny Hamilton.

Seated at a round table, C.C. took up a red leather menu and began to study it. Buddy Hester nudged him. "Look at that little pretty at the next table."

Lazily C.C. lifted his eyes. A young woman with silvery blond hair, porcelain-white skin, and ripe, voluptuous curves was sipping red wine.

Her eyes, big and brown, met C.C.'s and he felt his chest tighten. Since his marriage to the beautiful Caroline, there had been other women that caught his eye in passing, but there was something irresistible about this lovely platinum-haired girl. Never had he seen a female who looked quite so fuckable.

One glimpse and it was easy to forget he was a married man. He wanted her.

C.C. smiled at her. She lowered her eyes and turned slightly in her chair. The movement caused her flowing silver hair to spill over a shoulder and her shimmering brown silk dress to pull and bind over high, full breasts.

C.C. fought the attraction, turning his attention to the menu. But he continued to be acutely aware of her presence and when half an hour later she rose and walked out of the restaurant, it was all he could do to keep from running after her.

The next night C.C.'s road manager, Guy Stearns, threw a pre-performance party at the lavish Beverly Wilshire suite, inviting friends, musicians, entertainers, movie stars, and lots of ambitious pretty girls.

C.C. spotted her across the room. Staring, he tossed down the last of his iced vodka and smiled, feeling a tingling excitement. Sure she would make her way to him, he stood his ground and waited. He caught her eye and winked. She smiled, but promptly turned her attention back to a small circle of laughing people.

C.C. was annoyed and impatient. A waiter brought him another iced vodka. He waited a while longer, hoping she would come to him. She didn't. Another vodka and he went to her. Extracting himself from the admiring women surrounding him, he made his sure way to the beautiful blonde.

As though she could feel his commanding presence at her side, she turned and looked up at him. C.C.'s heart pounded.

"I kept waiting for you to come over," he said, his dark eyes caressing her. The message was unmistakable.

For a long, heated moment she held his gaze. "I never hunt with the pack," said she, handed him her glass, turned, and left.

Dumbfounded, immobile, he watched her walk away. No woman had ever turned him down. He grinned and drank the last of her wine, debating whether or not he should go after her. It was too late. She was gone.

C.C. paced the floor that night after the party, irritable, disturbed, obsessed with the elusive blond beauty. At 4:00 A.M. he picked up the phone and buzzed Buddy's room, explaining his dilemma. "I don't know who she is, Bud, but you've got to get the boys together and find her. See to it she's at the show tomorrow night."

"Right, boss," Buddy said sleepily.

C.C. had long since quit trying to get any sleep before sun-up. He prowled the suite alone all night, turning down offers of company from his crew. At dawn he finally stepped into his shower to get ready for bed. And when he came out, toweling his black hair dry, he blinked in shock, and dropped the heavy towel.

There upon his bed was the gorgeous blonde.

Propped upon the pillows, she was as naked as he, her long platinum hair spilling over her ivory shoulders and full breasts, her pale, shapely legs curled to one side.

"They found you," he said foolishly and came to the bed, his erection already complete.

"I was never lost," she reached for him.

He moaned and fell onto the bed with her. In seconds he was buried deep inside her and when the telephone rang beside them, neither paid any attention. It was picked up in the other room while the hot pair on the bed rocked in raunchy rapture.

At first they ignored the loud knocking on the bedroom door. But C.C. was trapped when Buddy's apologetic voice said through the door, "Sorry, C.C., but it's Laura Kay on the line. She wants to talk to her daddy."

Locked in lust with the platinum blond, C.C. jerked up the phone, "Hiya, sweetheart."

"Daddy, good morning," came the sweet, childlike voice, "What are you doing?"

"Ah . . . I . . . honey, I was just getting into bed," his slim hips continued the grinding, thrusting motions while the pliant woman beneath him playfully bit at his chin and his throat and pressed her pelvis to his.

"I wish I was out there with you," said Laura Kay.

"Me too, sweetheart . . . I . . . aaaah . . ."

"Daddy, why are you groaning?"

"I . . . darlin', daddy's tired. I'll talk to you later."

"Okay, daddy. Do you want to say hello to Mommy?"

"When I wake up, baby. When I wake up. Bye."

"Bye, daddy." The dial tone hummed in his ear.

Ryker Rawley took the key to room 214 of the La Fonda Motel in West L.A. and climbed the stairs, a small vinyl suitcase in one hand, a morning paper in the other. When he'd closed the door, he shrugged out of his clothes and stepped into the shower.

Later, a towel wrapped around his hips, he lay on the bed in the air-cooled room and checked his revolver. He smiled. Tonight was the night. The night to get C.C. McCarty.

Ryker Rawley kept up with the Chief's career better than the most avid of fans. He knew that this was the last show. No more personal appearances were booked; not after tonight at the Hollywood Bowl.

It was impossible to get near the star when he was in residence at Musicland. Musicland, now more than ever, was an armed camp. He could never reach him there. The movie lot was almost as bad. He couldn't get past the gate guard, much less onto the soundstage where McCarty kept himself surrounded by boot-licking cronies.

Ryker shoved another cartridge into the chamber and grinned.

There was only one place where a star of McCarty's magnitude could not be fully protected.

On stage.

He was vulnerable up there performing live before an audience. Nothing to shield him from harm. No burly bodyguard standing in front of him. No defense against a well-aimed bullet to the chest.

"McCarty," he said to the whir of the loud window air conditioner, "you have less than twenty-four hours to live. I hope you're using the time well."

CHAPTER TWENTY-ONE

LAURA Kay hung up the receiver, sighed unhappily, and buried her dark head under the covers of her silk-hung canopied bed. She missed her daddy. She shut her eyes tightly. It was only seven o'clock. She would go back to sleep and then she wouldn't miss him so much.

Her eyes came open. She jerked the covers off her head and sat straight up in bed. Daddy said he missed her. It was Saturday. Why couldn't she and her mother go to California?

Excitedly, she bolted from her bed and sailed out of her room. Dark tangled hair falling into her eyes, white choirboy nightgown held up past her dimpled knees, Laura Kay dashed down the hall to her mother's bedroom.

She paused outside the closed door. Her mother didn't like being awakened early on the weekends. It might be wise to wait until Caroline came down to breakfast. Laura Kay quietly eased the big door open and peered in.

"Hi," her mother's soft voice was warm. She sat at the dressing table, brushing her long golden hair.

"Mother," Caroline shrieked. "You're awake."

Caroline nodded, smiling, and held her arms wide. Laura Kay hurried happily into them. "I couldn't sleep. I miss your Daddy," Caroline murmured against her child's glossy dark curls.

"You too, Mother?"

"Hmmm."

"Let's go out to see him," Laura Kay pulled back to look at her mother, dark eyes gleaming with hopeful anticipation.

Caroline considered it for only a moment, smiled, and picked up the phone. "Did I wake you. Sorry. Brad, this is Caroline. Is the BAC 111 available?"

"Yes, Ma'am, it's fully serviced and in the hangar at Love Field," said C.C.'s ready back-up pilot, Brad Hemphill. "The chief and crew went out in the Caravelle."

"Please prepare to fly Laura Kay and me to L.A. this afternoon."

"Sure thing, Mrs. McCarty."

"Thanks, Brad. We'll see you around two." She hung up.

Laura Kay hugged her mother, then clapped her hands and jerked up the telephone receiver. "Who are you calling, honey?" Caroline asked.

"Daddy. I'll tell him we're coming."

Caroline shook her golden head. She smiled. "Let's surprise him."

C.C. McCarty was like a young man who had just discovered sex. He couldn't get enough of the blatantly erotic Venus with the long platinum hair and the total lack of inhibitions.

To the deceptively innocent-looking blond beauty, C.C. was a god and she used every trick she had ever learned to give him exquisite carnal pleasure.

She did things to him he'd forgotten people did to each other. She did things to him no one had ever done before. She did things to him that were an intoxicating blend of mild pain and exotic pleasure.

Never had he known a woman who knew more ways to use her body, her fingers, her lips, and tongue than the angelic-looking silver blonde with the big, melon breasts and strong, silken-skinned legs.

They fucked throughout the morning, oblivious to the stirrings from the outer room where C.C.'s entourage was gathered. They ignored the impatient knocks and the repeated warnings from the road manager, Guy Stearns, that C.C. was to rehearse at two o'clock. At two, rehearsal was the furthest thing from C.C.'s mind.

The wanton blonde had him on his back in the smoke-mirrored, white-carpeted bath. She was sitting on her heels between his spread legs. Her well-oiled forefinger was inside his anus making lazy, lust-inspiring little circles while C.C. moaned and gritted his teeth and begged her to do something with the swollen, aching tumescence jerking on his bare belly.

At three o'clock she ordered food from room service so he could keep up his strength. C.C. inhaled the raw oysters and the thick steak and the champagne and reached for the rich concoction of fresh sugared fruit dripping with thick cream. The blonde smiled naughtily, took the large bowl from him, and, looking straight into his black eyes, poured part of the gooey sweet onto his smooth chest. Open-mouthed, he stared at her while bits of fresh pineapple and raspberries and peach slices trickled down his naked chest onto his stomach and into the thick curly hair of his groin.

She poured the rest over herself and they spent the next forty-five minutes eating their dessert, laughing and licking and loving.

It was just past four in the afternoon and they were at it again. C.C. was seated on a straight-backed desk chair, knees apart, bare feet braced on the carpeted floor. The voluptuous blonde was astride him, doing most of the work. Her very skilled vagina gripping and grabbing him so that his black eyes were glazed and he could feel himself getting bigger and harder by the second.

His wrenching climax was close at hand.

A laughing Buddy Hester answered the knock on the hall door, expecting a uniformed hotel porter with the nuts and chips and beer he had ordered.

The laugh died in his throat. His face grew blood red and he thought he was surely going to choke to death.

"What's wrong, Buddy," Caroline smiled up at him, "aren't wives and daughters welcome at the party?"

"Sure . . . ah . . . gosh, yeah," he stammered, his big chest tight with terror, his heartbeat hammering in his ears.

"They most certainly are welcome," came the calm, even voice of C.C.'s road manager, Guy Stearns. He stepped around Buddy. "Only trouble is, the Chief's not here, Caroline. Steve McQueen stopped by in his new Lotus and they went for a spin. Steve said he would drop the Chief off at the Bowl for rehearsal."

"Let's go on to the Hollywood Bowl, Mother," Laura Kay couldn't wait to see her daddy.

"No, Laura Kay," Caroline vetoed the idea, stepping inside the spacious suite. "It's hours until showtime. I want to rest and freshen up." She smiled to the crowd of men who had fallen deathly silent.

"Hello, Caroline, Laura Kay," offered Benny Hamilton. "Mrs. McCarty. Laura," they all mumbled greetings.

"When did you get in, Caroline," Guy Stearns asked, and his voice was much firmer than the others. Loud enough to carry into the bedroom.

C.C. heard.

But C.C. was coming at that moment and there was no stopping it. Feeling the loud groan of release building in his chest, he savagely pulled the blonde's mouth to his and kissed her. And while he pumped furiously into the girl, his lean hands clutching her bare white bottom aggressively, he heard Guy Stearns say apologetically, "Caroline, uh . . . this is a little embarrassing. You see, one of the boys . . . ah . . . has a young lady in there right now and . . ."

"They're using C.C.'s room!" Caroline's voice was shrill with shocked disgust.

"I'm sorry . . . C.C. wouldn't like it if he knew and . . ."

"I should think not," said Caroline indignantly. She took Laura Kay's hand and jerked her toward the hall door. "I'll book another suite. Have a limo call for us at seven!"

"Sure thing, Caroline."

"And Guy," Caroline added as an afterthought, "don't tell C.C. we're here. We'll surprise him. He'll look out and there we'll be in the audience."

"He'll be thrilled."

Crowds had been gathering at Hollywood Bowl since early afternoon. A vintage Bentley limo arrived at ten minutes before eight and pulled to a stop at valet parking. An expensively dressed, slender young woman and a pretty little girl with jet-black curls stepped from the spacious back seat.

The pair were escorted through the screaming, cheering fans. A tall, dark-haired man with cold gray eyes and pale skin was in that crowd. He looked, not at the gilt-tressed woman—he stared at the black-haired child. A flash of her pretty pink skirts up over an olive thigh gave him a fleeting glimpse of the black star birthmark.

C.C.'s daughter was whisked through the crowd and out of sight.

Ryker Rawley calmly went to find his seat, a loaded pistol concealed beneath his jacket.

The show was a smashing success. C.C., grateful his wife knew nothing of his indiscretion, put something special into his performance. Feigning surprise and joy when he stepped on stage and saw Caroline and Laura Kay seated down front, he directed all his love songs to them. Caroline knew she had made the right decision by flying out.

C.C. had been as lonely as she.

She smiled, catlike, and shivered. She could hardly wait to get her husband back to the hotel. She would make it a memorable night for them both.

C.C. went into his closing number. Flashing that brilliant smile, he took from his tux's lapel the trademark red rose.

Screaming women clamored to be the lucky one to get the rose. But on this night, this special night when he had had such a close call and been blessedly reprieved, C.C. intended the rose for his beautiful, trusting wife.

Ryker Rawley's slim hand slid into his coat. He was no more than fifty feet from the unprotected entertainer. His heart pounded with excitement.

C.C. started to the lip of the stage. And when he stepped down to hand the rose to Caroline, Ryker Rawley eased up out of his seat, gun drawn, gray eyes deadly, saying silently, "You're on your way to hell, McCarty!"

From the corner of his eye, the ever-alert Buddy Hester saw Ryker draw and leaped from his seat at Caroline's side to throw himself in front of C.C. Ryker fired. The bullet ripped into the bodyguard's massive back. Buddy gave a gurgling little "arrgh" sound and collapsed atop a horrified, frozen C.C.

Screams filled the open-air auditorium as pandemonium broke out. Armed police emerged from nowhere to wrestle Ryker Rawley to the ground, while he continued firing, the shots going wild, hitting empty seats.

The terrified crowd scattered, fleeing in their panic. People were knocked down and trampled as thousands of frightened fans rushed the exits. Still others, stunned by the chaos, remained in their seats, crying softly, their eyes on the stage where all three McCartys were being hustled away by Bowl security, C.C.'s tuxedo covered with the blood of his bodyguard.

The high whine of the arriving ambulance was accompanied by a chorus of police sirens. The sirens, the red flashing lights of the ambulances, and the blue spinning lights of the cop cars cast an eerie pall over the mass confusion.

C.C., against all advice, insisted on riding to Cedars Sinai in the screaming ambulance with his loyal, unconscious friend. Caroline and Laura Kay, both shaken and sobbing, were rushed back to the Beverly Wilshire where round-the-clock guards were stationed outside their suite.

Six guards shadowing his every step, C.C. smoked and paced the hospital corridor and prayed to his childhood God—the God Gracie McCarty had taught him about—that Buddy Hester would not die.

Buddy lived.

And no one was more relieved than C.C. McCarty. Unless it was his wife, Caroline. Grateful he had saved C.C.'s life, remorseful that she had always treated Buddy like a barely tolerated intruder, she vowed it would be different in the future.

And so when, after only seven days in the hospital, the big bodyguard was released and flown home to Dallas, she insisted he convalesce at

Musicland. And not out in the gatehouse quarters he shared with Michael Shephard, but in one of the many spacious bedrooms of the mansion.

Buddy was overwhelmed. And very pleased. He quipped to C.C. that he had spent eight years trying to win Caroline's approval when all he had to do was get shot.

Laura Kay, who had always loved the rowdy, affectionate Buddy, took it upon herself to keep the invalid entertained. Each afternoon when she came in from school, she raced through the house, shouting his name, assuring him that she was back and ready to read to him. Or play gin rummy or crazy eights. Or to push his big wheelchair outdoors and get some sun.

Laura Kay loved her Uncle Buddy and liked hanging around with him. And she was overjoyed that her mother no longer seemed to mind. Caroline stopped to watch the pair from her upstairs window one unusually warm October day. Buddy and Laura Kay were out on the back terrace in the bright autumn sunshine. Laura Kay was pretending she was an entertainer. Like her daddy.

"Ladies and gentlemen," said Laura Kay in her best announcer's voice, "I'm happy to present the world's greatest entertainer, Miss Laura McCarty." Laura Kay giggled, flew out of sight, then came strolling back, bowing and smiling while Buddy grinned and clapped enthusiastically.

Taking up her imaginary microphone, Laura Kay began singing— "You've Lost That Lovin' Feeling," one of C.C.'s hit songs—and her rapt audience of one was nodding his big sandy head appreciatively.

Caroline felt an unsettling chill. Suppose her child should become an entertainer. She knew all her father's songs. She was mimicking his brilliant smile, his easy, casual stance, his sensual intonation.

Caroline shivered as her only child stood in the crisp fall sunshine and "performed." And she made a mental note to speak to C.C. when he got home. It was his fault. He had put the notion into Laura Kay's head. Surely after almost losing his life at the Bowl, he wouldn't want Laura to become an entertainer. He wouldn't want . . .

The ringing telephone broke into Caroline's thoughts. Her father, seventy-eight-year-old Commodore Mansfield, had suffered a fatal heart attack.

"Young man, I'm not happy. Not happy at all," Valentina tapped a well-shod foot on the black-and-white marble and glared up at Benny Hamilton.

Benny pushed past her, strode into her living room, lifted the stopper from a crystal decanter, and poured himself a drink. "You have no right to be unhappy," he told her calmly. "My cousin will be moving to Dallas after the first of the year. He had to wind things up, I told you that."

"I am not a patient woman," said Valentina. "And it's not just the slow-moving doctor we're talking about here. You promised our gorgeous blonde was going to bowl the Chief over. What happened?"

"The timing was bad. First he's got her in bed and his wife walks into the suite, almost catching them. That's enough to cool off any man. Then he gets shot at the same night. Timing, lady, timing."

"You mean Caroline McCarty walked into the hotel while the Chief was in bed with the girl?"

"She and the kid showed up unexpectedly at the suite. C.C. was in the bedroom banging the broad."

"Then why didn't you allow Mrs. McCarty to go into the bedroom and see for herself what—"

"I wasn't the only one there, Valentina. Most of the guys were in the suite. Guy Stearns quickly covered for C.C., saying he wasn't there."

"Damn! We could have had him the first time he crawled in the sack with somebody." Her brown eyes blazed. "Why couldn't that nosey Stearns mind his own business."

Benny Hamilton stared incredulously. "For chrissake, Valentina, there was not a man in that room who would have allowed his poor unsuspecting wife and daughter to walk in on something like that."

Valentina moved closer. "Listen to me, Hamilton. If such a golden opportunity ever again arises, I'll expect you to see to it that that haughty little Highland Park princess is allowed to see exactly how her wrong-side-of-the-tracks, half-breed husband acts when he's out of her sight."

"Now, Valentina I don't . . ."

"What happened to the blonde?" she cut in. "Think we can get them back together and try again?"

"Not a chance. The chief loves his wife. Nearly being caught scared the shit out of him. It's going to be a while before we can get him back in bed with anybody."

"Hmmmm. Perhaps you're right." She smiled suddenly. "Actually I needn't worry all that much."

"Giving up?"

"Not at all. He's taken the plunge and next time it will be easier for him. You say there's always beautiful girls around him. We'll let him choose his own the next time."

"I don't think . . ."

"You certainly don't. Get that snail-assed cousin doctor to Dallas. This attempt on McCarty's life has surely left him jumpy. The man needs pills. Let's get him some pills."

Buddy Hester, twenty pounds lighter, joined his boss in Hollywood in mid-November. And he basked in the glow of more attention than he had received since his football-playing days at Crozier Tech. He was a hero and some of the groupies looked with favor on the big man.

A short brunette who had, in the time he had been away, come on the scene and slept indiscriminately with half the entourage, set her sights on Buddy. A couple of nights with Lorene Morris and the responsive bodyguard was foolishly in love. Really in love. And no one had the heart to tell him about Lorene.

So they told the Chief.

"Bud," C.C. eased into it. "Don't you think this thing with Lorene has happened a little fast?"

Buddy gave him that foolish grin, his eyes twinkling happily. "Seems to me that's what I said when you met Caroline. I love this little girl, C. C., and she loves me. There's never been a pretty woman loved me before." He shook his sandy head, disbelievingly. "And she is pretty, ain't she? Just a little doll. I never been so happy in my life!"

C.C. studied the florid face of his best friend, the man who had saved his life. He couldn't do it. He couldn't be the one to break a heart as big as Buddy Hester's. Maybe the girl would change once they were married, be a decent wife. "She is pretty, Bud. You're a lucky guy. Promise I'll be your best man."

"Shitfire, C. C., who else would I want?"

And so Buddy asked little Lorene Morris to marry him, telling her truthfully that he was crazy about her and that although he didn't make all that much in salary, he personally owned four percent of the Big Chief Corporation, a company worth millions. He never noticed the new gleam that leapt into her eyes.

"Buddy, let's don't wait. Let's get married this week," Lorene suggested, giving him a big kiss.

Two days later they became man and wife.

The trial began in December. C.C. insisted that all newspaper articles be kept from Laura Kay and the subject never mentioned in her presence. The assailant's name was not spoken at Musicland.

He didn't want his child worrying and having nightmares.

But he did agree with Caroline that it might be wise to discourage Laura

Kay's plans of following in his footsteps. The thought of someone harming her made his chest tighten in terror.

With cold fingers, C.C. unfolded the *Times Herald*.

Charles E. Rawley's picture was on the front page. A Dallas native who had spent time in a Home for Boys in Gatesville. C.C. studied the dark-haired, twenty-year-old man. The cold, clear eyes staring out at him were filled with deep hatred and defiance.

But why shoot at me? wondered C.C. What have I ever done to Charles E. Rawley?

The answer was clear. Rawley was a psycho. One of thousands loose on the streets who could, for no logical reason, pull the trigger and end his life. It wouldn't do to think about. Like Kennedy had often said before his assassination, "If they want you, they can get you. And there's not a damned thing you can do about it."

CHAPTER TWENTY-TWO

THERE were good times.

There were bad times.

Long, halcyon days at *Cielo Vista* or the beach house on Padre Island or the newly purchased stucco in Palm Springs.

Glorious Texas autumn days of horseback riding—the three of them, C.C., Caroline, and Laura Kay—through the tall cottonwoods and loaded pecan trees and out across the rolling, sprawling prairie. Silvery, magical nights lounging on the moonlit balcony of the seaside villa in South Texas, the safe soothing sound of the waves crashing rhythmically to the sandy shore, the cool Gulf breezes tickling the almost-naked flesh of the contented McCartys, exhausted from a long summer's day of frolicking together in the surf. Clear, bright, shimmering hot days on the Mojave desert, when all three wisely remained cloistered inside the palatial thick-walled dwelling, shut away from the world, happy to laze about in air-cooled comfort until the blazing sun had set behind the distant mountains.

But there were days—weeks at a time—when C.C.'s shooting schedule kept him away from his family. In his absence, Caroline's mother, the widowed Lenore Jesse, spent a great deal of time with her daughter. The two had never been close, but Caroline felt sorry for the older woman. And she tried, very hard, not to let her mother's worrisome habits upset her.

Since the Commodore's death, Lenore Jesse had rewritten history. Theirs had been the perfect marriage. Caroline knew better. Lenore Jesse, in the final years of the old man's life, had barely tolerated him, complaining constantly that he was underfoot, senile.

"We had forty-eight wonderful years together," said Lenore Jesse, smiling wistfully.

166

"Yes, Mother," said Caroline.

"There's nothing as fulfilling as living with the man you adore." She smiled suddenly and added, "That reminds me. They say True Youngblood and his wife just returned from three months abroad. She's his second wife, a beautiful girl. The first marriage lasted less than a year, but then you know that. Anyway, this girl is . . ."

Caroline ground her teeth. Was it possible to be in her mother's company for longer than an hour without hearing about the latest adventures of True Youngblood? It made no difference that she had reminded her mother time and again that she was not particularly interested in what True Youngblood was doing.

C.C. was lonely without his family. And he was bored. Terribly bored. He had come to hate the movies he was grinding out—two or three a year—and longed for the excitement of personal appearances. He needed to be before an audience, he complained to Ash Ashford.

"Making these stupid movies is tearing my guts up, Ash," C.C. told his manager, pacing restlessly in his Beverly Hills Hotel bungalow. He flung himself down into a chair. "This is no way for a man to make a living. Let's go back on the road. I need to see the fans, I need to . . ."

"These stupid movies are making you a very rich man," Ash, unmoved, calmly told his star. "You'll be before your fans when the time is right." The silver-haired manager rose and smiled down at the scowling C.C. Glancing at the gold watch on his wrist, Ash added, "Got to go, C.C., I'm . . ."

"Aw, stick around. We'll go over to the Troubadour for a drink."

"I've got to get on out to LAX, C.C. See you when you get back to Dallas."

Frowning, C.C. lifted dark eyes to Ash. "Going over to Vegas?" Ash nodded yes. C.C. started to grin. "You promised Charmaine you had given up the tables."

Ash grinned with him. "I did. Trouble is, they won't give me up."

C.C. stood up. "I'll come with you."

"I don't like company when I gamble." Ash crossed the room. "Besides, you know damn well you couldn't walk into a casino without getting mobbed. Take it easy, C.C.," he said and left.

C.C. sagged dejectedly back down into his chair, hooking a long leg over the arm. He sighed. And once again, he was bored. And lonely.

The stomach pains that had plagued C.C. intermittently became all to regular. When he returned to Dallas, he consulted his physician. Dr.

Thomas sent him to a gastroenterologist. Tests were run. C.C. was told the lining of his stomach was highly inflamed. The doctor suggested a more sensible diet than the one C.C. preferred. And he told C.C. to stop drinking.

"Jesus, Doctor Brady," C.C. argued, rebuttoning his shirt. "I'm no drinker. A glass of vodka now and then. Surely that can't . . ."

"No liquor," the white-haired, ruddy-faced specialist looked him straight in the eye. "Cut down on fats. Eat more poultry and fish and . . ."

"You sound like my wife."

The short physician put a hand on C.C.'s shoulder. "You want to live a long life, Mr. McCarty, you'll have to change your habits." His hand fell away. "That, of course, is entirely up to you."

C.C. changed his habits.

For about a week. He ate steamed vegetables and broiled fish and drank nothing stronger than ice tea and complained that he was starving to death. "Belle, darlin'," he knocked on the door of Musicland's stocky black cook one midnight, and stuck his head inside. "I'm so hungry I can't stand it. Reckon you could fry me a steak?" The big black woman beamed at the tall man she loved like a son, hefted her great weight from the bed, and headed for the kitchen.

So C.C. continued to sip vodka almost nightly and to eat the red meats he so loved. The stomach pains returned, but he paid little attention to them. He now had pills that eased them immediately.

The new member of his growing entourage had given them to him.

Dr. Stuart Hamilton had come to Musicland one winter's day with his cousin, Benny. Benny introduced the young, pleasant-looking man to C.C. Dr. Hamilton shook C.C.'s hand and said, "Ever anything I can do for you, Chief, let me know."

A couple of weeks later C.C. and the crew, including young Dr. Hamilton, were on the West Coast. C.C. had a stomach ache. Dr. Hamilton produced a pill he guaranteed to give instant relief.

"Why suffer, C.C.? Take it," urged Dr. Stuart Hamilton.

C.C. popped the small green capsule in his mouth and within minutes, all pain had disappeared. "What was that?" he asked, slurring his words, smiling, and having trouble focusing on the helpful Hamilton.

Hamilton didn't answer. Just smiled at him. C.C. smiled back. He felt relaxed and a wonderful sense of well-being settled over him.

"Better get him to bed, Buddy," C.C. heard somebody say later and that was the last he knew.

The next morning C.C. felt drugged and hung over. He sat on the edge of his bed, dark head lowered, wondering how he could make it through the first day of shooting on his picture, *Surfs Up*. A soft knock; the bedroom door quietly opened and young Dr. Stuart Hamilton came in.

"How you feeling?" he inquired solicitously.

C.C. lifted his head with difficulty. "Like shit. There's no way in hell I can make it to the studio."

But he did make it.

The obliging Dr. Hamilton gave him a blue pill and within minutes great bursts of energy surged through C.C.'s lean body. He sang loudly in the shower and looked forward with great expectation to the day's shooting.

C.C. had not yet met his co-star.

Surfs Up was to be Belinda Townsend's first starring role. A beauty queen from Sioux City, Iowa, Belinda was terribly excited about playing opposite MGM's reigning male sex symbol. And Belinda let C.C. know it.

C.C. was in a jovial mood all day. Loaded with unspent energy, he clowned and teased and put the nervous Belinda at her ease. And when a tenacious photographer somehow slipped through the protective barrier surrounding the valuable star, C.C. obliged and posed, much to the delight of Metro's publicity department.

And much to the chagrin of his wife.

Caroline's days, even with her mother's visits, were not filled as they had been when Laura Kay was a baby. There were too many lonely hours to fill now. Too much time to feel increasingly left out of her husband's life as well as her daughter's. Time to wonder what C.C. did when he was as lonely as she.

So Caroline was genuinely hurt when she opened the Dallas *Times Herald* to the entertainment section to see a half-page filled with pictures of her husband in various affectionate poses with his pretty brunette co-star. She was sure she read something telling in C.C.'s black expressive eyes. Her husband was embroiled in a red-hot affair with the dark-haired actress.

Upset, Caroline called C.C. and accused him of misbehaving. C.C. denied it hotly. It was not true. Belinda Townsend was a sweet, well-brought-up young girl, and he felt nothing more for her than a brotherly protectiveness.

He loved her—Caroline—and no one else. He was lonely and anxious to get back to Musicland. There was to be a break in shooting in a couple of weeks. He'd fly home and they would all go over to *Cielo Vista* and spend a few days.

"Alright, C.C." Caroline felt a little better. "Call me tomorrow."

"You know I will. Love you, baby." He hung up the phone.

And he looked at the sensuous young woman curled up on the brown suede couch in his luxurious dressing room. C.C. hadn't lied to Caroline. He had not touched the tempting, teasing Belinda.

C.C. rose and poured himself a tall vodka on the rocks. He stood, a hip against the bar, studying the provocatively beautiful Belinda.

"You ought to go," he said and took a drink.

She smiled. "There's an old saying in Sioux City, Chief. 'If you've got the blame, might as well have the game.' "

He grinned. The smile fled and he stared intently at the girl. And he mentally told himself, Aw, what the hell. "Yeah," he said in a low, caressing voice, "might as well." He set down the half-empty glass and went to her.

It was to become the pattern of his life.

At home in Dallas, C.C. was the loving husband, the doting father. But away from Musicland, in Hollywood or on location in such exotic places as Hawaii or Singapore or New Orleans—where the pills and liquor flowed and the party never ended and the women shamelessly played up to his passionate nature—he strayed with ever greater frequency. And he suffered great pangs of guilt for his indiscretions.

The mobs outside the Music Gates had grown through the years. Twenty-four hours of the day the faithful stood, their hands gripping the tall steel bars, hoping for a fleeting look at the magnificent man who resided in the big white mansion.

On an April afternoon when Laura Kay was not expected home after school—she was to sleep over at Missy's—Caroline returned alone to Musicland, the melancholy mood that had sent her forth on a shopping foray to Neiman Marcus still with her.

The crowds around the gate were unusually heavy. Tony Zoppi's column had reported that the Chief's latest movie had wrapped. He would be coming home any day. When the crowd saw the long black Rolls approaching, they just knew the Chief had returned.

"Who is it? Can you see? Is it him? Is it the Chief?" shouted eager gawkers, and a loud buzz of excitement swept through the crowds swamping the slowing Rolls. And then: "Oh, it's nobody, it's Caroline. It's nobody."

"It's nobody." The words resounded long after the locked gates had closed behind Caroline and she was inside the silent house. For a long time . . . far too long . . . she had been a nobody.

Caroline walked straight down the corridor into C.C.'s library, the heels of her I. Magnim pumps clicking on the marble floors. Calmly she removed the emerald-and-pearl earring from her right lobe, picked up the telephone and dialed. A cheerful female voice answered. "Good Afternoon. Youngblood Oil Company. May I help you?"

Caroline drew a deep breath. "Let me speak to True Youngblood."

CHAPTER TWENTY-THREE

THEY had lied. Those friends who had, over the years, confided to Caroline that an occasional fling had been just what the doctor ordered. Their lives, and their marriages, had benefitted, had become richer, fuller, more satisfying after a few stolen hours in the arms of a man who was not their husband. It was exciting, immensely invigorating to steal away to some pre-appointed rendezvous and meet a passionate tennis pro or bartender or med student for a little illicit lovemaking.

Caroline felt nothing but guilt and shame after her one clandestine afternoon in a Carrollton motel room with the very married True Young-blood. She had made a mistake in going to him. It was too late for them; ten years too late. Sadly, she told him as much when they were dressing to leave, and to her mild disappointment, True Youngblood had merely shrugged, smiled, and said, "Why the long face, Caroline. We had a little fun, passed an afternoon; no harm done."

But there was. She had broken her marriage vows and she felt miserable about it. Nursing her terrible guilt, Caroline vowed that she would never again betray C.C.

She would stay busy and out of mischief.

So that's just what she did. She chaired society balls, served on fund-raising committees, lunched often with old friends, redecorated the guest rooms at Musicland, and spent more and more time at *Cielo Vista* Ranch around her prized Arabian horses.

And around likeable, good-natured, boyishly appealing Donny Wheeler, the divorced ranch foreman.

* * *

172

Valentina Trent was laughing.

She sat behind her imposing desk high in the Republic Towers, laughing merrily, tears of joy filling her eyes.

In her long championship bout with C.C. McCarty, she had just been awarded another round. The arrogant singer was losing the match. She would still be on her feet long after he had collapsed to the mat.

True, things were not progressing as rapidly as she had hoped, but they were progressing nonetheless. Her inside man, Benny Hamilton, reported that the Chief had been involved with at least a half-dozen beautiful women. And that the singer was growing dependent on some of the potent pills Dr. Stuart Hamilton helpfully supplied.

Those, granted, were minor victories.

But this morning's was a major one. She had just purchased, for an astronomical sum, four percent of the Big Chief Corporation from the greedy young wife of C.C.'s right-hand man, the foolishly-in-love Buddy Hester.

She now owned seventeen percent of C.C.'s company. A long way to go, but getting there was half the fun. And she was confident that she would soon have her hands on the other three percent held by supposedly faithful employees.

And finally, one sweet day, one way or another, on Ash Ashford's whopping forty percent.

What pleasure it would be when she was in total control of the holding company, when that high-flying, ungrateful superstar they called The Chief, was once-and-for-all working for her!

Valentina laughed louder.

Buddy Hester, ever honest, told C.C. what Lorene had done. "I swear to God, C.C., I never meant this to happen," the big man shook his head, his florid face contorted with misery and shame. "I never thought about it when Lorene asked me to put her name on the stock. It was in case something happened to me . . . Shitfire, I never dreamed she would up and sell it. Especially not to Valentina; I've told Lorene how you feel about that woman."

C.C. grinned at his worried friend and told him to forget it. "Lorene might invest the money in something a lot more lucrative than yours truly."

Buddy tried to smile.

But Buddy cried like a baby when Lorene, not a week after the stock's sale, cleaned out their joint bank account, packed all her clothes, and left him. Wiping his red eyes, he said sadly, "I don't know what I'll do without her; she was just the cutest little thing I've ever seen, C.C."

"I know," said C.C. for want of something better to say, "I know, Bud." And he wrapped his oldest friend in a tight consoling hug, thinking how he would feel if Caroline ever left him.

For as long as she could remember, Laura Kay had known that her daddy hated the rich redheaded society woman at Bluebonnet Records. She never knew the reason why he hated Mrs. Valentina Trent, though she had asked time and again. His answer had always been, "Darlin', she's not a very nice lady."

C.C.'s language was much stronger when, not knowing Laura was awake, he stood in the doorway of Caroline's bedroom late one night. "That vile bitch Valentina's got another four percent of Big Chief. Bud's wife sold it to her."

From Caroline: "I told you, C.C., all those years ago that you were making a mistake."

"So you did. Thanks, sweetheart, for reminding me."

"Get angry if you want to, but you have to admit I was right. I was also right when I warned you about allowing the 'boys' to roam at will through this house. One of them took your Sears guitar and God knows what else."

"You still harping on that, Caroline?"

"I'm not harping on anything. I know how much that guitar meant to you. I'm just saying I was right about—"

"Ah, well, darlin', aren't you always?"

"Must we argue on your last night at home?"

"Cut!"

"Sorry."

"It's okay, Chief, okay." The director came forward. He put an arm around C.C.'s wide shoulders. "What is it, Chief? You feeling bad today? Want to start fresh tomorrow?"

C.C. jerked the hated white turban from his head. "I can't finish this stupid picture. I can't. I won't." He stripped the heavy white robes from his body and slammed them to the sand while his big-eyed, big-bosomed co-star stood staring at his bare brown legs and chest. Her hands on voluptuous hips clad in revealing harem pajamas, she blew bubbles with her gum.

"Goddammit, I refuse to deliver one more idiotic line like 'My little vixen, I will carry you over the burning sands to my tent,' and then burst into an asinine song in the middle of a desert!"

"Chief, you aren't the first major star to play a role like this. Valentino and Doug Fairbanks and—"

"I don't give a damn if John Wayne did. I'm through," he turned and stalked to his trailer, wearing nothing but his jockey shorts, the astonished eyes of actors, cameramen, and grips following him.

"Take a break, everybody," called the director. He had never seen his star behave the prima donna. He didn't know what to do. He got on the phone to Ash Ashford.

Ash got in touch with his client. The picture, *Burning Sands* was the final in a three-picture deal. If C.C. would finish *Burning Sands* with no further fuss, he, Ash, would promise it would be the last one for at least a year, perhaps two. C.C. agreed, put his hot white robes back on and sang hated songs, delivered foolish lines, and made love before the cameras to the bubble-gum-chewing harem girl for the next three months.

The picture had wrapped.

C.C. was in residence at Musicland. It was blistering hot in Dallas, Texas, but C.C. didn't mind. Caroline found him stretched out on the hot cement beside the pool, like a lizard sleeping in the sun.

"Put on your suit, darlin'," he smiled up at her.

"Too hot," she said and sat down on a padded chaise. "C.C., I understand Valentina Trent has gotten another one percent of Big Chief and—"

"Jesus H. Christ, Caroline, will you give it a break. I'm not home two days and already you're—"

"Mommy, Daddy, are you fighting again?" Laura Kay, clad in a red swim suit, stood on the terrace steps above them.

They looked from their daughter to each other and back. "No, sweetheart," said C.C., lithely rising to his feet. "Mommy and I were discussing daddy's business."

"Big Chief?" said Laura.

"Big Chief," he confirmed, plucking the child up and into his arms. "And if I want any of your advice, puddin', I'll ask for it, alright?" he grinned and she giggled. "Now hold your nose because we're going in the pool."

Laura Kay gripped her turned-up nose with one hand, her daddy's neck with the other. He jumped into nine feet of water, submerging them. When they surfaced, both were laughing and Laura Kay sputtered happily, "Mommy, Mommy, come in the water and have fun with us."

"Yes, Mommy," said C.C. affectionately, "come in and have some fun with us."

Before she could answer, Ash Ashford, silver hair gleaming in the sun, was crossing the terrace, calling to them. He was smiling broadly. C.C. and his daughter climbed out of the pool and went to greet him.

"What's up?" C.C. could tell by the gleam in his eye Ash was in high spirits.

"Vegas," was his one-word reply.

"Vegas!" C.C., dripping water, paced restlessly back and forth, hands rubbing together in anticipation, wide, happy smile lighting his face while his manager elaborated. "Caesar's! That's great. You know how anxious I've been to get back on deck." Then, pausing; "Jesus, Ash, it's been a long time. Maybe we ought to go on a shakedown tour first."

"No time. You open August 19."

"Can we go, Daddy?" asked Laura Kay.

"Will you go, darlin'," C.C. asked his wife.

"We'll all go," said Ash Ashford.

After Ash left, and Caroline had gone back inside where it was cool, C.C., his mind racing, sat staring into space, smoking one cigarette after another. He felt a small hand on his forearm. He turned to look at his daughter.

"Don't be nervous, Daddy," said Laura Kay, "you'll be a boffo, socko hit!"

CHAPTER TWENTY-FOUR

ADING desert sunlight glinting on its silver fuselage, C.C.'s customized 707-320 touched down at McCarren Field and taxied to a stop out and away from the terminal.

Laura stepped from the plane. Dry desert heat blasted her in the face, taking her breath away. When she got it back, she dashed, squealing, for Caesar's air-conditioned limo waiting on the tarmac. The driver, uniformed in crisp white cotton, swung open the heavy rear door and Laura bounced inside. Nestled on the blue velvet upholstery, she giggled happily when her daddy, handing her mother inside, crawled across her, stretched his long legs, winked, and said, "Hotter than the hinges of hell, huh, sweetheart?"

All eyes, Laura asked question after question as the sleek white limo crawled down the traffic-clogged Strip. "What's that hotel? And that one? Look over there! Oh, daddy, see that billboard. Frankie Avalon is at the Desert Inn. Can we go see him? Please, daddy, say yes."

"You bet, baby," said the happy man who had not felt so vibrant, so alive in years. "We have a couple of free nights before I go to work." He reached a hand across the seat and affectionately squeezed Caroline's shoulder. She turned and smiled at him.

"Daddy!" Laura's voice had raised to a screech. Just ahead, on their left, Caesar's Palace—the grandest of all the Vegas hotels—sat far back from the Strip, its entrance partially obscured by a half-dozen cascading fountains shooting water up into the dry desert air.

The limousine turned into the long drive, passed the colorful Roman statuary, and rolled to a stop before the glassed entrance. The limo door

177

opened. A purple-and-gold-uniformed doorman flashed a bright smile and said, "Welcome, Chief, Mrs. McCarty, Miss McCarty. Great to have you at Caesar's."

The doorman signaled a quartet of purple-and-white-uniformed bell-boys. They hustled forward to unload the luggage, while from out of nowhere, a pair of huskily built, hotel security men materialized to escort the McCartys out of the overwhelming heat and into the cool interior of the giant hotel casino.

Inside, Laura watched, fascinated, as a swarthy-skinned man stepped forward to shake her daddy's hand. Hawk-faced, he had swept-back, solidly silver hair, heavy lips, riveting eyes, and a voice that sounded like sandpaper rubbing against wood. He wore a pin-striped suit, white-on-white shirt, white silk tie, and a diamond on his pinky finger so big it reached his knuckle.

"Chief," rasped the hawk-faced man, "It's a great day for Caesar's." White teeth flashed against the swarthy complexion. "You're pre-checked, of course. We'll get you right up to your suite."

With bellboys trotting behind and security men on either side, the dark-suited man led the entourage directly through the hotel casino before anyone had a chance to realize who the arriving guests were.

The star treatment.

Hurrying to keep up, Laura, eyes wide, took it all in. The Vegas she had heard so much about from Uncle Ash. He was right. It was exciting.

One-armed bandits cranked and crunched and spit out coins. Tiny white balls clattered around spinning roulette wheels. Cards shuffled and flicked at the blackjack layouts. Dice shaken and flung at crap tables. Croupiers chanting, "Get your bets down—the dice are coming out." Gamblers laughing and shouting and cursing.

The Checkmates, a musical group, warming up in Nero's Nook. The hotel operator paging, "Princess Fatima. Princess Fatima, please call . . ." Curvaceous cocktail waitresses in brief gold-trimmed white togas and golden highheels. Handsome dealers in snug black pants and blousey sleeved white shirts, gold medallions swinging from their throats. Players in dark, expensive suits, chewing cigars and peeling off hundred-dollar bills to buy black chips while tall, heavily made-up women stood at their elbows, smiling broadly, and pressing possessively close.

Quivering with excitement, Laura stepped into the private elevator and was whisked up to the penthouse. The hawk-faced man threw open the doors to show them the most opulent suite in the hotel. Bedrooms were upstairs, overlooking the enormous two-story high living room with its front wall of gleaming glass. Laura rushed across the deeply piled royal purple carpet to survey the glittering city below.

The hawk-faced manager, the smiling bellboys, and the huge security men left them at last. Caroline went upstairs to unpack. C.C. came to stand beside his daughter.

The broiling desert sun was rapidly setting behind the low, distant mountains, turning them a cool violet hue against the clear, darkening sky. Dusk was descending over Vegas and the dazzling lights on the marquees of the hotels were now ablaze, spelling out the headliner's names.

Laura stood entranced. So did Laura's daddy.

Eyes never leaving the towering hotels and the crowded casinos and the never-ending lines of cars streaming down the Strip, Laura reached for her daddy's hand. "Will I have to wait until I'm twenty-one to appear in the main showroom, daddy?"

She lifted big dark eyes to his. He held her small hand in both of his own and smiled down at her. "Honey, you're going to be there at my opening."

Laura shook her head. "That isn't what I mean, Daddy. When can I be a headliner here at Caesar's?"

They came from as far away as Hong Kong, Singapore, Tokyo, Europe, and Mexico City. And as close as California and Arizona. The highest rollers. In town to see The Chief.

The waiters had cleared the tables. The lights began to dim in the big showroom. The drum rolls started.

It was show time in Circus Maximus.

Laura, seated beside her mother in the white-trimmed violet leather banquette, felt the arousal of the crowd build. Her heart thudded against her ribs and she nervously squeezed Caroline's bare arm. Caroline, too, felt it. The shimmering bodice of her pink Grecian gown trembled with the rapid rising and falling of her breasts. She wet her dry lips and unconsciously patted at sleek, blond hair that was carefully dressed into a diamond-and-pearl-bedecked French twist at the back of her head.

The room had grown very quiet and still. The house lights were dark. All eyes were riveted to the stage. The heavy purple curtains slowly lifted while the crowd held its collective breath. The stage, too, was dark, only the shiny brass instruments reflecting beams from the tiny mounted musicians' lights. Nothing on stage was moving.

The drum rolls ended. There was absolutely no sound. On stage or off. Thirty seconds of silence elapsed.

Then a tiny pinpoint of light appeared at center stage. The baby-blue spot caught and framed a delicate blood-red rose in a circular pool of illumination. Slowly the circle of light grew larger. And larger. Until beneath the scarlet rose, a black tux jacket and a snowy white shirt became visible.

The awed audience made not a sound.

The light continued to pull further back, further back, revealing a darkly handsome face.

The Chief stood there in the spotlight, in the silence. Moving not one muscle. And before the audience had a chance to begin shouting, the orchestra's string section began playing. Lifting the gleaming mike close to his lips, he sang one of his biggest hits, the haunting, "I Remember You."

And if he remembered them, they certainly remembered him. He did not disappoint. At thirty-five, C.C. was sleek and poised and suave. Impeccably groomed, rich raven hair gleaming in the spotlight, lithe body taking up that arrogant stance, he exuded a steamy kind of sex appeal that rendered every female totally helpless. He had never looked better. He had never sounded better.

Bending a long arm, C.C. brought the mike up against his lips to finish the song. Lids sensually low over dark shining eyes, he sang in soft caressing tones, his voice rich and deep, the dropping inflection of tone causing many a feminine heart to beat faster.

> "When my life is through
> And the angels asks me to recall,
> the thrill of them all,
> Then I shall tell them I remember you."

There was a shriek of delight from a woman far in the back of the hall. Quickly followed by another from the opposite side of the cavernous room. Then the massive crowd was on its feet, screaming and shouting and applauding. Total pandemonium broke out as C.C. moved about the stage, bending to shake hands, a dazzling smile on his handsome face, dark, dark eyes glittering.

And behind him, the band began its sledgehammer riff, further whipping the excited audience into a frenzy. The locomotive pounding grew louder and louder until fans begged their worshipped Adonis to sing.

"Come on, Chief, more! 'Flaming Love'! Sing, Chief, sing!"

Casually, taking his time, C.C. straightened and sauntered to center stage. Winking at his audience, he pointed a lean forefinger at his conductor and went immediately into his earliest hit, the song that had charted a dozen years before.

"Flaming Love" still excited.

C.C., too, was excited. In a state of euphoria, he sang all his old and new hits, one after the other, his voice rich and resonant, exhilaration and happiness sending great surges of energy through his tall, lean body.

He loved his audience and it showed. The audience loved him back with a devotion reserved for him alone. He belonged to them, they felt, this gleaming god was theirs and he had been away from them too long.

Now The Chief was back!

The blatant sexuality was as potent as ever and women, some now middle-aged and married, others young and beautiful, swooned and screamed and behaved as though they were experiencing orgasmic delight. And more than one highly aroused female wet her pants.

Caroline was still a fan. She watched her husband perform and felt the same intense stimulation as those around her. Mesmerized, she watched the Comanche-dark man with the velvet voice, the man she had lived with for more than a decade.

Onstage he was The Chief. A powerfully compelling male, as sleek as a panther, and so handsome it made her weak just to look up at him. Unconsciously, Caroline crossed her legs beneath the table as a strong flutter of pure desire rippled through her lower belly and made her squirm with anticipation.

And when, as pre-planned, she and Laura Kay were guided to a side door as the hour-and-a-half performance was ending, she glanced back for one last look as The Chief leaned down to give the red rose to an admiring fan. The woman, a gorgeous brunette gowned in shimmering blue silk, rose to meet him. He handed her the rose; she pulled his dark head down and kissed him hotly on the mouth.

Caroline gritted her teeth.

At the opening night party, stars from the other rooms along the strip— Vic Damone, Totie Fields, Jimmy Durante, Keely Smith—came by to congratulate C.C. The dressing room was packed with well-wishers, and C.C. made it a point to shake hands with every one of them.

Laura was allowed to remain at the party for a brief time before Buddy Hester hustled her, protesting loudly, off to bed.

Caroline remained with C.C. Possessively, she stayed at his side, reluctant to leave him for a minute. She kept a hand casually pressing his shoulder or his arm or his back throughout the evening and each time C.C. looked down at her, he saw smoldering desire in the depths of her beautiful emerald eyes.

He knew what his wife wanted. Like the other women in the audience, she wanted to make love to The Chief. Not to him. Not to C.C. Not to her husband. To The Chief.

He wondered just how badly she wanted it, how much like a groupie Caroline would behave. "I've a hunger," he whispered, leaning close, "have you?" He almost hoped she would say, "C.C. behave yourself," or "Someone might hear you," or "you can't leave your own party."

"Yes," she said, breathlessly, "when can we leave?"

"Not for a while, but there's a large bath," he inclined his dark head.

"Let's go," she said, grabbed his hand and led him hurriedly, anxiously across the crowded room.

Five minutes later Caroline, her beautiful pink Grecian gown shamelessly pushed up around her waist, firm naked bottom on the cold marble of the vanity, wrapped long, tanned legs around her standing husband's back and writhed in ecstasy, the mirrored walls multiplying their mating images.

Dozens of pink-gowned Carolines made love to dozens of tux-clad C.C.s. Those half-dressed Carolines couldn't get enough of what the well-endowed C.C.s were giving them. And when the ultimate rapture was attained, all the Carolines called out in their ecstasy. But none of the C.C.s received their accolades.

"Oh, Chief," gasped Caroline, breathlessly, "Chief, Chief, ooooh, Chief!"

C.C. felt a twinge of resentment shoot through his pounding, pumping heart.

CHAPTER TWENTY-FIVE

VARIETY   August 20, 1971
The CHIEF opened last night at Circus Maximus before a cheering,
sold-out crowd. Like a tribal shaman of old, he cast a powerful spell,
taking his enrapt followers—the highest rollers—on a wild ninety-
minute ride.
The Chief opened with . . .

THE Vegas run broke all existing records for casino take and Caesar's
begged C.C. to hold over for an additional week. Flushed with success,
vitally alive, he was tempted, but he turned the offer down. The
reason? He wanted to go home. Caroline and Laura Kay had remained
in the hot desert city for only three days. Those days had been golden for
C.C. The hours with his wife had been some of their best. He was anxious
to get to Dallas to pick up where they left off.

Back in Dallas, he found Caroline just as eager.

When the pair came down the stairs one morning, wonderfully
exhausted from a wild night of lovemaking, Buddy Hester and three
members of the crew were on the back terrace overlooking the shimmering
pool.

Resenting the unexpected intrusion, Caroline pulled her robe securely
around her, smiled forcedly, and sat down at the glass-topped table. She
paid little mind when Buddy mentioned that C.C.'s old music teacher at
Crozier Tech was dying of cancer in a San Antonio charity hospital. Her
husband's reaction, however, drew her undivided attention.

His handsome face wore a stricken expression as he silently mouthed the
word, "Gail." Then: "Bud, send one of the jets down to move her to M. D.
Anderson in Houston. I want her to have the best medical care available.
We'll take care of all expense."

"You'll take care of it?" Caroline spoke up. "Why?"

C.C. gave her a dark look. "You heard Bud. She's dying."

"It might take her months to die. That could cost thousands."

"I don't give a damn how much it costs," his voice was cold, controlled.

Hers was not. Eyes flashing, she said hotly, "Really? That's very interesting. Just who is this woman who makes money no object?" Upset, oblivious to the tight masculine faces around the table, she went on, "Is she someone special, C.C.?"

"Yes," C.C. said calmly, "Gail is special."

It was not the answer she had wanted. Hurt, she struck back. "I see. And does she love you like all the rest of the women in the world?"

"Hush now, darlin'," he said softly, embarrassed that his wife was challenging him in front of his friends.

"I won't hush," she said through thinned lips. "I asked you a question, damn you. Did she love you too?"

"Yes," he said, losing his temper, grabbing her arm, and pulling her close. "She did love me. And she loved me before I was The Chief. She loved me when I was nothing more than West Dallas trash." He released her arm and shot to his feet. His angry dark eyes still on her, he said, "Bud, roust out the pilots. I'm flying to San Antonio." He shoved back his chair and walked away.

Caroline jumped up. "You are not!" she shouted, tears gathering in her eyes. "You're not going to some ex-lover's bedside. I will not have you make a fool of me!" She ran to him, grabbed at his arm, and jerked violently.

"Sweetheart," he said, "you're doing a pretty good job of that yourself."

Ignoring his remark, she threatened, "C.C. McCarty, you go to that woman, I don't want you back in this house."

C.C. sadly smiled. His voice lowered to a whisper so that only she could hear. "No. But you'll always be more than willing to fancy fuck the famed Chief, right, sweetheart?" He removed her hand from his arm and walked away.

Twenty-four hours later C.C. returned to Musicland. Without knocking, he entered his wife's bedroom. Caroline, reclining on a plum-colored chaise, book in her hands, slowly lifted her eyes to his.

He stood, hands in his pockets, looking down at her. "I'm sorry I made you unhappy, Caroline. Gail Bradford is an old and dear friend. She's alone, no family. I had to help her out. I hope you can understand that. You're right, it's going to cost a great deal of money, but I had to do it."

Caroline was silent, hadn't said a word. He ventured further into the room. "To make it up to you, I thought maybe we'd buy a corner apartment in the 3525 down on Turtle Creek." Several times Caroline had mentioned buying an apartment for guests in the luxury high-rise. He knew she was referring to his crew. She didn't want them at Musicland. "You can fix it up anyway you like. Even antiques." He smiled boyishly, lifting his wide shoulders.

Caroline exhaled. The book slipped to the floor. She got up and flew to him, crying, and telling him she was sorry. He held her close and said gently, "It was my fault, darlin', all my fault. Don't cry, baby."

Tightly she hugged him. And against his shoulder, she said, "C.C., can we really buy at 3525? Greer Garson lives there . . . I can go to New York with my decorator, Gene Sparks, and see if Christie's has any bargains . . . heard at the Dallas Symphony Orchestra League luncheon that one of the penthouses is for sale . . ."

Caroline got her penthouse. She also got an expensive colorless diamond pendant from Corrigan's, a full-length Black Diamond mink from Koslow's, and dozens of smaller mementos from the husband who dreaded the thought of leaving her and Laura Kay behind when he went on an international tour in October.

Gail Bradford was never again mentioned and when Caroline, wearing the lush dark mink, said good-bye to C.C. on a cold, cloudy October day, she kissed him and said she would keep busy decorating their new 3525 Turtle Creek penthouse.

She had every intention of doing just that. But when, after C.C.'s departure, she went straight to the Terrace House and found Gene Sparks not home, Caroline, disappointed, with a long, lonely day to fill, went to *Cielo Vista.*

Alone.

She found him at the back barn.

Bare-chested, he was lifting bales of hay from the pickup bed. He didn't hear her approach. She stood, quietly watching him work, the chill north winds riffling his light hair and chapping his lips.

Hands in the deep pockets of her new mink coat, Caroline sauntered inside the dim barn just as Donny Wheeler looked up, a huge bale of hay held high over his head. He smiled. And slowly lowered the hay.

Caroline felt a strange tremor of excitement rush through her body. Instinctively, she backed away from the ranch foreman, farther into the barn. Purposefully, he strode toward her, stopping directly in front of her. Holding her gaze, he removed his heavy work gloves, stuffing them into the hip pocket of his tight Levis.

"I was thinking about you," he said.

"You were?" her throat was tight. It grew tighter still when the slim cowboy wordlessly nodded, pushed the supple lapels of her expensive fur apart and unceremoniously began unbuttoning her blouse.

A soft gurgle of emotion surfaced when Donny Wheeler easily unhooked her front-closing sheer bra and ran calloused thumbs over her rapidly peaking nipples. "Kiss me," he said and lowered his mouth to hers.

For months, even years, Caroline had been around this handsome young horseman and nothing like this had happened. It couldn't be happening now. It couldn't. It made no sense. She had just left her husband at the airport. They had been getting along better than usual. She couldn't do this.

"Jesus, I've wanted you for so long," said Donny Wheeler, lips dropping to the soft flesh of her throat. "And finally you're ready."

"I don't know what you mean. I'm not, I can't . . ."

"You are. You can. You've wanted it for a long time, just as I have. I've seen it in your eyes. You came out here today for this."

"No. That's not true," she gasped as his lips slid along the top of her right shoulder. And all the time she protested, she wondered, was he right?

In seconds they were both naked and Donny was moving atop her. "How long is he going to be gone?" he asked as he slid into her.

"Two . . . two months," she murmured, gripping his sweat-slick shoulders and wincing with pain and with pleasure.

"Tell me I can make love to you every day while he's away."

"No . . ." she weakly objected. "I don't know why I . . . this has to be the only time . . ."

"Say it. Say I can have you every day while he's gone."

Breathlessly, she whispered, "Yes . . . yes, you can."

"I can what?" his eyes bore into hers, his body poised.

"You can have me every day while he's gone."

Donny kissed her. He started moving his slim hips in slow rotating motions and running a calloused hand down her slender body, savoring the soft, feminine curves that heated at his touch.

While a cold winter rain began falling and great raindrops dripped from the eaves of the barn, Caroline, wearing nothing but a glittering diamond necklace around her throat, made warming, wonderful love to the muscular ranchhand atop a soft, luxurious bed of lush black mink.

On that same cold October day, a Military Air Transport 707 landed at Dallas' Love Field. A pale-skinned, dark-haired, heavily decorated young warrant officer, an ebony cane in his slim right hand, limped down the 707's passenger off ramp and into the cold, biting rain.

An enlisted driver stepped forward, saluted the emaciated officer, and escorted him to a waiting olive drab Army station wagon. Alone in the back seat, the wounded officer removed his rain-speckled Green Beret, let the cane fall between his bent knees and drew a Pall Mall from the inside of his wintergreen uniform blouse.

Gray eyes squinting, he lit up.

"Sir, I'll have you across town to the V.A. Medical Center on Lancaster in minutes," said the driver. His eyes lifted to the rearview mirror. "Pretty rough over there in Nam?"

The slender officer slowly exhaled. "As opposed to what?"

"Oh . . . I see. Don't want to talk about it? Forget I asked."

"Forgotten."

"Still . . ." the driver couldn't quell his curiosity. "My cousin writes that it's the worst thing he's ever been through. Said he . . ." His words trailed away when he heard deep laughter coming from the strange man in the back seat.

"Your cousin obviously led a sheltered life," said the officer in a flat voice. "I found the Army and Vietnam not a great deal different from what I was used to. But then, from the time I was a kid I've been locked up."

"You have?"

"Gatesville School for Boys when I was twelve. Behind the walls of Folsom Prison at twenty-one. I might have been there forever if my attorney hadn't made a bargain with Uncle Sam."

"Sir?"

"Three years ago I was released from prison and sent straight to Vietnam. I've been there since . . . helicopter pilot. After I got shot down, I was discharged, and here I am, a free man."

All eyes and ears, the young driver swallowed hard and said, "Is there . . . is there anything special I can do for you, sir?"

"Matter of fact, there is. How far out of the way would it be to swing by Hockaday?"

"Hockaday? I'm afraid I don't . . ."

"Hockaday School out on Midway Road."

"No problem. You got a kid sister out there?"

No answer.

It was break at Hockaday, but most of the students remained inside the building, out of the rain. Two little girls did not. Bright yellow rain capes and hoods protecting them, the giggling twelve-year-olds skipped across the water-soaked quadrangle, straight toward the idling olive drab station wagon.

The rain-streaked back window of the automobile slowly rolled down; the wounded officer peered intently at the two young girls. One, the taller of the two, impulsively shoved her rain hood back off her head and shook her long dark hair about, laughing happily. She jumped agilely across a wide mud puddle, sending her rain cape and green wool uniform skirt high. Exposing a slick, tanned left thigh with its black star birthmark. She whirled and dashed rapidly back to the school building.

Gray eyes gleaming, the young warrant officer slowly rolled up the car window and settled back, a hint of a smile lighting his too-thin face. "I'm ready," said Ryker Rawley, calmly. "Let's go to the V.A. hospital."

The first public word of trouble was in *Daily Variety*. Army Archard's column asked, "War clouds over the big teepee on the Texas plains?"

From his Connaught Hotel suite in London, C.C. denied things were less than rosy between him and Caroline. He laughed off reports of bitter arguments behind closed doors at Musicland. "My wife and I have never been happier," stated a confident C.C. McCarty.

But six months after the rainy morning with Donny Wheeler in the *Cielo Vista* barn, Caroline asked C.C. for a divorce.

It was a clear March day. C.C. had just come in off the extended European tour. Shouting eagerly, "Honey, I'm home. Caroline. Caroline," he swiftly mounted the stairs.

She appeared on the landing. C.C. paused to look up at her. Heart hammering in his chest at seeing her again, he smiled and held wide his arms.

"C.C.," she said, not moving, "we . . . I have to talk to you."

When she closed the doors of the library and turned to face him, C.C. felt he couldn't get a breath. "There's no easy way to say this," she began immediately. "C.C., I want a divorce."

Thunderstruck, he stared at her. His hand gripped the mantel of the fireplace and he tried to clear his head. Carefully, as though he were just learning to talk, he chose his words. "Why, sweetheart? What's happened?"

Caroline, head bowed, sighed. "There's someone else." She lifted her eyes to his. "I'm in love with someone else, C.C. I'm sorry."

He swallowed. "In love," he said foolishly. "Who's the lucky guy?"

"Donny."

"Donny?" he repeated, incredulously. "Donny Wheeler? My ranch foreman?"

"Yes. We're in love and we want to get married."

"You're married to me," he said, "you're my wife and I love you."

"Not the way he loves me, C.C."

"How many ways are there to love someone," he asked, "I worship you, I always have."

Caroline shook her golden head, longing to pass on part of her own guilt. "C.C., I know there's been other women. Lots of other women."

He looked pained. "I love you," he repeated, "I never loved any other woman." She gave no reply. "But you never really loved me, did you, darlin'?"

Her eyes filled with tears. "I'm sorry."

For a long moment he was silent. Then: "What about money?"

She frowned. "I don't know what you mean."

His voice flat, he said, "I may have been a big enough fool to let some other man steal my wife, but surely you don't expect me to keep Donny on the payroll."

"No, of course not," she said nervously, "we . . . I . . . thought perhaps you would allow us to keep the ranch and . . ."

He smiled. "That'll solve it all? I give you the ranch and you live happily ever after?"

"Donny's a very good foreman and I . . ."

"Caroline, you have never been without money in your life. Lots of money. You actually think you'll be happy as the wife of a poor ranch hand? *Cielo Vista* has never turned a profit, or didn't you know that?"

"I don't care." She was growing more upset. "I'm in love with Donny and I don't care about money. We'll get along just fine and . . . and . . ." Her voice trailed away, tears splashed down her cheeks.

"Ah, don't cry, baby." C.C. took a step toward her, stopped himself. "You can have the ranch. It's not your fault. None of it's your fault. I was gone too much. You had no life, I know that."

She wiped at her eyes, "I never meant to hurt you, C.C."

"I know you didn't, Caroline." He smiled at her. "I'll be fine, don't worry."

"I . . . I'll have my attorney get in touch with yours." She nervously laced her hands together. "I've packed a few things and I thought if you didn't mind, I'd have Robert drive me out to the ranch."

"Sure," he said, "whatever you want."

She gave him a grateful smile. "Thanks, Chief," she said, backing away, and it hurt him, just as it always had, when she called him by that name. He watched her go, his heart squeezing painfully in his chest.

Morning sunshine played in her long gold-gilt hair. Emerald eyes shone with a teary brightness. Cherry red lips were turned up into a nervous smile. She was, he noted, every bit as "dazzling" as the very first time he had seen her, when she was an angelic-looking eighteen-year-old deb.

* * *

C.C. carefully concealed his heartbreak and remained a good friend to Caroline. And on the day the divorce became final, those around him were relieved to find him in a relaxed, almost carefree frame of mind. The crew was waiting at Musicland when he returned from the final hearing.

When asked how he felt, he flashed them that famous, brilliant smile and said, "As Martin Luther King, Jr., said, 'Free at last, free at last, thank God Almighty I'm free at last.'"

But when the laughter had died and the boys had wandered away and C.C. was at last alone, he slowly lowered his long-limbed body tiredly down into his worn easy chair and violently threw his half-full vodka glass crashing into the cold fireplace.

And when Caroline dealt him the final blow, it was almost more than C.C. could bear. She was awarded custody of Laura Kay. His cherished child was to board at Hockaday during the week and spend her weekends at *Cielo Vista* with Caroline and her new husband.

When Laura Kay heard the news she cried brokenheartedly and clung to her daddy's neck. Feeling as though he were letting down the only person on earth who loved him, C.C. held her and said truthfully, "Sweetheart, it's the only way. You know you can't live with me. I travel all the time and stay in hotels."

"I know, Daddy," she sobbed, "but sometimes I wish you never had to leave me again. I wish you could just stay at Musicland with me."

He hugged her tighter. "Want us to give it all up? Say the word."

She pulled away, blinked back her tears, "Never!"

"That's my girl."

CHAPTER TWENTY-SIX

THE temperature clock in the Sahara Hotel tower read 8:47 P.M. The time disappeared and the temperature was flashed—106 degrees. August in Las Vegas.

A morose man, lids low over bored dark eyes, thick, black hair disheveled, stood unmoving before the two-story glass in Caesar's penthouse suite. In his hand was a tall glass of vodka on the rocks. He wore nothing but a white towel around his hips. It was only thirteen minutes until the dinner show.

The man moved at last, picked up the telephone and said into it, "Send Dr. Feel-Good in here."

In seconds Dr. Stuart Hamilton, now a permanent part of C.C.'s entourage, entered. In his right hand was the ever-present black bag. He smiled at the sullen, near-naked man.

"Give me a couple of dexamyls," ordered C.C., yawning sleepily. "Those Placidyls you gave me at noon have left me drowsy." The young doctor nodded. C.C. placed a flattened palm on his bare belly. "I need a Hycodan too, my stomach's killing me."

Ash Ashford walked into the suite as C.C. was swallowing the pills. He gave Dr. Hamilton a harsh look and said, "Goddamn you, Hamilton, you trying to kill him?"

Dr. Hamilton shrugged. "Just a couple of dexamyls, Ash. No harm."

Ash glared at him. "Get the fuck out of here and take that bag with you." To C.C., "Do you have to be watched twenty-four hours a day? You're due downstairs, it's showtime."

"I know," said C.C., "that's why I needed the dexamyls. I'm sleepy, I don't feel like going on." He shoved long arms into his white dress shirt.

191

Ash snorted. "You take enough downers to knock out an elephant and complain of being sleepy." He lit a cigarette. "C.C., you've got to knock off the pills, it's a sucker's game and . . ."

"You should know all about sucker's games, Ash," C.C. interrupted, "how much you down at the tables?"

Ash colored. "Thirty, forty grand. That's just money, we're talking about your health."

C.C. stepped into his black trousers. "I'm alright. Stop worrying." He picked up his tux jacket and left the suite, still yawning.

Ash remained in the rapidly darkening room. Buddy Hester joined him after escorting C.C. downstairs.

"Ash," Buddy's florid face wore a worried frown, "C.C.'s changing. Sometimes I hardly know him. What's wrong? What's happening to my old pal?"

Ash motioned Buddy to a chair. Ash sighed. "Bud, life can become boring, when, like C.C., you've lived too long in the high-speed world of the rich; private jets, expensive hotels, exotic movie locations, and scores of beautiful women." He looked at Buddy. Buddy, mouth agape, stared at him. Ash smiled, "What I mean, Bud, is that C.C. has had it all since age twenty-one. The new has worn off for him. It happens to superstars."

"What can we do to help?"

Ash said, "That's a hard one. He was bored making movies so I put him back on the road. For a while that did it. Now it's been a couple of years and he's already tired of the tours, tired of Vegas."

"It's more than that, Ash."

Ash sighed. "Yes. He misses Caroline and Laura. What happened? I thought the kid was flying out for tonight's opening."

"She was supposed to, but Caroline changed her mind. Wouldn't let her come." Suddenly he smiled. "God, I'll bet Laura Kay threw a real shit fit."

"Laura, unlock this door," Caroline said heatedly.

"Go away," came the shouted response.

"I mean it, I don't want to have to call Donny in here. Open the door."

Minutes passed. Caroline waited. Finally the door opened a crack and a tall, slender, teary-eyed young girl stood before her. Three days short of her fourteenth birthday and Laura Kay McCarty looked more like her father with each passing year.

"Laura, I know you're disappointed, but . . ."

"It's opening night and you said I could go! He was counting on me."

"There'll be plenty more opening nights. He understands. He's not upset."

"That's what you think, Mother. You never could tell when Daddy was upset about anything."

"Perhaps not," Caroline admitted, "but C.C. told me on the phone that it's just as well you're not going to be there." She added, as an afterthought, "He'll be busy with the backstage opening-night party . . ." she made a slight face, "and all that goes with it."

"If you are referring to women, Mother, I'd like to remind you that if you hadn't left him there would be no other women."

"Don't judge me, Laura, I won't have it. You don't know what you're talking about, and I've never said an unkind thing about your daddy."

"And he's never said anything bad about you either," Laura's chin lifted defiantly.

"No, I'm sure he hasn't," answered Caroline. "C.C. is a kind, dear man." She smiled.

Laura saw a glimmer of hope. She rushed forward, taking her mother by the arms. "Oh, Mother, he is. He truly is. Don't you think you could . . ."

"Laura, I'm married to Donny, and I love him. I'm sorry that I never loved your daddy the way I love Donny. Truly I am."

Laura hung her head. "Me too."

C.C. had became increasingly grave, no longer charmed by life and fame. He missed Caroline. He missed Laura. He missed Musicland. He found little joy in a world without them.

His dependency on uppers, downers, and painkillers steadily grew, altering his personality. Too many downers and friends would find him drowsy and fatigued, sometimes confused and deeply depressed. Other times, when he'd taken too many uppers, he couldn't sleep; he was restless and talkative, easily irritated and hard to get along with.

And then there were the painkillers. His stomach trouble had grown much worse since the divorce and hardly a day passed that he did not need something to ease the burning ache. Demerol and Percodan became his favorites, despite their side effects of dizziness and light-headedness.

Women, who had always pursued him, even when he was married, now threw themselves at him mercilessly. Hurt by Caroline's rejection, C.C., foolishly needing to prove his masculinity, sought solace in their arms. A constant parade of exotic, beautiful women, longing to please him, moved through his life.

He never sought them out; it was the other way round. Shamelessly they stalked him, bribing hotel employees to let them into his suite, calling round the clock, hiding in his dressing room, throwing panties and keys to him on stage.

The dexamyl had worked. C.C. had shaken off his lethargy. He gave an electric opening-night performance. He gave yet another one in his king-sized bed later that night.

Two beautiful dark-haired, dark-eyed women, who looked so much alike he assumed they were sisters, were seated ringside at the dinner show.

Later he watched in interested appreciation, while the two, Jean and June Barlow, sensuously disrobed in his bedroom. Swallowing a couple of orange dexamyls and washing them down with iced vodka, he stood at room's center, nodding his approval.

When both were bare, they laughingly attacked him, jerking at buttons and unzipping his trousers. In seconds he was as naked as they, the glass of vodka still in his hand. Jean stepped into his arms, kissing him and erotically rubbing her breasts and pelvis against his leanly muscled body. Not to be outdone, June Barlow stepped up behind him and pressed her soft, naked curves to his back, wrapping her arms around both him and Jean.

Not wanting to play favorites, C.C., after several long, hot kisses from Jean, turned within the grasping, hugging female arms and began kissing June, his erection already complete. June, bolder than Jean, put her hands between their bodies and stroked him, sighing happily into his mouth. And when at last he lifted his dark head, she said frankly, "I've wanted to suck your cock from the day I first saw you fifteen years ago."

"It's all yours," he grinned, then amended, "yours and Jean's."

Under the mirrored ceiling, he stretched out on his back. While June's warm, wet mouth slid down over his pulsing shaft, Jean, growing increasingly excited, leaned close to his face and murmured, "Do to me what she's doing to you," and before he could answer she nimbly threw one leg over him and was seated astride his shoulders.

Looking straight into his eyes, she slowly raised herself to a kneeling position a few inches from his face. And threw back her head and sighed with ecstasy when his hands clasped her bare buttocks and he guided her wet, dripping cunt to his dexamyl-dry mouth.

Soon the women changed places in their share-and-share-alike quest for pleasure. Later C.C. screwed June, who lay upon her back, while Jean, kneeling beside him, kissed him hungrily, then fed him her big, hard-nippled breasts.

It was Jean's turn to be screwed. She rode astride him while the equally big-breasted June teased at his lips with her rocklike nipples, brushing her soft breasts back and forth until he reached out and grabbed one and sucked as much as he could into his mouth.

Pushed by the pills, he was an insatiable lover and the girls had the time of their life. When finally tiring, they were dressing to go, C.C.—eyes too bright, heart beating too fast—was still after June. From behind her, he was trying to push his swollen member up into her while she was trying to lower her rumpled black dress.

He won.

Wadding the half-on, half-off dress in her hands, she moved her high-heeled feet apart and leaned forward, winking at Jean. C.C. pumped into her with the vigor of a young boy with his first piece and Jean, watching them, became so excited, she dropped down into a chair, ripped off her underpants and began stroking herself.

June climaxed deeply and alerted Jean that C.C. had not yet come. Jean rushed forth to take June's place with such agility, C.C. hardly knew he had changed partners.

As the sun was rising he kissed them both good-bye. "May I say the beautiful Barlow sisters have given me a most pleasurable night."

Jean and June looked at each other and giggled. June spoke, "Chief, honey, we're not sisters. I'm Jean's Mama. She's sixteen and I'm thirty-three. Everybody thinks we're sisters."

"God in Heaven," said C.C., suddenly feeling nauseated. "My daughter's sixteen. Laura's sixteen," he said, closing the door behind the giggling mother-daughter pair. He headed straight for the vodka bottle. Naked, he sat and drank, alone in the bedroom.

When he could no longer remember June and Jean Barlow, or any of the hundreds of other pretty faces that had passed through his life, he rose and wobbled tiredly to the bed.

There was only one face he saw when he closed his tired, blood-shot eyes. An angelically beautiful face with large emerald eyes and cherry red lips and gold-gilt hair.

The dazzling Caroline.

C.C., smiling foolishly, fell into a deep sleep.

Laura was almost as unhappy as her daddy. She desperately missed him and their happy times at Musicland. And to make her life even more miserable, her dearest friend, Missy Graham, had transferred from Hockaday to the co-ed Greenhill.

"I'm tired of nothing but girls," Missy had confided, "I want to be where the boys are!"

Laura begged her mother to allow her to transfer with Missy. Caroline refused, reminding her daughter that she would be the third-generation Mansfield to graduate from Hockaday. There was tradition to uphold.

"But I'm not a Mansfield," lamented Laura, "I'm a McCarty."

It had done no good. She remained at Hockaday while Missy left her behind and was soon going out on dates with handsome young Greenhill boys and regaling Laura with tales of parties and fun and kissing.

On weekends Laura was chauffeured to *Cielo Vista* where she was further shut off from friends her own age. There was no one she wanted to bring to *Cielo Vista* but Missy, and Missy had too much going on in town.

On rare occasions, C.C. flew into Dallas to spend a few days at Musicland and these times were golden for Laura. She was allowed to stay with him at the mansion and C.C., longing to make up for all the time he was away, spoiled her, catering to her every whim. Laura was, Caroline complained, always harder to live with once C.C. had been in town.

C.C. was harder to live with, as well. He loved his child. Leaving her behind seemed never to grow any easier and for days after a reunion at Musicland, he was more depressed than ever, snapping at old friends, complaining over little things, restless and unhappy.

The pill popping continued. The vodka consumption increased. The steady stream of women never subsided.

Those closest to him worried. Ash, ever sensitive to his client's suffering, saw C.C. grasp his stomach one afternoon, his dark eyes dim with pain.

"C.C., I wish you'd let me call in a specialist. That stomach is giving you a fit, isn't it?"

The intense pain passed, C.C. grinned and made light of it. "Girls, guitars, and gastritis. They're all part of the music business."

A few nights later, after Ash had flown back to New Orleans, C.C.'s road manager, Guy Stearns, came into the dressing room and found the star not dressed. It was only minutes before he was to step on stage.

"Chief, better shake a leg," he said.

"I'm sick," said C.C. "I can't go on."

Guy Stearns walked to the door and called for Dr. Hamilton. The doctor quietly entered with his bag.

He took out a hypodermic needle. "Here's a little something that will make you feel better, Chief," he said.

C.C. looked up at him. "It's Doctor Dope."

Hamilton, ignoring his sarcasm, raised the needle to C.C.'s right arm. "This will do the trick."

"That's right," said C.C., "shoot old Slick up and send him in."

Buddy, standing outside, overheard. He bounded in just as Doctor Hamilton discarded the used hypodermic. "What the hell you giving him?" Buddy said, chin pugnaciously jutting forward.

"Not a thing, Bud," answered a smiling Guy Stearns. "That's just his pillhead paranoia talking. Get him dressed, will you, we've got a show to do."

Buddy Hester saw his best friend rapidly deteriorating before his watchful eyes and there was nothing he could do to stop it. C.C., always lean, was now skinny. His cheekbones became more prominent. So did his hipbones. There was a sadness in his dark eyes that never quite left and the brilliant, winning smile was less in evidence.

More and more with the passing of the years, C.C. had become a prisoner of his fans. He sadly told Buddy that he had bought a Circle suite in the Cowboys' new Irving Stadium, but that he would never be able to see a game. He had a fleet of vintage cars and couldn't even go out for a drive. He had played Vegas dozens of times and had never held a hand of blackjack or tossed the dice.

He longed, he said gloomily, to lie on the banks of Turtle Creek when the azaleas were in bloom and listen to the Sunday afternoon concerts. He wanted to go to the Texas State Fair and ride the roller coaster and win a teddy bear and eat cotton candy. He'd like to attend one of those teas or recitals at his daughter's fancy school.

"Willie and Wayland invited me to their Fourth of July picnic last summer in Austin," C.C. said. "God, I'd have given anything to have been there. Do you realize, Bud, that I can't even walk outside except within the walls of Musicland? Jesus, how can a man live like this?"

"I don't know," said Buddy truthfully. "I just don't know." And thought to himself, If C.C.'s not happy, what chance do the rest of us have?

For hours—sometimes days—at a time, C.C.'s speech was slurred, his breathing was labored, and his restlessness was so severe, he paced like a caged animal. In the grip of too many ingested Quaaludes shoved at him by the helpful Doctor Hamilton. Both Ash and Buddy would run the doctor off, but it did little good. C.C. demanded him there with his never-ending supply of pills.

The Chief was in bad shape.

*   *   *

"The Chief is in bad shape," announced Benny Hamilton to the red-haired woman seated in a dimly lit cocktail bar just off the Las Vegas Strip.

She smiled. "How bad?"

"The poor bastard is really hooked, Valentina. He can't go on anymore without a handful of dexamyls to wake him up. Then he can't go to sleep without large doses of Valium."

"What about women?"

"Jesus Christ, when he can't sleep he's at it till dawn. Nights when I can't sleep, I sneak into his bathroom and watch. It's the damndest thing you've ever seen." He knew she loved this part of their conversations. She never tired of hearing all about The Chief's busy love life.

Her breathing speeded. She picked up her Tanqueray and tonic and drank greedily. "Tell me about it, Ben. What do they do?"

And Ben would give Valentina a blow-by-blow of the bedroom action while she squirmed and perspired and licked her lips.

"Is there any way you could sneak me up there so I could watch too?"

"Not a chance. I have to wait until Buddy drifts off myself. He'd beat the living shit out of me."

"Damn," Valentina whined. "I would so like to see it."

"Hell, admit it. You'd like to climb in the sack with him."

The very thought so excited her she felt light-headed. But she said, "Don't be silly," and shook her head distastefully. "How long will it be before the pills and booze and broads so take their toll he can no longer perform?"

Ben Hamilton tossed down his drink. "The days are surely numbered."

CHAPTER TWENTY-SEVEN

TEXAS, our Texas, all hail the Lone Star State . . ." Laura strummed her guitar and sang the words of the state song. She stood before the full-length mirror in her *Cielo Vista* bedroom in a pair of tight jeans, a navy western-cut shirt, a red kerchief at her throat, and hand-tooled cowboy boots. "Texas, our Texas, so glorious, so great . . ."

A knock on the door interrupted. Laura frowned. "Yes?"

Caroline stuck her head into her daughter's room. She smiled at the tall, coltish girl with masses of rich, ebony hair. "You sound like him, honey."

Laura grinned. "Do I, Mother? Really?"

Caroline nodded. She came inside. "Laura, I've two things to tell you. Bad news, good news. Which would you like to hear first?" She sat down on her daughter's bed.

"Get the bad over with."

"Alright. Donny feels it's a mistake for you to sing at the Weatherford rodeo next month and he . . ."

Laura's black eyes flashed with anger. "But mother, I've been looking forward to it. It would be my first real appearance outside school programs. I've practiced this song for weeks and I . . ."

"I'm sorry, but Donny feels, and so does your daddy, that you'd be too unprotected out in the middle of the arena. We've talked it over with your bodyguards; they agree."

Laura crumpled to the floor in a disappointed heap. "Damn! Damn! Damn!" she shrieked loudly.

"I know you're disappointed, but—"

"Disappointed? I'm heartbroken! I'll tell you one thing, just as soon as

199

I'm of age, I'm going to be a singer, whether you or Donny or Daddy or my damned bodyguards like it or not. Ooooh!" She folded her arms atop the guitar and buried her face.

Caroline, smiling, said, "Ready for the good news?" A slight shrugging of slender shoulders was all the response she got. "How would you like to live with Daddy for a year?"

Early September in New York.

Crisp, clear days. Cool, sweet nights. Perfect for sleeping. But C.C. never slept nights. He slept days, fitfully.

He was dozing in his Hotel Pierre suite when Caroline called from Texas shortly after four in the afternoon. Buddy Hester knew C.C. would take her call. He opened the door and crept into the darkened bedroom.

"C.C.," he said gently, "Caroline's on the phone."

C.C.'s dark arm shot out, he grabbed up the receiver and cradled it between his face and bare shoulder. "Caroline?"

"How are you, C.C.?"

"Great, hon," was his immediate answer, although he was physically and mentally exhausted, his weight far below the normal one hundred eighty, his stomach afire. "How ya'll doing. Laura okay?"

"We're fine." Caroline paused. "C.C., how would you like Laura to live with you for a year?"

C.C. sat straight up in bed. "You mean it? Jesus, you mean it, Caroline?"

Tinkling laughter came from the other end. "Yes, I do. Donny and I . . ."

"Daddy, daddy," Laura had jerked the receiver from her mother's hand. "Isn't it wonderful? I can be with you for a whole year!"

"Darlin'," said C.C., "it sure is. When will I see you? You want to fly up here and . . ."

"No, I can't, Daddy. Here's the deal. Mother and Donny are going down to Argentina to spend a whole year. Donny's in on a Texas A & M project to study breeding exotic horses. They leave on the twentieth of this month; I go to Musicland and wait for you there. Your tour ends the night of the twentieth at Red Rocks in Denver, doesn't it?"

"That's right, baby."

"Yippee. Fly on home after the show. I'll wait up and we'll have a real Texas blow-out at Musicland!"

"You got it, sweetheart," C.C. gladly agreed. "Mark your calender. September 21, 1975 is going to be one great day."

When he hung up the phone, C.C. McCarty threw back his head and laughed out loud. Buddy laughed with him. Dr. Hamilton knocked and swiftly entered. Buddy Hester blocked his path.

"He don't need you today, Hamilton."

"He's right, doc, I gotta get in shape. I'm getting my kid back. Bud, call room service. I'd like a big plate of bacon and eggs."

Buddy warned, "Bad for your stomach, C.C."

C.C. grinned at him. "Make it cereal and fruit and whole wheat toast," said C.C., nodding. "I'm getting my kid back."

He had gained back eight pounds. His blood count was better. His memory had improved. KHOW Radio's Hal and Charlie said on their morning show that The Chief never sounded better.

Those closest to him marveled at the miraculous turnaround.

Happy, relaxed, looking forward to the next day's reunion at Musicland, C.C., having a haircut and manicure in his Denver Brown Palace hotel room, nodded yes when one of the crew told him Ash was on the phone from L.A.

More good news.

After weeks of hard negotiation, Ash had just signed a contract with Columbia pictures for C.C. to star in the remake of *The Jolson Story* for two million and a percentage of the profits.

"None of that travelog silly fluff, C.C.," said Ash, "a real honest-to-God part with a chance to do some acting."

"Ash, you don't know how much this means to me. Wait til I tell Laura. Hey, why don't you meet me at Musicland later tonight? Call your wife, have her fly in from New Orleans. We'll all . . ."

Laughter from the other end. "C.C., you know me. I'm going to celebrate in Vegas. I'll be in Dallas in a couple of days."

"Win a bundle."

"That's in the script." And he hung up.

Overjoyed, C.C. shared his good news with the crew, laughing at Ash's plans to hop over to Vegas. To celebrate, they ordered up chilled champagne, but "good boy" C.C. didn't partake. He was, he told them happily, concerned with his health. Amidst the gaiety and laughter and congratulations, nobody noticed Benny Hamilton slip away to his own room.

There he quickly called Valentina Trent at her Dallas office. He told her of C.C.'s good fortune. And he told her that one Ash Ashford was on his way to Vegas.

"You sending someone out to watch Ash like always?"

"No," said Valentina, "I've got a hunch. I'll fly out myself."

* * *

If the giant DFW airport had not been completed in 1974, it might have made all the difference. Or if C.C. McCarty, in a good mood, hadn't decided at the last minute that he wanted to land at the far-out airport instead of Love Field, explaining boyishly, "I've never been to DFW; let's set it down there," he might have made it.

But the vast, safest-in-the-world airport had been built. And C.C. McCarty did instruct his pilots to land there. Inside the terminal, he bought stuffed animals and candy and souvenirs, just like any other traveler, having a good time, happily signing autographs for the few startled late-night passengers in the gift shop.

Arms full of foolish presents for Laura, he and Buddy boarded the waiting limo into Dallas. It was shortly after two o'clock.

"I expect she'll still be up, don't you, Bud?"

"Shitfire, C.C., nobody could make Laura go to bed with you coming in."

"No. She's as excited as I am." He absently stroked the star birthmark on his cheek, reached out and grabbed up a soft stuffed puppy. "I'm one happy man and . . . and . . ." He stopped speaking.

Buddy's eyes were on his face. Blood bubbled from C.C.'s slightly parted lips. The stuffed toy slipped from his fingers. He clutched his stomach and moaned.

"Jesus God!" said Buddy. Then: "Get us to Parkland immediately," he shouted to the driver. "C.C., hang on . . . hang on, old pal. You'll be okay. We'll get you there."

C.C. tried to speak, couldn't. There was fear and pain in his eyes. Blood continued to bubble from his lips.

"Goddammit, hurry!" screamed Buddy and wrapped massive arms around his friend.

C.C. didn't make it to the hospital. It was too far. The ulcer that had never healed, perforated. He hemorrhaged. His stomach burst. He died on the way to Parkland in Buddy Hester's arms.

In Vegas, Ash Ashford stood at a dice table in the penthouse casino where only the highest rollers play. After one early flurry that caused him to think this was surely his night, Ash had lost consistently. A man possessed, he had doubled-up-to-catch-up all evening, signing markers, and betting astronomical sums of money.

And losing.

Valentina Trent was in her suite below the penthouse casino, watching television, sipping her gin and tonic and boredly zapping the channels, when the bulletin came.

"We interrupt our regular programming," said a KLAS-TV newsman. "This just in from Dallas, Texas. The Chief has passed away. Details are sketchy, but sources say the world-famous entertainer—C.C. McCarty— was dead on arrival at Parkland's emergency ward. First indications are that the Chief hemorrhaged. No other information was available at . . ."

Valentina stared at the tube. The remote control dropped from her hand to the carpet. She downed the last of her gin. Shaking uncontrollably, she murmured, "No . . . no . . . you weren't supposed to die. I never meant you to die. I loved you, you were the only man I ever loved. It could have been so different. It could have been . . ." Her eyes filled with tears. "Damn you, damn you, C.C. I told you you'd pay. Damn you to hell." She rose and drew a long, slow breath. Then she grabbed up her evening bag. Feeling at once deeply grieved and gloriously elated, she left the suite, hurrying to the cashier's cage.

Ten minutes later, in the penthouse casino, she sidled close to the crap table where Ash Ashford, broke, desperate, was frantically begging the tight-lipped pit boss for more credit. He was turned down.

Red-faced, wild-eyed, Ash banged a fist on the table's chip rim, pleading for only a few more thousand. Ten. Twenty. That's all.

Valentina tapped Ash on the shoulder. "Running a little short, Ash?"

"Leave me alone," he snapped, and again asked for more credit.

"Ash," she continued, undaunted, "how would you like to have five hundred thousand spot cash?" That got his attention. "I've got it right here. Five hundred thousand dollars." His eyes went to the large black handbag. "You put up your forty percent of Big Chief Corporation for collateral and you've got the money. Right here. Right now."

Ash raked fingers through his disheveled silver hair. "Big Chief is worth millions." His eyes flicked to the table. Some lucky roller had just shot another eleven. "How soon do I have to repay the loan?"

She smiled, catlike. "Twenty-four hours."

"Make it forty-eight. I'll have no problem getting the money at Republic Bank on Monday."

"You got it, Mr. A."

The deal was done.

Valentina got a signed note stating forty percent of Big Chief belonged to her if the loan was unpaid in forty-eight hours. Ash got five hundred thousand cash. Certain his luck had changed, he bet the limit on the line. The shooter got six for a point. Ash backed up his pass line bet and covered all the back numbers—ten thousand each. The shooter sevened out. Ash had lost eighty thousand dollars on one roll of the dice.

He jerked his necktie loose and unbuttoned his shirt collar. He kept playing. He kept losing.

He had only ten thousand left. He put it all on the pass line. The shooter rolled an eleven. Ash let the twenty thousand ride. And just as the shooter reached for the dice, the house lights dimmed. The stickman swiftly scooped up the dice and brought them back to the center of the table. A voice over the loudspeaker said, "Ladies and gentlemen, we've just received word that the Chief has died in Dallas, Texas. Let's have a moment of silence in his memory."

Stunned, disbelieving, Ash stared at the square red dice on the green felt table. The minute of silence passed and still he stood, silent, shocked, heartsick.

The shooter tossed the dice. "Seven out," shouted the stickman, "line away."

And in the skies over Vegas, an American Airlines pilot, descending to land, radioed the tower. "Hey, the Strip's gone dark. We got a power black-out down there?"

"Worse than that," came a flat controller's voice from McCarren Control. "The Chief is dead."

CHAPTER TWENTY-EIGHT

ROLLING *Stone* was bordered in black.

The governor of Texas declared a day of mourning and ordered flags at all state buildings flown at half-mast.

From all over the world, Laura received thousands of cards and letters of sympathy.

From Wichita Falls to Laredo, from El Paso to Texarkana, Texas was sold out of red roses.

A shocked nation wept for its fallen idol. Heartbroken fans gathered at the Music Gates, bewildered, lost, murmuring, "What are we going to do? How are we going to live? We'll be lost, so lost without him."

The funeral was to be held in Highland Park Presbyterian, but swarms of saddened fans descended on Dallas and the pastor and the family decided to move it to Moody Coliseum.

The services were scheduled for 3:00 P.M. on Thursday, September 26. Trucks arrived carrying flowers—thousands of red roses and huge arrangements, some in the shape of guitars with the word "Chief" spelled out in glittering gold. Throngs lined the streets for miles and mourners—over one hundred thousand crying people—stood in the scorching September sun to watch the long black Mercedes hearse bearing the body of The Chief.

When the doors were closed to the coliseum, ten thousand people were inside. At the very front, below the stage, Laura, eyes red-rimmed, face pale with grief, sat between her mother and stepfather. Ash Ashford and his wife Charmaine sat just behind them. And all of the Chief's crew, musicians, drivers, house servants—his close friends.

The heavy bronze casket, covered with a blanket of red roses, was now closed. It had been open since ten o'clock and in that time thousands of weeping fans had filed by for one last look at their beloved Chief. Women fainted and some had fallen onto the casket, to be pulled away by security guards.

Elvis and Linda Ronstadt sang the haunting hymn, "Amazing Grace."

The pastor wisely made the service brief, concluding with the comforting statement, directed to the family, "Legends live forever."

Then Buddy Hester rose and solemnly recited the only poem he had ever learned:

> *Smart lad, to slip betimes away*
> *From fields where glory does not stay*
> *And clearly though the laurel grows . . .*

Buddy's voice broke, but he continued,

> *It withers quicker than the rose.*

At graveside, Laura was handed a lone red rose from atop the bronze coffin. She lifted it to her breast and silently repeated, "It withers quicker than the rose."

"Good-bye, Daddy."

CHAPTER TWENTY-NINE

O N SUNDAY morning, September 21, C.C. had died.
On Monday morning, September 22, Ash Ashford had hurried into
Republic National Bank. He had less than twelve hours to come up
with the money to pay back Valentina Trent. Or lose his forty percent
of Big Chief.

Perspiring, hands trembling, Ash was ushered into the plush offices of
the senior vice president, Will Abernathy. Abernathy shook Ash's hand,
offered condolences on the Chief's untimely death, and indicated a chair.

Ash came right to the point. He had to have five hundred thousand
dollars immediately. He couldn't believe his ears when Abernathy, shaking
his balding head, said, "Sorry, Ash. Everything's changed now, what with
the . . ."

"My God, Will, what are you saying? Big Chief is worth millions and all
I want is five hundred thousand dollars."

Abernathy, unmoved, explained that the bank couldn't loan that kind of
cash until the late singer's estate was settled. The board would need to know
who was to be in charge of his holdings, who would be running Big Chief,
how much C.C.'s death would effect the profitability of the corporation.
"C.C. *was* Big Chief Corporation. With him gone, everything is on
hold."

Ash Ashford remained in Abernathy's office for more than an hour.
Other bank officers were called in. All agreed with Abernathy. They
couldn't give Ash the money, at least not now. Perhaps after the funeral,
when the will had been read and . . .

Ash walked wearily out of the bank, got into the elevator, and rode
straight up to the offices of Bluebonnet Records. Valentina was behind

her desk. She smiled when he entered and offered him a drink. Ash declined.

"You know why I'm here, Valentina," Ash dropped down into a chair opposite her.

"I've a good idea," she admitted. "Sorry to hear about the Chief." She shook her auburn head and clicked her tongue. "I suppose when you live like that wild Comanche, you can't expect to reach old age."

Ash wanted to hit her. He said, "Valentina, I've come to ask for an extension on my . . ." She started laughing. Desperate, he pressed on. "When I borrowed the money I never dreamed that . . . I could never have guessed that . . . that . . ." His words trailed away. Suddenly it dawned on him. "My God. He was dead when you made me the loan. And you knew." His eyes narrowed with hate.

"Of course, you fool." She leaned forward, still smiling. "But would it have made that much difference, if you had known he was dead? You're a sick, degenerate gambler, Ash. You'd toss your own daughter on the table for one more roll of the dice."

"You bitch, you purposely—"

"Bitch?" She laughed happily. "Perhaps, but a smart bitch, you'll give me that. I don't allow my weaknesses to destroy me the way you and that West Dallas singer always have."

Angry, reckless, he said, "Don't you? Lady, everybody in the business knows you keep young studs between your legs by dangling contracts before their starstruck faces."

In calm control, she responded. "Ah, that's true, Ash, and some mighty good lays I've had, I assure you. I like my fucking, same as the next person, and I'm good at it. But I'm also good at business. I keep brilliant executives with my company and pay them well for their services and their loyalty. I have the best talent scouts in the country on my payroll and they bring money-making artists into Bluebonnet. I'm far too smart to allow my company to suffer from my peccadillos." She leaned back in her chair, pleased with herself. "I'm always in control, Ash. C.C. was not and he's dead. You are not and you've lost Big Chief." Again she laughed.

It was true, and it made him hate her all the more. Swallowing his pride, he agreed. "It's true, Valentina. Everything you've said is true. I was a fool and I'll admit it. I'm asking you to give me a little time . . . a week or . . ."

"Ashford, you have until exactly 2:00 A.M. tomorrow to deliver to me five hundred thousand in cash or lose your company."

"I could give you several thousand now and—"

"Five hundred thousand."

He was sweating. "I can't raise that kind of money until . . ."

"That's your problem, Ashford. You're dismissed. Don't come back until you bring the money. All of the money."

Ash, desperate, did something he hated himself for. He begged. "Please, Valentina. Please give me some time. You're leaving me with nothing. Nothing."

Valentina nodded happily. "You've crapped out. Now get out."

The funeral was over.

Friends, paying their respects, milled about in the antique-filled rooms of Musicland. A buffet was laid out on the English pedestal table in the dining room. White-gloved waiters circulated carrying trays of hot hors d'oeuvres.

At the back of the house, behind the closed library door, Laura and Caroline sat holding hands as C.C.'s will was read. Everything he owned was left to his daughter, to be held in trust for her by Republic National Bank until she reached her twenty-fifth birthday. Caroline was to be consulted by the trust officers on any transaction concerning the vast estate. For her trouble, she would be given a small percentage of the proceeds derived from such ventures.

The reading was over in a matter of minutes and when Caroline and Laura stepped out of the library, a grave-faced Ash Ashford was waiting.

Clearing his throat needlessly, he said, "Laura, honey, could I have a word with you in private?"

"Of course you can, Uncle Ash," She hugged him and Ash felt like the world's biggest heel.

Never in his life had he done anything as hard as telling her that, because of his personal weakness, her father's company was now controlled by Valentina Trent.

They stood in the backyard under a tall oak tree. The sun was setting in the west. The hot September air had begun to cool.

She said, "I can't believe he's gone, Uncle Ash."

"Sweetheart," he said, "your daddy went down at his absolute peak. Not many men can be that lucky."

She tried to smile at him through her tears.

Ash looked at the tall, black-eyed, beautiful young girl and felt his heart kick against his ribs. She looked so much like her daddy. Like the innocent young C.C. McCarty he had signed up one rainy night in Shreveport, Louisiana.

"Laura, I've done a terrible thing."

He explained exactly how and what had happened, speaking slowly, precisely, making no excuses for his actions. She stared fixedly at him from eyes that had cried too much in the days just past. Finally she spoke.

"You allowed my daddy's company to fall under control of the horrible woman he hated?"

"Yes, Laura, I did." He inhaled. "I don't suppose you'll ever want to see me again." He waited.

Her lips trembled. Her slim hands balled into fists at her sides. "No," she said, "I don't believe I do."

Ash nodded understandingly, pivoted, and walked back to the house.

That night at his apartment behind the Pink Wall, he watched his wife packing to leave for New Orleans. On Monday morning, as soon as she had arrived in Dallas, he'd told Charmaine about the gambling and Valentina and losing Big Chief. She'd said little at the time; only that they would talk about it after the funeral.

Now as she meticulously folded silky underwear and placed it in her open bags, she told him what he had been dreading he'd hear all along.

"I'm leaving you, Ash. I should have left long ago, but . . . you see I love you very much."

Ash came to her. "Then don't do it, Charmaine. I need you, I love you."

She shook her head. "You're sick, Ash. You need help. I can't help you."

"Honey, just give me one more chance and I promise I'll . . ."

Sadly, she smiled. "You've promised for years. No more, Ash. No more, I'm divorcing you."

Dallas Times *Herald*   September 27, 1975
                 THE CHIEF IS BURIED
The death of America's best loved rock and roll star stunned and saddened millions of devoted fans. Tens of thousands of those fans were in Dallas yesterday to say good-bye to their chief. C.C. McCarty was a handsome, talented . . .

Valentina handed the newspaper back to Neil Allen. He carefully folded it and placed it atop his desk. He said, "It's finally over, Valentina. You can hurt him no more. C.C.'s dead."

Valentina smiled. And said to her vice president, "Ah, but there's still C.C.'s daughter."

Ryker Rawley sat drinking beer in the Kentucky Bar in Juarez, Mexico, with his old Vietnam buddy, Billy Bledsoe. Bledsoe, owner of a small commuter plane service across the border in El Paso, had offered Ryker a job. Ryker was considering it.

The two veterans knew all there was to know about each other. There were no secrets between them. Bledsoe said idly, "Well, looks like the booze and broads got to McCarty before you. You can't get him now, the bastard's dead."

Ryker took a long pull from his icy *cerveza*. "But there's still C.C.'s daughter."

PART TWO

★

PART TWO

CHAPTER THIRTY

THE gleaming private jet began its gradual descent. At twenty thousand feet its nose punched through the thick blanket of clouds and bright, pervading sunshine filled the cabin for the first time since leaving Dallas. Laura smiled and lifted her head from the high-backed ivory leather seat. Leaning toward the window, she looked down and her smile widened.

The plane was crossing the rimrock of the Guadalupe Mountains. She was less than eighty miles from the vast *Roja Rosa* ranch and Missy. Less than an hour away from two glorious weeks of freedom. She still couldn't believe that her mother had at last allowed her to come alone to El Paso.

Smiling, she felt a sense of well-being wrap itself around her as she neared the west Texas desert town of perennial sunshine and heat and Mexicans and dramatic mountain scenery. And freedom.

Laura glanced at the slim gold Omega, her high school graduation present. Ahead of schedule. An hour early. Good! She'd take a taxi to the Graham ranch and surprise Missy. Never in her life had she ridden in a taxi, Laura absently mused. It sounded like great fun.

When the jet touched down at El Paso International and rolled to a stop on the baked tarmac, Laura cast off her seatbelt, ran forward to the cockpit, and told her two pilots a little white lie.

"The Graham limo will be waiting for me."

The pewter-haired pilot didn't look up from his clipboard. The co-pilot looked at his wristwatch. "Honey, you just relax a minute. I'll take you inside. You can't go running about an airport without—"

"Damn you, Gregory," Laura exerted her independence. "I'll be eighteen years old in three weeks! I'm tired of being treated like an infant. I am

215

getting off this plane alone, walking into the terminal and out again, straight into the Graham limo."

The pilot's eyes widened in surprise. "Laura, you'll have to wait for your luggage so—"

"Send it to the ranch. I'm leaving. Open the door."

Reluctantly the shirtsleeved co-pilot twisted and crawled out of his seat. In moments he stood at the open jet door, hands on slim hips, watching the beautiful young woman rush across the heated cement to the terminal, her thick, raven hair gleaming in the hot sunlight. Unease filling his broad chest, Nick Gregory returned to the cockpit. Sinking back down into the right-hand seat, he said skeptically, "You sure he's not in El Paso?"

"Relax, Nick. Buddy says he's in Mexico, and believe me, Buddy keeps close tabs on him."

"The guy's a pilot, Bert, and as slippery as an eel. He might . . ."

"She'll be safely back in Dallas before he returns. He'll never know she was here."

"I suppose, but I don't like it. If anything should happen to her . . ."

"Nothing's going to happen. Bennett Graham will keep an eye on her."

Speeding along Interstate 10 in the hot backseat of a rattling border taxi, Laura felt like a true free spirit. The driver, a smiling, happy Mexican, spoke accented English. His dark eyes kept lifting to the rearview mirror and Laura realized he was flirting with her. And not because she was C.C. McCarty's daughter. But simply because he found her attractive. Smiling at him, Laura briefly considered moving to Mexico.

Laura took a long, deep breath of the dry, clean air when the aging taxi drove through the towering white archway entrance of *Rojo Rosa*. From the Texas sabal palms lining the road, to the huge white brick ranch house at its end, to the irrigated gardens and whitewashed stables beyond, *Roja Rosa* rose like an oasis in the desert, shining and magnificent in the broiling west Texas sunshine.

Laura was calling Missy's name by the time the taxi rolled to a stop before the sprawling ranch house. She paid her cab fare, tipping generously, and waved good-bye to the driver. Then she dashed across the flagstone patio to the house. "Missy, Missy, I'm here."

A Mexican maid told her that Senorita Missy had not expected her to arrive so early. The senorita was at the payshack at the back edge of the stables. "You wait here and drink iced tea, *si?*"

"No, I'll go find her," said Laura and left the servant looking after her as she hurried down the wide, sunny corridor, the heels of her white summer sandals clicking on the brick floors. Impulsively, Laura kicked off the shoes. Barefooted and laughing, she went through the back door, once again stepping out into the scorching sunshine.

Laura crossed the terraced yard and headed determinedly toward the distant cluster of whitewashed outbuildings and stables. In seconds her top lip was beaded with moisture and her long, thick hair clung hotly to her neck. She could feel her lacy slip sticking to her thighs and perspiration wetting the back of her knees. A fierce sun directly overhead beat down atop her head and caused her to squint in the harsh, punishing glare.

On the far side of a huge, hay-filled barn, a lone man lounged lazily in the hot, noonday sun. A tall, hard man. Strong and lean. Black hair, light skin. Hooded gray eyes that held the look of a man who had seen almost everything there was to see. And disliked much of it.

The droopy lids of those cynical eyes rarely lifted to look at anything. Habitually sleepy-eyed, his expression was one of disinterest, bordering on boredom. His mouth, full and wide, was the only soft feature in a hard-planed, hawkish face. Taut, fair skin seemed to be stretched too tightly over high prominent cheekbones, making his face appear to be chiseled from cold ivory marble. The high, intelligent forehead was largely obscured with a shock of wiry, black hair falling rebelliously to permanently arched, thick brows. A smattering of silver flecked the black at his temples.

A rangy body matched the immobile face. Hard and angular, not an ounce of extra flesh. He leaned against the corral, one foot crossed over the other. Faded Levi's molded tightly over sinewy thighs and across hipbones and down long legs. Long arms, crossed over his chest, were exposed by the rolled-up sleeves of his dark shirt. The shirt fit snugly across a hard chest and a thatch of crisp black hair curled from the throat of his open collar.

Laura rounded the barn. Abruptly she halted, although why she felt compelled to stop was a mystery. She stood very still and stared while the man remained unaware of her presence. Immobilized, she couldn't take her eyes from the silent, unmoving man who stood, bareheaded under the hot sun and looked to be as cool as if he were in an air-conditioned room. No circles of sweat stained the fitted black shirt, no moisture gleamed on the pale face. Not even above the heavy, sensual lips.

All at once Laura realized the perspiration above her own lip had dried and there was a strange coldness in the pit of her stomach. Confused by her reaction to the stranger, she idly wished for the familiar presence of her faithful bodyguard, Buddy. At the same time, she was glad no one was with her. She was uneasy, yet excited. This lazily lounging man both frightened and fascinated her.

She wanted very much to attract his attention. She wished his harshly carved face would turn her way. That those nearly closed eyes would see her and widen. Unconsciously smoothing at her white skirt with nervous, clammy hands, Laura started toward him.

Any second he would look up and she would ask—though she already knew—where the ranch payshack was located. She drew closer to him. His head didn't raise, eyes didn't lift.

Maybe he still had not seen her. She was barefooted, she made no noise on the sandy soil. Laura raised her hand to her mouth and purposely coughed. Still he did not look up. Never moved. Now she was determined. She was directly even with him. She slowed and glanced directly at him. Nothing.

She rushed on, her heart pounding against her ribs. Was he looking at her now that she'd passed? She could almost feel the cold eyes on her back. Abruptly she whirled around, intent on catching him staring. His head was tilted at the exact same angle it had been from the first minute she saw him. He'd not moved. Still stood with one foot crossed over the other, arms folded over his chest. Looking bored and distant. And scary.

Missy Graham never failed to shock the sheltered Laura, and Missy delighted in it. Less than an hour after Laura's arrival, Missy lighted a Pall Mall cigarette, flopped down on a deep brown leather sofa in the cedar-beamed, Spanish-decorated den, and said nonchalantly, "I've decided to screw only policemen this summer."

Laura shook her dark head incredulously. "What about the *vaqueros?*"

"That was last year," Missy waved her cigarette dismissively.

Missy Graham had eagerly parted with her virginity in her sixteenth summer. Swimming alone in a stock pond at the back edge of *Roja Rosa* on a hot June afternoon, she had seen a rider approaching and smiled when she recognized handsome Juan Guitierrez, *Roja Rosa's* newly hired horse trainer. The nineteen-year-old cowboy dismounted, smiled, and coolly undressed right down to his brown skin.

"Not bad," said the adventuresome Missy and smiling calmly, rose from the water and peeled off her swimsuit. Eyes pointedly fixed on his groin, she challenged, "You intend to do something with that thing or don't you know how?"

She quickly found out that Juan knew exactly what to do with it. She called Laura that night and told her all about it. And by the next time she saw Laura, there had been two others.

"I like Latins best," she had said casually. "They get it up and keep it up for hours."

"Missy Graham!"

"It's true. Dance close with a Mexican early in the evening; he'll get a hard-on and keep it way past midnight."

"Stop it," Laura had shaken her dark head and pressed her hands over her ears. "I don't believe one word you're saying. You just like to shock me."

"I've switched to cops this summer," Missy continued, enjoying, as she always did, the look of disbelief in her virginal friend's dark eyes.

"Any particular reason?" Laura skeptically wondered if half of what Missy told her actually happened.

Missy snuffed out her Pall Mall. "The first week I was at the ranch I got stopped for speeding. A cute cop . . . you know, those tight britches and shiny black knee boots." She laughed low in her throat, remembering. "He was tall, my Ferrari low. When he stepped up to the car, his crotch was at eye level. It looked pretty good. Then he squatted down and I saw his face. It looked good too."

"So did he ask you for a date?" Laura questioned.

Missy howled with laughter. "No. He brought out his little pad to write a ticket, so I stepped on the gas and drove off. He jumped in the squad car and followed me, siren blaring. Straight to the La Quinta Inn." She sighed softly. "Since that day, it's been nothing but policemen for me. Once they get those tall boots off . . ." Her words trailed away and she asked, "What about you? Still as pure as the driven snow?"

Laura reddened. "I'm not in love and . . ."

"What's love got to do with it?" Missy said flippantly. Then, "Oh, yes, did I tell you . . . Daddy's not at the ranch."

"Downtown?"

Missy shook her head. "Benjamin. Won't be back for five days."

"But if your mother is in the South of France then . . ."

Missy was nodding. "We've got the place to ourselves."

Laura laughed. "If mother knew your daddy was away, she'd have a conniption."

"Well, she won't know, so relax." Missy rose from the couch. "Let's get you unpacked. We're going down to Juarez tonight. I fixed you up with a guy who is—"

"A policeman?" Laura interrupted.

"No. I sleep with cops, I don't date them."

*　　*　　*

Laura's date was a neighboring rancher's muscular, blond twenty-two-year-old son. Stoney Butler was loud and fun-loving and on his way to being drunk by eleven that night. The foursome were upstairs in the Jockey Club at the Hippodromo race track in Juarez, Mexico. Stoney downed his fifth tequila and squinted to read his racing program, an arm possessively draped around Laura's slender shoulders. Laura, oddly restless, let her eyes wander over the crowd.

They came to rest on a black-haired man seated alone at a table in the blue section, two tiers down from her own. At that instant a pair of hooded, gray eyes lifted and Laura stopped breathing.

The man from the corral!

Laura immediately ducked her head. Her breath returned but she shivered, unaccountably cold. Her heart speeded alarmingly. Her hands shook and her throat felt dry and she wondered at the curious sensations this stranger aroused.

She allowed several moments to pass before she ventured another look. Pretending to be casually glancing around the room, she looked at him. He was studying a menu; she studied him.

He wore a tan gabardine summer suit that fitted his broad shoulders so well, it had to have been tailored for him. His shirt was white, tie a dark brown silk. Black gleaming hair was neatly combed back off his high forehead and he was freshly shaven, the fair, hawklike face shiny clean. Long pale fingers held the menu. On his left wrist, a shiny gold watch reflected the overhead lights.

The hooded gray eyes lifted.

He caught her staring, but she was incapable of looking away. He stared back, unsmiling. He coolly held her gaze and Laura felt hypnotized; as if he were silently commanding her to look into his strangely beguiling eyes. And she felt the same sense of danger she had felt when first she had seen him at *Roja Rosa*. This quiet stranger evoked conflicting feelings of extreme uneasiness mixed with sensations of unfamiliar sexual excitement.

It was time for the next race. The overhead lights dimmed and a voice said over the loudspeaker, "Here comes Rusty!" and the crowd collectively looked toward the starting box. The greyhounds broke from the box and flew onto the track. Shouts and whistles accompanied them. Laura had a bet on the six dog. It's distinctive gold color was out in front; he was leading the pack. She didn't care. Her eyes left the speeding dogs and returned to the strange man's table. And he was not watching the race. He was looking directly at her.

He pushed back his chair and rose and Laura knew he was coming for her. And she knew that she would go with him. Anywhere.

Calmly, strangely resigned, she watched him take some bills from his pocket, toss them on the table, and nod to the white-jacketed waiter. Unhurriedly, he made his way up the steps toward her. Laura turned to her date and said, "I'm sorry, Stoney. I have to go."

The tall stranger reached her. He stood at the table, his narrow gold belt buckle inches from her face. Laura smiled up at him and rose. He reached out and masterfully, silently, took her arm and escorted her away from the table.

"What the hell—" Stoney sputtered, but the pair had gone.

His arm wrapped tightly around her waist, the man wordlessly guided Laura across the marble floor, down the suspended spiral walkway, and out to a waiting black Oldsmobile. He handed her inside, circled the car, and slid into the driver's seat. Turning to face her, he casually dropped his right hand to the hem of her beige linen skirt. Long, deft fingers slowly pushed the fabric up over her knees and higher, midway up her thighs. Gently insistent, he urged her tightly closed legs to part. Glittering gray eyes lowered leisurely to her lap.

Laura, her breath coming in shallow little gasps, waited, unable to move, unable to speak, her awed gaze on his hawkish face, while sure male fingers swept caressingly over her bare, sensitive flesh. Abruptly, those fingers stopped and came to rest on the trembling inside of her bare, left thigh.

Directly atop a small, black star birthmark.

A pleased, lazy smile touched his full lips. Almost reverently, he spread a possessive hand over the star and the tanned, smooth flesh beneath.

With only the gentle pressure of his fingers on her thigh, he drew her to him, slowly bent his dark head, and kissed her softly, his breath warm and smokey against her lips.

"Laura McCarty, I'm Ryker Rawley. If you don't want me to take everything you have, get out of the car and run."

He waited. Gray eyes flashing in the hard, demonic face. Terrified, intoxicated, Laura swallowed convulsively. And she laid a hand upon his hard, trousered thigh.

"You can't take it from me, Ryker. But I'll give it to you."

CHAPTER THIRTY-ONE

AURA asked no questions of the mysterious man with the chiseled cheekbones. She was neither surprised nor suspicious that he knew who she was. The whole world knew who she was and everything about her. She knew nothing of him, save his name. Still, she knew all she needed to know. She knew, just as she knew that the sun would rise come morning, that this powerfully compelling man was taking her someplace to make love to her.

A Mexican hotel in Juarez, a motel room back in El Paso, his home . . . apartment . . . it made no difference. She wanted him to hold her. To hold her and love her all through the night. To make her a woman. His woman.

Ryker Rawley left his fingers resting loosely on Laura's bare leg. One-handed he drove the Oldsmobile northward through the noisy Juarez streets toward the International Bridge. And as he drove, he spoke softly, reassuringly, the sweetness of his words strangely at odds with the image he projected, but welcome and thrilling to the young, attracted girl beside him.

"I saw you this afternoon at the Graham ranch," his gray, magnetic eyes flicked to her, then returned to the street. "I wanted to talk to you, to stop you, but I was afraid. You're so beautiful, so . . . young. I wanted you. I want you now." Those forceful eyes came back to her. "Be my girl, Laura McCarty."

Laura was thoroughly enchanted. "I will, Ryker. I'll be your girl." But even as she said the words and studied the hard, sculpted profile with its sharp nose, full mouth, and strong chin, Laura felt an icy heat spread from the top of her scalp to the tips of her toes. Ryker Rawley was a strange

222

paradox; handsome-ugly, shy-aggressive, magnetic-repelling, obvious-puzzling.

He had the eyes of a saint.

He had the eyes of a satyr.

They reached the bridge spanning the muddy Rio Grande that would take them back into Texas. Ahead, a long line of cars waited their turn to pass through customs. Ryker braked the car to a dead stop and turned to her. Those steady, satyr's eyes exerted an almost physical pull.

Laura gazed into his awesome eyes and experienced a sudden, overwhelming urge to leap from the car and run from him, just as he had told her to do. For an instant she was filled with an unreasonable fear of such intensity, she felt her body temperature plummet. A tremor shot through her and a strangled gasp of terror rose up to choke her. Unconsciously, she moved toward the car's door.

But Ryker reached for her. His lean, firm fingers gently captured her quivering chin and tilted her frightened face up to his.

"Trust me, baby." His lids lowered sensually over rapidly softening gray eyes and his wide, full mouth, warm and persuasive, covered her trembling, parted lips. Tenderly, languidly, he kissed her with mild, undemanding pressure. Her fear evaporated.

Laura softly sighed and allowed her head to fall back against the supportive arm that had swiftly come around her. Her hand lifted to Ryker's chest, slipping purposely beneath the tan suitcoat to skim caressingly over his silky shirtfront. Beneath the soft, white fabric, hard muscle and crisp hair teased her sensitive fingertips. Moving her fingers outward over the width of his chest, she felt a smooth leather band going over his left shoulder and down under his arm.

Laura was familiar with gun holsters. Her bodyguards wore them, were never without them. But why should Ryker Rawley be wearing a gun? What kind of man was he that . . .

Ryker's hand captured hers. His lips went to her cheek. "Laura, I operate an airplane charter service. For the protection of my passengers, I wear a gun. If it bothers you, I'll take it off."

"No. No, it doesn't," she said quickly.

His mouth came back to settle gently on hers in a long, warm kiss of heartstopping tenderness. Horns honked impatiently behind them and a disgruntled man shouted, "Come on, buddy, move it. You're backing up traffic!"

Unruffled, Ryker gave her lips one last little biting kiss, lifted his head and smiled down at her. "Remember where we left off, sweet."

"I will," said a starry-eyed Laura. Any traces of apprehension were gone. There was only a growing anticipation. A gentle longing. A woman's yearning to be alone with this man whom, before today, she had not known existed.

The couple cleared customs and Ryker accelerated, quickly picking up speed on the Interstate. He drove with a long arm securely around her, telling her of his plans for them. "I'm a pilot, Laura, a good one. I want to fly you out of town for a couple of days. To have you to myself. We can leave tonight and spend . . ."

She listened dreamily, head resting on his shoulder, loving the sound of his deep, mellow voice. When finally he wheeled the Oldsmobile to a stop before a small tin building on the west perimeter of El Paso International, Laura clung to his hand and followed him into the darkened building. Ryker flicked a switch on the wall. Fluorescent lights shimmered on overhead. He pointed to a cluttered desk at the back of the room, indicating the phone.

"You'll need to make calls. Tell anyone who should know, we're flying down to Mexico." She smiled up at him, nodded, and went immediately to the telephone.

"I'm staying with the Graham's. Missy—the girl I was with at the dogtrack—won't be back at the ranch yet but I can leave a message with her maid."

"Do it," said Ryker and shook a cigarette from a near-empty package of Marlboros. He drew a gold Dunhill lighter from his pocket and lit up while she dialed.

Excitedly, Laura explained to the Mexican maid that she was going to Mexico with an old and dear friend. "Tell Missy to cover for me please."

"Si," came the automatic reply. "I tell Missy you go to Mexico with friend."

"Thank you, Rosita."

"Si, Senorita Laura. You want Rosita should tell—"

Laura missed the last half of the chattering maid's sentence. Ryker, his cigarette quickly pinched out in an ashtray, had quietly stepped up behind her and slipped his arms around her waist, locking his wrists in front of her. Head lowered, he nudged the summer blouse off her shoulder with his face and his open lips were scattering kisses over the flesh he had bared. His solid chest and hard thighs were pressing her back and Laura couldn't think clearly.

"Say good-bye," urged Ryker, unclasping his hands and allowing his spread fingers to move down over her flat stomach. "Tell her you'll be back in a few days."

"Rosita, tell Missy I'll be back in—" Ryker took the receiver and hung it up.

Laura turned in his arms. The uneasiness was returning. "I really shouldn't go, Ryker. Missy will worry."

"Will she?" Ryker's voice was flat, impassive, his eyes vaguely amused. He released her, circled the desk, plucked at the sharp creases in his tan gabardine slacks, and sat down in the tall-backed leather chair, swiveling it about. Laura turned to face him. The aura of menace emanating from him was sexually exciting. "Perhaps you shouldn't go, Laura" he said calmly. His eyes grew hard for an instant, then he softened them and smiled. And he reached out and wrapped his hand around her leg, behind the knee. "Maybe you're afraid to fly to Mexico with me." His eyes held hers as his fingers slowly, surely, moved up the back of her leg beneath her skirt.

Midway up her thigh, the hand paused, squeezed gently, then fell away. Ryker abruptly rose from the chair, stepped past her, and walked to the door.

He turned. "Come on. I'll take you home."

"No," she flew to him, throwing herself into his arms and saying, "Take me to Mexico, Ryker. Please, take me."

He smiled. "Anything you say, sweet."

The green twin-engine Cessna, with Ryker at the controls, descended over Ixtapa, Mexico. It was past four in the morning. A big, romantic Mexican moon bathed the small coastal village, enhancing the fairyland beauty of the remote seaside resort. Tall hills and dense jungles surrounded high-rises on strands of beautiful, gleaming beaches. Great white cliffs crashed down to the sea and huge ceiba trees and cactus encircled the bay in a lush private paradise.

At the tiny airport, Ryker guided Laura to a waiting taxi. The slumbering driver awakened when Ryker tapped his shoulder and said, "Take us to the Camino Real, *amigo?*"

Built into the side of a cliff, hanging precariously over the ocean, the spectacular hotel, with hardly a light on, appeared to be sleeping in the moonlight. But the huge pools and pastel-lighted waterfalls and fountains rushed and spurted and sprayed and plummeted in the still July night.

A yawning uniformed Mexican ushered the arriving pair to a luxurious suite of rooms decorated tastefully in earth tones. Double doors, at the far end of a spacious living room, stood open to the bedroom beyond. A wide sundeck stretched the length of both rooms; the Jacuzzi, directly adjacent to the bedroom, churned up white foam of hot water.

Ryker generously tipped the bellman and closed the door behind him. Laura wandered to the mirrored bar, turned and half-sat, half-leaned on a tall leather barstool, unsure what to do next.

Ryker, shrugging out of his tan suitcoat, tossed it to a chair. Leisurely, he crossed to Laura. Cautiously removing the revolver from its shoulder holster, he placed the gun atop the counter. Laura's eyes were fixed on the gun. There was something strange about the weapon. Something different. Momentarily she realized what it was. The pistol had no front sight on top of the barrel.

"Ryker, your gun . . . it has no sight?"

Ryker grinned. "I'm surprised you noticed. Most women know nothing about weapons."

She looked up at him. "You're forgetting. I'm Laura McCarty. Daddy sometimes carried guns. And I'm constantly in the company of bodyguards who wear guns."

"Ah, that's right. I forgot."

"What happened to the gun sight?"

"I filed it off."

"Why?"

His smiled enigmatically. "You'll see."

He put out his hand. She took it, and experienced a dreadful attack of anxiety. Would he take her at once to the bedroom? Would she have to undress with him watching? Would he refuse to wait until she . . .

A soft knock on the suite door startled her. Ryker pulled her gently into his embrace. "I ordered nice cool drinks. I thought it might be pleasant to sit on the balcony and watch the sun rise over the mountains. Then a big breakfast and perhaps a swim."

Relieved, enchanted, Laura nodded violently against his throat.

They shared a wide padded deck chair on the moonlit balcony. An arm around her, Ryker held Laura loosely back against his chest, her head resting on his shoulder. Their legs were stretched out the length of the chaise. On a small glass-topped table beside them sat a large, cold pitcher of delicious frozen daiquiris.

In her right hand, Laura held a stemmed glass filled with the frosty pink concoction. It tasted wonderful; cold and sweet and good. She drank thirstily, as though it were Coca Cola.

"Tell me everything about yourself, Laura McCarty," Ryker's white teeth flashed in the moonlight. He sipped his daiquiri.

Laura blinked up at him and shrugged. "Everybody knows everything about C.C.'s daughter. My father's fame is something that—"

"Not your father, sweet. You," he interrupted, "I'll never know enough about you." His expressive eyes were warm, smokey. "I want to know how many times your heart beats per minute. Which side of the bed you sleep on. Which hand is largest, the left or the right. How many men I should be jealous of?"

Flattered and thrilled by his words, she was quick to assure him. "Ryker, there's no one. There's never been anyone." She drained the last of her daiquiri.

Ryker was pleased. It was just the answer he wanted to hear. There'd been no man before him. His victory would be sweet indeed. She was untouched. Before he had finished with her, she would have had things done to her she could never have imagined.

C.C.'s daughter would not soon forget Ryker Rawley.

Wordlessly, he lifted the frosty silver pitcher and refilled her glass. She turned it up immediately, taking a big, sweet swallow.

"I'd go easy, if I were you, sweet," said Ryker. "There's rum in that drink."

"Yes . . . yes, of course," she said, smiling. She liked him calling her "sweet." She'd been called every other pet name under the sun, except "sweet." It sounded special, coming from him. His voice was so warm and deep.

She sipped her drink. Ryker lit a cigarette with his gleaming gold lighter. "I'll bet," he said, "that you were walking by the time you were nine months old."

"Ryker! How did you know?" she twisted about to look up at him. "I did walk very early . . . at eight months, actually. My mother and daddy were so attentive and . . ."

Laura was rapidly becoming drunk. But she did not know it because she had never been drunk before. She knew only that she felt very relaxed and sure of herself and that she was obviously a very entertaining, interesting person because the sophisticated man beside her hung on her every word and nodded appreciatively, encouragingly, laughing at her amusing anecdotes and shaking his dark head wonderingly at some of the secrets she shared with him.

". . . and when I was four, Daddy taught me to read from *Variety*." She laughed giddily. "I could recognize words and expressions . . . boffo . . . socko . . . blockbuster . . . opened to a weak 25 G's . . ."

She told Ryker about life at Musicland. How she'd been given everything

she ever wanted for as long as she could remember. About learning to sing
her father's songs when she was only three. About her favorite birthday party
for her and a half-dozen of her dolls when she turned six. They were in the
Fairmont Hotel in San Francisco; her daddy was appearing at Candlestick
Park. He had allowed her to order from room service, anything she wanted
and she had called for caviar and champagne and chateaubriand and Baked
Alaska and Pepsi Cola and chocolate cake and strawberry ice cream—for
eight. A trio of red-coated waiters had transported the mountains of food
and drink to the penthouse suite and she and her daddy and her dolls had
celebrated royally.

She had ridden in a long black limousine to her first day of school at
Hockaday, and every day thereafter until she graduated the past spring.

She said she had never really wanted to be anything but a successful
entertainer, like her daddy. She was only waiting until she turned twenty-
one and could do as she pleased. She fully intended to follow in her famous
father's footsteps.

Impulsively, Laura raised her skirt up over her left thigh. "See that,
Ryker? It's a star birthmark exactly like the one my daddy had on his face."
She tapped the tiny asterisk with a manicured nail. "My daddy said the
birthmark means I'm special."

"I intend to show you just how special, sweet."

The moon had gone down. The morning sun had risen and turned the
silvered sea a shimmering vivid pink. And Laura McCarty, lounging lazily
in the summer dawn with an attentive Ryker Rawley, sighed and stretched
and nodded yes when he asked if she was ready to go inside.

Skillfully, Ryker had relaxed his young companion, just as he had
planned. Just as he would continue to do. He had no intention of shattering
her illusion of romance too soon.

Indoors, Laura sank down onto a comfortable custom sofa of striped
beige-and-white linen. Ryker did not sit down beside her. He switched on
the radio, searching until he located a Mexican station with clear reception. Soon a rich baritone voice sang softly in Spanish. Satisfied with his
choice, he crossed to Laura, drew up an armless chair and sat down facing
her, so close his long spread legs trapped hers inside.

"You're not afraid now, are you, sweet?" Before she could answer, he
leaned forward and kissed her. While his lips moved on hers, his hands
eased her blouse up out of the waistband of her skirt. The kiss ended. He
unbuttoned her blouse and pushed it apart. She was braless; her small, high
breasts spilled out. Ryker smiled and touched a soft nipple with his fin-
gertip.

He took the blouse from her and laid it on the cushion, stood and removed his shirt. Laura's eyes were fastened on his broad, bared chest. Thick, black hair, in a fanlike pattern, covered his torso from collarbone to belly.

Ryker dropped back into his chair. He clasped her knees and gently drew her forward to the edge of the sofa. "You're so beautiful, Laura, that I'm almost afraid to touch you."

"I want you to touch me, Ryker," said Laura truthfully.

"Do you, sweet?" he murmured and kissed her. His arms slipped around her to press her close. The crisp, dense hair of his chest tickled her breasts and Laura sighed into his mouth. His lips slid to her cheek, then to her right ear, while his hands moved enticingly over her bare, silky back. Her breath grew short and her pulse quickened when his mouth, open and warm, pressed kisses to the side of her throat, her bare shoulders.

Ryker kissed her and kissed her and Laura marveled at how tender and worshipping his lips were on her tingling flesh. Awed, she watched the dark head moving over her. Hands now gliding ahead of his mouth, he urged her arms away from her sides and kissed her heated underarms, the insides of her elbows, her fragile wrists, the palms of her hands.

And while he kissed her Laura sighed and trembled and arched her back. He kissed a path along her ribs and the thick hair of his head grazed her left breast. Laura moaned.

Ryker lifted his head. He drew both her hands to his lips, turned their palms up, and kissed them. And placed those hands in his hair at the sides of his head. Silver eyes hot, voice deep and sensuous, he said, "Show me, sweet. Put my mouth where you most want it."

Laura shivered, uttered a choking little sigh and anxiously guided his face to her aching left breast. "Ryker," she gasped as his warm, moist lips enclosed the straining nipple. Her hands continued to cling to his dark hair, pulling him closer while she unconsciously pushed her swelling breast against his hot face.

Ryker's lips pulled gently on the erect nipple and he heard her murmur breathlessly, "Ryker, oh, Ryker."

Ryker Rawley knew women. He knew that all of them tremendously enjoyed this part of lovemaking. Couldn't get enough of it. And because they did, he had sucked on every kind of female breast under the sun. Big, pillowy, mountainous breasts that smothered and choked him. Small, flat little ones he could hardly get a hold on. Young, firm pretty ones with large nipples of pink satin that tasted sweet and grew pebble hard beneath his lips.

Like the one now enclosed in his mouth.

He could tell by her sighs and movements and the flushing warmth of her skin that young, trusting Laura McCarty was exactly like all of her sisters. She liked a man's mouth at her breasts.

So Ryker gave her want she wanted. He sucked harder and harder on the sensitive flesh while she squirmed and purred, loving it. He released the throbbing bud and ran the tip of his tongue around and around it and her breath came in rapid little pants. He took the nipple back into his mouth and sucked gently, barely pulling with his lips. Again he released it, only to nibble, to bite on it, teasing at it with sharp, white teeth.

Laura's hands slid from Ryker's dark head. Weak arms fell to her sides and she gave herself over to him, passion-dazed eyes opening and closing in shocked wonder. Never had a man seen her bare breasts, much less kissed them, and she was astounded by the pleasure. Guiltily she looked down at Ryker, thrilled by the sensual, erotic sight of his hot mouth enclosing her breast. His lips released her. She whimpered softly and tossed her head.

His hands came up to clasp the breast and he began licking it. The more he licked, the harder the tiny bud became, the darker its color. He stroked it vigorously with his tongue as though he were holding a sweet ice cream cone that would surely melt unless he lapped it all up.

Again he covered the darkened nipple with his mouth and began to suck greedily, loudly, and Laura threw her head back and leaned to him and wondered fleetingly why, when it was her breast his lips clung to, did she feel the sweet, aching pull between her legs.

Ryker abruptly released the nipple and lifted his head. In one lithe movement he rose and scooped Laura from the sofa and up into his arms. Crossing the deep pile carpet, he stepped through the double doors to the bedroom.

Blackout drapes were pulled against the bright morning sunshine. It was cool and dim and quiet. Pale blue sheets of silky percale had been turned down earlier by the hotel staff. A half-dozen fat, blue-cased pillows rested against the dark walnut headboard. Beside the bed, a gleaming vase of Waterford crystal held two dozen fragile white rose buds, their delicate fragrance sweetening the air. Soft, romantic music from the radio was the only sound, save the wild, wild beating of Laura's heart.

Laura inhaled deeply and thought how perfect it all was. The romantic Mexican seaside resort. The quiet early July morning. The man like no other in the whole wide world.

CHAPTER THIRTY-TWO

RYKER paused midway into the room, kissed Laura, and lowered her to her feet. Looking down into her upturned face, speaking in a low, soothing voice, he told her what he intended.

"I'm going to undress you, sweet, and put you in bed." His hands were already at her skirt's zipper. "I know you're tired; that's alright. You can lie back and relax while I make love to you." The skirt fluttered to the carpet. Laura stood in the dim light in her white, lace-trimmed half-slip, heart pounding wildly beneath uncovered breasts.

The slip came over her head and Ryker tossed it aside. He peeled her bikini panties down over her hips as she stepped out of them. A wave of embarrassment overcame her and she took a step backward, turning from him. Ryker caught her and pulled her back into his embrace.

"Put your arms around me," he murmured softly. Nervous hands stole up around his neck as he drew her closer.

Naked, she stood in his arms.

He kissed her softly, sweetly, the thick, crisp hair of his bare chest pleasingly abrasive against her tingling breasts.

His hands, so masterful, so warm, moved over her narrow waist and gently flaring hips to her bare rounded bottom. He cupped her caressingly, kneading and stroking. And then, with long fingers spread beneath each firm, creamy cheek, he slowly lifted her straight up before him until her bare toes left the thick carpet and her young, glowing face was above his own. Holding her this way, he kissed her deeply, then walked with her to the bed.

Laura closed her eyes and felt the soft mattress beneath her back as Ryker laid her gently atop the cool, clean sheets. Hardly daring to breathe, she waited for him to undress. He didn't.

Ryker sat down on the bed's edge and removed only his shoes. He twisted his lithe body about to face her. "Look at me, Laura," his voice was rich and deep. She obeyed, and with those eyes that possessed the power to mesmerize, he held her gaze. Slowly, gently, he reached out a hand to touch her flushed cheek. He drew a finger down the side of her face in a tender caress. He stroked her long, dark hair and let his gleaming silver eyes roam slowly over her body. Unhurriedly, he studied her nakedness and Laura felt a surge of new excitement electrify her body.

Floating in a strange, sensuous daydream, she watched him from beneath fluttering lids while his eyes, so intense and potent, touched her flesh caressingly, admiringly. She experienced a glorious sense of feminine power over the chisel-featured man. Ryker was making love to her with his eyes and it was unbearably exciting. Unconsciously, she stretched and purred and raised her arms above her head, an unclothed nymphet allowing her love slave to feast his eyes on her fairness.

Ryker could feel the arousal rising from her like a glow. She was moving sensuously on the pale sheets, undulating, offering herself for his homage. There was about her a naive sexuality that was devastatingly appealing and he was not unmoved. Not immune. But neither was he blinded by her charms. He had had other young beauties with petal-soft lips and dark, sultry eyes.

A muscle jumped in his lean jaw and his broad bare chest constricted. Below him, lovely jutting breasts still pinkened and tender from his kisses, were undeniably tempting, as was the rest of her long-waisted, slender young body. Narrow ribcage leading symmetrically into a tiny waist. Flat stomach with proudly rising hipbones made the shimmering little belly concave. Thick tangle of raven curls between sleek, satiny thighs. Long, shapely legs and slender feet.

Ryker put a hand to the bed on each side of her, leaned down, and kissed her open, succulent lips. "You're so very sweet, so beautiful, I'd like to keep you just as you are at this moment." His lips softly brushed her cheek, her ear. "I shouldn't touch you, should never make love to you. Just content myself to adore your innocent naked beauty and allow you to remain totally unspoiled." His gray eyes grew wistful.

Laura caught her breath. And said exactly what he knew she would say. "No . . . no, Ryker. I want you to make love to me. I want to belong to you."

"God," he breathed. "Do you know what it means to hear you say that?" He shook his head, as though in wonder. And swiftly stretched out beside her and dedicated himself to giving Laura McCarty one of the most glorious mornings of her life. He would introduce her to love, teach her the delights of passion and all the sweet methods of joy. He would willingly be her teacher; patient, kind, caring. He would painstakingly lift her to the heights of ecstasy.

His reward would come later.

Laura remained deep in her beautiful love dream. Ryker held her and she lay pliantly in his arms and stroked his long back and loved the feel of smooth flesh and hard muscle, the deep cleft running down its center. His skin was warm, his lips were hot, his tongue arousing. He kissed her for a long, lovely time, his kisses changing as his ardor grew. Soft, gentle kisses of affection turned to deep, probing kisses of passion. When his lips slipped over her chin and pressed the sensitive hollow of her throat, Laura sighed expectantly. And murmured his name when his dark head started a slow downward plunge.

He was at her breasts again, lingering there, biting and nibbling and thrilling her. Chewing teasingly on a rigid nipple, he let his hand, sure and determined, sweep over her, touching, caressing, enkindling. Laura squirmed and clutched at the sheet and felt new heat consume her.

Ryker's lips enclosed a breast and he sucked vigorously, hungrily, taking as much of the milky mound into his mouth as possible. Laura exhaled raggedly and closed her glazed eyes. And enjoyed the strong pull of his lips, the erotic sounds of sucking.

His lips came back to hers and she kissed him anxiously, and when, deep in the heated kiss, her lids fluttered restlessly, she found his gray, gleaming eyes wide open. It was wildly exciting.

His hand gently stroked her bare belly. Hotly, deeply he kissed her now, his tongue plunging insistently, rhythmically while his fingers trailed along the insides of her thighs, teasing, igniting, molding.

When Laura's slender body began to writhe and she felt as though she were afire, Ryker shifted beside her. He slid across the bed and Laura was certain he would undress and take her at last. She closed her eyes tightly and eagerly waited.

And her eyes flew open wide in shock.

Ryker was over her, kissing her stomach. Slacks still on, he slid steadily downward, parting her legs, moving between them. He laid on his stomach and put his arms beneath her, filling his hands with her rounded buttocks while his lips scattered kisses on her belly.

Startled, mortified, Laura rolled her shoulders up from the mattress, resting her weight on her elbows. "Ryker," she gasped weakly as his mouth moved over her stomach, leaving wet, quivering flesh in its wake. "Ryker, don't do . . ."

He lifted his head. "Sweet Laura, aren't you mine?"

"Yes, but . . ." Her face flamed feverishly as heated arousal warred with embarrassed shame.

"Then trust me, baby," said Ryker, his silver eyes molten. "You're so beautiful, let me kiss you, baby. Let me taste you."

Laura shook her head violently, but watched, transfixed, when his face lowered into the thick black curls between her legs. He nuzzled there, playfully, familiarly, blowing hot, moist breaths against her.

"No . . ." she whispered again, and came up off her elbows to lean on stiff arms in a sitting position.

"That's it, baby, watch me. Watch me love you," and his face moved lower and burrowed into the thick, protective hair.

She did watch. She couldn't keep from it. She sat there in that bed, and watched the dark head bending between her parted legs. A strangled cry tore from her shocked throat. His open mouth covered ultra-sensitive flesh, enclosing her warmly. Her entire body spasmed when his tongue touched her, and swept slowly upward.

Her stiffened arms grew limber and she fell back. A fist went to her mouth and she bit her hand while Ryker Rawley lay between her thighs and gently kissed her. She could feel his warm mouth against her burning flesh, the abrasiveness of his day-old beard brushing the insides of her thighs, tickling her.

After the initial touch of his tongue, he withheld it from her. He kissed her, close-lipped, tenderly, lightly, over and over again, expertly teasing her.

After several minutes of sweet play, he kissed her open-mouthed, allowing her to feel the tip of his tongue against her, but purposely keeping it virtually still. Tiny little plucking kisses. Brief, fleeting, toying.

Laura's head tossed frantically on the pillow and she felt both wonderful and miserable. It was the most sensational pleasure she had ever experienced, yet she was hurting. A part of her wanted him to continue forever, another part wished he would stop the torture at once. She longed for . . . for . . .

Hands tightening on her buttocks, Ryker lifted her to him. Mouth open wide and hungry, he gave her all that she needed, kissing her, licking her, loving her completely.

"Yes . . ." Laura gasped breathlessly and pressed closer to the masterful mouth feasting on her. "Ryker . . . oh . . . oh . . . Ryker," she murmured through fevered lips and felt as though he was surely devouring her and that it was exactly what she wanted. Unconsciously she opened her legs wider and reached down to clasp his hair to pull him to her.

Ryker paused for a moment.

"No . . . please . . ." she was excited, practically sobbing, a deep pulsating growing almost painful.

Ryker smiled and began to lick her again, running his tongue over silky flesh, circling, probing. Then finally kissing and sucking, burying his face in her, intent on taking her over the edge.

Laura lost all awareness of her surroundings. She forgot completely where she was and who she was and what she was doing. She didn't think; she didn't know, she didn't care. Only responded as Ryker Rawley expertly pushed her helplessly toward release.

And when it started, it took her totally by surprise. Her eyes widened in disbelief. Her thighs tightened on his dark head. Her hands clasped his hair, frantically pulling. The first orgasm of her life was one so deep and pleasurable, she could feel it to the roots of her hair and the tips of her fingers and the soles of her feet.

Her blood was liquid fire and it seemed to rush headlong to that searing point between her legs where Ryker kissed her. It felt for all the world as if she were pouring out her lifeblood into the tight, hot seal of his mouth. She screamed and let it flow.

Ryker stayed with her, mouth fused to her, until all the little tremors and aftershocks subsided. He moved up beside her, pushed her wildly tangled hair back off her face and leaned down to kiss her temple.

"Ryker" she purred breathlessly, "I . . . I feel so . . . wonderful."

Ryker smiled in quiet amusement. "I know, sweet." Stroking her hair, he drew her against him. "Laura, you'll find toilet articles in the bathroom. And a new terry robe. Have a nice hot tub and I'll order breakfast."

The linen-draped breakfast table had been placed on the sundeck overlooking the calm Pacific. A hot July sun climbed higher into the cloudless sky, turning the endless ocean into a million tiny gleaming mirrors of light. The subtle scent of fresh gardenias floated up from the flower-filled swimming pool below.

A sterling silver bud base at the table's center held a lone white rose. Large, linen napkins, folded into perfect pleated fans, rested atop silver-plated holloware serving dishes. Cut crystal salt and pepper shakers matched a pair of crystal candleholders.

Two tall hand-blown champagne flutes were filled with freshly squeezed orange juice mixed with chilled Dom Perignon. Beneath silver-domed lids were light, fluffy cheese omelettes, a rasher of crisply fried bacon, and golden brown waffles. A silver basket was filled with tarts and sweet rolls and hot Mexican breads. A small crystal bowl held wonderful preserves made from large chunks of apricots and mirabelles in sherry. Rich creamery butter, molded into tiny oncidium orchids, rested atop a bed of chipped ice. There was strong black coffee and fresh strawberries in thick cream and thin crepes filled with blueberries and a rich flan custard.

Laura, glowing, famished, fresh as the perfect July morning in a knee-length white terry robe, sat across from Ryker and smiled, her face flushing with happiness and embarrassment.

"Hungry?" he said, taking her hand and rubbing the fragile knuckles with his thumb.

"Starving," she admitted, the word punctuated with happy, nervous laughter.

He laughed with her, squeezed her fingers and urged, "Eat plenty, baby. You are going to need it." And he winked at her.

Laura could not remember having such an appetite. Nor could she recall food ever tasting quite so delicious. She ate heartily, taking at least a few bites of everything, thirstily washing it down with the champagne-laced orange juice.

Ryker pushed his plate away and lit a cigarette. Leaning back in his chair, he watched the happy young girl. There was a wonderful abandon in the way she leaned forward and caused her robe to shift so that a firm, bare breast was in view. He felt his stomach muscles tighten with desire. Swiftly he looked away, silently cursing himself for his weakness.

Squinted eyes on the sea, he said, "Do you want to sleep after you finish your breakfast?"

Laura, gleaming olive breast still exposed, chewed a mouthful of sweet, rich flan and shook her dark head. "I'm not sleepy. I shall never be sleepy again."

Ryker's gaze came back to her. "Want to go exploring?"

"Could we?" Her dark eyes danced with delight.

They strolled hand in hand down the powdery beach, pausing at the pier to watch the native children play volleyball on the hot sand. Laughing, they climbed into a rickety wooden taxi boat and went across the bay to a tiny island where they collected seashells under the steamy tropical sun. They whiled away the gorgeous afternoon at the open-air restaurants on La Ropa Beach, drinking Tecate, nibbling Paquitas, and playing gin rummy.

They found a small cantina where a young guitar player strummed Latin ballads. Barefooted, they danced on the dusty floor, their long-limbed bodies swaying together lazily, sensuously. A trio of young Mexican men watched and the boldest of the three stepped up, and tapped

Ryker's shoulder. "*Con permisso*, I would like to dance with the lovely senorita, *si?*"

Fierce gray eyes fixed the brown-skinned youth and Ryker's volatile temperament surfaced. "You can't even look at her, pal!" He pressed Laura's face to his throat, trapping her. "Stay the hell away from her." His sharp-featured face hardened dangerously. "Go on, get out of here!"

"Ryder . . ." Laura couldn't believe her ears.

The stunned Mexican backed away, hands lifted, palms out. "I'm going man. No hard feelings, *si?*" He and his companions hastily retreated.

Ryker's gaze swung back to the girl in his arms. He saw alarm clearly written in the big, dark eyes. His face softened at once and he grinned disarmingly. "Who does he think he is? Julio Iglesias?" He laughed and added, "Sorry, sweet, I'm jealous because the guy is younger and better-looking than I. Afraid I might lose my girl."

Laura relaxed and laughed with him. His self-mocking wit made it easy to forgive his brief show of temper. "You'll never lose me," she said and locked her hands behind his head.

The lovely, lazy day passed. Shadows lengthened. The pair strolled back toward their hotel. Native women were selling colorful beads on the beach. Ryker stopped, bought some for Laura, and draped them all around her neck at once until she was weighted down with bright reds, blues, and yellows dripping over her bare throat and linen blouse. Smiling sunnily, she fingered the beads and told him, honestly, that she loved his present more than any she had ever had before.

The sun was setting across the Pacific, turning the restless waves into fiery sheets of color, when the tired pair reached their hotel. Inside the large, westward-facing suite, the sliding glass doors and heavy drapes were open wide to the dying day. The rooms were bathed in a vivid orange glow. A gentle ocean breeze cooled the still air.

Without a word the pair walked into the bedroom and undressed, watching each other as they disrobed. Curious, excited, Laura forgot her many strands of colored beads. Naked, save the beads, she stood in the gloaming and looked at tall pale man with the jet black hair covering his chest and belly and groin. Ryker allowed her to study him for a time before he smiled, moved closer, and hooked a long finger under a string of bright yellow beads resting on the swell of her bare breasts.

Slowly, by the beads, he pulled her to him. He put his hands in her hair at the sides of her head and kissed her. "Like the beads so much you want to wear them to bed?"

"I forgot. I must look foolish." She lowered her head to look at the tangled necklaces.

Ryker chuckled and put a finger beneath her chin, lifting her face to his. His laughter stopped abruptly and his gray eyes turned to silver. "No, sweet, you look just about good enough to eat."

Laura flushed.

CHAPTER THIRTY-THREE

DON'T you want me?" Laura breathed excitedly, lying naked beside him in the sun-pinkened bed. She couldn't understand why, when his body was unquestionably ready, he waited. He seemed in no hurry although he was clearly aroused.

"I will want you, sweet. But not until you want me."

"But I want you now, Ryker."

"No. No, you don't. I'll know when you want me." He turned her to face him, drawing her long, slender leg up over his hip to curl around him. His hand traced her spine from neck to lower back while he looked into her dark eyes. Long, deft fingers roamed down over the swell of her bottom, moved to the crevice, and slipped between, seeking out sensitive, concealed feminine flesh. He touched her and her breathing changed. He caressed her coaxingly while his eyes trapped hers.

They lay there like that, Laura, colorful beads spilling about her naked shoulders, hips undulating against his hand; Ryker, hot silver eyes holding her gaze, knowing fingers rubbing, circling, working magic.

A silky wetness began to flow from Laura. He kissed her deeply and his stroking grew more rapid, more insistent. They strained together, twisting and turning in the blazing sunset, she becoming as brazen as he. Her hand slipped from his shoulder down the hair-covered muscles of his chest, exploring, inquisitive. Eyes still locked with his, her slender fingers moved steadily to the rigid rod of power throbbing between their heated bodies. She touched the tip and gasped when it jerked involuntarily. She liked the smooth, hot texture and felt she could not wait another second to have it inside her.

Ryker shifted their positions. Laura found herself on her back, her legs widely parted, Ryker between them, his long, lean body and wide shoulders looming above her. He guided himself into her and stopped. He lay still for a long moment, leaning to her, kissing her lips, her eyes, her ears. And began moving once more. Little by little, in slow careful stages, he sank into her and Laura was so passionately aroused, she felt no pain.

She astonished the man above her by straining anxiously up to meet his thrusts, eager for him to push farther, to fill her completely, to make her his own. Her hands clung to his upper arms as she surged against him and murmured his name, urging him on, brazenly looking straight into his eyes.

Inflamed, he plunged deeply into her and saw a brief joyous smile touch her kiss-puffy lips. It was all he could do to keep from climaxing.

Laura luxuriated in the loving. Better by far than anything she had ever dreamed of, being loved by this silver-eyed man was sheer ecstasy and she wanted to lie naked beneath him for all the rest of her life. She winced with heightened rapture when he began to move back and forth within her, rhythmically, erotically. He was piercing her, stretching her, filling her to overflowing. It was exquisite. Wonderful. Extraordinary pleasure. And she loved him for it.

"Ryker," she whispered breathlessly, "I love you. I love you, Ryker."

His answer was a deep, devouring kiss and a gradual increasing of his thrusts. Faster and faster they moved, their heated bodies gleaming with perspiration, their breaths hot and ragged, their lips seeking naked flesh. Innately passionate, Laura's quest for fulfillment was primitive. She bucked and lunged and clasped his slippery shoulders and gave as good as she got.

And when she came, she was like a young wildcat, scratching him with sharp punishing nails raking down his back, biting at his slick throat and crying out as his climax began and he exploded deep within her.

Spent, they lay entwined in the now darkened room. And Laura McCarty, open and honest as only a naive seventeen-year-old can be, told Ryker Rawley that she was in love with him and would be in love with him for the rest of her life.

"Do you love me, Ryker?" her dark, liquid eyes flashed in the darkness.

"What do you think," said Ryker and kissed her.

They splashed about in the steamy hot tub, got out, took a cold shower together and ordered a late supper. Over thick sirloins and chilled Cabernet Sauvigon, Ryker smiled lazily at a glowing Laura while she chattered happily.

"I always knew there would be a Ryker Rawley in my life," she told him honestly. "I've daydreamed about you for ever so long, darling." She lifted her robed shoulders and sighed contentedly. "Now you're here and I never want to be out of your sight. Never." She reached suddenly for his hand. "You want me with you always, don't you?"

Ryker smiled warmly, squeezed her hand. "I want you with me, sweet."

"We'll be so happy, Ryker. I know we will. I never really wanted to go to college, although Mother has always insisted. Now I won't have to. There's not much she can do about it after we're married."

"Sweet, eat your dinner. It's getting cold."

Laura shook her dark head, and looked at the plate she had hardly touched. "I'm full, darling. Can't eat another bite." Laura stuck a forefinger into the Fresh raspberry Bavarian cream wreathed with Kron white chocolate, licked disinterestedly, then pushed the rich dessert away.

But she said yes to after-dinner Armagnac because Ryker urged her to do so and she wanted only to please this magnificent man she loved. She felt the warm, silken brandy float over her palate and into her throat, down into her chest and out into her arms.

They carried the brandy bottle and two glasses to the bedroom. The moon had risen; light streamed in the open balcony doors but did not quite reach the big, tumbled bed. So they didn't get into the bed.

They stripped and stretched out on the thick carpet. In the silvery moonlight they sipped their brandy and kissed and talked and made slow, languid love. They dozed there on the floor; waking long after midnight to make wild, uninhibited love, as from below the hotel club's orchestra drummed out a loud, thrumming beat in rhythm with their pagan mating.

They bathed again and got into bed. At dawn Laura awakened, turned her head on the pillow, and saw a pair of hypnotic silver eyes looking at her. Without a word, Ryker kissed her and at once her bare body was aflame, ready to accept him. He moved atop her, slid easily into her and began the slow, sensuous movements of lovemaking. Together they climaxed as the new day began and fell back to sleep having never uttered a word.

Laura awoke cold.

Naked, she lay atop the sheets in the dark bedroom. Alone. She shivered and had the unsettling feeling that the frigid air conditioner was not solely responsible for her chill.

"Ryker." It was little more than a whisper coming from her tight throat. No answer. Laura swung her legs over the bed's edge and reached for the terry robe.

Squinting in the darkness, she shoved her arms down into the sleeves and tied the sash securely at her waist. Immediately she crossed to the sliding glass doors, jerking almost frantically at the drapery cord.

And she blinked owlishly and felt a great measure of relief when bright, blinding sunshine filled the too-cold room. She had thought it still early morning.

It was the middle of the day. Ryker had awakened, didn't want to disturb her, and had quietly gone into the other room.

Laura rushed toward the living room, as anxious to see her lover as if it had been weeks instead of hours. Smiling sunnily, she jerked open the interior door and called his name breathlessly.

"Right here, sweet," came the deep, calm voice from the depths of the long linen sofa.

It was as hot in this room as it was cold in the other. The air conditioner was not on. The drapes were open wide to the glaring Mexican sun, but the glass doors were tightly shut. Laura frowned.

"I woke up and missed you," she said, circling the sofa to him. He sat at one end of the striped couch, a long leg hooked over the sofa's arm. In his hand was a glass of Scotch and a lighted Marlboro. A half-full bottle of J & B was on the side table at his elbow.

He wore only a pair of black bikini jockey shorts. Into their low riding elastic waistband, his pistol was shoved, butt resting on a naked hipbone. He was perspiring heavily, moisture beading the furred chest; bare arms and legs gleaming. He still had not shaved and his black, thick beard had grown rapidly. There was about him a decidedly sinister air and Laura again experienced a chill, despite the oppressive heat of the room.

"Did you, sweet?" His eyes were on her and Laura felt their erotic pull, just as always, despite his menacing appearance. "Then come here and kiss me good morning."

She hurried to him, bending to meet his raised lips. Ryker pulled her down onto his lap. Laura put her arm around him. "Ryker, you're so warm. Let's turn on the air or open the balcony doors."

Ryker shrugged bare, gleaming shoulders. "I hadn't noticed the heat."

"Well I'll go . . ."

"No, stay here," he gently ordered and she did.

"Have you eaten?" she felt edgy. A loaded gun touching her thigh made her extremely nervous. Why did he have the revolver sticking in his shorts? "Want to clean up and go down to the restaurant?" She waited hopefully while he stared at her, those silver eyes deep and unreadable.

He ignored her question.

"Laura, do you love me?"

Laura tilted her head. "Of course I love you, Ryker."

He smiled at her. "How much do you love me, sweet?"

She was unsure what he wanted from her. She leaned to him, hugged his head to her breasts. "More than I've ever loved anyone in my life. I love you, Ryker. Only you. I love you, I love you." She pulled back to look at him.

"If you love me, then you want to please me." His fingers toyed with the tightly tied sash of her robe.

"Certainly! Always."

"You'll do anything I ask?" Nervously, she laughed. "Answer me, Laura."

"Y-yes, Ryker."

"That's my sweet girl." He untied her sash and slowly, methodically parted the white terry robe, exposing her nakedness. Laura felt a rush of desire as his eyes traveled intimately over her.

But it was gone in the blinking of an eye.

Ryker pulled the pistol out of his shorts and, elbow bent, held it pointed toward the ceiling. "Know anything about gun clubs, honey?"

Nervously pulling her robe together, Laura said, "I . . . I've heard of them. Missy's daddy . . . Mr. Graham . . . belongs to the National Rifle Association."

Ryker grinned wolfishly. "I'm not speaking of that kind of gun club, sweet." He slowly lowered the pistol, pushing it teasingly beneath the lapel of her robe.

Growing steadily more apprehensive, Laura, wide eyes on the gun, said, "Then wh . . . what do you mean? I don't understand."

"I'm speaking of my gun club. Ryker's special gun club. I want you to be a member."

Truly frightened now, Laura cautiously pushed the revolver aside. "Put that gun away! It's dangerous." She tried to get up.

He jerked her back. "Not half as dangerous as defying me."

Her heart pounded. "I . . . I'm not defying you, Ryker, but I . . ."

"Ah, sweet, don't disappoint me." He softened his eyes and smiled at her. "Join my gun club?"

"Alright," she murmured uneasily. "How do I join?"

"First you open your robe." She looked at him skeptically, but obeyed, drawing a shallow breath when once again her body was uncovered. He leaned to her and kissed a quivering breast, raised his dark head and commanded, "Part your legs, sweet."

"Ryker, please . . ."

"Do it."

She let her thighs fall apart. "Alright, but that gun is . . ."

"Is going to make you come, sweet." And he lowered the gun, twisting his hand about, to place the smooth gleaming barrel directly between her thighs.

"My God . . ." she shrieked, shocked, revolted, afraid. Through her mind flashed the recollection of asking him why he had filed the sight from his gun. *You'll see*, he'd told her. Dear Lord! He was going to use the smoothed-barreled pistol to . . .

Ryker pressed the gun against her flesh. "There you go. Feel good?"

"No! Move that gun this minute."

"Shhh, Laura. Don't fight it. Become a member of my gun club."

Outraged, horrified, Laura began to struggle, and found him unbelievably strong and determined. Tears streamed down her hot cheeks and she pleaded. But all in vain. Their scuffling continued, Laura desperate to get free, terrified the gun would discharge. It was child's play for Ryker. In truth he enjoyed the fierce wrestling; it excited him—just as it always did.

She tired at last, unable to fight anymore. For her physical surrender, she was rewarded with a deep, thrusting kiss from her captor. Ryker held her head immobile in his spread fingers and kissed her, the gun remaining safely stationary between her thighs, until he got the response he sought. Only then did his lips release hers. He cradled her back in the circle of his arm and slowly slipped the gun up and down between her legs.

"That's better," he praised, when she attempted no further escape. "Yes . . . baby . . . enjoy it."

Laura felt the pistol's smooth steel barrel slowly move up and down against her sensitive flesh. She gritted her teeth and endured it, her anger white-hot, her disillusionment crushing. From tear-heavy lashes she looked at the man meting out this unusual punishment.

His eyes, fixed in queer pleasure, were demonic. A satyr's smile was on his lips. He was sweating profusely, rivulets dripping down his lean whisker-darkened cheeks. He looked like the devil himself.

The strange stimulation continued. And continued. And with it calm, low words of encouragement from Ryker. And much to her self-disgust, Laura was growing more and more aroused.

"You can do it, baby. I know you can," Ryker praised. "You'll be in the club. All you have to do is come on my gun. That's it Laura, rub up against it. Push your pelvis, sweet. Yes . . . yes . . . you're so hot and wet, you're about to come. Come for me, baby. Let it out."

Laura, tears dried on her cheeks, robe pushed completely off her arms, wasn't sure if he was mad, or if she was. Or were they both? And for the moment, she didn't care. Excited, on fire, she pressed anxiously against the stroking, teasing metal cylinder, making love to it with her heated, perspiring body, her lips widening into a wanton smile when Ryker whispered, "God, you're a little beauty. My gun loves you; I love you."

It started then, triggered by his words. She climaxed deeply, riding the gun frantically, savagely, while he lauded her. "You're the best, baby. Mmmmm, yes, that's beautiful . . ." until all the wrenching tremors had ceased. She went limp against him then, her head falling back onto his shoulder.

Eyes closed, panting for breath, she heard him say coldly, "Congratulations, bitch, you're in the club." He chuckled then, a low, demonic laugh. "If I had a dollar for every woman I've brought to climax on this gun, I'd be as rich as you, C.C.'s daughter."

CHAPTER THIRTY-FOUR

A TERRIFYING nightmare had begun for Laura McCarty.

For three tortuously long days and nights, Laura, naked and defenseless, was virtually held sexual prisoner by a cruelly vindictive beast disguised as an appealingly virile man.

She knew—by the contemptuous tone of his voice when he called her C.C.'s daughter—that he despised her.

Too late, she learned Ryker Rawley's true identity. The extraordianry lover who had taken her virginity and her heart was the man that had attempted to kill her daddy.

Did he mean to kill her too?

Speechless, Laura lunged from his lap, but he was too swift. Quick as a cat, he reached for her, the muscles beneath his pale skin coiled and corded. Ryker jerked her back with such force her teeth rattled in her head. With deft ease he stripped the loosened robe from her arms and sailed it across the room.

He deposited her on his left knee, trapping her legs between his. He tossed the gun onto the sofa beside them and grabbed her shoulders. It stunned her into quick thought. "Ryker, I have money, I'll give it to you and—"

"Just like your daddy, aren't you," he cut her off. His lean hands came up to frame her frightened face, clamping it viselike between his palms. "Money solves everything." His lips thinned dangerously. "Something you don't like; pay to get rid of it, is that right?"

"I don't know what you mean, but—"

"When I was twelve years old my sister died," he said through clenched white teeth. "She was murdered. Linda was the only female I have ever known who was not a tramp." His eyes shone from narrow slits of hate. "She was sweet and good, but she was unlucky. She met your famous daddy. He seduced her, got her pregnant, then tossed her aside like a used condom."

Horrified, Laura said, "Ryker, I know nothing about it and I . . ."

"You're going to know all about it, so shut up and listen. Linda, my sweet Linda, was an innocent . . . untouched. The Chief violated her. And then he killed her."

"No . . . no . . ." Laura choked.

"Oh, yes. She was carrying his bastard. He sent her for an abortion; she bled to death with only me at her side."

"That's terrible . . . I . . . I'm sorry about your sister, Ryker, but I can't see what . . ."

He smiled suddenly. A harsh, menacing smile that stretched his lips wide. " 'An eye for an eye,' the Bible says. That's all I want, an eye for an eye. If I had managed to kill your daddy, the score would have been settled, but he always had bodyguards around and I couldn't get to him." His hands slipped from her face down to settle on her trembling shoulders. "So you'll have to pay. I've taken your virginity, just as he took Linda's. And I'll keep you here with me until I make you pregnant. Then you can have an abortion and . . ." He shrugged bare shoulders, smiled coldly at her.

"My God, you're insane," she struggled anew, desperate to be free. "Let me go!" she shouted, near hysterics.

"You're wasting your breath. This is a fine hotel; the walls are thick and soundproof. No one can hear you." He continued to smile.

"I am leaving and you can't stop me," her voice was high and weak, panic steadily increasing, her hands pushing frantically on his hair-covered chest.

"You're going nowhere and I'll do exactly what I want with you, my beautiful little whore."

The word stung her. Foolishly, she defended herself. "I'm not, I love . . . loved you and . . ."

He snorted. "You fly to Mexico and shack up with a man you just met and you'd like me to believe it's because you love me?" He threw back his dark head and laughed. Laura struggled furiously. Abruptly the laughter stopped and his chiseled face was inches from her own. "You're no good. Just like my mother. Just like all the rest. All but Linda." He suddenly urged her up off his lap, rising with her. "You act like a bitch in heat, so that's the way I'll treat you."

Confused, frightened, she looked up into his cold silver eyes. Obviously he was crazy. She would play along with him; it was her only chance. "You're right, Ryker, I'm a bitch and . . ."

"Get on all fours, bitch," he commanded heavily and roughly pushed her to the floor, following her down. Outraged, terrified, she fought him valiantly. They wrestled and rolled about on the carpeted floor, she crying hysterically, he laughing demonically.

She clawed at the carpet, wild to escape, tears streaming down her hot cheeks. She managed to rise to her hands and knees; tried desperately to crawl away. She felt the crush of his weight as he draped himself over her back and covered her body with his.

She screamed, she jerked, she pleaded, she threatened.

He waited.

She tired long before he did and when she could no longer lift her arms to strike at him, nor her legs to kick at him, she collapsed, trembling, her face dipping wearily to the carpet. Ryker Rawley smiled and rose to his knees. He knelt behind her and with grasping, punishing hands, spread wide the cheeks of her bare buttocks.

Ryker forced his throbbing tumescence into her, clung to her narrow waist and recited in his head a childhood poem while his gray, glassy eyes stared out at the sun-splashed balcony and shimmering Pacific beyond. He was not about to allow himself to climax too quickly. Difficult as it was to hold himself in check, he was bent on doing so and had plenty of practice controlling his body. What worked best for him was a poem he had had trouble memorizing as a boy. The verse was tricky and he had to concentrate in order to recite it perfectly.

So he silently recited and kept his eyes averted from the fragile female back and lovely buttocks and lustrous dark hair. And when the poem was completed, he repeated it twice while the terrified girl below him wept in pain and heartbreak.

Pleased, thrusting cruelly, deeply, he leaned over Laura and coldly commanded, "Now bark, bitch. Bark for me. Bark." Finally, he quit taunting and then there was nothing but the sound of Laura's strangled, heartbroken sobs and his loud breathless grunting.

It was only the beginning.

Minutes later, when Laura cautiously turned over onto her back, Ryker, standing, smiled at her, leaned down, and jerked her to her feet.

"No," she screamed, and pulled away, her strong spirit and determination to survive surfacing. "I'm getting out of here, you sick bastard. I hate you, I hate you!" She rushed at him, kicking and hitting.

He laughed and held her off with one muscular forearm. And when she tired he forced her up against his bare, hard body. Effortlessly holding her to him, he said, "My fun is only beginning. You've so much to learn. So much," and he grabbed her long, tangled hair and twisted her face up to his. Laura looked up into those cold silver eyes and felt the blood in her veins congeal.

They stood there like that, eyes locked, for what seemed an eternity to Laura. And then Ryker's hands were atop her bare shoulders, applying pressure, slowly forcing her down and against his hot body. Laura's mouth and nose were trapped against his hairy chest. She could scarcely breath. His strong hands were clamping her to him, closer, ever closer.

Slowly, he continued to urge her down. Her open lips grazed his ribs, his belly, before he pushed her slightly back away from his body. She was on her knees before him. He was gripping her head, long fingers entwined in her flowing hair. Roughly, he tilted her face up, and looking down into her frightened eyes, ordered coldly, "Make it hard again, bitch. Do it." She gave him a half-angry, half-questioning look. He chuckled. "How? You take it in your mouth, that's how."

Laura gave a little strangled cry of despair before he pressed her face to his damp groin. She attempted to appease him with half-hearted, fluttering kisses to the pulsating member. It wasn't enough. He made that clear. It wasn't what he wanted from her. She would give him what he wanted or suffer the consequences.

Laura learned fast. She had no choice.

Ryker got what he wanted. And when it was over, she crawled away, choking, dazed, foolishly searching for the discarded robe. He snatched it out of her reach, put it on, and lit a cigarette. She started to rise from the floor; he told her to stay where she was. He took a seat on the linen sofa.

She couldn't believe her eyes when not a half-hour later, Ryker rose, slipped off the robe and came to her. He took her hand and laid it on male flesh that was rising again.

"No," she hissed, "I will not—"

"Shut your mouth and open your legs," said Ryker.

He took her over and over again, reminding her each time he was in her, that he was determined to make her pregnant. It seemed to Laura that, for hours, he lay atop her in the too-hot room, thrusting in and out, hurting her, using her, humiliating her.

There was no escape.

Ryker ripped up all of her clothes and threw them in the trash. At mealtime, he ordered from room service—raw oysters and rare steaks and scotch—and made her sit, wearing only his white dress shirt, beside him on the sofa, his gun poking her ribs, while the food was served. When she showered, he showered with her. She was not allowed out of his sight for a minute.

He was insatiable. A demon lover, tirelessly taking her with a bloodless passion that sickened and terrified her. He wanted more than to make her pregnant. He meant to degrade her in every conceivable way and he was a master at it.

Night fell.

Ryker took her into the bedroom, dumped her on the bed, and tied her hands over her head with his necktie. He left her, returning an hour later to find her tiredly struggling. "Hate me, do you, sweet?" he quizzed, standing above her, laughing at the look of fear and anger in her dark eyes. "I thought you loved me."

"You're an animal and I despise you," she managed, straining at the tight silk securing her hands to the bed's headboard.

"Do you now? Is that any way for the mother of my child to talk? I don't believe my little whore really hates me. I'll prove you don't." She didn't answer. Her body stiffened. What was he going to do now?

He fell on the bed with her, pushed her legs apart, and lowered himself between them. He slid all the way down until his face was between her open thighs. He lay there like that, on his stomach, hands stroking her inner thighs, silver-gray eyes watching her boredly, contemptuously.

His gaze went to the star birthmark on her left thigh. A forefinger rubbed back and forth over the tiny black imperfection, while his icy eyes stared at it disdainfully. "Just like the one on that arrogant bastard's face," he muttered coldly. He bent his head and kissed the birthmark. Then licked it. Then sucked it so forcefully, Laura cried out in pain. At last he lifted his head.

He shifted slightly, and lowered his face once more. Languidly he nuzzled the tight triangle of raven curls between her thighs. Laura tensed and tried to jerk away. He laughed and went to work. And he didn't stop until, against her will, her body afire from his intimate kisses, Laura was close, very close, to climaxing. So close she was straining upward against his hot, wet mouth, lost in the urgency of the moment.

Abruptly Ryker stopped, raised his head, and smiled. Her eyes flew open and she searched his demonic face. "I'm tired," he said, flatly, flipped over onto his back beside her and closed his eyes. Burning, hurting, Laura fought bitterly at the silk chains that bound her, ashamed, frustrated, in misery.

Minutes passed and her urgency with them. The throbbing subsided and stopped. The longing agony eased. The flushed skin cooled.

And when Ryker was certain, absolutely certain, that his unwilling playmate was no longer suffering, he took up his post between her legs once more and, deaf to her cries of fury and despair, once again caressed her with his mouth. And again he led her up, up, up, until she was aching for total release, blinded by animal passion, craving the ultimate ecstasy.

Mercilessly, he halted in mid-tongue-stroke and rolled away from her, taking up a cigarette, and lazily lighting it while she lay thrashing beside him, hurting. The pattern was repeated for a full two hours until at last, when he lay teasing her with his tantalizing tongue, bringing her once more to the brink, he said meanly, never lifting his lips from her flesh, "Beg me for it or I'll stop again. Beg me, bitch."

"Please," she whimpered desperately, feeling as though she would die if he took his mouth from her, "Please, Ryker. Please."

"That's my whore," he murmured and allowed her fulfillment at last.

Ryker continued to drink heavily of scotch and the flashes of violence he had shown grew more frequent, more alarming. His kisses were too forceful, his teeth on her nipples too sharp, his hands on her body, insensitive. He was a dangerous, drunken animal, a sexual sadist, subjecting Laura to a never-to-be-forgotten ordeal of perversion in a plush, hot chamber of horrors.

She was no longer allowed to shower. He liked her dirty, he told her, it suited her. She behaved like a South Ackard streetwalker, he wanted her to smell like one. Soon she did, because Ryker insisted that the air conditioner be left off, the balcony doors tightly closed. It was stifling hot inside the suite; the scent of sweat and sex heavy in the stuffy air.

It did not dampen his animalistic ardor. His depravity grew with each passing hour, with each glass of scotch, with the growing ripeness of their unwashed bodies. On the last day of her captivity, Laura lay, from the time the sun came up until it finally sank below the horizon, in the big rumpled bed while Ryker Rawley did every depraved, abnormal thing to her he had ever learned.

And when that endless day finally drew to its close, Laura McCarty's slender body was marked with bruises, as was her spirit. When Ryker fell from her at last, she was too tired, too hurt, to move. But when she heard soft snores rising from the naked, corrupt man, she determinedly dragged herself out of bed.

Too terrified to risk a bath, she crept quietly into the other room. She pulled on Ryker's soiled white shirt, grabbed her handbag and headed for the door. So sore and stiff she could barely walk, she let herself out of the suite and went at once to the boutique in the hotel lobby.

Jerking the first dress she saw from its hanger, she stumbled to the dressing room while open-mouthed clerks stared at her. She pulled the bright orange cotton dress down over her dirty, aching body, paid with a credit card, and hurried outdoors to the cab stand.

At the airport she had a bit of luck. The last plane for El Paso was leaving in fifteen minutes. Passengers stared at the young, pretty barefoot girl with the dark disheveled hair and the circles under her eyes and the bruised arms and legs, but Laura was oblivious to their curiosity.

It was not until she was in the air that she began shaking uncontrollably. She ordered a drink and was told by a smiling stewardess, "Sorry, hon, you're too young." Laura wanted to shout at her that she wasn't, that she would never be young again, that she was old and used. But she did not.

Laura laid her head back and closed her scratchy eyes.

She no longer wanted to be a singing star like her daddy. That dream was dead. Now she knew what he had meant when he had told her wistfully, on more than one occasion, that fame's price was high.

It had killed him. And now she had lived through unspeakable agony of a kind she could never have imagined. All because he had been a superstar.

Laura shifted a little in the seat. A burning, stabbing sensation shot through her groin. Softly, she moaned, and hoped against hope that she was not pregnant. Silently she wept for her lost innocence. Her lost youth. Her lost dreams.

CHAPTER THIRTY-FIVE

STEPPING onto the bare concrete porch in the scorching sun, Missy Graham gasped when she saw the bruised and battered Laura step from the rattling taxi. Arms open wide, Missy ran to meet her.

Babbling foolishly, "You'll be okay, Laura, we'll fix you up, don't worry. Don't worry. That bastard! That rotten bastard. He hurt you. They say he's mean to women and likes to beat them up and he . . . he . . . oh, Laura, speak to me. Are you alright?" Missy urged Laura into the cool ranch house.

While Laura soaked her aching body in a tub filled with bubbles, Missy pleaded with her to see a doctor, to call the police, to have the animal thrown in jail. Laura refused.

Zombielike, she reclined in the hot, steaming water, her eyes staring fixedly. "You know Ryker Rawley?" Laura asked quietly.

"I know of him. He's a sadistic bastard that likes to play devil-stud who . . ."

"He tried to kill my daddy." She lifted her eyes to Missy's. "He shot Buddy out in L.A."

Missy gaped. "That I didn't know. My, God, you're lucky to be alive. The man's a killer. I'm calling the police." She jumped up from the velvet vanity stool.

Eyes wild, Laura bounded, dripping suds, up out of the tub. "No! You are not, Missy Graham. No one is ever to know, do you hear me? If you're any friend of mine, you'll keep my secret."

Missy nodded, jerked a huge white towel from the rack, and swirled it around Laura's bare, bruised body. "I agree. But how can we be sure he won't come after you again?"

Laura said, "I've been a trusting fool; never again. Buddy will be close from now on." She sighed, then, and added, "Even without Buddy, Ryker Rawley won't bother me anymore."

"How can you be sure?"

"He's satisfied. The man's no fool; he knows I'll never report him because I couldn't bear the shame. And he knows, after what he did to me, I'll never be the same." She drew a shallow breath. "And if . . . if . . ." She closed her eyes and shook her head.

"If what, Laura?"

Laura's eyes came open. "If I am pregnant, well . . . Ryker Rawley will always be with me, won't he."

"Holy shit."

They were all there.

Mr. and Mrs. Toddie Lee Wynne, Jr. The Morgan Mayfields. The Jack Vaughns. The Henry Kyles. Clint Murchison. Mitch Lewis. The Gordon McClendons. The T. A. Rippeys. The Dave Scribners. The Cecil Triggs. The Hunts. The Meadows. The Johnsons. The Grahams.

And the younger set. Tanned, laughing Hockaday girls in pretty summer dresses. Tall, smiling young men, graduates of Greenhill and Southern Methodist University. Texas royalty gathered at the Mansfield Armstrong Parkway mansion for an outdoor gala.

A birthday party for Laura McCarty.

A fabulous fete thrown by Lenore Jesse and Caroline, an evening meant to be remembered by Laura all the days of her life. It would be, but for an entirely different reason.

Laura, in a stunning white sundress, stood looking cool, unruffled, and demure on the wide cement steps above the pool. The bruises had faded from her deep olive skin, her blue-black hair was parted in the middle and brushed straight down her bare back. She was not flashing her brilliant smile, nor chattering with Missy and the rest of her girlfriends.

There was about the sad young woman a new wistful quality that stirred the boisterous, red-blooded young men who turned to stare at her. There was a mystery about her. A depth to her that had not been there previously. An invisible appeal that drew them to the girl who was now more woman than they had recalled.

The last thing Laura had wanted was a birthday party. She had said as much a half-dozen times in the past week, and Caroline had questioned, "What's bothering you, Laura? You've not been the same since you got back from El Paso. Did something happen down there?" And her grandmother,

Lenore Jesse, had said, "Of course, you'll have a birthday party, I've sent out the invitations."

So Laura, forcing a smile to her lips, drew a deep breath and descended the steps beneath a canopy of hundreds of pink-and-white balloons, thinking morosely that black-and-blue would have been more appropriate. Dutifully she danced and made small talk and pretended a gaiety she did not feel. From a gauntlet of waiters parading about with silver trays, she lifted a glass of sparkling Tattigers and she visited the pink-and-white tent set up on the lawn, to sample the Beef Wellington and lobster and quail.

And at midnight, she blew out eighteen tall white candles atop a giant pink birthday cake.

"Did you make a wish, darling?" Her mother embraced her.

"I did," said Laura, thinking, Oh, did I.

The wish she made was a very private, very desperate one. It had been exactly eighteen days since she had been with Ryker Rawley. She had had no period since. She was late. Eight days late.

The birthday bash went on until the wee small hours. Tired, worried, Laura let out a loud sigh of relief when the last of the guests finally departed.

It was too late to return to *Cielo Vista*. They stayed the night at Armstrong Parkway; Donny and Caroline and Laura. Alone in bed, back aching, thoughts tumbling, memories flooding, Laura couldn't sleep. So she did what her daddy had done on more than one sleepless night. She slipped into a white spandex swimsuit and went down to the pool.

She dove gracefully into the lighted water and swam back and forth several times. Exhausted, she climbed lithely from the pool and went for her towel. Dripping, she stood drying her long dark hair when a tiny drop of blood fell on the smooth cement between her feet.

Laura's eyes widened.

She dropped the towel and excitedly examined herself. Her white suit, between her legs, was stained a bright crimson.

It was the best birthday present of all.

Caroline was puzzled, but pleased. The morning after the birthday party, Laura told her that she no longer wanted to sing. She wanted a college education. She was enrolling for fall classes at Southern Methodist, just as Caroline has always hoped she would.

Laura informed her mother that she intended to move back into Music-land. That way she would be close to the campus. Buddy would live there with her, keep an eye on her.

It was Laura's turn to be puzzled.

Caroline's flawless face had taken on a tight, strange expression. Apologetically, Caroline explained that it would be impossible for Laura to take up residence at Musicland. She and the trust officers had decided to open up the mansion to the paying public for conducted tours through the rooms and grounds between the hours of noon and dusk.

Laura was furious. The very idea of strangers tromping through Musicland! "My, God, Mother, you can't do it," Laura shook with anger, "Daddy never allowed strangers inside Musicland. It was his home. My home."

"Laura, it will bring a great deal of money into the estate and . . ."

"I don't care if it brings in millions! Daddy left plenty of money and even if he hadn't, I wouldn't want people going through Musicland."

"I'm sorry you feel that way, but I . . . and your trust officer feel it's in your best interest. Musicland will open to the public the weekend of the State Fair."

Laura said, "Well the date is fitting. You're making a carnival of my daddy's home, of his life. Set a ferris wheel up on the lawn. Pitch a freak tent out by Daddy's grave. Sell hot dogs and popcorn!"

At Arlington's Greenhouse, where Valentina Trent was spending a week of shaping up and slimming down, her breakfast was served to her in bed. A properly uniformed woman—simple black dress, white pinafore apron, black stockings, and black mid-heel shoes—quietly entered carrying an attractive white tray covered with a powder blue linen placemat. A matching napkin was folded beside a white porcelain bud vase containing a single yellow rose.

"Your breakfast, Mrs. Trent." The young woman smiled and placed the tray across her knees.

Valentina looked at the meager fare and wrinkled her nose. Another thirty-calorie breakfast. She was starving. Starving. Dispiritedly, she picked up the small crust-trimmed whole wheat toast and shoved half of it into her mouth.

The phone rang. Her secretary at Bluebonnet. She had, Viola told Valentina, received a call from Laura McCarty. Miss McCarty would like an appointment at Valentina's convenience. Should she set something up?

"You didn't tell her where I am, did you?"

"I've told everyone you're someplace in the Caribbean on the *Valentine*. Just as instructed."

"Good." Valentina was vain. She didn't want anyone in Dallas to know that she was at the establishment her friends referred to as the fat farm. It was

to be kept a secret, as was her recent visit to a famed plastic surgeon in
Buenos Aires. Only her secretary and Neil Allen knew where she was.
"Inform Miss McCarty that I'll be delighted to see her next Monday when
I've returned from my cruise."

She hung up the phone, more than a little curious. She drank her black
tea and pondered the possibilities. A brisk knock on the door broke into her
thoughts. It was time to begin her exercises. How could she exercise when
she was so weak from hunger?

"Do come in, Miss McCarty," Valentina, all smiles, welcomed the
young woman into her office. "What can I do for you?"

Laura studied the slightly overweight woman whom her father had so
disliked. "Mrs. Trent, I've come to buy my father's company back from
you."

"I see," said Valentina, still smiling. How like her daddy she is, thought
Valentina, contemptuously. Not only does she look like him, she's arrogant
too. Thinks she can march right in here and have her own way, just like
him. "Miss McCarty, it's not your father's company. It's mine."

Laura shook her head negatively. "Not really. Big Chief was built on his
talent, his hard work, his tremendous popularity. You have Bluebonnet,
Mrs. Trent. Sell me Big Chief."

"Correct me if I'm wrong. I was under the impression your fortune is tied
up in trust."

"It is, but I'm positive I can get my trust officers to release enough money
to buy back the company. I understand you purchased it for a mere five
hundred thousand dollars." Valentina gave no reply, just smiled and leaned
further back in her chair. Laura continued. "I realize you should make a
profit. I'll be glad to pay you a million dollars. Doubling your money in two
years should be satisfactory."

"Well, thank you, Paine Webber," Valentina said. "Let me tell you
something, dear. I wouldn't sell you my shares in Big Chief for five million.
How do like them apples?"

Laura flushed. "But why? Why do you insist on—"

"It's mine, that's why. It was always mine, or should have been. I gave
your daddy his first break, and what did I get for it? A slap in the face. A
'thanks, but no thanks.' An insult and desertion, that's what!"

"I never knew that—"

"There's a lot you don't know about your daddy. Shall I tell you a bit
about him? You're a big girl, don't you think it's time you got your head out
of the sand?"

"Mrs. Trent, I am not interested in hearing—"

"You're going to hear, because I'm going to tell you. You think he was a great man? Ha! He was weak, a loser who died because he couldn't stay off drugs." Laura's eyes widened. Valentina laughed and continued. "Oh, yes, The Chief was 'living better through chemistry.' One of the biggest pillpoppers in the business."

"No . . ." Laura felt sick.

"Yes," Valentina liked the stricken look on Laura's face. "And I orchestrated the whole thing, in case you've any doubts about my power."

"That's absurd. You were never around my daddy."

"No, but the first pills he took, I ordered given to him. So were the last. He was a weak, helpless puppet on a string. I pulled the string all his life."

Shaking her head in bewilderment and anger, Laura said, "How could you . . ."

"Easy. C.C. had no willpower. None. Besides the pills, there was the booze. He was a lush. I can't take credit for that." She smiled. "Remember all those glasses of ice water you saw in his hand. Vodka. He swilled it night and day and I'll tell you what else he had a weakness for. Women. Couldn't get enough. Stayed in bed more than he stayed on stage. They say he would stick it in the crack of dawn if he could rise in time. He was so bad that he . . ."

While Valentina rambled, the truth dawned on Laura. Suddenly it was very clear why this vindictive woman hated her daddy. She wanted him for herself.

"Now I understand," Laura, interrupting, slowly rose to her feet and gripped the desk's edge. Leaning over it, she said, "All these years I've wondered. Now I know."

Valentina, flustered, blinked up at her. "Know? Know what?"

Laura calmly smiled. "There was one woman he wouldn't stick it in, huh, Valentina?"

"I . . . I don't know what you mean. He was an animal, he . . ."

"Not animal enough to give you any, bless him. That's why you hated him. Why you wanted to destroy him."

"That's a lie! I never wanted him, I . . . I . . ."

"It's the truth and we both know it." It was Laura's turn to laugh. She did, throwing back her head in merriment, while Valentina sputtered and cursed and denied everything. When she'd calmed, Laura said coldly, "Listen to me, you pathetic old bitch, and remember my words. Never have I been as proud of daddy as I am now. He refused to touch you even though it would have meant instant stardom. He wasn't for sale. The man had even more class than I knew. But, then, class is something you know nothing about."

"You can't talk to me like that!" Valentina struggled to her feet. "That's no way to get what you want. You're as stupid as he."

"You'll see how stupid I am. Get ready for a long, bloody battle, Mrs. Valentina Trent, and you'll tire much sooner than I. You're already looking fatigued. How old are you? Fifty? Fifty-five?"

"Of all the—"

"You'll wish you had never heard of me or my daddy. I'll take artists away from Bluebonnet and I'll—"

"You don't scare me one bit."

"I'll give you a run for your money, believe it. And then sooner or later, I'll get Big Chief back. One way or the other, I'll get it back. Perhaps not next week or next month, but I'll get it back."

"You little fool, get out of my office. You'll take nothing from me, nothing!"

"Oh, yes, I will, Mrs. Trent. Count on it."

"Out!"

The eight-room 3525 Turtle Creek penthouse had never been furnished. Laura contacted a brilliant young builder whose unique designs were the talk of Dallas.

Harvey Ritche was happy to help out and soon plush, comfortable pumpkin couches and chocolate ultra-suede chairs dominated the spacious living room. Overstuffed, soft pillows were scattered all over the deep beige carpet. Glass-and-chrome tables gleamed in autumn sunshine.

Laura, in an effort to mend fences, solicited her mother's help in picking household items. Caroline was delighted.

She insisted Laura have several pairs of fine Irish linen, hand-embroidered Frette sheets as well as custom Porthault tablecloths for the gleaming rosewood dining table. She chose Wedgewood's Ulander Powder Blue china, Buccellati silver, and Baccarat crystal.

Champagne-and-powder blue towels soon hung in the baths, and a padded headboard, covered in blue raw silk, graced Laura's king-sized bed. Blue-and-white Chinese porcelain vases dotted tabletops and small Oriental rugs added pattern to the rooms.

It was an elegant, attractive apartment. A warm, comfortable dwelling. A beautiful place. Still, it wasn't home.

It wasn't Musicland.

CHAPTER THIRTY-SIX

CATTLE and crude was the answer.

Where did ya'll's money come from? was the question.

Missy Graham had adopted the reply for her own when she was no more than three years old. Seated atop the knee of her strapping rancher daddy, Bennett Graham, she heard him use those words to a wide-eyed eastern reporter when the man had visited their biggest ranch, a seven-hundred-thousand-acre spread just outside Benjamin, Texas.

The simple declarative statement had brought a wide grin to the young columnist and a devilish twinkle to her daddy's sun-squinty eyes. The very next day when Missy climbed in the pickup and went to town with her daddy, she informed his coffee-drinking buddies at the Matador Cafe that, "We're rich from cattle and crude."

It brought howling laughter from the overall-clad farmers and denim-trousered ranchers. Bennett Graham laughed loudest of all.

It was fact.

Bennett Graham had been born and raised on the vast Benjamin spread. The year he went away to college at Texas Tech over in Lubbock, oil was discovered. He liked to joke that their white-faced Herefords had turned as dark as their Saint Gertrudis, what with all that crude spewing up out of the ground.

At Tech, Bennett met an attractive young girl from Andrews. Patsy Mayhan happened to be the only child of a man who owned not one, but three Texas cattle ranches. The home place was near Andrews, a smaller spread down close to Pecos, and another—that they called *Roja Rosa*—thirty miles outside El Paso.

With the wedding of Bennett Graham and Patsy Mayhan, two of the largest ranching empires in all Texas merged. Bennett took Patsy home to Benjamin. Missy was born there a couple of years later. At first Patsy was content, but she soon got "uppity ideas," Bennett Graham complained. She was bored with living on a ranch; she wanted to move to the city.

"Well, hellfire," said Bennett, "let's go on over to Lubbock and buy us a big home then."

Patsy snorted. "Lubbock is still the sticks. I've thought it all out, Ben. We'll move up to Dallas."

"Dallas?" thundered Bennett, "Why in the Sam Hill would anybody want to move to Dallas? Let's go down to San Antone."

Patsy quickly explained to her husband that in San Antonio there was a definite, ruling "old guard." Families that had been there since the Alamo and would not accept newcomers into the inner circle. But in Dallas, most of the big money had come with the oil boom. Patsy said that if a person was rich enough and dropped enough into the charitable coffers, it didn't matter if he'd just been in Dallas a week. A sizable contribution to the symphony or the art museum would probably do the trick.

Instant members of Dallas' elite.

"Patsy, honey, you telling me that by just me donating a chickenshit little dab of money to their charities you'll be gettin' invitations to their homes?" Bennett sucked on a Camel.

"That's what I hear."

"Well, hell, if it'll make you happy, let's get on up there and find us a big home."

The Grahams were warmly welcomed into the drawing rooms of Dallas. No one minded that Bennett Graham cussed a blue streak, told off-color stories, and showed up at black-tie events in his shiny western suits and a Stetson. Nor that Patsy Graham talked and laughed too loud, and asked blunt, probing questions, and drank her bourbon straight.

A palatial home in Highland Park, a fleet of long Cadillacs, hot-and-cold running house servants, and deep, deep pockets from which to donate generously to a never-ending stream of civic causes established for the Grahams an unshakable position in Dallas society.

Bennett and Patsy hadn't changed much over the years, except that they had grown richer. And they had grown apart. Patsy liked her long, social lunches with the girls, her spring shopping trips to Paris, her summers in the South of France. And her bourbon.

Bennett, the maverick, a man born to the big outdoors, felt stifled in Dallas. He preferred riding horses to riding in his Cadillacs, wide-open spaces to city limits. And the company of his of cattle to most people. He spent more time on their four ranches than he did in Highland Park.

All who knew Patsy and Bennett Graham agreed that the flamboyant Missy was a fiery blend of them both, with only a few of the rough edges polished away. Mischievous, inquisitive, and perceptive, Missy, from early childhood could get away with murder. With her parents. With her teachers. With her friends.

Behavior that would have been considered outrageous and unforgivable in any other young girl was overlooked, indulged, even applauded, in Missy Graham. As plainspoken as her mother and as fearless as her father, Missy went on her merry way doing exactly as she pleased. She was, she pointed out more than once to Laura, Missy Graham, only heir to one of the biggest fortunes in all Texas. If that didn't grant her carte blanche, what the hell did?

If her daddy couldn't buy it for her, then it just couldn't be had, was the way she looked at it.

Missy said what she had on her mind, did anything she took a notion to do, and paid no attention to raised eyebrows and whispered gossip. In her teenage years she blossomed into, if not a beautiful girl, at least an attractive one with her thick blond hair and flawless white skin and a ready smile.

She and Laura made a striking pair. Both tall, Laura was dark, slender, and exotically beautiful. Missy fair, voluptuous, and appealingly pretty. Both were outgoing and fun-loving, although Laura was more graciously well mannered than the charmingly crass, spoiled Missy. Strange bedfellows, some people commented, as different in character as in looks.

Missy lay stretched out in the living room at 3525, hugging a powder blue throw pillow. Laura sat on one of the pumpkin couches, meticulously painting her toenails. And relating everything that had taken place at Valentina's. Missy, interrupting often, listened with excited interest.

When Laura had finished, Missy was sitting up, clapping her hands in admiration. "Anything I can do to help you lampoon that viperous old redhead, let me know. Any enemy of yours is an enemy of mine."

"Do you suppose," mused Laura, "that Valentina has anybody fooled? Does Dallas' upper crust . . . including Grandmother Mansfield . . . have any idea . . ."

"You have to hand it to her, Valentina is one shrewd old broad. She shows up at all the important civic events on the arm of her company vice president and behaves as though he's the only man in her life. She never drinks to excess, never flirts with anybody's husband, never does one unladylike thing. And, most importantly, she contributes large sums of money to the charities."

Laura sighed. "I'm going to get Big Chief back, Missy. The thought of that woman owning daddy's records and movies makes me physically ill. Damn her. And damn Ash Ashford."

"You're being too hard on Ash. The poor guy's probably more upset about it than you. Good Lord, he lost everything. The company, his wife, everything. I feel sorry for him."

"I can't forgive him, Missy. Of all the people he could have sold to, he sold to Valentina."

"Oh, come on, Ash is a sick gambler. Valentina was there at the opportune time. Under the circumstances, he would have sold to the Devil."

"Valentina *is* the Devil."

Missy laughed. "Let's forget her. In two hours I have a date with a simply gorgeous Dallas Cowboy rookie receiver. He's got a real cute teammate. Why don't I tell him—"

"No," Laura said calmly, "I have to study."

Missy made a face. "Don't use that word in front of me, I find it offensive. Take a break; we'll all go out to Gordo's."

"No, Missy."

Missy was worried about her friend. "Laura, you've got to forget about Rawley and what he did to you."

"Sure," Laura said sarcastically. "Nothing to it."

"Okay, okay, so it will take a while. But you could use a little fun. These guys are sweethearts. Say you'll go."

"Some other time."

Laura stayed up past midnight, pouring over her business law books. Exhausted, she climbed into bed, yawned, switched off the bedside lamp, closed her eyes, and fell asleep.

"Laura, honey, you alright?" Buddy Hester, banging loudly on her door, awakened her an hour later from the terrifying nightmare that had caused her to cry out.

Hair wringing wet with perspiration, heart pounding in her chest, Laura threw on a robe and hurried to the door. Opening it wide, she apologized, "Bud, I'm sorry. It was a dream, just a bad dream."

His worried face relaxed. "You okay, hon? Want to wake the cook and have her fix you some hot chocolate or something?"

"No, thanks. I'm fine, really I am."

He smiled. "I ain't gonna let anything ever happen to you, Laura. No need for worrying."

"I know. Night, Bud."

"Sleep well, hon."

She closed the door and returned to bed. And lay awake a long troubled time, trembling in the darkness, in the grip of the nightmare's terror. Each time she closed her eyes she saw a pair of demonic silver eyes and heard a cruel, deep voice. And experienced once more the pain and shame of being used in the most grotesque ways.

Laura's brilliant, beautiful smile was less in evidence, her eagerness for life and adventure, sadly diminished. She felt unclean and hollow, as though she would never again be whole. Those who knew her best worried and commented on the change, but Laura shrugged off their questions of concern with the shake of her dark head.

The opposite sex, who had always found her appealing, now were helplessly drawn by her dark, smouldering beauty, her mature sexual allure. Where before she had been a happy, giggling young girl, she was now, overnight, a mysterious, magnetic woman, whose strangely wistful eyes held a secret in their depths that every red-blooded male longed to uncover.

At eighteen, Laura McCarty exuded the same potent animal sexuality that had made her father irresistible to women. The aura of mystery about her added to that charm. Men wanted her, desired her instantly, longed to make hot, passionate love to her. At the same time, there was about her a cool and distant air that made all but the boldest afraid to approach her.

Laura was sure that the only reason males pursued her was because she was C.C.'s daughter. It never occurred to her that she was a beautiful young woman who would have attracted attention had she not been the offspring of a famous entertainer. She knew she looked so much like him that the entire world realized she was C.C.'s daughter the minute they saw her. That's why men wanted her. How many, she wondered, were like Ryker Rawley. How many secretly hated her and wanted to make her pay.

In the three years she studied for her business degree at SMU, she dated less than a half-dozen times. And all with the same disastrous results.

Over-sexed, over-anxious males with nothing on their minds but getting her into bed so that they could brag that they had slept with C.C.'s daughter. Frightened, disgusted, Laura vowed each time she would never again go out on a date. Their heated lips on hers, their rough hands pawing at her body brought back all the frightening horror she associated with sex.

She was having none.

Missy Graham, on the other hand, was having more than her share. A freshman cheerleader, she laughingly told Laura her acrobatics on the football turf were nothing compared to the ones in the back seat of her boyfriend's parked car.

Dave Lovell, she noted, had fallen for her the minute he found out she was sole heir to the Bennett cattle and oil fortune. Missy didn't care. He was devastatingly handsome and as horny as she—an unbeatable combination. He didn't like studying; neither did she. He cut all his classes. She did too. While their friends poured over books and wrote themes and gave speeches, Missy and Dave studied sex. Together.

Dave Lovell flunked out of school at midterm. He blamed it on Missy. Missy decided she couldn't possibly care for a man who was so ungallant. After all, she had flunked out, too, and she didn't blame him.

Far from being heartbroken over the loss of Dave or of college, Missy took a much-needed vacation to New York, and on the return flight sat next to a distinguished, forty-six-old electronics executive who found her delightful. When the plane landed in Dallas, Missy climbed into Walt Davis's waiting limo and went with him to his condo in far North Dallas.

"Look, Walt," she pointed in passing to a huge salmon stucco building under construction and barely visible at the end of a small country lane, "why are they building a hotel way out here?"

He laughed. "That's a private home, Missy. Some rich Venezuelan fellow is building a villa."

"Jesus, it's so huge, he must have a dozen kids."

"No," said Walt Davis, "they say Arto DiGrassi is a confirmed bachelor."

"And you?" Missy ventured.

Walt laughed. "Been married three times already." He reached for her. "And I still like to play house."

Laura graduated with honors at age twenty and promptly called a meeting with her trust officers. She was going into business, she told them. She intended to start up a recording company and she needed money.

The two middle-aged trust officers tried to hide their amusement. A twenty-year-old child running a company. Why, the idea was preposterous. They were paid to look after her best interests. Allowing her to borrow against her trust fund for such an improbable undertaking was simply out of the question.

Laura McCarty could be very persuasive when she wanted something badly. And she wanted to start a record company. If Valentina Trent had control of Big Chief, why then she, Laura, was going into direct competition with Valentina's Bluebonnet Records.

Laura remained in the Republic Bank offices throughout the afternoon, presenting her well-thought-out plans to the two astonished officers. Like a seasoned businesswoman, she showed them a detailed business plan, explaining cost estimates, assuring them she could get capable people to work for her, pointing out that some of the talented people her daddy had worked with over the years would be available for the new project.

Laura lifted her fluted champagne glass and smiled. Joined by her five full-time employees, she drank to the first anniversary of Lone Star Records.

It had been a long, sometimes disappointing year, but she had made it. Working day and night to make it go, Laura had spent almost all her time at Lone Star's offices on North Central Expressway. And now, after losing money consistently, she could see light at the end of the tunnel, and with any luck, Lone Star's second year would actually produce a small profit.

Laura talked and joked with her employees, thanked them all for their loyalty, and promised salary raises soon. That brought applause.

"I mean it," said Laura. "I'm sure Paul's single will be a hit." Her dark eyes twinkled. "If it charts, everybody starts getting bigger paychecks."

More applause. Laura, smiling at Paul Peterson, accepted another glass of champagne, and waved aside Paul's whispered worry that he might let them all down.

"You won't, so relax," she told her newly acquired recording artist.

Paul Peterson was not yet a big name, but Laura was delighted to have him under contract at Lone Star. A nice, likeable man, he was terrifically talented, hard-working, and anxious to be famous. Best of all, he had been snatched from under Valentina's nose twenty-four hours before he was to sign a Bluebonnet contract.

Laura glanced at her watch. One o'clock. She was late. She had promised Missy she would pick her up at one. Handing her half-finished glass of champagne to Paul, she said, "I'm sorry, I have to leave, but ya'll go on partying. Better yet, lock up and go home if you like. I won't be back this afternoon." More applause.

At the Graham home, a maid let Laura in. Laura sauntered into the high-ceilinged living room. She paused. A man, his back to her, was crouched before the fireplace, his head half-hidden in the flue. Laura cleared her throat. A blond head ducked out of the fireplace and he rose to his feet.

"A little early to be expecting Santa, isn't it?" teased Laura.

"Not really," said the man, eyes pointedly sweeping over her, "looks like old St. Nick has delivered exactly what I asked for."

Laura felt herself blushing.

His face broke into a broad grin. Tall and slim, he had thick, sun-tipped blond hair, a narrow, suntanned face, piercing blue eyes, an aristocratic nose, and a very appealing mouth. He was dressed casually in a V-necked sweater of ice-blue wool, a pair of impeccably tailored gray wool slacks, and well-polished black shoes.

And he was very handsome.

He came forward, hand outstretched. "I'm Stephen Flynn, and believe it or not, I don't make a habit of snooping around in people's fireplaces."

"Laura McCarty, Mr. Flynn," she took his hand. "I hope I can believe that."

He refused to release her hand. "I'm an architect, Laura. Patsy Graham wants me to design a lake house for the Bennetts. She wants fireplaces like the one in this room."

Laura, smiling, extracted her hand from his. "Have I heard of you, Mr. Flynn?"

"Stephen. No, I'm sure you haven't. I've been in Europe for the past eight years. I returned to the states last month."

Laura nodded. "I hope you'll be staying for a while."

"He will," it was Missy's throaty voice. "Patsy'll keep him tied up for a year." She stalked into the room, buttoning the cuffs of her blouse. "Stevie, want to come to lunch with Laura and me?"

Laura held her breath. She hoped he would say no.

"No, thanks, Missy. I was just leaving. Nice to meet you, Laura."

CHAPTER THIRTY-SEVEN

DAWN was breaking over the Chihuahuan desert. El Paso and Juarez were slowly coming to life. At the outer perimeter of El Paso International Airport, Billy Bledsoe unlocked the door of Bledsoe Charter Service.

"Ryker? Where are you? Ryker, you here yet?" Bledsoe flicked on the lights, glanced at his watch, and cursed under his breath. Ryker Rawley was scheduled to fly an El Paso stockbroker to San Diego at 6:30 A.M. "That bastard," Bledsoe said, "he's at it again. Son of a bitch!"

Across the border a tiny clapboard shack, painted a nauseating shade of chartreuse, sat nestled deep in a barren arroyo. The house rules were posted in plain sight in the dusty front yard. "Check your gun at the door." The shack was open twenty-four hours of the day, seven days a week, and there were always at least a dozen people inside. Customers.

Ryker Rawley had arrived at the house shortly after 3:00 A.M. Drunk when he walked in the door, he focused with difficulty on the tiny tinfoil-wrapped pellets displayed on mirrors. He picked up one, studied it, replaced it, and chose another. He smiled and nodded his head.

Next he chose a woman from the four pretty, young Mexican women standing stiffly against the wall like suspects in a police lineup.

Choices made, he ordered a bottle of scotch, took the whiskey, the cocaine, and the woman back to a tiny partitioned cubicle in a rear room. There, he shed all his clothes and ordered the woman to disrobe. Naked, he sat spraddle-legged on the narrow, unsheeted bed and drank the scotch while the woman kissed him and stroked him and tried her best to arouse him.

Bored with her attempts to please, Ryker knocked her rudely away and produced the tiny pellet that would make his ugly, sordid world a beautiful, sparkling place. Eyes glazing, he freebased the cocaine, smoking the pipe with eagerness, waiting for the euphoria this god he worshipped could produce.

Within seconds the ultimate high came. Ryker reached a summit of pleasure ten times as powerful as any he'd attained when he merely sniffed the coke.

Unlike most freebasers, the love of coke did not kill his sex drive. The incomparable highs had the opposite effect.

He reached for the pretty brown-skinned girl. For the next supremely pleasurable seven minutes—while the incredible high lasted—he aggressively took her, shoving her down on her back, slamming her knees up against her chest and pounding into her with a rapid driving force that brought the seasoned prostitute to shuddering climax. He continued, wild-eyed, in paradise, thrusting, bucking, sweating, until the magical seven minutes ended and he crashed back to reality with a painful thud.

With the come-down came immediate depression. And anger. Still buried deep within the panting girl, Ryker snarled his disgust and slapped her hard across the face. She didn't make a sound, though blood spurted from her split bottom lip. She didn't dare complain.

Ryker Rawley was one of the house's most frequent customers, spending large sums of money. Her brother, the enterprising Mexican who operated the house, had warned her never to make trouble, to satisfy Rawley at all costs. To make him happy. She tried, just as the other girls did, and had said nothing on the occasions when Ryker had beaten her, blackened her eyes, and left bruises and teeth marks on her breasts and belly and the insides of her thighs.

It wouldn't have done any good. Her brother was in the next room. He heard and did not care. He would have beaten her if she displeased his best customer. Blood wiped away on a rag, the uncomplaining girl spent the next three hours in the close cubicle with a pleasure-seeking Ryker Rawley. He drank more Scotch. He smoked the cocaine pipe again. He used her again. And again. And again.

And when finally he dressed to go, he cursed her for keeping him from his appointment. "You goddamned whore," he said, "you knew I was supposed to be at work by dawn." He grabbed her arm and snatched her up off the mattress. "I ought to kill you. I ought to . . ." He flung her away from him. She landed across the bed. His mood immediately shifted. He grinned suddenly, leaned down, and kissed her on the mouth. "I'll be back to see you tonight, baby. Clean yourself up for me."

He lifted the curtain and was gone.

* * *

He was in the depths of depression when he showed up, an hour late, at Bledsoe Charter Service. Spoiling for trouble, he found it in his old pal, Billy Bledsoe.

Heated words passed between the two Vietnam buddies and a few punches were thrown. Bledsoe, far the bigger and stronger of the pair, quickly overwhelmed the slender, strung-out Rawley.

He said, "That's it, Ryker. No more. You're a damned coke head and I'm fed up with you. Find somebody else who'll put up with your shit, I'm tired of it."

"You mean you're firing a decorated veteran of your country?" Somewhere far behind the dead mean eyes was the hint of a self-mocking smile. This time it didn't work on his old friend.

"I've had it. Get out," said Bledsoe.

"Fuck you."

"Fuck you."

"I don't need you, Bledsoe," Ryker said. "I'm a good pilot. I'll go somewhere else and get a job."

Bledsoe snorted. "You can't get anything in El Paso."

"Fuck El Paso. I'm going to Dallas."

The phone rang in Laura's Lone Star office. Distracted, thoughts on the afternoon's upcoming recording session, she said, "Yes?"

"How did you know the answer when I've not yet asked the question?"

"Well, I . . . Who is this?" Laura frowned, unable to place the voice, though it sounded slightly familiar.

"Steve Flynn. I want to buy you lunch; you just said you'd go."

She laughed. "I did no such thing."

"In case you've forgotten me, I'm the guy you found up the Graham's fireplace."

"I remember."

"Will you have lunch with me?"

"Yes."

"Good. Pick you up at 12:30." And he hung up.

Slowly, Laura replaced the receiver. It had been months since she had met Stephen Flynn at Missy's. She had halfway expected him to call. He never had and she was glad. Now he had called. And she was glad.

It was her favorite restaurant. The Mansion on Turtle Creek. A few blocks down from her penthouse apartment, the expensive eatery was a restored 1920s mansion. Marble floors, carved fireplaces, inlaid wood ceilings, and paneled walls echoed the glory of a grander era. The food was excellent—Laura ordered the sauteed Dover sole while Stephen chose roast quail—and the ambiance, quiet and genteel, was conducive to relaxing and enjoying the meal.

Laura did just that.

She sat across the intimate, pink-draped table and sipped white wine while Stephen Flynn amused and entertained her with tales of his failures and triumphs of the past eight years designing country homes for Europe's wealthy landed gentry.

"Why did you decide to return to the U.S.?"

He shrugged. His blue eyes twinkled. "I woke up one morning in London. It was raining. As usual. I couldn't take it anymore." He grinned, boyishly. "I'm a Texan. I like the sun. I look better with a tan, don't you agree?"

"Very fit," she replied, thinking he looked gorgeous.

The conversation got around to her work, her life. She wondered how much he knew about her, about her daddy. She mentioned her daddy's name several times. Stephen Flynn seemed not all that interested, not all that impressed. Laura was relieved. She liked this tall, slim handsome man. She wanted to see him again. She wanted him to want to see her again.

And not because she was C.C.'s daughter.

Time swiftly passed and neither realized they were the only people remaining in the elegant room. It was nearing 3:30. A patient busboy, hands clasped behind him, stood beside the kitchen door, waiting for them to leave.

"Is he trying to tell us something?" Stephen indicated the white-coated man.

"He needs to get to work. And so do I," said Laura.

"I really enjoyed it, Laura," said Stephen Flynn, when he dropped her at the office. "Let's do it again and soon."

"I'd like that, Stephen."

It was weeks before he called her again. Late one Friday afternoon. He said he'd been busy. She said she had too. "Let's put on our jeans tonight and go over the Casa Dimingous for some good Tex-Mex food?"

"I'm wearing jeans right now."

"I'll be there in half an hour."

They had fun, just like before, and Laura was only a little nervous when, returning to her apartment, Stephen invited himself up. She needn't have been. He was the perfect gentleman. They drank coffee before the fire and talked until the wee hours.

When she could no longer stifle her yawns, Stephen smiled and rose. He urged her with him to the door and there in the foyer, bent his blond head down and kissed her. His lips were soft and warm. And undemanding.

"Get some sleep, sweetheart, I'll call you tomorrow."

"Please do," she said, and meant it.

He did. Soon they were inseparable. She shared her hopes and plans with him. Told him about her struggle with Valentina Trent. Told him she was bound and determined to get Big Chief back somehow, someway. Any way.

He told her he had come from an old and highly respected San Antonio family. That he'd studied architecture at Rice University, and that upon graduation, he had gone immediately to New York. After five years there he moved on to Paris and London. Told her that he was thirty-three years old and had never found the right time, or the right girl, to marry.

Laura liked Stephen Flynn very much. He was kind and considerate. Fun and mischievous. Industrious and talented. Well groomed and handsome.

Best of all, he didn't scare her. The exact opposite of Ryker Rawley, Stephen neither frightened nor excited her. There was no danger in his beautiful blue eyes, no coiled power in his trim frame. She felt no tingle of alarm or desire with him, she felt only comfort and warmth.

His kisses were never fiery and forceful, as Ryker's had been. They were warm and pleasant. Affectionate.

The relationship was good. She had her work. He had his work. They were the best of friends.

"I'll do you now," said Mr. Frederick, the pencil-slim hairdresser at the exclusive beauty salon, "Best Tressed."

Laura laid aside the copy of "D" magazine, slipped the Hermes scarf from her hair, and followed the diminutive man across the deep rose carpet, through the burgundy velvet-draped archway, and into the gold-and-rose work rooms of the exclusive salon.

When Laura emerged from the shampoo room, she came face to face with Valentina Trent. Valentina smiled as though they were old friends.

"I've some news for you, McCarty," Valentina said, reaching out to take Laura's upper arm.

Laura, black eyes leveled like a laser on Valentina, said calmly, "Take your hand from my arm."

Valentina promptly obeyed. "Aren't you interested in my news?"

"Nothing you do interests me, Mrs. Trent." Laura stepped around Valentina.

"Oh, I think this will," Valentina called after her. "I'm pulling all the C.C. McCarty videos and records off the market. Withdrawing the performing rights to C.C.'s repertoire from radio, TV, cable, and live performance.

Laura stopped in her tracks. She whirled about, the towel slipping from her wet, heavy hair to the thick rose carpet. "You can't do that."

"Oh, but I can," smirked Valentina, her rose smock gaping open to expose the tops of her big breasts. "I control Big Chief, remember."

"But you wouldn't," Laura said. "You'd lose more money than I and . . ."

"I've plenty of money, child. I don't need the piddling little amount those movies and records earn. Bluebonnet makes my fortune." She laughed softly. "But you need the residuals and performing royalties, don't you, dear? Even with your underhanded stealing of my artists, I'm sure Lone Star Records hasn't made a profit, nor will it." She clicked her tongue. "The way you spend money, you'll be broke when Big Chief quits producing."

"Is there no limit to how far you'll go to get even because my daddy wouldn't screw you?" Laura said, turned, and started toward a hair dryer.

Valentina looked nervously around the crowded hair salon. "Keep your voice down, you little bitch." She rushed forward and again took Laura's arm. "You don't know what you're talking about and I—"

"Sure I do," said Laura and again removed Valentina's hand from her arm. She sat down beneath a dryer, smiled up at Valentina, and added in a pleasant, even voice, "and so does everyone in Dallas." She pulled the dryer down over her head.

Seething, Valentina jerked the dryer right back up and snapped, "You hateful hussy, there was never anything between your no-good daddy and me! He was poor white trash and in case you don't read the columns, I go about with the elite of Dallas!" She gave Laura a smug smile, slammed Laura's dryer back down and took the one next to her.

Laura waited until the plump redhead was comfortably settled. Then she reached over, turned off Valentina's dryer, and said, "You may go about with the Dallas elite; you go to bed with contracted Bluebonnet entertainers." She calmly turned Valentina's heat back on.

Furious, Valentina shoved up her dryer, then raised Laura's. "That is the most derogatory, absurd statement I've ever heard. Where do you get off saying—"

"In the business," Laura smoothly cut in, "every singer and musician from Corpus to Chicago knows what it takes to make it at Bluebonnet." She lowered her dryer.

Her brows knitted, her blood pressure shooting sky high, Valentina shouted to be heard, "It takes extraordinary talent, that's what!" She ducked back under her own dryer, and added indignantly, "C.C. McCarty was a mediocre talent at best, so there was no place for him at Bluebonnet!"

Laura grinned and pulled Valentina's dryer up. Speaking in pleasant, conversational tones, she said, "Come off it, Valentina. There was no place for him at Bluebonnet because there was no place for you in his bed." Laughing easily, she moved again under her dryer.

Valentina angrily jerked it back up as soon it was down and, red-faced, threatened loudly, "You'll pay for that, you foul-mouthed little slut! I'll ruin you, just like I ruined him. You're two of a kind and I'll fix you good!" A smile spread over her face when Laura's laughter stopped abruptly. She waited for Laura to speak. But Laura said nothing. Extremely pleased with herself for having had the last word, Valentina sighed with satisfaction, picked up a magazine, and put her head back under her dryer.

Laura drew a deep, slow breath. She lifted her dryer. She reached up and flipped off Valentina's. She said, her voice level, determined, and loud enough for all to hear, "That's where you're wrong. Pull the records and movies off the market. Withdraw the performing rights from radio and television. Do anything you can dream up, but you won't stop me, Valentina. You're underestimating me if you think you will. You say I'm just like my daddy, well you've misjudged me. I'm not nearly as kind and forgiving as C.C. McCarty. Or as weak." She leaned closer, her face only inches from Valentina's. "You fucked him over until he died. You won't fuck over his daughter for long."

And she cranked Valentina's hair dryer up to Ultra High—let her bake.

Missy said to her, "Laura, I'm glad you came over for dinner. I hate to eat alone."

"Patsy and Bennett both out of town?"

Missy nodded. "Mother's in New York. Daddy's in Benjamin." She led Laura into the living room.

"Stephen's in San Francisco so I was glad to come, Missy. I'm starving. Will it be long?"

"A phone call away," replied Missy.

"Oh, no," said Laura, "we're eating out?" She knew eating out to Missy meant fast food.

Missy grinned.

Ignoring the fleet of cars in the garage, Missy called up Southwest Limo. She squinted at the liveried driver. He was a new one. A young man she'd never seen. Missy knew most of the drivers in Dallas.

"The Burger King on Lemon," she instructed the visored chauffeur and turned to Laura. "I want to go down on a Whopper, how about you?"

"Has anyone ever told you you're nuts, Missy?"

"Lots of guys. That's why I wanted you to come over. My love life is a shambles. I need help fast."

"I'm hardly the one to—"

"I desperately need a date for Saturday. I've wracked my brain and can't come up with anybody."

"That shouldn't be too big a problem. Where's the hip squad hanging out these days?"

"Joe Miller's Bar down on Maple, but I went there last night. No luck. Time's running out."

"I thought you were seeing the Preston Hollow tennis pro."

"No more. We have a love-hate relationship. I love him. He hates me."

"Missy, Missy. What about that banker you were . . . ."

"I warned him there would be a substantial penalty for early with-drawals," Missy said, eyes twinkling.

Laura laughed. "Walt Davis?"

"Old saggy balls? I got tired of him over a year ago."

Accustomed to Missy's mouth, Laura glanced at the driver; he was grinning. "You mentioned you met a good-looking man out at Northpark a couple of weeks ago. What ever happened—"

"Skip Davidson. Sure he looked great that day at the Mall. I made a date with him and he showed up with clocks on his socks." She made a face.

"I give up . . . I don't . . . oh, I know. What about old megarich Thomas Murphy, I read he's back in town and—"

Missy opened her mouth wide and stuck her forefinger into it, making the gesture of gagging. "He is ugly and doesn't shave everyday. I'd rather spend a weekend in bed with Yasser Arafat."

Laura was laughing; so was the chauffeur. Laura leaned forward and said to the man, "How about it? Can you help out my friend? She's having trouble finding a date."

The driver turned around, put an arm along the seat, and looked at Missy. "I'm Brad Thompson. My balls aren't saggy and I shave twice a day. Want to go out with me?"

Missy tilted her head thoughtfully. He was not handsome, but he had a strong chin, nice eyes, and good smile. "Take off your cap," she said. A shock of dark hair fell over his forehead. "Saturday," she told him. "The Corrigan's Cup at Willow Bend Polo and Hunt Club. Pick me up at noon and wear something casual."

"Yes, ma'am." He passed the burgers back to them.

Missy grinned at Laura, sank her teeth into the Whopper, and sighed with satisfaction. "Mmmmm, pair-o-dise," she said as she did each time she ate something she enjoyed. Or made love to a man she enjoyed. Already she was sizing up the man in the driver's seat.

"Now that you've found a date for Saturday," Laura said, "tell me why it's so important that you go to the Corrigan's Cup. I didn't realize you liked polo."

"I don't know one chukker from another but Arto DiGrassi, the rich Venezuelan everyone's talking about, is throwing a big party at his villa after the match. I'm dying to meet him and to see the place." She lowered her voice to a whisper and cut her eyes at the driver. "Think it's alright for me to show up with Brad the limo driver?"

Laura laughed. "Whatever blows your skirt up!"

CHAPTER THIRTY-EIGHT

K NOW whose birthday this is, Susie?" KVIL Radio's Ron Chapman asked his morning show partner, Susie Humphries.

"Oh, God," replied Susie, "It's yours and I forgot to get you anything."

"No," said Chapman, laughing, "it's not mine. It's Miss Laura McCarty's. Laura, honey, happy twenty-third birthday from Susie, me, and all the KVIL staff. And if I could just play one of your daddy's hits to celebrate, but . . ."

Stephen glanced at Laura, turned off the car radio, and braked to a stop before his house on the banks of Lake Roy Hubbard, twelve miles east of Dallas. He turned, took her hand in his, and said, "Happy birthday, Laura." He leaned across the seat, kissed her softly on the lips and murmured, "Let's get married."

"When?" was her reply.

"A week from today. Next Saturday. That'll give us both plenty of time to tie up any loose ends. Say you will."

"I will."

"Twenty-eight hundred dollars to American Express. Thirty-six hundred dollars to Mastercard. Forty-two hundred dollars to Visa." The trust officer's gray eyebrows lifted. "Eighty-seven hundred dollars to Universal Air Credit. Fifty-three hundred dollars to Torrie Steel." He looked at Laura over his glasses.

Smiling sheepishly, she said, "Can't a girl have a pair of shoes?"

"Miss McCarty," said Elias Denton, "I've cautioned you time and again

277

about your spending. You must learn to discipline yourself. Since Mrs. Trent's puzzling action—holding your father's films and music off the market—you know very well that great sums of money are no longer pouring into the estate. You will have to practice frugality if you wish to—"

"Alright, alright," Laura waved her hand, dismissively. "I'll do better, I promise." She rose. "I really have to go now, I'm meeting my fiancé for dinner." She smiled suddenly, "Did I tell you, Mr. Denton, that tomorrow I'm getting married?"

He looked stricken. "You most certainly did not. My dear child, we must make arrangements for—"

"No arrangements, Denton. Steve's family has plenty of money, he won't be trying to get his hands on mine, so relax. You may have heard of them . . . the Winston Flynns of San Antonio."

Immediately he relaxed. "Of course. Old money and lots of it. My best wishes for your happiness."

"You mean it?"

"But of course, why I . . ."

"In that case, I'll tell you, I spent seventeen thousand this afternoon on a trousseau."

He smiled. "When's the big day?"

"Tomorrow."

"Tomorrow," Stephen said softly. "We're getting married tomorrow."

His companion reached across the table for Stephen's hand. The couple sat in a secluded booth at the back of a dimly lit club on the outskirts of Dallas. "Don't do it. It's a mistake. We both know it is."

Stephen stared at the hand gripping his own. "It's not. Laura's as kind and warm as she is beautiful, we get along very well. We'll be happy."

"It won't last. You'll come back to me, I know you will."

"No. No, I won't. It's over between us. I've told you that. You have to face it."

"What we had was too beautiful for . . ."

"It was beautiful, but it's over. I'm marrying Laura McCarty in the morning and I'm going to be a good and faithful husband to her."

"No . . . no . . ."

"I'm sorry, really I am." He pulled his hand free. "I have to go. Laura's expecting me." He stood up, tossed several bills on the table.

"Kiss me good-bye." Sad brown eyes looked up into his.

Stephen glanced about, sighed, leaned down, closed his eyes, and felt the lips he knew so well open beneath his own, pulling him in, devouring him, exciting him. With an effort, he jerked free, straightened, and hurried away.

Mrs. Stephen Flynn, extremely nervous, awaited her bridegroom in the luxurious bedroom on board the customized Boeing 707. She had been sipping champagne since the noon wedding reception in Dallas, a small intimate gathering of only their family and closest friends.

They had continued drinking champagne when they boarded the plane and climbed high into the clear summer sky. They had laughed and kissed and grown increasingly tipsy.

Now, their cruising altitude of 35,000 feet reached, halfway across the Atlantic, Laura—her tall, slim body draped in a seductive gown and matching kimono-sleeved robe of ivory silk charmuse and lace—felt as though she had never tasted a drop of the bubbly wine.

She was terrified.

Any minute Stephen would walk through the door and take what was his. There was no escape. She was high over the ocean with the man who was now her husband. He could do anything he pleased to her and there was little she could say about it. Even Buddy had remained behind in Dallas to give the honeymooners absolute privacy.

A gentle knock. Laura flinched. Stephen opened the door and entered. His suit coat was missing. His white shirt was opened down his bronzed chest. He looked boyish and not at all dangerous.

She smiled and lifted her arms to him.

Laura lay naked beneath the silky sheet, an arm flung above her head. Stephen had showered, dressed, and left the cabin to see about an early supper for the two of them.

He had made love to her. The act itself had been brief and not that fulfilling for either of them, but it hadn't mattered. They had held each other and Stephen had apologized, explaining he was tired and nervous and she understood perfectly. The closeness was wonderful, the holding each other, the trust, the caring. He'd not left her feeling used and dirty. He'd not hurt her and whispered vile things in her ear. He had not punished and abused and done disgusting things to her.

Laura sighed and stretched. She was a woman, a married woman whose husband cared for her, respected her, cherished her. Together they would learn to be lovers.

✳ ✳ ✳

It had been three months since the wedding. In that time they had never had a cross word, no disagreements. Both were busy with their own work, but shared their interests with one another. Laura told her husband that things were slowly turning around at Lone Star. A couple of musicians that had been with her daddy in the old days had come to work for the company. A talented songwriter, Bailey Watson, a man who had turned out a string of hits from his tiny office in the Brill Building, had recently walked into Lone Star, said he was moving to Dallas, and wanted to work for her. Her fledgling company was fixing to fly.

Stephen was rapidly gaining a reputation for his innovative building designs and Dallas' wealthy were clamoring for his services. When not at his Meadows Building office, where he occasionally worked past midnight, he was before a drawing board at home.

When Laura and Stephen married they agreed to divide their time between the 3525 apartment in town and the secluded lake house on Roy Hubbard. Weeknights they stayed at the Turtle Creek residence, weekends at the lake.

A long weekend was coming up. Thanksgiving. Laura and Stephen had made the necessary excuses to friends and family. They were exhausted from their heavy work schedule and wanted only to rest and relax at the lake house.

On the Wednesday afternoon before the long holiday, Laura, sitting in on a recording session, became irritated with her long, black hair. It kept falling into her face. She kept pushing it out of her eyes, back over her shoulder. It refused to stay put, and she became increasingly annoyed with the bothersome mane.

When she returned to her office, Laura whimsically rang up Mr. Frederick and asked that he dash over and cut her hair. It was driving her nuts. She could stand it no longer. Mr. Frederick had, for ages, been trying to convince her to shorten her thick, wild hair into a more fashionable, carefree style.

The scissor-happy hairdresser snipped and clipped, brushed the thick short locks back on either side of her head, away from her face, leaving the front to wave appealingly low over her high forehead. When he was finished, Laura looked like a smaller, softer version of her famous father. She shook her head about and smiled happily; she liked it. It was neat and stylish and would take little care.

Driving to the lake house that evening, she wondered, suddenly, if Stephen would like it. Perhaps she should have asked first. She hadn't even thought about discussing it with him before doing it. She was not used to asking anyone before acting. Now she felt bad. What if her husband hated the way she looked?

"Laura, darling," he said, when she walked into the beamed living room. "Your hair."

Apprehensive, Laura ran her fingers through the shorn locks and began apologizing, "Stephen, I'm sorry. I should have—"

"I love it," he interrupted. "You've never looked better." His eyes were glowing. He took her in his arms and kissed her in a way that he'd never before kissed her. Not even in their bedroom.

"You don't think I look like a skinny boy?" she said and laughed when his lips lifted from hers.

His answer was to kiss her again, mouth open wide, tongue thrusting deep. Then he murmured against her lips, "It's going to be a wonderful holiday."

Later, in the kitchen, they laughed at everything the other had to say and bumped into each other as they went about preparing the next day's feast. Agreeing they'd allow no servant to rob them of the fun, they had left their staff in town at 3525. They were alone at the lake, Buddy to arrive later and spend the night down at the guest house.

It was great fun cooking together, especially since neither had ever cooked before. Sipping white wine and singing love songs, they went about stuffing the twenty-pound turkey that Stephen had chosen. By the time the bird was in the oven, Laura was feeling the effects of the wine. She was pleasantly tired and relaxed. She couldn't remember feeling so good in a long time.

Their moods a mixture of mellowness and playfulness, they strolled back into the firelit living room, harmonizing loudly. And Laura quickly agreed when Stephen suggested she sing for him. Put on a show, he urged. A show just for me. Please. The request had been made before, and always turned down.

This night she was willing. Eyes sparkling, she said happily, "Want me to do my impression of my daddy?"

Stephen, settling himself on the floor before the fire, smiled lazily. "Why not?"

"Stay where you are," she cautioned. "Don't move. I'll be right back."

Stephen smiled and lifted his glass of Chablis. They had not eaten and he, too, was feeling the warming, loosening effects of the wine. He inhaled deeply and stared dreamily into his glass.

Loud music blasted from the stereo and his head snapped up. Before him stood Laura, dressed in one of his tuxedoes, the black trousers tight around her hips, the stiff white shirt minimizing her breasts. She went immediately into one of her daddy's favorite cuts, a cover of the Impressions big hit, "The Way You Do the Things You Do."

She stood perfectly still, feet slightly apart, mimicking C.C.'s arrogant, sensual stance. She put as much fire into the suggestive lyrics as her father before her, all the while holding her husband's astonished gaze. With her short, short hair and the man's tuxedo, she knew she looked like C.C. Even sounded a lot like him. She played it for all it was worth, enjoying the joking imitation in the privacy, and safety, of her own home with her husband. And enjoying to the ultimate the exhilaration of performing.

The response she received both delighted and puzzled Laura. Stephen was not laughing and applauding her silliness as she had expected. Instead, he watched, mesmerized, an intense expression in his eyes.

When she finished the performance, Laura thought sure her husband would at last laugh heartily, shout "Bravo," and whistle and carry on as playfully as she had. He did not. He rose from the floor, crossed to her, and taking her face in his hands, stared at her, murmuring softly, "Darling, I want you, I want you."

His open lips were on hers and they were burning hot. Laura wrapped her arms around his neck and kissed him. Ardently they kissed, their tongues meeting and mating, their bodies straining together. Their lips separated. Her husband lifted her in his arms and carried her up the stairs to their bedroom. Leaving the lamps dark, he stood behind her and undressed her.

The tux jacket was shed. He slipped his arms around her, unzipped the trousers and slid them down her hips. Unbuttoning the white shirt, he leaned to her and kissed the back of her neck. She trembled when he pulled the shirtsleeves down her arms. He unhooked her bra and peeled it away. He pushed her panties down and off. Her breath was loud in her ears.

He took her to their bed. She lay there on her back, waiting, excited, anxious. Stephen hurriedly undressed and joined her. She smiled and turned to him, but he kissed her quickly, hotly, and turned her on her side, facing away from him. He lay down behind her, kissing the side of her throat, his hard, heavy cock pulsating against her buttocks. Laura felt her desire quickly escalate.

Stephen's warm lips moved from her neck to her shoulders. Over and over he kissed her tingling flesh and Laura sighed and felt her whole body catch fire. He moved on to her waist, kissing, caressing, his hands gripping her ribcage. She shivered deliciously when he slid lower and she felt his tongue go into the crevice of her bare bottom.

His hands were gripping her firm, rounded buttocks, gently spreading her and he was kissing her, his tongue dipping in, tracing, drawing a line of fire between the rounded cheeks. It was strange, but wonderful, and Laura, her passions erupting, pressed back against that exploring mouth, feeling herself becoming wet and very hot.

Her breasts were aching, the nipples hard and erect, so sensitive that the sheet felt abrasive against them. She squirmed and pushed, unconsciously trying to urge Stephen's mouth to move further down, to desert its target and go to that distended, throbbing nub of flesh that cried out for his touch.

Stephen remained where he was. Kissing and sucking, sticking his tongue into her, kneading the flesh of her buttocks with his long fingers. She was panting and rotating her hips against his lips, a silky wetness from deep within her mixing with the wetness of his open, questing mouth.

And then he was sliding back up behind her, his fingers between her legs, gently massaging her clitoris. Laura's eyes closed in bliss. She felt his hard, hot penis pushing into her yielding flesh and her husband's lips were again sprinkling tender kisses on her slender back as they moved together.

Laura clutched at the edge of the mattress and ground her bottom against his thrusting pelvis, finding his rhythm. His lips continued to press kisses to her short, dark hair, her neck, her shoulders and back.

There in the darkness of their bedroom, they climaxed together, a deep, shuddering release. And Laura, sated, exhausted, drifted dreamily into sweet slumber locked in her husband's arms.

CHAPTER THIRTY-NINE

VALENTINA closed her Louis Vuitton briefcase.

The department-head meeting had been brief; they were clearly anxious to get home to their families for the long holiday weekend. She could tell she had lost their attention after an hour, so she dismissed them.

She took her leather handbag from the bottom drawer and rifled through it, searching for aspirin. Her open wallet spilled onto the leather desk pad. Forgetting the aspirin, Valentina dropped down into her chair, picked up the billfold and studied, wistfully, a worn photograph.

A young man with sandy hair, a wide, infectious grin; aviator's goggles swinging from his sunburned neck.

She said aloud, "Daddy, I never knew you. I wish you were spending Thanksgiving with me. I'm so alone." She shook her head, closed the wallet and dropped it back into her bag.

She looked out her office window at the darkening night sky. She had no desire to go home. She buzzed Viola. "Has Neil left yet?"

"He's just locking his office, Valentina."

"Tell him to come in here for a minute."

"Will do." Viola looked up. "Ah, Mr. Allen, Mrs. Trent wonders if she might have a word with you."

He nodded and made his way to Valentina's office. "Need something, Valentina?"

"Come in, Neil." She smiled at him and circled her desk, "Big plans for Thanksgiving?"

"You know better than that, Val."

"I have no plans either." He remained silent. "Neil, let's order in and

284

work through the holidays. Stay right here at the office and audit the books, set our goals for next year, discuss doing some videos. There's a million things that need tending. What do you say?"

"Why not?"

"Good. I'll have Viola call out for dinner and we can get right to it. Where shall we begin? Have you started on the promotion packages for the first quarter? I've some ideas. I also have some plans on trimming the fat around here and . . ."

She kept Neil at the office past midnight. They returned the next morning—Thanksgiving Day—at ten to start again. He didn't mind; he was glad to have something to do. His apartment was quiet and lonely, he hated being there. But he wondered why Valentina hadn't found something better to do.

True, she thrived on the business, but she liked to mix her work with play, and play to her meant entertaining one of her recording artists in her office. Or in her limo. It had been months since she had fired Bossman White, a colorful country-and-western singer with whom she had been sleeping. Since White's departure, there had been nobody.

Neil glanced at her. A pair of reading glasses balanced on the tip of her nose, cigarette dangling from her lips, she sat at the conference table, reams of paper scattered around her, her rapt attention on long columns of figures on the computer printout before her.

Friday night they were still holed up in Valentina's office, hard at work. Neil saw her rub her neck. He suggested a change of pace. Why didn't they go down to the recording studio for a while? A singer he had found in a small Austin club was cutting a demo. Valentina yawned and nodded her head yes.

Neil watched Valentina closely when they reached the studio. The singer, a good-looking, dark young man, was on a stool in the middle of a small orchestra, headphones on, singing his heart out. The boy was just the type Valentina preferred. Neil expected to be dismissed, while Valentina remained behind to invite the singer up to her office for a drink.

"He's good, isn't he?" Neil said.

"Very talented. Thank you for finding him."

To Neil's surprise, she said no more. In minutes she whispered she was ready to get back upstairs. Neil felt foolishly relieved. And boyishly happy when, at midnight, Valentina, telling him goodnight, said, "We had fun today, didn't we?"

"I did."

"Me too." She smiled, raised herself on tiptoe and kissed his cheek.

"Ah . . . will . . . are you going to be here tomorrow?" Neil asked.

"Only if you'll join me."

"I'll be here by nine o'clock." He handed her into the limo, leaned down, and said, "Sleep well, dear." And felt his heartbeat quicken when she again kissed him. This time on the lips.

He stood in the cold night air, watching, until the limo's taillights disappeared. Maybe, just maybe, his time had finally come.

A bright red Ferrari streaked down the North Dallas tollway at eighty miles an hour. The driver, an attractive blond twenty-three-year-old woman, was laughing. The passenger, a darkly handsome, thirty-seven-year-old man, was cursing in Spanish, his dark eyes flashing with fear and anger.

"Arto, darling," Missy said, "relax. I learned to drive when I was four-teen."

"You never learned to drive, Missy," muttered Arto DiGrassi, "pull over before you kill us!"

Missy slammed on the brakes, almost throwing Arto through the wind-shield. When the Ferrari came to a complete stop on the shoulder, Arto DiGrassi exhaled heavily, and slumped back in the seat.

"You are never to drive again! I take this car away from you today," he said. "You drive like madwoman; you cannot behave!"

Missy saw that he was truly angry. Still, she wasn't all that worried. She knew how to sweeten his mood. She had from the very beginning.

Grinning, she put a hand on Arto's thigh and murmured, "I'm sorry, Arto, honey. Kiss me and say you forgive me."

"Missy, you are foolish girl. We are on public street; I will not . . ." Her lips silenced him and her kiss made him forget his anger and where they were. Just like always. It had been that way from the time they had met three months before.

Missy and Brad the limo driver had arrived late for the Corrigan's Cup polo match at Willow Bend. It was between chukkers. The players were off the field, changing horses. She spotted Arto at once. He looked just like his pictures, only better.

Helmet tucked under his muscular arm, dark hair gleaming in the midday sun, he was very appealing with his smooth dark skin and his tight white trousers tucked into tall black boots. She liked his strong, handsome face. She liked his broad, deep chest. She liked his trim waist. Her eyes dropped to his groin. A tightly packed crotch made it unanimous.

A look inside his many-roomed villa made Missy determined to become

Mrs. Arto DiGrassi. At the party, she watched every move the man made. She smiled seductively at him. Her eyes never left him for a minute.

She was growing worried though; he paid her no attention. All evening long she had been staring at him and not once did he look up and catch her.

My God, what would she do if he didn't want her?

Missy was frantic. Excusing herself from her date, she hunted the nearest phone. She'd call Laura. Laura would tell her what to do.

"Laura, Missy. My life is coming to the end."

"Again?"

"It's not funny, damn it. This is serious."

"Sorry. What's the problem? I thought you were going to—"

"I did. I am. I'm here right now at Arto DiGrassi's party and I want him. God, he's beautiful and so is this house. Forty rooms! Dark eyes and hair. Jesus, Laura, the damned floors are marble inlaid with mahogany and . . ."

"Missy, which is it you want? The man or the house."

"Well, both, of course, but I'm worried. Everybody is after the rich Venezuelan."

"Including you. I'm sure you've been flirting with him and—"

"I have not! I've just glanced at him a time or two and . . ."

Laughter from Laura. "Well, quit 'glancing' at him, I've seen the way you glance at men. Ignore Mr. DiGrassi. Maybe he'll notice and be intrigued."

"I don't know. I'll be in deep shit if that doesn't work. The party can't last much longer. I'll just go up to him and tell him I—"

"Never. He's a Latin. They like to be the aggressor, to make the first move."

"Hey, you're telling Miss Noah about the flood. I was screwing Latins when I was sixteen, remember." Then almost wistfully, "Nobody keeps it up longer than . . . oh, Laura, are you sure?"

"Let DiGrassi pursue you."

"What if he doesn't?"

"Then you'll have to accept it and be satisfied with Brad the limo driver."

Missy sighed heavily. "Couldn't I just asked Arto to autograph my boobs or something?"

"Listen to me, Missy, for once in your life, act prim. It will work."

"You're right. Sorry I bothered you this late. Kiss Stephen for me."

Missy hung up the phone and floated back into the party. She swept right past Arto DiGrassi and she didn't so much as sneak a peek at him. For the next hour her eyes never strayed in his direction.

She visited the powder room and when she came out, Arto DiGrassi was leaning against the wall outside the door, arms crossed over his chest. Wordlessly, he took her elbow and guided her masterfully up the stairs and into his spacious bedroom.

"Why," he asked, "are you no longer interested in me?"

Silently thanking Laura, Missy said demurely, "Sir, what makes you think I was ever interested in you?"

His hands were grasping her bare shoulders. "But you looked at me as one looks at her lover. Then you stop. I am forlorn."

Missy could hardly keep from smiling smugly. "I'm sorry, Mr. DiGrassi, if you got the wrong impression. Now if you'll please let me go, I'll return . . ."

"No," said Arto DiGrassi, "you must not leave me, Missy. I will tell your escort you are staying here with me."

Melting under the heat of those dark Latin eyes, Missy fought to keep her wits. If she remained it would mean a hot night in DiGrassi's king-sized bed. But if she left, it might mean many.

"Mr. DiGrassi, I cannot stay." She widened her eyes, as if in shock. "I don't know you, and I am here with a very nice young man. It would not be proper if I . . ."

"Is true, is true," he said sadly. He released her shoulders, took one of her hands in his, lifted it to his lips and kissed it tenderly. "I apologize for making such a ridiculous proposition to a beautiful, refined young lady. You will, I pray, allow me to call you on the telephone."

"695-4524," she blurted out before she thought.

"It is recorded in my heart," said Arto DiGrassi.

The phone was ringing when she got home. Would she meet him for breakfast at nine the next morning? If she did not, he would surely perish.

She met him. But she was distant, mysterious, and turned down his request for a dinner engagement. And lay in her room that night cursing herself because she had done it. Playing hard to get was a real pain in the ass.

The cat-and-mouse game lasted for a full week before Arto's patience and Missy's resolve ran out. The typical hot-blooded Latin, DiGrassi, beside himself with desire, showed up outside the midday chapel wedding of Laura McCarty and Stephen Flynn.

When bridesmaid Missy came dashing down the steps, laughing and throwing rice, a determined DiGrassi strode purposely forward, took her arm, swept her away and into his waiting limo. Feigning outrage, Missy was sped to the pink stucco villa. And when they were alone inside the huge house, Arto DiGrassi spoke what was on his mind.

"I am burning with desire for you, Missy Graham. I intend to have you." His mouth covered hers in a kiss of steaming passion. When breathless and dazed, their lips separated, Arto's eager hands were cupping her firm, full bottom.

"Touch it, Señor, and you gotta buy it," said Missy, forgetting her new persona.

"Then I will marry you," declared Arto. "But it must be very soon, because I long to make love to you."

"Very soon, darling," said Missy, "Oh, Arto, kiss me, kiss me." In minutes they were up in Arto's bed, their clothes discarded on the stairs. And when Arto said, "*Dios*, darling, no woman has ever made me feel this way," and then, immediately, "never let me catch you look at another man!" Missy knew she had him.

His warning was unnecessary. He had her too. She was going to behave the lady. Except, of course, with Arto DiGrassi.

"Want me to do that again, Arto?" she purred and the enchanted Latin nodded eagerly.

CHAPTER FORTY

ER short, gleaming hair, black like the records her fortune was built on, was swept back behind her small ears. She wore a tailored white gaberdine Adam Beall trimmed in purple leather. On her arm was an Elsa Peritti gold wrist cuff. At her throat was a Van Cleef and Arpels solitaire diamond on a delicate gold chain.

She was seated behind her white marble desk in her gray carpeted, suede-walled office. A smoked lucite jar, filled with clotted creme candies, sat on the right corner of the shiny marble. Her Mark Cross pigskin briefcase, contracts neatly stacked inside, rested on the left corner.

She was beautiful. She was brilliant. She was rich.

She was unhappy.

Laura rose from her chair. The lush white gaberdine, lined with silk and fitted perfectly over her hips, whispered softly as she crossed the room. She stood before the floor-to-ceiling windows in her Lone Star office. It was a warm, sunny day, almost like spring, although it was early February. Arms crossed over her chest she squinted, picking out, in the distance, her 3525 Turtle Creek high-rise where she had left Stephen sleeping.

Laura closed her eyes. Opened them once more. She drew a slow breath and went back to her chair.

Something was wrong with her marriage. Very, very wrong. It was time she faced it. Too long she had made excuses to herself for their passionless union. She could count on her fingers the times they had made love in the six months since their wedding.

She couldn't understand it. She had felt sure, after that holiday night at the lake house, that everything was going to be as it should between them.

How wrong she had been. That night was the only time Stephen had touched her all through the long, rainy weekend.

And since then . . . twice . . . three times . . .

Laura again rose and paced restlessly. The doubts she constantly pushed to the back of her mind surfaced. There was another woman. That had to be it. All those nights Stephen said he was at his office working, he was actually with a lover.

Laura sighed. If he was, if there was someone else, wasn't it possible that it was as much her fault as his?

She was not deeply in love with Stephen, had never been, not the way she had always dreamed of being in love. She loved Stephen, cared for him certainly, but she had never been mad about him the way Missy was about Arto DiGrassi.

A smile played briefly on Laura's lips recalling the first time she had visited the newly married Missy at the ostentatious DiGrassi villa. Missy, barefooted, had answered the door herself, waving away the disdainful British butler.

Laughing sunnily she had said, "It doesn't have the snob appeal of the 75205 zip code, but we like it." She pulled Laura along with her on a tour of the downstairs rooms, showing her the many treasures.

"Look at that, Laura," Missy pointed to a clock of rock crystal and gold. "It once sat in Eva Peron's living room. Arto got it at an auction. One hundred-fifty thousand dollars. And over there," indicating a silver-inlaid rosewood side table, "Napoleon Bonaparte's. Straight from Versailles. How does that grab you?"

She went on, before Laura could respond. "There's an Austrian Beidermeire secretary in the library that costs sixty-five thousand dollars. Beauvais tapestries in the music room and a two-hundred-year-old Georgian Sheffield silver coffee service in the dining room and . . . and . . . This house is full of goodies, Laura. The closets are filled with china and silver, enough to serve one hundred guests at once. There's cases of Mouton Rothschild in the cellar and pounds of fresh Beluga Malassol caviar and French goose liver in the pantry."

"Out in the garage there's a Maserati and a Ferrari and a Lotus and a Mercedes and three Rolls and . . . and . . . oh, come on upstairs," Missy rushed Laura up the winding marble staircase and right through the huge master suite to one of the two gigantic master bathrooms.

"Look!" she commanded, "look at that, Laura. Heated towel racks of polished gold. Twelve thousand dollars apiece and there's a dozen in both baths, I counted. Add that up real quick."

Laura was laughing. Missy would never change. She always told the price of everything, always had.

Delighted with her friend's obvious pleasure with the new castle, Laura said, "I'm impressed, Missy, truly I am. It's a beautiful place."

"Come with me," Missy grabbed Laura's arm and propelled her back into the bedroom. "See that?" she pointed to a shiny gold figurine adorning the smooth gold-and-white marble surface of a night table. "Know what that is and where it came from?"

"Afraid not."

Missy picked up the heavy, gleaming object and rubbed it. "A fertility god that belonged to Empress Carlotta. The story goes that she kept it by the bed at Chapultepec, hoping it would make her conceive." She grinned and added, "Or, probably just hoping old Max could get it up." She laughed and replaced it. "Now, let's see . . ."

Laura interrupted. "You forgot something."

"I did?" Missy frowned.

"How much?"

"Oh, god, so I did. Seventy-five thousand dollars."

Missy stepped up to the king-sized bed and jerked back the hand-quilted ivory silk chantung counterpain. "These sheets came from Italy. Hand-embroidered hems. Ten thousand dollars a pair and there's twenty pairs in the linen closets." She happily threw herself down on the bed, laughing.

"We need a lot of sheets, Laura," she confided, "Arto and I spend so much time in bed." She fell over onto her back and ran her palms over the silk crepe de chine. Dreamily, "My God, Arto is the best lover in the world!" She bounded up. "Isn't it fun to fuck the man you love? No, no . . . I take that back. Isn't it wonderful to 'make love' to the man you love, and know that he's your husband?"

"Wonderful," Laura said, and hoped she sounded convincing.

"I'm so in love with Arto and he's so in love with me. I've never been this happy in my life. Aren't we fortunate, Laura, you and I? Both madly in love and married to handsome, successful, passionate men."

"Yes, fortunate, very fortunate."

"Fortunate, very fortunate," the words ran around in her head on this sunny February morning. She was feeling less than fortunate. Her life was not exactly the way she would have had it. The way she had always dreamed that it would be.

The four things she most longed for deep down in her heart of hearts, were not hers.

To live at Musicland. To control Big Chief. To be a singing star like her daddy.

To love and be loved by the one man in all the whole wide world meant just for her. A man she'd recognize in a minute if ever she met him. A man who adored and desired her. A man who loved her the way her daddy had loved her mother.

Laura mentally shook herself. It was time to stop this nonsense. She could hear Missy saying, "Knock it off, Laura, you're crying with a loaf of bread stuffed under each arm." And Missy, of course, was right.

She had a good life and she was being foolish, childish. Everything was alright. She and Stephen got along far better than many married couples. She was being silly with her schoolgirl notions of romantic love and sexual fantasies.

Laura picked up the phone and dialed the apartment. Stephen's sleepy voice came on the line.

"I wanted to say good-bye, Stephen," Laura said. "I'm leaving for the airport in a few minutes."

"I'm glad you called. Have a good trip, Laura. I'll hold down the fort."

She smiled. "I'll be back Saturday if nothing goes wrong."

"I'll count the days. Call when you get to Nashville."

"I will. Bye."

She hung up, feeling better. Time permitting, she'd do a little shopping in Nashville. Pick up a couple of sexy new nightgowns, and when she got home, she'd subtly seduce her husband. Other women did it all the time. Why shouldn't she?

Stephen replaced the receiver, yawned, and shoved a blue-cased pillow up against the raw silk headboard. And again picked up the phone.

He dialed. A broad smile came to his lips when it was picked up on the other end. "Hi," he said, cradling the receiver between his chin and bare shoulder. "What are you doing?"

"You really want to know?"

"Yes?"

Low laughter over the wire. "I'm lying here on my bed, looking at the picture we had made last winter when we were down in Barbados. Remember the night we danced on the beach and then made . . ."

"I remember." Stephen said. "What are you wearing right now?"

More laughter. "Hold on. Just a minute, Stevie." Stephen could hear the faint rustle of clothing being discarded. Then, "I'm naked, darling. Totally naked."

"My wife's on her way to the airport," said Stephen, his voice lowered. "Can you go with me to the lake house in an hour?" A breathless yes. "Good. You know what to pack. Don't forget."

"I won't, darling. How long will I be there?"

"Until Saturday morning. Laura gets home Saturday afternoon."

Laura's spirits lifted considerably when she reached Nashville and the Country and Western Radio Stations Broadcasters' Convention. Her itinerary unfolded with efficient precision. She auditioned and signed two talented new singers, had meetings with two more, interviewed a noted promotion man, caught Larry Gatlin at the Grand Ole Opry, and dined with industry friends she had known since childhood.

On the last day in Nashville, Laura, with Buddy at her side, found a chic lingerie shop near the hotel. The big man stood sentry outside the door. While laughing at his staunch refusal to come inside, Laura hurried into the salon and purchased a couple of daringly beautiful nighties.

It was Friday evening. The last night of the Nashville stay. Laura dressed for her eight o'clock engagement with her daddy's old friend, Bill Mack. She was to consider Mr. Mack's proposal of Lone Star producing country and western videos with him as the host. Ready early, she called up Stephen. They talked for half an hour and when she hung up, her phone immediately rang.

It was Buddy. Bill Mack had called; the line was busy so Mack had left a message. He couldn't make it for the dinner meeting. He had offered apologies and said he would fly into Dallas in a couple of weeks.

"That's fine with me," said an exhausted Laura, kicking off her black Ferragamo pumps. "I'll just order from room service and watch television and . . . no . . . wait . . . Bud, are the pilots in?"

"Yeah," Buddy said, "I just came from Bert's room. He's laying up and Nick's down in the coffee shop."

"Bud, let's go home. To Dallas."

"Tonight?"

"We could get in by midnight."

"Sure, hon, sounds good to me. The plane's all fueled up. Let's do it. I'll go tell Bert."

Smiling happily, Laura rose to start packing. Sat back down and picked up the phone. She'd tell Stephen she was coming in early. She replaced the receiver without dialing. No. She wouldn't call. It would be fun to surprise him.

※   ※   ※

A bright winter moon was sailed high in the clear sky, turning the placid waters of Lake Roy Hubbard a shimmering silver. The weather had turned; it was icy cold and Laura, approaching the lake house, smiled to herself thinking that their big warm bed sounded awfully good to her on this chill February night. She would slip into one of her provocative new nightgowns and . . .

Buddy at the wheel, they rounded the last curve and saw the lights of the house winking from the downstairs rooms. Her smile broadened. Stephen was awake. Maybe they could scramble some eggs before they went up to bed.

"Bud, Stephen's up so you needn't come in. I know you're tired, drive on down to the guest house and get some sleep."

"Want me to bring in the luggage, hon?"

"Tomorrow will be fine. I'll just take my carry bag." She smiled at him. "My new goodies are in it."

Laura, still smiling happily, let herself in the redwood gate and paused, puzzled. Her father's distinctive voice was coming from the stereo inside. It was very, very loud. Why did Stephen have the volume turned up so high? And why, at midnight, was he alone listening to her daddy's records?

She reached the front door and lifted the brass door knocker, giving it a resounding bang. Nothing. She tried again, banging the knocker briskly against the plate, but realized he couldn't possibly hear it above the smooth, rich sounds of her daddy's recorded voice.

Laura raised her Balenciaga drawstring handbag and searched until she found her door key. She let herself in, calling, "Stephen, Stephen." No answer.

She stood in the middle of the brightly lit and very empty living room calling his name, an eerie sense of unease enveloping her. She threw down her bags and hurried to Stephen's studio. The lights were all on, but he was not there.

Breath short, she rushed back to the living room and headed for the stairs. Up three stairs she paused, and again called his name. And heard nothing but the loud, provocative beat of the music and her daddy torching a sensual, suggestive rock and roll song.

Laura climbed the stairs.

Before she reached it, she could see that the door to their bedroom was partially open. A dim, strange glimmer of light came from within. She stopped calling Stephen's name. She crossed the wooden landing, neared the half-open door and stopped, a cold nagging fear causing her heart to pound violently in her chest.

Above the music, she heard a man speaking. "Baby, baby." It was Stephen's voice and there was little doubt left what he was doing. Then gasping and moaning and the slapping of flesh upon flesh.

Her husband was making love to another woman in their own bed.

Feeling sick and angry and hurt, Laura told herself to turn and flee back down the stairs, to run out of the house and never look back.

Hot blood pounding in her ears, eyes round with outrage, she looked inside. And her pounding heart stopped and the blood in her veins congealed. In one dreamlike, freeze-frame, unforgettable instant, she saw it.

A ghost.

There was only one light; a track light in the ceiling over the bed, pouring a small circle of bright white illumination down directly on her daddy, kneeling, knees spread, naked in her bed.

Paralyzed with shock and disbelief, she stared at him, wordlessly murmuring his name. But it wasn't him, she realized; it was a man pretending to be her daddy. The kneeling man had the same olive skin; his bare chest and arms and legs very dark. His hair was blue-black and on his dark cheek, a black star. He was purring words of passion to his partner.

Choking, heartsick, it registered on Laura. Someone lay below the thrusting, grinding impersonator, shoulders and head concealed in the shadows. But it was clear the person was a male. He lay upon his back, a pillow beneath his bare bottom, his legs folded back on his chest and thrown over his lover's shoulders.

His hands were clutching, clawing at the dark man's hair-covered chest, at his waist, his hips and thighs, pulling him closer, deeper.

And from the shadows he was babbling in a high, breathless voice, "Oh God, baby, baby . . . force it in deeper . . . let me have it all . . . bury it in me, honey . . ." and then, "aaaah, yes, yes . . . don't baby, I'll . . ." Shocking, intimate words coming from the faceless man who Laura knew was her husband, Stephen.

No, her brain silently screamed, no, no, dear god no, as spellbound she watched the dark man, his painted black star now streaking down his cheek with a rivulet of sweat. He leaned forward and pulled his panting lover up into his arms.

And Laura's screams surfaced when the blond, handsome head of her husband entered the pool of white light and the pair passionately kissed. She never knew she was screaming until both heads—dark and light—snapped around and the two men froze there, melded together, their bodies joined, arms around each other, mouths gaping open in surprise.

Then it was all a blur.

Laura, screaming loudly, was running back down the stairs and Stephen, naked and shouting to her, was following. He caught up with her midway through the living room, grabbed her arm, and jerked her to him. She fought him, slapping at him, sobbing now, desperate to have him out of her sight.

"Please, Laura," he too began to cry, "It's not like you think. You've got to give me a chance to explain."

Her answer was more frenzied struggling, the violent shaking of her head, tears choking her.

Stephen refused to release her. He talked as fast as he could, tears streaming down his flushed cheeks, terror and regret in his eyes. "You'll understand when I explain. I know you will. You're such a kind, loving person and I do love you, Laura, I do."

"Let me go!" she pushed on his sweat-slippery chest, "Dear God, let me out of here."

"No, wait, Laura, please . . . please . . . it's . . . it's hard to . . . I am— was madly in love with your father . . . with the Chief . . . and he . . ."

"No," she shouted, hysterically, "you're lying! You're lying! My daddy never—"

"No. No, he didn't. I loved him but he never knew I existed. I followed him around the country and I tried to . . . I . . . He refused to have anything to do with me. I would have done anything for him, anything, and he wouldn't have me." Stephen was sobbing loudly now, his bare body shaking with emotion. "I tried to forget him, but I couldn't. I went to Europe after his death and told myself I'd get over him. I couldn't. I couldn't, even though he was dead."

"I don't want to hear it," Laura was beating on his chest, "let me go, Stephen, I can't stand this, I can't . . ."

"Wait. You must wait. I want you to know everything, Laura. I returned home and heard that C.C.'s daughter had grown up and looked exactly like him. Exactly. I knew that was my answer. I could have him through you. I found out everything I could about you and . . ."

"You mean you deliberately set out to . . . oh, God, you bastard, you heartless bastard."

"I'm not, Laura. I'm not. I loved you the minute I saw you. You look just like him. Don't you see, I can love you the way I loved him and we'll—"

"My god, you're sicker than I thought," Laura sobbed. "You're gay and you married me so you can pretend I'm my daddy! I'm a woman, Stephen! Damn you, damn you, I'm a woman. You want men . . . you want . . ."

"No, no, it will work. You'll see. This is the only time I've strayed since we married. You must believe me, you must. It won't happen again, Laura. I'm sorry . . ."

"Sorry? You're sorry?" Laura was completely hysterical now. Her voice was shrill and her face was fiery red. "You marry me because my daddy would never take you to bed. Then you bring your lover to our house and have him paint a star on his cheek so you can pretend you're making love to my daddy, and you tell me you're sorry." She shuddered with pain and with shock and with nausea. "Dear god, this can't be happening to me . . . it's not fair . . . it's too horrible, too . . . too . . . let me go. Damn you, Stephen, let me go."

With one last surge of strength she threw off his hands and lunged away. She was across the room when he caught her. At the front door they struggled anew, Stephen crying and pleading and clinging, Laura screaming and shoving and hitting.

Again she managed to free herself. She jerked open the front door and ran out into the cold moonlit night. Stephen frantically followed. Laura sprinted across the yard and out the front gate, heading toward the guest house.

Stephen was a few steps behind her, blubbering and begging and running as fast as he could, mindless of his nakedness, his bare feet, so bent was he on catching her, on making her understand. The strange pathetic chase continued until Laura ran headlong into the solid frame of an advancing Buddy Hester.

Collapsing into his big, comforting arms, she heard Stephen still sobbing pitifully, "You can't leave me, Laura, you can't."

CHAPTER FORTY-ONE

IT WAS at a loud party in a musician's Oak Lawn apartment where she first saw him.

Valentina had come, on the arm of Neil Allen, because she was bored. Extremely bored. She had no recording artist-lover, had not had one for more than a year. She went everywhere with Neil. Even, occasionally, to bed.

Neil Allen was ecstatic. In love with the aging redhead since the first time he'd seen her in Green's drugstore, he felt sure Valentina was finally his. It had been worth all the waiting, all the hurt, all the humiliation. The past few months had been the happiest of his life. She depended on him more and more to run her business, and she had even allowed him to make love to her on special occasions.

He felt like a young boy again.

But Valentina was bored on this night and she told Neil she wanted him to take her someplace exciting. He took her to a late supper at the Fairmont's Pyramid Room. She told him that was hardly her idea of exciting. Desperate, he mentioned a party at one of their house musician's.

"Supposed to be real wild," he confided.

"Take me," she commanded.

They reached the party. It was wild. Drunks everywhere. Marijuana smoke heavy in the air. Coke sniffers. Couples humping and grinding on the dance floor while the stereo blasted out raunchy rock and roll.

Sipping a gin and tonic, Valentina sat on a long sofa beside Neil and watched. Bored. She was about to suggest they leave.

Then she spotted him. He stood with his back to her, talking to a trio of women. He was tall and slim and he had thick black hair and wide shoulders. There was something about his stance, his posture.

299

Her heart began to beat faster. She silently commanded the tall, dark-haired man to turn around. He didn't. He continued to stand, feet slightly apart, white shirt pulling across his shoulder blades. A fourth female approached him. A beautiful, light-skinned black; she laid her hand on his arm. He turned and Valentina stared as the chisel-featured man unsmilingly pulled the black girl close, tilted her chin up and lowered his open mouth to hers.

It was a long, hot, sexual kiss and by the time it ended, Valentina, eyes never leaving the provocative pair, felt the familiar dampness between her legs.

"Neil, darling," she said, "that tall, hard-looking man. I want him." She finally tore her eyes away, and looked at her crestfallen companion. "Go over and tell him to be at my home tomorrow night at exactly nine o'clock. Give him whatever he asks."

"I refuse," said Neil Allen.

"Then I'll have our host tell him." She searched the faces for her house musician. Catching his eye, she motioned him over and told him what she wanted.

"I'll do it, Valentina, but I can't guarantee anything. I don't know the guy. One of the chicks brought him and I'm not . . ."

"My house at nine tomorrow evening. You understand me?"

"Yes, ma'am."

Valentina was in high spirits the next morning when she lay upon the massage table in her over-warm, white exercise room. Commanding Davy, the huge, talented black masseur, to, "Make my skin as elastic as that of a young girl," she threw off the covering sheet and picked up the white telephone.

She rang up La Lingerie in New York, a newly opened Madison Avenue boutique that carried exquisite European-made intimate garments. She needed, she told them, the most beautiful nightgown they had. That would be, they informed her, an incredibly gorgeous hand-embroidered silk gown and peignor set that went for fifty-seven hundred dollars. She'd take it, she happily shouted into the phone. Super, they said, they would put it in the mail immediately. No, she practically screamed, it had to be flown to Dallas that day so that she could wear it that night! They would, they assured her, love to accommodate, but they didn't think that . . .

"I'll send a plane to New York to pick it up; all you have to do is messenger the gown out to La Guardia," said Valentina.

The next call she made was to Mr. Frederick at Best Tressed. "You must come, darling Frederick," she ordered, "and bring your staff. I want the works. Be here no later than five this afternoon!"

After her massage, Valentina swam in the pool, had a light lunch served on the back terrace, and asked her personal maid once again if she and the servants had their instructions clear.

Sniffing, Della nodded and repeated Valentina's orders. "After the servants have finished with an extra-thorough housecleaning, they are to retire to their quarters and remain there until summoned. I am to stay and answer the door when your guest arrives, show him immediately up to your bedroom, and then disappear."

"You're leaving out something," accused Valentina.

"I . . . oh . . . at approximately ten minutes of nine, I'm to bring up a magnum of iced Dom Pérignon in a crystal ice bucket, two crystal champagne flutes, a silver bowl filled with fresh imperial caviar and a silver platter of tiny rounds of hard toast." She paused, "I believe that's exactly the request you made."

"Yes," said Valentina, smiling, "exactly." As an afterthought, "Oh, and Della, add a crystal pot of strawberry preserves. No, no, forget that. Make it a silver pitcher of chocolate syrup and place a couple of pastry brushes in a linen napkin."

"Ma'am?" Della wore a puzzled expression. "Chocolate syrup and pastry . . . ?"

"Never you mind," Valentina interrupted. "It just might come in handy." She rose, sighing with satisfaction. "I'm going up for a nap; don't disturb me. You can change the sheets—use the ivory satin ones—and clean the bedroom while my hairdresser's here."

"Yes, ma'am."

Valentina, as happy as a young girl, napped the long, quiet afternoon away, determined to look as rested, and as youthful, as possible. She roused about the time Mr. Frederick and his entourage arrived.

Ordering Valentina into her large bath-dressing room, the renowned hairdresser, issuing orders like a drill sergeant, went to work. In a matter of minutes, Valentina sat naked upon a sheet-draped chair in the mirrored room while Mr. Frederick clipped, colored, and curled her gray-streaked red hair.

At the same time, his female assistant gave Valentina a manicure and a pedicure. And the third member of the group, a full-lipped, lisping young man with perfect features and long, slim fingers, sat on his heels between Valentina's plump, parted thighs and, with the aid of tiny tinfoil strips and a small paint brush and his own bowl of henna, worked as an artist on a priceless painting, dying Valentina's thinning pubic hair the same shimmering shade of red as that upon her head.

Those tasks completed, the trio went to work on her makeup. Mr. Frederick applied a smooth, ivory base and added a peach blusher to the cheeks and chin while the girl did Valentina's eyes, smudging a smokey eyeshadow to the lids before applying eyeliner and black mascara. The pretty-faced young boy took care of the lips, outlining them with a thin brush dipped into a pot of bright red, then filling in with a softer, apricot shade.

Pleased, he moved on. To her nipples. Dipping the tip of his little finger into a tiny tray of pink, powdery blush, he skillfully applied it to a big, soft nipple, bent on making this aging woman—who was paying them a fortune—look like the young girl she wished she was.

They were finished. She was ready. They stood her in the middle of the room, ordering her to turn round and round. All were nodding and chattering. Mr. Frederick stepped forth with his lifter, to give the crown of her shining red hair one last finishing touch. The girl, the manicurist, rechecked Valentina's nails before taking up the perfume bottle to fritz Valentina's throat and elbows and behind her knees.

Pretty boy's eyes were on Valentina's crotch. He took a baby's hairbrush from one of the many bags and dropped to his knees before her. Brushing gently at the newly re-colored pubic hair, he wet his thumb and finger and gave a couple of fiery coils a finishing swirl, before leaning back to survey his handiwork.

"Out, out," Valentina ordered at last, the time of her guest's arrival rapidly approaching. She floated into her bedroom while they packed away their things.

She waited until they had left to put on the new luxurious gown. She didn't want anybody to see it but her new lover. The expensive, flown-in-from-New-York gossamer garment was for his eyes only.

When she was alone, she slipped on the beautiful gown, arranging the delicate bodice over her big breasts so that her pink-rouged nipples would show appealingly through the ivory lace. She smoothed the full, filmy skirt down over her thighs, pulling it tight, making certain the freshly tinted triangle of flaming hair was seductively visible through the silky folds of wispy fabric.

She drew a deep, shuddering breath and got onto her ivory satin-sheeted bed. Sitting up against the padded headboard, she again took pains to arrange the beautiful gown, spreading it in a lovely fanlike pattern, allowing only her bare, well-tended feet to peak from beneath the hem.

＊   ＊   ＊

He wheeled the car into the pebbled drive and looked up at the imposing Victorian house. He pushed back the car seat, reached into his jacket pocket, and took out a tiny vial of white powder. He sniffed some of the powder up both nostrils, and replaced the vial. He waited only a minute, then placed his right hand on his groin. He slid lower in the seat, laid his dark head back, closed his eyes, and conjured up his most-used—but still effective—erotic fantasy.

A young beautiful girl, her black long hair swinging about her lovely face, was upon her knees before him. He was fucking her in a hot hotel room in Mexico.

It never failed to work. He was hard. He bounded out of the car, the vision still clear in his head, desire building.

Valentina heard the doorbell ring downstairs and was beside herself with anticipation. She'd left the bedroom open a crack so that she could hear.

"Mrs. Trent says you are to go right up," she heard Della say, listened for his reply, and heard no answer. But she did hear his sure, swift steps on the stairs coming closer and closer. He entered without knocking. Without closing the door behind him.

Hand at her throat, Valentina watched as he crossed the room to her, his hard-featured face wearing a menacing expression that excited her. He came to the bed, stopped, but said nothing. His sinister demeanor kept Valentina silent as well.

He undressed carelessly, casting off his suit jacket and jerking his shirttail from his trousers. She watched, enrapt, pleased by the sight of all that thick black hair on his chest. And she couldn't believe her eyes when he pulled off his pants and shorts, and he was already impressively hard, huge and ready to give pleasure. Automatically her hand came up off the mattress to reach for what she couldn't wait to have inside her.

His hand shot out and grabbed hers. She winced and her eyes locked with his. He jerked her up, put a bare foot on the bed, and holding her close, viciously ripped the expensive new gown in two. A gurgle of excited fear tore from Valentina's throat.

He bent his dark head and buried his face in her full, nipple-tipped bosom and Valentina almost sobbed with joy.

Abruptly, he flung her down onto her back, swept back the tattered gown, pushed her shaking legs apart and lowered himself over her, his eyes, looking straight into hers, frighteningly cold, yet hot.

Valentina gave a choked cry of delight when he forcefully entered her, penetrating her deeply, savagely, causing her searing pain and rapturous joy.

He threw everything he had into her and while he hunched, he said the dirtiest, most obscene things to her she had ever heard. It was, to her, the beautiful language of love.

She sighed and gasped and moaned and sobbed while he brought her to multiple orgasms. Tirelessly he pumped into her, his slim hips driving, his passion-hardened lips murmuring a litany of lust.

Never had she been so carried away, so near to hysterics. She fleetingly wondered if this god of love was going to kill her with his deep, filling thrusts. It didn't matter. This was all she ever wanted, all she longed for, and if she were to die impaled by this fair-skinned demon lover, well, she had already reached Paradise.

At last he exploded within her and Valentina screamed with delight as she felt the hot gushing liquid spurt into her and overflow. "Darling, my darling," she shouted out in her ecstasy.

He fell away from her, panting, exhausted, his long, pale body gleaming with sweat. And Valentina, madly in love with him, determined to keep him forever at any cost, placed a possessive palm on his concave belly and purred, "Tell me, my big-dicked darling, what's your name?"

CHAPTER FORTY-TWO

BUDDY Hester was worried.

He had never seen a woman cry as long and as hard as Laura cried that cold February night. She cried all the way back into town; she cried the night through in her 3525 living room. She was still crying when the first gray tinges of dawn lightened the Dallas sky.

"I'm calling a doctor," Buddy said more than once during that long, painful night, only to have Laura beg him not to do it. "But, sweetheart," he said, "you're making yourself sick. You need help and I don't know what to do."

"Pl-pl . . . please, don't . . . don't, Bud," she sobbed pathetically, "I . . . I'm al . . . right, alright . . ." And she continued to cry.

It broke his heart to see her this way. He loved her as if she were his own child; loved her as he loved her daddy before her. Big tears filling his own eyes, he held her, cradling her dark head in his big hand, and murmuring soothingly, "Okay, sweetheart, okay. Whatever you want, I'll do anything I can. There, there."

Eyes swollen almost shut, head throbbing with pain, Laura, pale and drawn, finally quit sobbing. Drained, face pressed against Buddy's tear-dampened shirtfront, she said tiredly, "I'm better. I'm okay now," and with effort she slowly lifted her head.

He smiled kindly, wiped the last of her tears away and said, "Want me to help you to bed?"

"No, Bud," she shook her head, "if I could have a couple of aspirin and maybe a cup of coffee." She tried hard to smile at the big worried man.

Used to being told what to do, Buddy Hester, on that day, stepped into a different roll. He took the reins from his beloved employer, his heartbroken friend.

"You're to take the day off," Buddy commandingly informed the housekeeper when she awakened and came into the kitchen while he was fixing the coffee. "Mrs. Flynn has returned from Nashville. She's very tired and wants to rest."

"But what about Mr. Flynn. Is he—"

"Get your purse, Mrs. Cunningham, and take the back way to the service elevator." When Mrs. Cunningham was gone, Buddy rang up the cook and told him he could have another few days off. "Mrs. Flynn will call when she needs you."

He went back into the living room, bearing a tray with the coffee and some slightly burned toast. Refusing the toast, Laura took her coffee, sipped slowly, and said, dry-eyed and stoic, "Bud, you're my friend, you won't . . ."

"Laura, I'll take it to my grave with me, I swear it."

"Thank you."

They talked the morning away. Laura pouring her heart out, telling Buddy all that Stephen had done and said back at the lake house. She told him of the other man . . . the man with a star painted on his cheek. She told him how her marriage had been a farce from the beginning and that she felt like the biggest fool in all the world.

"I wonder," she mused sadly, "if anybody will ever love me for myself."

Buddy felt his chest constrict. C.C. had said those same sad words to him many a time. C.C. had confided that Caroline had never really loved him. That no woman had ever really loved him for himself. And now, here was his sweet, beautiful daughter suffering the same tragic fate. No, worse. Laura suffered much, much worse.

"Laura, honey," Buddy told her, "you'll find the right man. One day you'll meet the one who loves you."

"No, Bud, the only two men who ever . . ." she caught herself and stopped. "I'm C.C.'s daughter; that's why Stephen married me. That's the only reason anybody would want to . . . to . . ."

"That's not so, darlin'. You ran into the wrong guy, but the right one is out there someplace waiting for you."

Buddy tried, in his own awkward way, to assure the sad young woman that there would be brighter days ahead. By noon Laura was yawning and so exhausted that she agreed when he suggested she try to get some rest.

"I think I will, Bud." She rose and crossed the living room. "If you want to go out for breakfast or anything . . . don't feel like you have to baby-sit me. If Stephen comes here, I'll just . . ."

Buddy said, "I'm going nowhere. Flynn shows up here, he'd better be prepared to face me."

She smiled at him. "Bud, promise you'll never leave me."

Broadly, he grinned. "I promise."

Laura undressed and slipped into her bed, her arms and legs heavy with exhaustion. She closed her swollen, bloodshot eyes and saw again the shocking scene at the lake house and felt her stomach turn over with nausea.

"Oh, God," she murmured aloud, "oh, my God."

And she cried once more. Wracking, painful sobs, muffled into her pillow so that Buddy would not hear. She cried and cried until she was choking and could hardly get her breath. And then finally, blessedly, Laura fell asleep.

Buddy Hester did not.

Like an old mama lion protecting her cub, he paced quietly in the living room, his big hands balling into fists at his sides, his insides churning with disgust for the man who had caused Laura such pain.

When he heard the key turning in the lock, he knew who it was. He was in the foyer by the time the door opened. Stephen Flynn stood there looking scared and ashamed.

"Buddy, I've come to speak with Laura."

Buddy crossed his arms over his chest and blocked Stephen's path. "You can't see her. Not ever again."

"That's not up to you, Buddy. I want—"

"I don't give a good goddamn what you want, Flynn. You've hurt her all you're ever going to. I ever catch your ass around here after today, I'll kill you with my bare hands."

"Look, I know she's hurt, but you're being unreasonable and—"

"Well, just call me an unreasonable kind of guy," Buddy said. "I guess I am, because anybody that hurts that little girl in there is on my shit list and you, pal, are right at the top."

Stephen said, "I understand. I feel bad about . . ."

"You feel bad?" Buddy echoed. "You feel bad? Let me tell you something, Flynn, you don't feel half-bad enough to suit me. No, siree, if I had my way you'd feel one whole hell of a lot worse. You'd hurt so bad, mister, your lover wouldn't be able to recognize you. Now get the fuck out of here and don't ever come back."

"But I . . ."

"Give me your key. Your things will be packed up and sent to the lake house. You'll hear from Laura's attorneys about the divorce. That about takes care of it, doesn't it?"

Stephen tried one last time. "Buddy, please, if I could just talk to—"

"Flynn," Buddy stepped closer, "as long as there is breath in my body, you'll never get near her again."

"You can't leave me, you can't."

"Yes, I can. And I am."

"No," Valentina pleaded, "please, Neil, I need you. You know I can't get along without you."

Neil, standing behind his desk, continued packing up his things. "You'll get along nicely, I'm sure."

Valentina came to him, gripped his suit lapel. "Dear, dear Neil, that's not true. You know it isn't." She smiled up at him. "You're being a very foolish boy and I forbid—"

"I've been a very foolish boy for the past thirty-nine years," said the balding sixty-year-old Neil Allen. "Finally, I've tired of it." He removed her hand from his lapel.

"Oh, you're just being silly because you're jealous. You needn't be, you know. My relationship with Ryker has nothing to do with us. I'll keep him away from the office and . . ."

"Keep him any place you please because I'm not going to be around."

"What have you got against Ryker?" she said, the mere mention of her lover bringing a coy little smile to her lips. "He's really a very nice man."

"No, Valentina, Ryker Rawley is not a nice man. He's mean and sullen and a dope addict. Since none of that matters to you, I can only assume the man is highly proficient in his chosen profession."

Her red eyebrows shot up. "What is that supposed to mean?"

"You're a clever woman. Figure it out."

"Are you insinuating that I pay Ryker to sleep with me?" she was indignant.

Giving no reply, he snapped shut his briefcase and picked up the cardboard box filled with mementos of thirty-nine years spent at Bluebonnet Records. With her at his heels, like a worrisome puppy, he made his way to the door.

"Oh, Neil, please don't go. I don't know how to run the business without you. Stay with me and I'll double your salary. Stay and we'll . . ."

"No, Valentina. No."

And Neil Allen was gone.

She stood in the doorway, stunned, afraid for the first time in her fifty-seven years. No one was more aware than she of Neil's value to the company. He was brilliant and industrious and knew the business inside out. He was, she knew, responsible for much of Bluebonnet's continuing success and high margin of profits.

"Well, go to hell, Neil W. Allen!" she shouted and slammed the door with a bang. Muttering to herself, she crossed to Neil's empty desk and was reaching for the phone when it buzzed.

Viola, her secretary, said, "Valentina, your . . . ah . . . friend is on line two."

A wide smile instantly spreading over her face, Valentina forgot about Neil Allen. "Darling?" she said breathlessly into the phone. "Ryker?"

"There's no goddamn Chivas Regal in this house," answered Ryker Rawley. "Either have a bottle here in half an hour or I'm leaving."

Panic-stricken, she said, "Honey, no, don't go. I'll call Marty's immediately. You'll have a case of Chivas within the hour."

"Good," came the cool reply.

"Darling, what are you doing this afternoon? Shall I come home and . . ."

"No. I'm going out after a while."

Valentina swallowed hard. "Oh? May I ask where?"

"Lady, you just rent me, you don't own me. I'll be back by dinnertime, so don't worry about it." He hung up the phone in her ear.

"Alright, darling," she said to the dial tone.

The phone rang at 3525. Buddy jerked it up, loaded for bear, ready to give Stephen Flynn an earful. But it was Delson Parks, one of the old hands from C.C.'s days, now a studio musician at Lone Star.

"Bud, I just heard something I thought you ought to know. Charles E. Rawley is back in Dallas."

"Jesus H. Christ!"

"Probably nothing to worry about," said Parks. "Just thought you'd want to keep an eye on him."

"Thanks for calling, Delson."

Buddy hired another bodyguard that very day, not bothering to explain his reason to Laura. "Hal Alcott's a good man," he told her, "big and strong and trustworthy." He grinned then and added, "I'm getting old, honey. I've lost a step or two."

He didn't tell her that Rawley was in Dallas. He saw no need to do so; there was probably no cause for alarm. The man had been out of prison for years and had never tried to get near her.

At least that's what Buddy thought. Laura had never told anyone, save Missy, what happened all those years ago in Mexico. Buddy had no idea that a trusting Laura McCarty had lost her innocence to the depraved, sadistic felon.

If he had, he would have killed Charles E. Rawley.

"I'm ready to leave," said Laura, "is the luggage loaded?"

"Yes, Mrs. Flynn," said her driver, opening the Rolls door and handing her inside.

Three days had passed since the night at the lake house. In those three days Laura had remained in guarded seclusion at the 3525, refusing to see anyone but Missy DiGrassi. She was leaving town today, getting away, going abroad to seek peace and privacy.

She would have left sooner, but this date was special. It was February 16. Her daddy's birthday. He would have been forty-seven-years old.

Laura pulled her sable tighter in the early dawn, drew a deep, labored breath and said, "Take me to Musicland."

CHAPTER FORTY-THREE

THE new black Mercedes limousine with its diplomatic license plates and official flag careened around the corner and braked to a stop before a fire hydrant in downtown Dallas. Dallas' prettiest member of the Consular Corps, swathed in black mink and dripping diamonds, bounded out from behind the wheel.

Long mane of blond hair gleaming in the Texas sunshine, bright smile on her face, the glamourous young Consul General swept up the steps of the Dallas County courthouse. She remained inside for half an hour. When she came out, a parking ticket was attached to the limo's windshield. Blithely, she removed the ticket, tore it in two, and dropped it in the gutter, dusting her gloved hands together.

Into the Mercedes she stepped and away she sped, while from the courthouse a grinning, slightly drunk Venezuelan geologist emerged, a brand new visa and a one-way plane ticket clutched in his hand.

International duties done for the day, Consul General Missy DiGrassi wheeled the shiny limo around the corner and headed for Fountain Place.

At Fountain Place, a gleaming new sixty-story prismatic-shaped glass building pierced the bright Texas sky. Allied Bank Tower with its dramatic, modernistic architecture and large public plaza was Dallas' latest and most successful attempts at designing a piece of minimalist sculpture.

On the forty-sixth floor of the fabulous new skyscraper, Laura McCarty, in a pair of Laroche navy flannel trousers and a Barry Bricken cotton sweater, her shoulder-length black hair tied back with scarf, sat cross-legged on the deeply carpeted floor amidst a sea of cardboard boxes.

Lone Star Records, having made respectable strides in the past year, had moved their studios into the Tower. The new studio was Laura's pride and joy. A world-class facility designed by Houston's genius acoustic expert, Russell Berger, it contained an SSL room—Solid State Logic console— one of a half-dozen in the entire country.

Only a week before, Lone Star had taken delivery on its Sony multitrack (twenty-four-track recorder) imported from Japan. And in Lone Star's underground garage was a new remote truck with a 600 Series MCI board.

With Berger's help, Laura had created a magnificent studio with splendid aesthetics from the reception area to the control room to the private offices.

Alone in the spacious, sunlit room she had chosen for her office, Laura was supposedly unpacking. In actuality, she reminisced about the past year of her life.

The year since the lake house horror. The year since the Montenegrin ecstasy.

Cutting her stay short, Laura had returned from Montenegro the day after meeting Griff Deaton. She had no desire to remain after the bittersweet night they spent together.

Taking full blame for what had happened, she stopped Griff when he asked that she let him explain about his marriage. Lifting her hand, palm up, she said, "No, Griff. No. It doesn't matter, really it doesn't. You're married. I'm married. Let's leave it at that."

"But, sweetheart, I want you to know why—"

"I'd rather not. Truly." She raised robed shoulders, allowed them to fall. "This wasn't your fault and I'm sure you love your wife very much. I don't know her, but I feel terrible for seducing her husband and I—."

"It wasn't that way. I'm a big boy. I wanted you. If there's guilt here, it's mine, not yours."

"You're kind, Griff Deaton." She started for the door.

Griff followed anxiously. "God, honey, don't go like this."

They were to the slate foyer; small puddles of water standing where they had dripped seawater earlier. "Should I stay then, Griff, and further complicate things?" she asked. "Want me to spend a couple of days with you before you go back to your wife? Shall we make love again and again so that parting will be painful?"

He looked tortured, his gleaming leonine head sagging, his sleepy blue eyes filled with frustration. "You're right, of course. You can't stay. I don't want you to stay."

Sadly, she smiled. "I thought not." She looked down at the big, black robe she wore. Lifting a terry lapel, she said, "I'll return this tomorrow. And say good-bye."

"Fine," said Griff Deaton. "I'll be here."

Laura turned away, opened the front door.

Over her shoulder, "Goodnight, Griff."

"Goodnight, Laura . . . I . . ." He let out a loud moan, grabbed her and swiftly pulled her around and up into his arms. His lips were on hers and Laura felt herself melting against him. Desperately, she kissed him back, standing on bare tiptoe, straining against him, mentally memorizing everything about him . . . the lines of his hard, powerful body, his marvelous mouth, the clean, unique scent of Griff Deaton.

When at last they broke apart, gasping for breath, Laura shoved on his chest and ran out the door, not stopping until she was safely locked inside her own villa.

She never returned Griff Deaton's big black terry robe.

She never saw him again.

Laura stayed awake that night, pacing restlessly, wondering why she couldn't have met Griff Deaton before Ryker . . . before Stephen . . . She quit pacing and reproved herself for continuing to be a foolish, hopeless romantic.

She was going to stop it. She was going to be like Missy was before DiGrassi came into her life. She would go back to Dallas, divorce Stephen Flynn, and start living for a change.

Why not face the facts here? She, apparently, was a hot-blooded woman. She wanted sex, not love. That should be no problem. It had certainly been no problem getting the very married Griff Deaton to take her to bed.

For now, she would get some sleep, return Mr. Deaton's robe to him come morning, and rest here a few more days before returning home to begin her new, exciting life. Surely there were plenty of amorous, good-looking men in Big D who would obligingly make love to her when she was in the mood.

But her eyes never closed that night and at five in the morning, Laura called Buddy at the hotel and told him she was ready to go home. Packed and waiting, she met him at the front door. Ahead of Buddy, she hurried to the waiting car in the still-dark morning, never looking up at the top villa.

Her first day back from Yugoslavia, Missy breathlessly imparted the news. "Ryker Rawley is in Dallas. What are you going to do about it?"

Calmly, "Nothing."

"Nothing?" Missy screeched, "Did you hear me correctly? I said that bastard Ryker Rawley's in town. You're not safe and I think you should—"

"I'm safe," said Laura, continuing to unpack, while Missy stormed around her bedroom. "Ryker Rawley knows how completely he made me pay. He's satisfied, believe me."

Missy stopped storming and stared at Laura. "You really think so? He wanted you pregnant, remember."

"He doesn't know I wasn't. Besides," Laura placed folded lingerie in a dresser drawer, "I'm no longer a starry-eyed eighteen-year-old. The man didn't kidnap me. I couldn't wait to go with him."

"Mmmmm, that's true," said Missy, "I guess with Buddy around you'll be safe. Still, Ryker might want to . . ."

"No. No, he won't. The things Ryker Rawley did to me in that Mexican hotel room 'punched my ticket,' as they say. What the man really set out to do was to shatter all my illusions, which he very successfully did. End of story."

"Then I guess you won't mind me telling you who Ryker's screwing now. None other than the old superslut, Valentina."

Laura merely smiled. "If ever a pair deserved each other."

"Ain't it the truth," Missy flopped down on the bed. "What about Stephen?"

"What about him?" answered Laura.

"Are you going to see him to . . ."

"Not if I'm lucky. My attorney has begun the divorce proceedings. I'll be free in sixty days."

"That's good, then you can . . . hey, what's this?" Missy reached into an open suitcase and drew out a black terry robe. She rose and held it up to her body.

"It's exactly what it looks like. A bathrobe."

"But it's big enough for two of you and . . ." She started grinning, "Were you a bad girl in Montenegro?"

Laura took the robe from Missy, not bothering to reply. She saw no need to tell Missy about Griff Deaton. After all, Deaton was to be only one in a long line of lovers. Nothing worth mentioning there.

Later, after Missy had gone, Laura, wearing Deaton's big, comfortable robe, climbed into bed and rang up her mother.

"I'm back, Mother. Safe and sound."

"Good, Laura. You feeling better? When will I see you?"

"Come into town and have lunch with me someday this week."

"I will, I sure will." There was a short pause. "Laura. Ah . . . there's something I've been meaning to tell you. I guess it can wait though until . . ."

"What, Mother?"

"Well, I hate . . . I know you're still upset over your breakup with Stephen and I'd rather wait . . ."

"Mother, what is it?"

"Well, honey, I've agreed to write a book. Doubleday offered me—"

"What are you saying?" Laura felt her whole body tensing.

"They want a book about your daddy's—"

"No!" Laura shouted into the telephone. "You can't. You can't do that, why would—"

"Laura, calm down. I've already signed the contract and promised them a manuscript. I'll just write about my life with the Chief . . ."

"My God, how could you? You're not talking about some glamorous stranger, you're talking about my daddy. Damn it, can't anybody let the poor man rest in peace!"

"Honey, you're over-reacting and—"

"Over-reacting? You write an exposé on my daddy and I'll never speak to you again!"

Laura was at Lone Star the next day, plowing through the mail that had piled up in her absence, when her secretary buzzed.

"There's a Mr. Neil Allen here to see you, Laura."

She didn't hesitate. "Send him in, Betty."

She rose and smiled warmly at the tall, slim, bald-headed man. "Mr. Allen, so nice to meet you," she reached a hand out to shake his. "Please, sit down," she indicated one of the gray suede chairs across from her.

Neil Allen sat down, looked directly into her dark eyes, and said, "Mrs. Flynn, I've come to ask you for a job."

Laura's jaw dropped. "But I thought . . . that is . . ."

"No. I'm no longer employed at Bluebonnet and I would like to work for you."

"But what . . . that is . . ."

He smiled. "I simply feel I need a change, a new challenge." Far too much a gentlemen to say anything derogatory about Valentina, Neil Allen explained that there were few challenges left for him at the powerful Bluebonnet. "I know your company is relatively new and I feel, with my background, I could be of help, have something to offer."

Flabbergasted but delighted, Laura nodded eagerly. "Mr. Allen, your reputation is legend. I speak for the whole staff when I tell you we'd be honored to have you at Lone Star. I'm afraid the money I can offer may not be as much . . ."

He waved a dismissive hand. "When do I start?"

"Today too soon?"

* * *

Now Laura sat in the new offices high in the Allied Bank Tower, thinking about the quiet, capable man. Working with Neil Allen had been like studying at the feet of the master. He'd forgotten more about the record business than most had learned.

A kind, patient man, he'd worked tirelessly, remaining in his office long after the others had gone home, wining and dining retail chains and jobbers, laying out budgets, dreaming up promotions, calling in favors, and doing one hundred other things at which he was expert.

He had made the difference. Lone Star Records was coming into its own and if she never recovered Big Chief, the future ahead was still bright.

At least, financially.

Her private life was another matter. She hadn't done as she had promised herself she would that night in Montenegro. Oh, she had come home and divorced Stephen, alright, and the last she heard he had moved back to Europe.

Free, she had meant to lead the glittering life with the Dallas swells, bed hopping as so she desired, laughing and loving with the best of them, feeding every hunger, skipping giddily from one lavish party to another, one sexy man to another.

She found she had no taste for it and after only a couple of months of letting down her hair and swimming in an ocean of vintage champagne, of falling happily into the arms of handsome hunks, she gave it up for lost.

In truth she never even made it as far as the bedroom. A few drinks of Lafitte Rothschilds and fewer heated kisses were all she ever shared with the steady stream of men who came to her penthouse apartment during that short, blurred period. All too soon she gladly passed the torch to someone else, withdrawing from the race.

And try as she might, she couldn't forget a big, brown-haired, sleepy-eyed man who had made exquisite love to her in a firelit cliffside villa high above the Adriatic sea. Night after night, as she reached for a big, black terry robe, she thought about its owner.

And she wondered.

Did Griff Deaton ever . . . ever . . . think of her?

Missy DiGrassi strode through the door of Laura's carton-filled office and walked in unannounced. Seeing her friend sitting on the floor, hugging her knees, a wistful expression in her dark eyes, Missy sighed and abruptly drew Laura back to the present.

"You've got that thousand-yard stare," said Missy, loudly, shrugging out of her lush sable and tossing it over a chair. Laura's head snapped up. Missy laughed at the startled expression on Laura's face. "What were you thinking about?"

Laura shook her head, smiled and rose from the floor. "Nothing, really."

"You're a lousy liar, kid. There's something you are not telling me. I know it just as sure as I'm the new Consul General to Venezuela."

Laughing, Laura turned the questioning around, unwilling to share Griff Deaton with anyone. "Tell me, Consul, just what do you important diplomats do?"

"Consul *General*," Missy corrected. "Please use my full title. Today I went to the courthouse, bailed out a drunk Venezuelan geologist, and got him a visa to replace the one he lost when some punks rolled him." She sank down into the chair. "After such a taxing morning, I'm totally exhausted." Laughing, she went on, "We help stranded tourists. We apply wax seals to coffins of foreigners who die in Dallas so their bodies can be shipped home."

Laura made a face. "Sounds gruesome."

"I also rub elbows with presidents and princes. I'm pretty important, Laura, no doubt about it."

"I see. And how, I wonder, was such an honor bestowed on one so young and inexperienced?" Her dark eyes sparkled.

"Gee, I don't know. Do you suppose the fact I'm married to one of the richest men ever to come out of Venezuela had anything at all to do with it?"

When they had stopped laughing, Missy told Laura she had heard through the grapevine that Bluebonnet Records, sans one Neil Allen, was on the downhill slide. She said rumor had it that Valentina was so enamored of her live-in lover, Ryker Rawley, that she had lost interest in her company. Said eyebrows all over Dallas were raising and Valentina's escapades were the main topic of conversation at the social lunches throughout the city. Told her that Rawley was spending money like an oil-rich Arab and snorting coke and ordering Valentina around as though she were his slave.

"A charming couple," was Laura's comment before changing the subject. "What do you think of my new offices? Think you'd like to work here?"

"Me? Work? Bite your tongue," said Missy. "It is impressive, though. I like it."

Laura smiled. "On a clear day . . ."

"Very modern." Missy looked at Laura, cleared her throat, and said, "I got my hands on an advance copy of Caroline's book. Have you seen it yet?"

Laura's dark eyes clouded. "No. Tell me, Missy. Is it . . . Does she tell all?"

"I'm afraid so. You two still not speaking?"

"Can you blame me?"

"I did," said Missy. "After reading the book, I don't. Are you going to read it?"

"I can't not read it. I fly down to Houston tomorrow; I'll take it along and read it at the hotel."

"Houston?"

Laura nodded. "The Houston Bar Association. Neil committed to serve on a copyright panel, but he's come down with a bad cold. I'm filling in."

"Sounds like fun," said Missy. "Attorneys are still mostly male, aren't they?"

Laura rolled her eyes heavenward.

CHAPTER FORTY-FOUR

GRIFFITH L. Deaton II, his massive chest bare, thick brown hair disheveled, stood shaving before the mirror in the master bathroom of his River Oaks home. As he shaved, the successful thirty-five-year-old criminal attorney practiced the speech he was to give before today's lawyers' luncheon at Houston's Hotel Warwick.

Not yet fully awake, Griff mumbled the words, punctuating his sentences with big openmouthed yawns. Griff was tired on this chilly February morning. He'd slept restlessly, waking at the slightest noise, throwing back the covers again and again to rise and hurry down the hall to Annette's room.

All the sudden wakings had proved to be false alarms. Heart hammering against his ribs, Griff, terror gripping his chest, had rushed into Annette's spacious white-and-beige bedroom to find her sleeping as peacefully as an infant.

Releasing a relieved breath, Griff had stood over the bed, looking down at the frail figure beneath the sheets, affection and pity overflowing, assuring himself she still breathed. And he would reach down to gently push a thin, wispy lock of faded chestnut hair from her drawn cheek, or pull the silky sheets about her thin shoulders or whisper silently, "Sleep, hon. Rest, darlin', I'm right here. I'll always be here."

Then he'd smile down affectionately at the slumbering woman, return to his own room and fall, exhausted, into troubled sleep. Until the next time he awakened, thinking she might need him.

So he was tired, as usual, on this morning, and wondered, like always, if he would make it through the day. He would make it, he knew he would. He had made it for the past four years. He could make it for another four. Or another forty. Whichever it turned out to be.

319

Griff Deaton was freshly shaven, impeccably dressed, and all bright smiles when he walked into the bay-windowed breakfast room half an hour later. Annette was there, her lifeless hair brushed, her pale, drawn face carefully made-up. Her short fingernails were painted. She wore an expensive, delicate pink robe that Griff had bought her.

"Hiya, sweetheart," said Griff, cheerfully, and bent to place a warm, loving kiss on her translucent right cheek. "My, my, you look pretty this morning," he said, nodding to the uniformed nurse. He winked at Annette, touched her hair briefly, kissed her again and took his place at the breakfast table.

Annette Deaton did not really look pretty. Annette Deaton would never look pretty again, though she was only thirty-three years old. Once a vibrant and beautiful woman, the former high-fashion model was trapped in a useless, unresponsive, and far-from-attractive body.

Eyes blinking, but following every gesture her husband made, Annette Deaton could not move. A narrow leather band, going around her forehead and attached to the high back of her wheelchair, kept her head from falling onto her bony chest. Her hands, those carefully manicured hands, were strapped to the arms of her chair. A seatbelt was fastened securely about her waist.

The tragic young woman's muscles would no longer obey her. She couldn't walk. Could hardly talk. A hand-embroidered bib was draped about her neck because Annette drooled like a baby, and without the bib, she soiled her clean, expensive robes.

Mrs. Griffith L. Deaton II was suffering from Lou Gehrig's disease.

Griff Deaton talked to his wife just as though she were as fit and as sound as she had been when first they met. He told Annette that his speech was finished . . . such as it was . . . and he hoped he didn't have an attack of stage fright when he got up there before all his peers.

He carried on a one-sided conversation with her throughout the meal, stopping to repeat something if she looked too puzzled. He joked and kidded and behaved as if everything in the Deaton household was completely normal and by the time he was ready to leave, Annette was smiling, her faded eyes holding a spark of remembered vitality.

"Lord, hon, I'm running late," Griff looked at his gold Rolex and shoved back his chair. He came to her, crouched down beside the wheelchair, and covered her hand with his.

"Sweet baby, I hate it, but I'm going to be late getting in tonight. I'm one of the hosts for the welcoming cocktail party at the Warwick. I should be no later than nine o'clock and if you're still up, we'll have a nightcap and listen to a little classical music, how does that sound?"

"Sounds good," managed the woman who had always had a weakness for fine wines and fine music.

"It's a date. Love you," he kissed her and rose, grabbing up his smooth calfskin briefcase and dashing for the garage, whistling happily.

Griff Deaton climbed into his bronze Mercedes, started the engine, and exhaled heavily. Gripping the steering wheel, he leaned his forehead against it, and said aloud, "Oh, God, if there is a God, take her soon. Listen to me, God, no more. No more, you hear me. She's suffered enough."

Laura McCarty was already in an agitated mood when she walked into the opulent marble lobby of Houston's Hotel Warwick. The flight from Dallas had been bumpy despite her expert pilots' doing their dead-level best to fly around ominous, water-filled clouds, rising to a ceiling of fifty thousand feet.

It was beginning to sleet by the time they landed at Hobby and Laura had the sinking feeling that this entire trip was going to be as bleak as the unexpected, nasty weather.

At the Warwick, it didn't help matters to find herself lost in a sea of business-suited men, all laughing and talking and checking in, mountains of luggage stacked throughout the lobby.

Waiting her turn in line, Laura grew more annoyed by the minute. When finally she reached the front desk, she was frowning. "McCarty," she said, exasperated.

"Oh, Miss McCarty," apologized the hotel employee, "so sorry for the inconvenience. I had no idea you were . . . there's an attorneys' seminar and lawyers are pouring in from everywhere. Racehorse Haynes is to address them as well as young, brilliant Mr. Deat . . . ah . . . but of course, you're not interested." He slapped his palm down on the bell. "Front, please," he shouted, though no bellmen were in sight.

"Can I please have a key? You can send the luggage up when a bellboy is available."

"Oh, certainly, Miss McCarty. Room 718." Laura took the key and made her way through the swarm of loud-talking lawyers, ignoring the turning of heads and looks of inquiry she evoked.

She let herself in the room, kicking her shoes off the minute she was inside. Shortly, a beaming bellman arrived with her luggage and handed her a complimentary newspaper. She tossed it on the bed and tipped him.

Laura undressed, put on the worn black terry robe, and curled up in an easy chair to read more of the book Caroline had entitled simply *Chief.* The more she read, the more upset Laura became. Her face grew fiery red while the hands that held the book were icy cold.

She couldn't believe that her mother told and allowed to be printed the most intimate details of her stormy marriage to the man she was quoted as saying, ". . . was certainly an expert in bed, but then he should have been, he spent as much time there as he did on stage. And I don't mean with me."

It got worse. Caroline told of his drug dependency, of missed studio appointments, of bitter arguments, of irrational behavior, of a burned-out, mixed-up man who became a stranger to her and to his friends in his last tragic days.

Laura slammed the book shut, her stomach churning with emotion. It was impossible to believe that all her mother told could have happened without Laura's knowing. It wasn't true. She refused to believe it. Her daddy was a good man, a loving and talented man, not some pill-crazed maniac who unwittingly committed suicide with his excesses.

Laura walked the floor of her suite, rubbing her arms and fuming. Upset, edgy, she went to the tall windows. The sky was blacker than ever and the sleet was now sticking to the streets and sidewalks.

She turned away. She had planned to spend the evening going over the notes Neil had drafted for her panel participation tomorrow morning. She drew the notes from her briefcase, glanced at them, sighed, and tossed them on the bed. She snatched up the *Houston Post* and flopped down on a sky-blue velvet sofa.

Scanning the lead stories—Ronnie and Nancy flying to the Western White House, the price of crude dropping around the world, the nominations made for the Academy Awards—she turned to the society pages to read Maxine Messinger's column.

". . . Dr. and Mrs. Grant Dickson held a lavish dinner party at their Memorial swankienda. The town's gay crowd . . . Wedding bells for Houston oiler, Brant Sherwood, and beautiful Sunny MacFadden in the . . . Back from another trip to Yugoslavia and settled once more in their River Oaks manse in the city's silk-stocking district, is attorney, Griffith L. Deaton II and his wife, Annette. Griff Deaton will be on hand for the Houston Bar Association outing beginning today at the Warwick. Deaton is one of a half-dozen of our town's most prominent attorneys who will be speaking before the group, as well as hosting a cocktail party in the Warwick's posh club at 5:00 P.M. today."

Laura realized she had not breathed while reading the column. She inhaled deeply and looked at the thin gold watch on her wrist. She began to shiver. Griff Deaton was in the hotel this very minute, under the same roof with her, in the same world with her.

And she was going to see him.

Dressed in a simple Calvin Klein black lamb's wool with a V-neck, her shoulder-length blunt-cut black hair worn straight, Laura stepped into an empty elevator and ascended to the top floor where the club was located.

It was half past five in the afternoon.

The heavy doors opened. She stepped out into the corridor and turned right, following the noise. At the club's open double doors she paused, eyes quickly scanning the room filled with dozens of laughing, talking men and a scattering of women.

It was easy to pick him out of the crowd. He stood head and shoulders above the others. His back was to her, but she'd have known him anywhere. That great, leonine head, those massive shoulders, that unruly brown hair.

Laura remained there on the threshold, despite friendly, hopeful invitations from a number of the lawyers, to come on inside and join in the fun. Her only answer was a shake of her dark head, and a sweet, declining smile. She didn't want to go inside. She didn't want to seek him out.

She wanted to stand here until he turned and spotted her. When that happened, she would know in an instant if Griff Deaton was glad to see her. Terrified, hopeful, she never took her eyes from him.

Griff, a half-full glass of bourbon and water in his right hand, gestured with the other. A great storyteller, he had a small, enrapt audience and he was entertaining them with a humorous anecdote. Grinning engagingly, he was coming to the punch line when he felt a peculiar tingling. The hair on the back of his neck stood up. He lost his train of thought, repeating, trying to pick up where he left off.

Faces turned up to his, waiting, his companions were puzzled when he stopped speaking, a strange light coming into his eyes. "I . . . excuse me," he said, and very slowly, Griff Deaton turned around.

He was looking at her across the crowded room and the answer Laura had so hoped to see was written all over his expressive face. Absently handing his liquor glass to a passing fellow attorney, he made his way to her.

The room was suddenly far too warm and Laura was afraid she might faint. Walking toward her was the only man that had ever made her feel like a woman. Bigger and handsomer than she had remembered, the potent maleness of Griff Deaton took her breath away. She wanted this man, had wanted him every night of her life, would want him for all the rest of her life.

He reached her.

They stood looking at one another, in awe, shy. She felt the nearness of his hand rather than saw it. He took her arm and the heat of his fingers seemed to burn through the soft lamb's wool sleeve and into her skin.

Wordlessly, he guided her down the corridor to the bank of elevators, ignoring the good-natured shouts of, "Hey, Griff, where you going?" and "Bring her to the party," and "Dinner later, Griff?"

The elevator was crowded, so they said nothing to each other. His hand was no longer on her arm. But his big, solid body was close to hers and Laura could feel his muscular thighs trembling against her.

The car stopped at every floor, discharging passengers, picking up new ones. She thought she would go mad. At last they reached her floor and she wordlessly produced a key. Then they were inside the suite. And still they stood, speechless, awkward, staring at each other while across the dimly lit room, heavy, freezing sleet pelted the windows with rhythmic repetition.

Griff slowly lifted a hand, placing it at the side of Laura's bare throat. His fingers curled around the back of her neck while his thumb touched her chin briefly before moving down to skim beneath the V of her dress.

The contact was so powerfully electric, Laura felt the jolt all through her slender body. It was as though nobody had ever touched her in quite the same way before.

For what seemed an eternity, they looked into one another's eyes, both trembling, both frightened of what they knew was going to happen. Had to happen.

"God, Laura . . . Laura," he said and slowly he wrapped her in his arms and pulled her to him.

"Griff," she breathed as his lips covered hers.

CHAPTER FORTY-FIVE

ADAM burst inside them both.

There was nothing and no one but each other. There was no yesterday, no tomorrow, only now. No world outside this room. No caution, no holding back, no sense of guilt.

Laura's mouth opened immediately beneath Griff's. She kissed him fiercely, starvingly, her shaking arms going around his back to pull him closer. Breasts crushed to his broad chest, she could feel his heartbeat hammering against hers, thrilling her, exciting her.

While his mouth devoured hers, his large, deft hands were unzipping the back of her black wool dress. The fabric parted to her hips, she shivered anew when she felt Griff's fingers worshipfully exploring her spine, his gentle, masterful touch causing her wildly beating heart to sing with fierce joy.

Their lips separated and Laura, as anxious as he, helpfully lowered her arms so that Griff could remove her dress. His sleepy blue eyes gleaming in the half-light, he swiftly swept the black wool down her arms and off. Caught there between their pressing bodies, the dress clung to Laura's hips.

Naked to the waist, Laura began unbuttoning Griff's white shirt, eager to have his hot bare flesh against her own. Reluctant to release her, even for a minute, Griff let her undress him. His hands remained upon her, on the silky skin of her slender back, her delicate shoulders, her narrow waist.

"Griff . . ." she whispered, "please . . . help me."

He kissed her. And one-handed, the other clinging to Laura as though afraid if he released her she might vanish in the air, Griff Deaton managed, amazingly quickly, to divest himself of suit coat, tie, and shirt while Laura slipped off her shoes and panty hose.

When he pulled her to him, Laura winced with pleasure at the startling contact of her swelling breasts against his warm, hair-covered chest. Her hands moved to his upper arms, her fingers curling tightly around his bulging biceps. She pressed her face close and allowed her lips to teasingly trace the edge of his collarbone, the hollow of his throat, his heavily cut chin. And all the while she murmured his name and told him exactly how she felt.

"Griff, Griff," she whispered, "I thought I'd never see you again. I thought you'd never hold me like this, love me like this . . . I wanted it . . . I wanted you . . ."

Griff's hand went into her dark shoulder-length hair and gently he pulled her face away from his trembling chest. "God, Laura, me too . . . me too, sweetheart . . ." He bent to her, reverently kissing her mouth, her eyes, her cheeks, her chin. "I've dreamed of this . . . lived for this . . . Laura, love me, love me, baby . . ." His lips moved down her long, slender neck to her shoulders and Laura threw back her head and breathed through her mouth, acutely aware of her own hair tickling her sensitive back, of Griff's hot, open mouth moving steadily nearer to nipples that were already hard and puckered.

Hands sliding down from her waist, Griff slowly slipped to his knees before her, sweeping the black wool dress from her hips. It fell to the floor at her feet. His mouth never left her flesh and Laura released a tiny gurgle of excited emotion and lowered her head when she felt his hot lips close over her left nipple and he began to gently suck.

She stood there wearing only her panties, her contracting belly and undulating pelvis pressing against his chest and shoulders as he knelt on the carpet, his mouth filled with her breast, his hands filled with the rounded cheeks of her bottom. She clung to the thick hair of his leonine head and sighed, gloried in the strong, erotic pull of his lips on her aching nipples. Knowing his was the only mouth she ever wanted at her breasts, his were the only hands that should ever slip so enticingly beneath her panties.

His lips at last released her tingling nipples and he rose, lifting her, an arm at her waist, the other beneath her knees. Laura wrapped her arms around his neck and left them there when he lowered her to half-sit, half-lie on the blue velvet couch.

They were kissing, straining against each other, Laura's hand moving between them to unzip his trousers and release him. Awed by the size and heat of him, she wrapped inquiring fingers around his jerking tumescence and began to adoringly stroke him.

But Griff's hand covered hers and moved it from him while his lips traveled down over her slender body, brushing kisses to her nipples and ribs and navel. And to her stomach, through the wispy panties she still wore.

Griff didn't take her panties off. Bending his head between her parted thighs, he kissed and nuzzled their soft, smooth insides and slowly worked his way down to her dimpled knees, her shapely calfs and on to her ankles, feet and toes, while Laura sighed and trembled and made involuntary little cries of choked excitement.

And then he started back up.

Suddenly holding her breath, clutching at the velvet cushions of the couch, Laura squirmed as his hot, arousing mouth moved steadily up her legs, kissing and gently biting, until he was back between her spread thighs. She released a labored breath and frantically wished she could rip off her panties before he . . .

His lips moved unerringly to that slick, damp band of nylon going between her legs.

Griff pressed his open mouth directly against the swollen sweetness before him, blowing his hot, fiery breath against her. Laura moaned and clutched at his thick brown hair, her back arching up, her head pressing back against the cushions, her half-closed eyes catching a fleeting glimpse of the icy beads of sleet pummeling the tall frosted windows beside them.

Gently, he began to kiss her through the covering of silky nylon, pressing soft, closed-mouthed kisses to her while he inhaled deeply, savoring the steamy sexual scent of her. Reeling with hunger for her, he opened his mouth and kissed her as though he were kissing those other lips, his tongue thrusting, tasting, molding the damp nylon to her burning flesh.

Laura felt unbelievable heat radiate from his mouth, engulfing her entire body. She pushed her pelvis closer, closer, her frenzied fingers entwining in his hair, grabbing at his ears, the contractions in her belly growing stronger, the wetness flowing from her like a fiery fuel to their unleashed desire.

Griff pushed the soaked panties aside and buried his face in her wet, throbbing heat. He licked her, moving upward, finding that slick, distended nubbin of throbbing flesh. Kissing and sucking, he felt her whole body rising and moving upward against his mouth as though she would have him eat her completely up. And he was so hot and hungry for the taste of her, he longed to do just that.

The licking, the lapping continued until Laura was shuddering, the tenseness building and, breathlessly calling his name, she urged him up, her hands seeking him, wanting him inside her. Griff rapidly shed his trousers and lifted her so that she lay upon the sofa. Kissing her wildly, he moved over her, slid into her hot, tight body and began at once the rhythmic movements of loving.

Laura, her eyes open wide, her restless hands dancing over his slippery shoulders, his furred chest, his corded ribs, gloried in his rapid, powerful thrusting, the sound of his labored breathing, the sight of his shadowed, passion-hardened face above her own.

The pressure was building to an unbearable crescendo, she could feel her muscles gripping him, squeezing him, and him becoming bigger . . . huge . . . with the onset of release.

"Griff . . . Griff . . . I'm . . . I . . ."

"Yes, baby. Come . . . come with me . . . ahhhh."

"Gr . . . Griff . . . Grifffff . . ."

"Laura, sweetheart."

Showered and relaxed, they lay naked beneath the sheets, no illumination in the suite's bedroom, save the diffuse glow of a rust-colored sky coming through the tall ice-crusted windows. The sleet had grown heavier, its harsh tattoo against the cold panes a strangely pleasing, provocative sound to the two sated lovers snuggled closely in the warm bed.

Griff, his arms tightly around Laura, said, "I can't stay, Laura. And I want to tell you why."

He told Laura everything, speaking calmly, leaving nothing out. Told her he had fallen in love with his wife when both were students at Rice University. That theirs had been a good marriage until Annette was stricken with Lou Gehrig's disease four years ago. When he met Laura in Montenegro, Annette was undergoing treatment in Belgrade.

Concluding, he said, "I want to know all about you, Laura. Your marriage, your life." He kissed her.

She told him there was no longer a marriage, that there never had been a real marriage. Told him when they met in Montenegro, she had just uncovered . . . in the worst possible way . . . the awful truth about her husband.

Griff had been right; she had considered jumping into the Adriatic. She was very grateful he saved her. She had desperately needed, she told him, to be held and loved on that night, so she had brazenly asked that he make love to her, never considering, or caring, whether or not he was married.

"I felt terrible about it afterward," she said, "not for my sake, but for yours. I know you felt guilty about betraying your wife."

Griff's arms tightened around her. "I didn't. Perhaps I should have, but I didn't. Still, I was sorry it happened, because I haven't been able to get you out of my mind and I was sure I'd never see you again." His lips pressed a kiss to her brow. "A day hasn't passed I didn't think about you. God, I had no idea who you were; I didn't even know where you lived, except that it was in Texas."

"I know," she turned onto her side and toyed with the crisp brown hair covering his broad chest. "It was the same for me, only worse. I couldn't remember your last name until I saw it in the newspaper today. Griff. That's all I could recall."

"Thank god you read the newspaper."

"Griff."

"Yes, sweetheart?"

"Will I see you again?"

He tilted her chin up so that she was looking at him. Eyes glittering in the semi-darkness, he said, "I won't lie to you. I'll never leave Annette."

"I don't expect you to, but you didn't answer my question."

"I can't offer you anything, Laura. I can't even see you often."

"I'll take it," said Laura.

His thumb brushed back and forth over her parted lips. "It's not enough. I want you to have more. I want you to meet some nice guy and fall in love and . . ."

Thinking to herself, I am in love, she said, "Why would I want to do that when I can have you."

"Sweetheart," he said, "I told you, you won't have me that often. It could be a mighty lonely existence."

"I won't be lonely. I have my company and I understand that you're not free."

"Would you understand if I told you that I can't even spend the night with you? That I have to leave in a few minutes and get back downstairs to the party before too many people miss me? That I have to be home by nine o'clock because I promised Annette?" His hand left her lips to move down and caress a bare hip.

"Yes, I would. How much time have we got?"

Griff lifted his head, looked over at the glowing dial of the bedside clock. "Jesus. None." He turned to her, kissed her deeply, quickly, and got out of bed.

Naked, she followed him into the other room and watched him dress, dying to, but not asking, when next she would see him.

Working at the knot in his tie, Griff came to stand before her. "How long are you staying in Houston, sweetheart?"

"I'm supposed to leave at noon tomorrow, but if the weather's still bad . . ."

He grinned. He pulled her into his embrace and she was keenly aware of the slightly abrasive texture of his flannel suit against her bare skin, of his hands skimming over her back. He said, "I have a couple of hours free tomorrow afternoon. If you're still here . . ."

"I'll be here." She pulled his mouth down to hers. "Even if there's a Houston heat wave."

Three days later, a glowing Laura McCarty returned to Dallas. The precious hours with Griff Deaton had been some of the most beautiful of her life. Not only was he a tender and expert lover, he was a kind and caring man and in his arms she felt safe and cherished.

It was a sensation so wonderful yet foreign to her, Laura warmed herself in it as one would toast himself in a soft, fleecy blanket. Instinctively she knew that never would she be lost and lonely again.

True to his word, Griff called her every day and saw her as often as possible. A day-long tryst at her Padre Island beach house. A stolen night of bliss in his Clear Lake A-frame. A hurried trip to Aspen. All in secrecy.

It was enough.

But Missy DiGrassi was worried about Laura. Missy knew nothing of Griff Deaton; she knew only that Laura never went out with men. She felt it was her duty to right the situation. She paraded a constant stream of eligible bachelors beneath Laura's nose and grew increasingly exasperated that Laura failed to take the bait.

"I have," Missy bossily informed Laura one sunny May afternoon, "arranged for the extremely rich and handsome Jeffrey W. Willingham to be your escort for the dinner party I'm throwing at North Dallas Forty in June. I picked him because . . ."

"No," Laura cut in.

"No? Why?"

"I went out with Willingham once, Missy. He's not my type."

"Not your type? Jeff's the most eligible bachelor in Dallas."

"He chews his fingernails and laughs too loudly."

Missy's hands went to her hips. "You, Laura McCarty, could pick fly shit out of black pepper."

Laura smiled. "I'm sorry, Missy. Jeff's okay, but I pass."

"You always pass, Laura. What's with you?"

Laura's slender shoulders lifted in a shrug. "Nothing, far as I know."

"Yeah? Well, I don't see it that way. You act weird, you know that. You sit around smiling like a Cheshire cat, but you never go anywhere except to work or on one of your infernal business trips. I tell you, Robin Leach could do a story on you and call it 'Lifestyles of the Rich and Fucked-up.'"

"I thought Arto told you to quit using that kind of language."

"Let's not get off the subject here. Tell me why you stay jailed here in this apartment. Is it what Stephen did to you? Are you still, after all this time . . ."

"Stephen who?" Laura replied, smiling.

"Okay, then, so what is it? It's like you know a secret and you won't share it with me. That's not fair, damn it. I tell you everything."

It was true.

The haunted sadness had left Laura's dark eyes, she laughed more often, she was more optimistic and relaxed, she was more like the carefree Laura of old.

She was a woman in love.

She was not the only woman in love.

Valentina Trent absolutely worshipped Ryker Rawley. Their unholy alliance was, for her, pure heaven.

It mattered little that Ryker was cruel and greedy and dangerous. Valentina went about with a foolish smile on her face, a smile his depraved lovemaking had put there. No sexual act was too perverted as long as he was doing it to her. No demand for clothes and cars and money too outlandish, as long as it would keep him with her.

She had met her match. And then some.

Ryker Rawley lived in coke-crazed splendor at Valentina's White Rock mansion. From the start, he had made it clear that if she wanted him to stay with her, she would have to cater to his every whim.

"I'll keep you coming as long as you keep the money coming," was the way he had crudely put it to her after the first night in her bed.

And she had. So he had.

Overnight he was the one in complete control, ordering Valentina about from his command center in the middle of her big rumpled bed.

"I'd like a half dozen Ceruiti suits," he informed her before a week was out. "A couple of dozen Armani shirts and a dozen pairs of Bally shoes."

"Of course, darling," twittered Valentina Trent, stroking his hair-dusted thighs and belly. "Anything you like."

A month later he demanded a white Porsche. He got it.

She didn't mind. She got a great deal more than a car and a few clothes. She got carnal surprises and multiple orgasms from this hard-featured man who knew more ways to make her come than any man she had ever met.

One of her favorites was a novel little trick with a loaded revolver.

CHAPTER FORTY-SIX

IT WAS a laughing Laura that pulled up before the locked Music Gates that blistering hot August day. Her twenty-fifth birthday. The day Musicland would be closed forever to the public.

Buddy Hester at her side, Laura swept into the mansion and swept out the intruders. And when the last patron had been escorted through the gates along with the uniformed tour conductors, Laura gave a great shout of joy and sprinted across the lawn to the gleaming white marble tomb.

She fell to her knees on the manicured emerald lawn. Impulsively she kissed her fingers and pressed them to the smooth, sun-heated marble. "Never again will the curious set foot on these grounds," she declared. Smiling, she rose and flew back to the house.

She moved into Musicland that same week, bringing with her the 3525 cook and housekeeper and locating and rehiring many of the old crew from her daddy's days at the estate.

When the phone rang on her first night in the mansion, she answered it in the master bedroom. It was Griff.

"You get moved in, hon?"

"Yes, Griff, darling, and it's wonderful. I hadn't realized how very much I had missed this house. My home."

"I'm happy for you, sweetheart. I don't suppose I could talk you into spending one night away from Musicland, could I?"

"When, Griff?" was her answer.

"Tomorrow in Denver. I have to fly up for a—"

"I'll be there."

"Good. The Brown Palace. Meet you there around noon."

*   *   *

"I can't do everything around here," snapped Valentina Trent, addressing the department heads assembled around the conference table. "I've spent my life at this office, night and day, for years. I'd like a little more free time." She looked at her watch. "I've a headache and I want to go home. Is it too much to expect you to take some of the burden off my shoulders?"

They looked at her. They looked at each other. They were worried about her and they were worried about the future of Bluebonnet Records. The company had become a ship without a captain and it was drifting, going nowhere, moving dangerously close to the rapids. Yet despite her demands for more help, Valentina refused to delegate authority as Neil Allen had done.

Jealously she guarded her position, while at the same time displaying a lethargy that spelled doom to the company's future. If her executives made no decisions, she upbraided them, if they made decisions, it was worse. Clearly, she was losing interest in the company that had meant so much to her. Every employee at the conference table knew the reason.

Ryker Rawley.

This man, they all knew, was no passing fancy as had been her artist-lovers of the past. He had a powerful hold on Valentina Trent and that fact was brought home to them on days like this one when, with profits tumbling, she refused to remain at the meetings, choosing to ignore the troubled company in order to rush home to Ryker Rawley.

"I pay you good wages," Valentina said angrily, "see if you can't come up with a few answers on your own!" And she stormed out of the room.

At her White Rock home she found Ryker and a business-suited gentleman in the living room. Ryker was looking at expensive watches from a jeweler's velvet tray. Cartier's had obligingly sent the man out from their Galleria Mall boutique. Valentina Trent would be paying.

"Darling," Valentina said, crossing to Ryker and eagerly sitting down beside him, a possessive hand going immediately to his thigh.

He didn't greet her nor introduce her to the jeweler. "Which one do you like best? This one or this?" he said, holding up two heavy gold timepieces.

"Mmmmm, this," she indicated the one in his right hand, sure it was the least expensive of the two.

Ryker tossed it back into the tray. "I'll take this one," he picked the watch she failed to choose. Clasping it on his pale wrist, he rose. "Write the man a check, Valentina," he said, over his shoulder as he left the living room.

Gritting her teeth, Valentina smiled at the Cartier employee, wrote out a check for forty thousand dollars, and showed him to the door. She needed a drink. She headed for the library and the long oak bar, noticing, as she did each time she came into the room, the naked wall above the mantle where C.C.'s Sears guitar had hung for so many years.

It was one of the many times she and Ryker had fought. She had come home one afternoon to find the guitar missing and, frantic, had rushed from room to room hunting for the treasure. While she searched, questioning all the servants, and considering calling the police, Ryker arrived home.

"I took the goddamned guitar," he coldly told her, "and I sold it to Slim down on Ervay street."

Hand at her throat. "But why? My God, why would you do such a thing, you know how much that guitar meant to me."

He laughed and poured himself a Chivas Regal. "More than me?"

"No, certainly not, but still . . ."

"I asked you to leave some money for me. You didn't do it. You went off to the office and left me without a cent."

"Dear god, couldn't you have called me and . . ."

"That will teach you to go off without giving me any money. Besides, I was sick of looking at that fuckin' guitar."

Furious, Valentina immediately called up the pawnbroker. But it was too late. A kid had come in off the street and bought it. Slim couldn't tell her who. It was gone.

Sipping straight gin, Valentina shook her head remembering that day, and how mad she had been at Ryker. She was mad at him again today. Forty thousand dollars for a watch! The nerve of the man.

She set down the half-empty liquor glass and rushed up the stairs. Ryker stood before the mirror, brushing his dark hair, the expensive watch gleaming on his wrist.

"Darling," she began, "while I want you to have the finest of everything, my company is not having one of it's best years and . . ."

Cold gray eyes turned on her. "Where's the problem? You control Big Chief. Put all those songs and movies back on the market."

"Never. I told you how I feel about that."

He lowered the brush. "Wouldn't it be satisfying for us to spend the money the bastard worked so hard to make?"

She shook her red head. "You're forgetting. That would mean his bitch daughter would get money too." She narrowed her eyes. "I'll keep that fortune tied up forever before I see her have one dime of it." She looked up at him. "Wouldn't you like to make her pay?"

Ryker smilingly recalled a sobbing, heartbroken young girl in a hot Mexican hotel room. "I have made her pay," he mumbled, his gray eyes slits of cruelty as he took a vial of snowy white powder from atop Valentina's dresser.

"What did you say?"

He sniffed some of the magic powder up his left nostril. "Nothing. I didn't say anything." He sniffed more up the other side.

Valentina touched the shiny new watch. "What do I get for buying you this, Ryker?"

"Fucked."

"Oh, darling, yes."

Deep in the heart of Texas it was celebration time. The Lone Star State's Sesquicentennial Anniversary. Festivals and rodeos and parades and fiddlers' contests and bar-b-ques and concerts and speeches and dances and tributes.

Texas' favorite sons were honored across the vast state. In Dallas, one of their most famous favorite sons would have been fifty years old on his state's one-hundred-and-fiftieth birthday.

The Sesquicentennial Committee asked if Laura would appear at a ceremony honoring her father. She agreed, and standing under the clear Texas sky on San Jacinto day, she graciously accepted a silver plaque shaped like the state of Texas; a gleaming gold star with diamonds denoting Dallas.

TEXAS SHINING STAR
C.C. McCARTY

"I accept, for my daddy, this honor bestowed by the people he loved most in all the world. Fellow Texans." She smiled and held the gleaming silver plaque high so the enormous crowd could see it. "I thank you. Daddy would have been pleased."

Laura descended the stairs of the raised, flag-draped podium to find her mother, emerald eyes bright with unshed tears, waiting at the bottom of the steps.

"Laura," Caroline said, "will you give me just a minute? That's all I ask."

Laura handed the silver plaque to Buddy. "Yes, Mother, I will. Where's Donny?"

"He's at the ranch. I . . . I wanted a chance to . . . I hoped you might . . ."

"Come on," she took her mother's arm and guided her through the crowd, Buddy and Hal Alcott running interference for them.

At Musicland, Caroline sat sipping iced tea in the high-ceilinged house where she once had lived.

"I know you'll never forgive me for writing the book about your daddy, but at least let me explain why I did it."

"Alright," said Laura.

Caroline drew a shallow breath. "Laura, from the time I was born, I never knew what it was like to be without money. I had everything I ever wanted. I married your daddy and had even more. Then when I divorced The Chi . . . when I divorced C.C. and married Donny, I . . . he . . . we didn't have much, just the ranch that C.C. gave us. I thought it wouldn't matter, that we could live on love." She lowered her eyes. "It was hard, Laura. Very hard. I didn't like doing without the things I was used to having." She raised her head and looked at Laura. "Have you any idea what it's like to fix your own hair, to do your own nails? Make your own bed?"

"Mother, I . . ."

"No. I mean it. I loved Donny. I love Donny, but we were having such a tough time and then Doubleday called me out of the blue and offered a half-million advance for a book."

"I understand," said Laura.

"I thought I'd write a nice little book about your daddy's triumphs but . . . they wanted more about his private life and then . . . Oh, Laura, I said things, told them things that . . . I don't know . . . When I saw it all in print, it sounded so much worse." Caroline had begun to quietly cry. She took a kleenex from her handbag and dabbed her eyes. "I said so many things that . . ."

"You said he used women."

"I know, and . . ."

"Mother, women used him as well," said Laura.

Caroline nodded. "I know. I know. Including me, I suppose."

"Why did you marry daddy when you didn't love him?" Laura's black eyes were on her mother's tear-stained face.

Caroline weakly smiled. And she said, "Have you any idea how very foolish and impressionable a sheltered eighteen-year-old girl can be? When I first met your daddy I was . . ."

Laura listened intently while Caroline explained how easy it had been for the handsome, worldly C.C. to sweep her off her feet so completely that she would have done anything, would have gone anywhere with him. And Laura's pain-hardened heart softened completely. She well remembered how effortlessly the compelling Ryker Rawley had done the same thing to her.

Could she blame her mother for behaving as she herself had done? Was it Caroline's fault that she'd wound up married before she had had time to catch her breath?

Feeling tears sting her eyes, Laura was beside Caroline on the Chippendale sofa, her long, slender arms wrapped around her mother.

"Don't cry, mother, it's alright. It's all okay. Don't cry anymore."

"Oh, Laura," sobbed Caroline, "I'm sorry. Can you ever forgive me?"

"Of course I can. I love you, mother. I forgive you."

An hour later a greatly relieved Caroline Wheeler descended the marble steps of Musicland. Laura stood waving, promising she would come out to the ranch soon, reminding Caroline that she could come and choose from any of the Musicland antiques and have them moved to *Cielo Vista*.

Watching the gleaming blond head disappear into Caroline's three-year-old Chevrolet, Laura felt good about their reconciliation. She didn't realize, until this afternoon, how much she had missed her beautiful mother.

Smiling, Laura went back inside. The phone was ringing. "I'll get it," she called and lifted the receiver.

"Laura, it's Griff. Annette passed away three hours ago."

"Oh, my darling, I'm so sorry."

CHAPTER FORTY-SEVEN

CHRISTMAS time in Dallas. Millions of colored lights decorated the city and downtown, silver tinsel, shimmering in the cold winter winds, stretched from lamppost to lamppost, across the busy streets. Faithful Salvation Army soldiers rang their bells and thanked passersby for coins tossed into their baskets. Christmas music boomed from strategically placed loudspeakers on the towering buildings, and laughing shoppers streamed in and out of stores, arms filled with packages.

High up in the Allied Bank Tower at Fountain Place, Lone Star Records employees drank eggnog and nibbled on canapes. Laura McCarty, smiling, had every reason to be happy this Christmas season.

The man she loved would soon be her husband.

"Neil," she leaned close to her vice president's ear, "I have to get to the airport and pick up Griff. Keep the party . . . and the company . . . going for me."

"Don't worry about a thing, Laura." Neil Allen smiled at her. "Be happy, dear."

"Thanks, Neil. Merry Christmas," she kissed his cheek and was gone.

Griff Deaton arrived at Love Field all smiles and kisses for Laura. In minutes the happy pair were at Musicland, stretched out on the worn sofa in the library, going over their plans for the holiday wedding.

Laura speaking: "Tomorrow, Christmas Eve, Arto and Missy are throwing a big reception at North Dallas Forty. Christmas day we have the turkey dinner here . . . Mother and Donny and everyone. Then midnight on Christmas, we get married in this room and leave immediately for Montenegro. Have I forgotten anything?"

"Yes," said Griff, grinning.

"What?" her well-arched black eyebrows lifted.

"I've been here almost an hour and you haven't told me how much you love me."

"Oh, Griff," she pressed her face to the curve of his neck and shoulder, "I do. I love you so much it scares me."

His muscular arms held her close. He kissed her gleaming hair. "It shouldn't. I love you, darling, and—"

"Griff, am I asking too much?" She lifted her head and looked down into his eyes. "Giving up a highly successful career in Houston. On top of that, living here at Musicland. Is it unfair? Is it too selfish of me?"

"Sweetheart, I've told you, if there were no you, I would still leave Houston. That part of my life is over and as for living here at Musicland," he grinned boyishly, "if it makes you happy, it's fine with me. I don't care where I live, as long as it's with you."

"Griff, I'll make you happy. I promise."

"Darlin' you already have. Make me happier. Kiss me."

While Laura and Griff were embracing, Buddy Hester, grinning from ear to ear, knocked on the doorframe and waited. Laura's dark head shot up and she blushed, frantically shoving her skirt down.

"Bud, come on in. Griff and I were . . ."

"Hate to bother you, but I've got some news I thought you'd want to hear."

"No bother," said Griff graciously, swinging his long legs to the floor and rising. "Fix you a drink?"

"Nothing, Griff. Laura, a musician pal just called. C.C.'s old Sears guitar has shown up in a Vegas pawnshop. Want to send one of the boys out there to get it?"

"Yes, Buddy," Laura said excitedly. "You're sure it's daddy's? I don't understand how . . . I've wanted that . . . Oh, Buddy call the pilots right away and get someone out to—"

"What the hell, it's Christmas," Griff cut in. "Why don't we fly out and pick it up ourselves?"

Laura's eyes sparkled. "You mean it? Griff, you just got in."

"I never felt better. Let's go to Vegas."

It was cold and dry in the desert. Crystal clear and sunny; shadows lengthening as the hotel limo eased to a stop before Ace Loan Company on Fremont Street downtown. Laura and Griff hurried inside. Impatient to have the sentimentally valuable guitar in her possession, Laura had to wait.

The man behind the counter was busy with a customer. The customer was a short, slim man. His disheveled silver hair needed cutting. He hadn't shaved in days. He was removing a wide gold band from his finger as he said, "Bill, what happens if I can't get you the money in time?"

The pawnbroker, eyes magnified behind thick glass lens, said, "It's the gas pipe for you, friend."

The borrower nodded his shaggy silver head and reluctantly handed the ring across the glass counter, his shoulders drooping beneath an ill-fitting jacket.

"Ash," Laura silently mouthed his name, recognizing the voice. Dropping Griff's arm, she hurried forward. "Ash. Ash Ashford!" She was shouting now.

Ash slowly turned. His face, in need of a shave, was thinner and not nearly as bronze as she remembered. He wore a thin, threadbare suit jacket, a cotton knit shirt, and a pair of frayed khaki pants. No socks on his feet. But he wasn't dirty.

"Laura?" he blinked, disbelievingly. "Little Laura?"

"You folks want to hold a family reunion, do it out there on the sidewalk," said Bill the pawnbroker, clasping the gold wedding ring in his fist, "this is a place of business."

Ignoring Bill, Laura said, smiling, "Yes, Uncle Ash, it's Laura." And impulsively threw her arms around him and hugged the man whom she had vowed never to forgive.

Ash Ashford swallowed hard. When she released him, his fingers with their ragged nails went up to graze his stubbly chin. "You just caught me on a bad day, Laura. I'm usually more presentable."

"You look good to me," said Laura and turned to the pawnbroker. "Give him back the ring."

"It'll cost you some interest," snapped Bill.

Griff shook hands with the small, unkempt Ash while Laura insisted Ash join them for dinner. Gratefully, he accepted.

So with Ash and the guitar in tow, they headed for Caesar's where they checked into a suite and ordered a lavish meal from room service. And Ash Ashford told Laura and Griff about the past ten years of his life.

"You know Charmaine left me." Laura nodded. "I came out to Vegas, shilled for a while over at the Riviera. Did okay, but couldn't quit gambling. They fired me and I moved on to the Silver Slipper and dealt blackjack for a couple of years. When I lost that none of the strip joints would give me a job, so I moved downtown." He talked on and on, telling without emotion how he had slowly but surely wound up where they had found him, hocking his last earthly possession, his wedding ring.

"It was a short step from the limo to the gutter." Ash laughed and they did too.

And before the evening was over, Laura had persuaded Ash Ashford to return to Dallas with them; to work for Lone Star.

"I need you, Ash," she told him.

Blinking back the tears of gratitude, Ash said truthfully, "Well, honey, you don't have to ask if I need you."

"I do," said a radiant Laura to Griff Deaton in the midnight Musicland wedding ceremony. Twelve hours later, Griff laughingly carried her across the threshold of the Montenegrin cliff house where they had met.

For a long, lazy week they remained in guarded seclusion, at peace with themselves and their world. They made love, slept, read, drank wine, and watched the sunset from the balcony high above the Adriatic. For the first time in her life, Laura cooked . . . or tried to. And was happily surprised to learn her big, masculine husband was an excellent chef.

"Is there nothing you can't do?" she asked when he placed before her a plate of smoked tenderloin of beef with vegetables in flour tortillas.

Pouring Pouilly-Fuissé into her wine glass, he nodded. "I can't sing." And he winked at her.

They lingered over their meal and when finally Laura rose to clear the plates away, Griff poured more wine and tuned in the radio to Radio Free Europe. Mellow music filled the room and Laura sang along while Griff stretched out before the fireplace.

When the song ended, he said, "You sure inherited your father's voice, sweetheart."

Laura smiled. She came to him. "When I was a little girl, all I ever wanted to be was a singer. I'd stand before the mirror and practice by the hour. I just knew I would be a big star like my daddy."

"You could be."

Violently, she shook her head. "I just want to be your wife. And to get daddy's company back from Valentina Trent."

"I could make you as big a star as C.C.," said impeccably groomed, deeply bronzed Ash Ashford as he looked across the desk at Laura one May afternoon. It was not the first time he had mentioned it. Ever the manager, he dreamed of seeing her up there where her daddy had been, with world tours and hit singles and platinum albums. And he knew, deep down, that she dreamed of it as well.

"Hmmm?" was her distracted reply.

"God he was magnificent," Ash went on. "Even now, thirty years later, I can vividly recall C.C.'s energy, strength, and presence of bearing when he stood on that stage in Shreveport. He was just a kid . . . nineteen years old . . . but what power, what looks . . ." His eyes clouded. He cleared his throat. "You have the same good looks, the same—"

"Ash," she put down her pen and looked him in the eye, "you've been with me six months now and we've been over this a dozen times. If anyone knows what fame can do to a person, it's you. And me. I'm happy, I love Griff, and I'd never do anything to risk losing him."

Ash, standing, pushed back his suitcoat and shoved his well-tended hands deep into the pants pockets of his custom-tailored suit. "It could be a whole different ballgame with you, hon. You're not—"

"Ash, no."

He sighed. "Okay, but answer me this, Laura. And answer truthfully. Aren't there times when you wish you were up there on Caesar's stage holding the crowd in the palm of your hand the way C.C. did?"

Only every day of my life. "No," she said. "No, there's not."

"Am I interrupting something?" It was Griff. He stood in the doorway.

Laura's face lit up like a Christmas tree and all talk of performing was forgotten. "No," she said softly, awed, as she always was, by the imposing, pleasing sight of him.

Grinning, he said, "Stay where you are, Ash," when Ash started for the door. "I finally have good news for Laura and I think it will interest you as well."

Laura tensed. She knew that her husband, from his offices in the LTV Center, had quietly been looking into Valentina Trent's life, hunting for anything that might be helpful in their struggle to regain Big Chief. She also knew that Griff was very busy, his newly established practice doing remarkably well due to his reputation in the Texas legal community. If it wasn't something important, he wouldn't have left his office in the middle of the afternoon.

She eyed the rust-colored accordion folder he held in his right hand.

"I've finally put it all together," said Griff, easing his big frame down into a guest chair, stretching his long legs out before him. "Valentina Trent is vulnerable on several counts. In the first place, she is not Valentina Trent. She was never married to Kirkland Trent."

"What?" Laura and Ash spoke in unison.

"Trent neglected to divorce his first wife. She left him, went East, and neither ever bothered getting a divorce. He married Valentina alright, but it was bigamy."

"I can't believe it," said Laura.

"There's more. Valentina was born in Mexico to a poor laborer and his wife. Her last name is Perez. The family entered the country illegally and worked in the Texas Valley as produce pickers. Valentina, when she was fourteen, hitchhiked to Dallas, giving her name as Jones."

"She's a Mexican?" It was Ash.

"Yes. She's Valentina Perez from Chihuahua, Mexico."

"Where the hell did she get that red hair and fair skin?"

Griff lifted wide shoulders. "I'd say some Anglo was more than friends with her mother."

"So smug old Valentina Trent has never been a wife or a U. S. citizen," Laura had risen and come around to lean back against her marble desk. "Griff, darling, you're wonderful."

"Sweetheart, I don't deserve all the credit. The beautiful Consul General of Venezuela had a hand in it."

"Missy helped you?"

"Missy got in touch with the governor of Chihuahua. Calls him by his first name. She called Gilberto and asked if he would do her one tiny little favor. He had met her at one of those consular functions and was so taken with her, he would have agreed to anything. He put a team of his people to work looking up birth records in the state." Griff laughed and shook his head. "Missy called me and said, '*Bueno nuevas, mi amigo, la Senora Valentina Trent ees Senorita Perez de Republica de Mexico. Hasta la vista!*'"

"Jesus Christ," said Ash.

"Halleujah," said Laura. She leaned down and kissed her husband and said to both men, "I do hope you two will excuse me, I've got some unfinished business to take care of."

Griff grinned, knowing exactly what she intended. He handed her the accordion folder. "It's all here." She nodded.

"Where you going?" asked Ash.

Jerking her Gucci bag from the credenza and slinging it over her shoulder, Laura, black eyes dancing, said, "Gentlemen, I'm going to get my company back!"

CHAPTER FORTY-EIGHT

LAURA'S anticipation rose along with the high-speed elevator whisking her up to Bluebonnet Records' penthouse suite. Smiling, she stepped out into the corridor, swept through the double glass doors, and ignoring the secretary's protests, marched straight into Valentina's office, calmly fanning herself with a cashier's check for five hundred thousand dollars.

"What in the name of God . . ." said a surprised Valentina. Then, into the telephone receiver, "No, no, not you, Ryker, darling . . . We'll talk later." She hung up and shot to her feet, pointing to the door. "I don't know what you're doing here, but get the hell out."

"I'm here to buy back Big Chief." Laura, smile firmly in place, extended her arm, presenting the check to Valentina. "A cashier's check for five hundred thousand dollars."

Valentina, smirking, sat back down. "May I suggest, Mrs. Deaton, that you'll want to crinkle that check up real good before you wipe your skinny ass with it." She folded her hands atop the desk.

"May I suggest, Miss Perez, that you firmly consider my offer." Laura took a chair, crossing her long legs, placing the rust-colored accordion folder on her lap, and tapping the check against her chin.

A brief look of confusion filled Valentina's brown eyes. Her smile slipped ever so slightly. "It's been ages since I was Miss anything and never was I Miss Perez."

Laura smiled and ceremoniously placed the cashier's check midway between herself and Valentina. She set the rust-colored folder atop the desk. "You were and are," she said, and opening the folder, drew from it a yellow sheet of paper. "Born Valentina Perez to Maria and Juan Perez in Chi-

344

huahua, Mexico on June 3, 1928." She set the birth certificate neatly alongside the cashier's check. "Perhaps this will help jog your memory."

Valentina took the document and hurriedly glanced at it, knowing all too well what it said. Her fear and her temper were rapidly rising, but she was determined not to let Laura McCarty Deaton know. Steeling herself, she lowered the item and smiled across the desk.

"Well, good for you," she said, nodding her head, "you and that pituitary case of a husband have finally uncovered something you think you can use." Calmly dropping the birth certificate on the desk, she laughed, deep in her throat. "Hardly. It doesn't make a great deal of difference where, or to whom, I was born."

"You're wrong, Valentina," Laura leaned back in her chair. "The first thing you'll have to do in a federal court is prove U. S. citizenship. You can't."

Valentina's brown eyes flickered only an instant. She steepled her fingers together and said, "But I can. As I said, it's been a long time since I was a Miss. I married a powerful U. S. citizen. Kirkland Trent. Correct me if I'm wrong. After marrying Kirkland, I automatically became a citizen of the United States." Again she laughed. "You see, your overgrown ambulance-chasing attorney husband is not the only one who knows a little about the law. You should give me more credit, don't you think? I am an American citizen," she tapped her silk-covered full breasts with a forefinger, "I'm Kirkland Trent's widow."

"No," said Laura, drawing from the folder an 8 × 10 glossy, "this is Kirkland Trent's widow."

Totally at a loss, Valentina, her composure slipping, snatched up the photograph. "What is this? What are you trying to pull, you little hussy?"

"Mrs. Kirkland Trent . . . and here's her marriage license," Laura carefully arranged the marriage license alongside the picture, birth certificate, and five hundred thousand dollar cashier's check, "is very much alive in Atlantic City, New Jersey and—"

"But . . . it can't be . . . she was just his first wife and I—"

"His only wife, Valentina. Trent may have gone through a quickie ceremony with you in Oklahoma, but he neglected to get a divorce first. He never sought a divorce. Nor did Nellie Trent. The only Mrs. Trent."

"No," screeched a horrified Valentina, "no . . . no."

"Yes," said Laura. "Poor Mrs. Trent. The old woman is in her eighties. She lives on social security, hardly makes ends meet." Laura went no further, allowing the threat to sink in.

Suddenly sick and dizzy, Valentina's shocked eyes scanned the damning documents, her mind spinning. "I don't care," she hissed, grasping at straws. "It doesn't matter. Trent wanted me to have the company, he loved me and—"

"He may have loved you, Valentina, but a federal court won't be swayed by sentimentality. He died intestate, his entire estate is legally his wife's."

"The hell with her. I was his common-law wife," Valentina was panicky. "That's it. I was Trent's common-law wife and deserve—"

"It won't wash. You lived with Kirkland Trent only five years. I don't know what the laws are south of the border, but here in Texas you must live with a man seven years to become his common-law wife. And then, of course, only if the man in question is not already married. Which Trent most definitely was."

Valentina's fair face had flooded with blood, it was fire engine red, except for a white line of anger around her tight mouth.

"Here," Laura poured a glass of water from a silver pitcher sitting on the edge of Valentina's desk. "Drink this, you look a little hot."

Valentina's hand shot out and knocked the water from Laura's, sending the heavy leaded glass sailing across the room, water spraying the carpet.

"Oh? Not thirsty?" said Laura, "Alrightee. Shall we talk now about Big Chief?"

Shaking with fright and anger, Valentina snapped, "I don't want to talk to you about anything, ever. I want you out of here!"

"You're boring me. Let's get this over with," said Laura, the smile now missing, and she drew from the rust-colored folder its final document. "You, Valentina are an illegal alien, in this country unlawfully."

"So what?" Valentina's heart was racing, "You can't blackmail me, you little cunt, because I never gave a good goddamn what Dallas society thought of me. I have what I want. Tell the world I'm a wetback, I don't care." She managed a smile. "And as I told you, take that check and—"

"You haven't been listening," said Laura, exercising great patience. "An illegal alien can't own a U. S. company, so Bluebonnet—"

"Damn you! Bluebonnet is mine!"

"And Big Chief is mine, Valentina. I want it back and I'm willing to pay you five hundred thousand dollars. Exactly what you paid for it."

"Big Chief is worth millions!"

"And it was worth millions when you stole it from Ash." Laura rose and, placing the transfer contract before Valentina, said, "Listen to me, you vindictive old bitch, all I want is my company. Nothing more. You take the check and sign these papers or . . ."

"Or what?" said Valentina, rising to face her.

"Lose it all," said Laura, "Big Chief. Bluebonnet. The yacht *Valentine*, the White Rock mansion." She paused, inhaled and softly added, "And Ryker Rawley."

"No," screamed Valentina. "Not Ryker. Not my darling Ryker . . ."

"Ryker Rawley won't stay with you five minutes if you're without Blue-bonnet . . . without money."

"He will. He loves me and . . . he . . ."

Laura smiled, leaned over, and punched in the intercom button, "Tell your secretary to come in to witness your signature, Valentina."

"He loves me, Ryker loves me," murmured Valentina.

"Yes?" came Viola's voice.

"Will you step in here a minute, please," said Laura.

Zombielike, Valentina scrawled her signature on the document selling Big Chief to Laura McCarty Deaton for five hundred thousand dollars. A disbelieving Viola witnessed and notarized it.

"You may go, Viola," Laura told the pinch-faced woman and Viola backed away.

Laura gathered up all the documents, stacked them neatly, and returned them to the rust-colored accordion folder. She picked up the cashier's check and handed it across the desk. Valentina, stricken, stared at it, never lifting her hands from the chair arms. Laura stepped around the desk and stuffed the check into the breast pocket of Valentina's silk blouse.

"Cheer up, Valentina," she said. "None of this will leave this room. I want no revenge; all I want is Big Chief."

"Ryker," Valentina was glassy-eyed. "All I want is Ryker. I couldn't bear losing him. You don't want me to have Ryker."

"Lord, are you mistaken there, Mrs. Trent. You'll never know how pleased I am that you have Ryker Rawley."

Overjoyed, Laura, the folder tucked under her right arm, walked from the Republic Tower to Allied Bank Tower, smiling all the way, nodding and speaking to strangers on the street, a glorious feeling of exhilaration giving an added spring to her step, a heightened beauty to the balmy Texas day.

Her life was finally what she had always hoped it would be. She was married to the most wonderful man on earth and he loved her as much as she loved him. Together they would spend the rest of their days at her beloved Musicland.

And she had her daddy's company back.

Within a week all C.C. McCarty movies and albums were on the market. You couldn't turn on the radio without hearing him sing in that rich, sensual voice, nor the television set without seeing that handsome face. Theaters across the country re-released his movies and people stood in line to see The Chief. A whole new generation of teenagers discovered him and his records topped the charts just as they had when he had first cut them.

Royalties poured into the Big Chief Corporation. Eleven years after his death, the Chief was earning millions and millions of dollars for the estate. More than he'd earned when he lived. Laura McCarty Deaton was once again one of the richest young women in Texas.

And one of the happiest.

With the loss of Big Chief, Valentina lost all interest in the world of business. She ignored her executives when they warned her Bluebonnet was in bad financial trouble. Her heart was no longer in it; she refused to "waste her time" in the company's day-to-day operations.

She had only one interest.

The cruel sexual athlete, Ryker Rawley.

Failing to see that she had done what she always congratulated herself on being too smart to do, she had, from the beginning, allowed him to become the buyer, she the bought. The money was hers, but he called all the shots, just as she had with Kirkland Trent.

Valentina reasoned that she had ordered Trent about, certainly, but she, in her own way, had also loved him. It was the same with Ryker ruling her, he liked to give her a hard time, but he loved her, just as she had loved Kirkland Trent.

She refused to believe otherwise.

So she endured it, and halfway enjoyed it, if Ryker slapped her around when he was angry. She didn't object when he charged expensive items to her accounts, or paid vast sums to drug dealers, or stole from the mansion.

And she certainly didn't object when he was in one of his moods for marathon lovemaking. Usually kinky and wild. Sometimes savage. Always profane, but immensely satisfying to her. How she savored those sordid sex festivals!

When he was in that frame of mind, she eagerly urged him up to their room and anxiously stripped. And saw to it he had all the raw oysters and rare steaks and Chivas Regal and pure cocaine he wanted.

She always grew breathless when he reached under the bed and drew out his gun. More than once she had watched him load it and felt a delicious shiver of anticipation skip up her naked spine.

And when he expertly aroused her with it, aiming for all sorts of erotic stimulation, the added danger was glorious, the excitement almost unbearable.

*　　*　　*

It was one of the rare days when Valentina was at Bluebonnet. She had come to sign the payroll checks. That task accomplished, she sat in her office, idle, feeling more than a little melancholy. And old.

I'm sixty years old . . . almost sixty-one, she thought sadly. And Ryker's only forty-one. She shuddered. How long would he find her attractive? How long could she hold him?

She took her handbag from the bottom drawer and rummaged through it, hunting a mirror. She shoved the purse aside and lifted the gold compact. Studying herself appraisingly, she caught sight of movement behind her. She swiveled her chair around.

A scaffolding with two coveralled men was lowering into place. Valentina smiled, fondly recalling the old days when she was young and desirable and Kirkland Trent had made love to her while workmen watched. Her heart began to beat a little faster. Why not? Why not brighten up their boring day and at the same time lift her sagging spirits, reassure herself she was still a sensual, attractive woman.

Patiently waiting until their rugged faces were visible through the plate glass, Valentina slowly lifted her skirt, an inviting smile curving her lips. The men absently glanced at her, nothing more. Disappointed, she went a step further. She wiggled out of her lace panties.

Nothing.

One workman just shook his head. The other never slowed the pace of his window washing.

Shocked, hurt, she whirled around, her ego suffering a brutal blow. How could she excite them? What would she have to do to . . .

The smile returned and she snapped her fingers. Jerking up the receiver, she dialed home. No, Ryker was not there, a servant said. She dialed the cellular phone in Ryker's new Jaguar twelve-cylinder X car and sighed with gratitude when he picked it up.

"Darling," she said, breathlessly, "how far are you from my office?"

"Around the corner," said Ryker, failing to mention he had spent the afternoon at the Anatole Hotel with a Dallas Cowboy cheerleader.

"Wonderful. Come up immediately."

"What for?"

She giggled girlishly. "To 'give me the gun.' "

In minutes he walked into her office, and seeing her seated there, barebottomed, legs spread, in plain view of a couple of window washers, he was at once repulsed and aroused.

Slowly, he drew the gun.

"Is it loaded?" asked Valentina, her whole body trembling with expectation.

"Yes," he said, crossing to her. He stood looking down at her, his eyes flat and dead, his lips thinned. "You're really a disgusting old bitch, you know that, Valentina?"

"Please, darling, hurry." Her breathing was heavy.

"Get on the desk," he ordered, and with a swipe of his arm, cleaned off its surface. Valentina's handbag, compact, and wallet went flying. A cracked black-and-white snapshot, falling from the wallet, fluttered down. Ryker reached out and caught it with his left hand.

A young man with sandy hair, a wide, infectious smile, and aviator's goggles swinging from his sunburned neck.

Ryker stared at the picture and felt his mouth go dry, his chest constrict. "Where did you get this?"

Valentina, seated on the desk's edge, was puzzled. "Why? I've had it since I was a child. My mother gave it to me."

"You're lying," his gray eyes lifted to impale her. "You stole this from me. This is my picture."

"Stole it from . . . Come on, darling, we're wasting time."

"Goddammit, what are you doing with this snapshot?" His voice was deadly cold and a vein was throbbing on his pale forehead.

"It's a picture of my father. My real father. I don't even know his name. I'm illegitimate, if you must know. A Texas cropduster, working both sides of the border, was spraying the fields outside Chihuahua one summer. My mother slept with him. I'm the result. That's where I got my red hair. Now, please, forget about my father and give me the gun."

Ryker's hand crumpled the fading photograph as he looked, cold-eyed, at the aging, offensive woman before him. He felt a chill wash over him, followed at once by a knot of fire in the pit of his stomach.

"I'll give you the gun." His voice was deadly cold when he added, "Big sister."

And, tired of her, tired of himself, tired of living, he raised the revolver, pointed it directly between her eyes, and squeezed the trigger.

She never even had the chance to scream, so sudden was it. Her surprised brown eyes flickered briefly and rolled upward. A tiny hole appeared in the center of her forehead. Dark scarlet blood trickled down her brow to the bridge of her nose.

Ryker dropped the revolver to the carpet and moved to the windows. While the two startled workmen clung to the cables in horror, he walked out onto the scaffolding.

And silently stepped to his death, forty stories below.

CHAPTER FORTY-NINE

CRESCENT Court's Beau Nash for dinner was Griff's idea. He liked the mixture of tall, painted ceilings and massive mahogany columns and the enormous bar at the restaurant's center. He liked the exposed kitchen where a line of talented chefs created tempting cuisine. He liked the unobtrusive service and the sophisticated atmosphere. He liked his choice for the evening's meal—succulent sliced breast of duck with melon and kiwi.

Most of all he liked the raved-haired woman seated across from him, and he didn't tease her when she asked him to order her usual, a sirloin strip, extra well done.

"Burn it," he said to the waiter and smiled at his wife.

By the time they were having their coffee and cognac, Griff Deaton was a relaxed and satisfied man. Laura was in a talkative mood and she was regaling him with tales about the private lives of her colorful recording artists.

Using her hands to embellish a particular story, Laura lifted her arms, causing the tank top of her white crepe Valentino evening dress to slip dangerously low on her splendid, smooth-skinned bosom.

Enchanted, Griff interrupted, "Laura, honey, let's go upstairs."

Laura read the unmistakable message in her husband's low-lidded blue eyes. She smiled at him. "Griff, we're only fifteen minutes from Musicland."

"I can't wait fifteen minutes. Let's check in."

As soon as the door closed on their Crescent Court suite, Griff, his eyes locked with Laura's, gently peeled the white crepe bodice to her waist. She shivered. And softly laughed when he picked her up and carried her through the palatial sitting room with its original art and antique porcelains and deep carpets.

His lovemaking was exquisite and Laura purred and stretched and reveled in the bliss of having his hands and his lips so knowingly caress her. And then, lying on their sides, facing each other, they culminated the act, her slender leg curled around his ribcage, one of his big hands cupping her bare bottom.

Later Griff lay in the tumbled bed, hands locked behind his head, a smile on his face. He was listening to the rich, sensual voice of his wife coming through the open bathroom door. Chin deep in a marble tub filled with bubbles, Laura sang a song her daddy had cut back in the late 60s, "Love Me With All Your Heart."

When she walked back into the bedroom, toweling herself, she was still singing. Smiling at her husband, she came to the line, "When we are far apart, or when you're near me . . ." She put exactly the same inflection, the same slow, subtle drawing out of the word near, as did C.C. McCarty on the recording.

"Laura, come here," said her husband.

Wrapping the towel around her slender body, sarong style, she climbed onto the bed and sat cross-legged.

"What is it?"

"Sweetheart, do you want to be a singer?"

"No, Griff. Why would you think that?"

He grinned. "No reason I can think of."

She flushed. "I guess I sing too much."

"No. Never too much. I love to hear you. Your voice is beautiful. So beautiful, you should share it with the world."

For a moment she was silent. She stared at him. Then she said, "No, Griff."

"Why, sweetheart? Why don't you give it a try? Ash says you could make it to the top just like your daddy."

Nervously, she laughed. "You trying to get rid of me?"

"Never."

"Griff, I won't deny there are times I think about it." She laughed at herself. "Who am I kidding? I've spent half my life thinking about it. But I'm afraid. I might lose you and I couldn't bear it. Without his career, daddy would never have lost mother."

"You have it backward, angel." He reached out and toyed with the towel's hem. "Without his career, he would never have had her."

She thought a minute and said, "I guess you're right." Her eyes clouded.

"But success killed him. It very nearly ruined my life. The price of fame is far too high." She shuddered.

Griff Deaton, knowing his talented wife—though frightened and doubtful—would never be fulfilled if she didn't pursue her old dream, reached out and drew her to him, enfolding her in his arms.

"Darling, your daddy was a poor, uneducated kid from the west Dallas projects. He was unprepared for his phenomenal success. Overnight he was a superstar with everybody wanting a piece of him. His fame just ate him up."

"You're a sophisticated woman," he went on. "You were raised in a totally different environment. You've had attention and money all your life. You've weathered disappointments and cruelties and tragedies, and came through them all with your sanity and courage intact. You're stronger than your daddy, Laura. Fame will never destroy you. You wouldn't let it."

He kissed her hair and added, "I won't let it."

She pulled away and looked at him. "Griff Deaton, I could live all my life without performing, but I couldn't live a single day without you."

"Why not, my love, have both. Me and singing."

"I don't know. I'd have to give it a lot more thought," said Laura.

"That's fine. I won't mention it again. But remember, if you want to give it a try, I'll be your biggest fan."

She smiled and said, "Kiss me, fan."

He kissed her softly and turned out the bedside lamp. In moments the steady rise and fall of his broad chest beneath her arm told Laura her husband was sleeping.

It was a long time before she slept.

Her mind raced. Filled with thoughts of the past.

Her tuxedoed daddy, his dark eyes flashing with elation, standing before thousands of cheering fans.

Those same dark eyes, deep and brooding, his marriage shattered, his health failing.

She thought of the dead Valentina Trent. A woman so in love with C.C., she would rather see him destroyed than with another woman.

Ryker Rawley's cruelly handsome face rose in the darkness. Ryker, murmuring filth in her ear, hurting her, despising her, because she was C.C.'s daughter.

Stephen Flynn, wanting her, marrying her, only because he was in love with C.C. McCarty.

Trembling, Laura pressed closer to the warm, solid body of her husband. Her arm tightened over his chest and she buried her face beneath his strong chin.

And she wondered, what would the answer be if she could ask her daddy, "Was it worth it?"

CHAPTER FIFTY

THE temperature clock in the Sahara Hotel tower read 8:57 P.M. The time disappeared and the temperature was displayed—106 degrees. August in Las Vegas.

The waiters had cleared the tables. The lights began to dim in the big show room. The drum rolls started.

It was showtime in Circus Maximus.

The room had grown very quiet and still. The house lights went dark. All eyes were riveted to the stage. The heavy purple curtains slowly lifted while the crowd held its collective breath in anticipation. The stage, too, was dark, only the shiny brass instruments picking up reflective beams from the tiny mounted musician's lights. Nothing on stage was moving.

The drum rolls ended. There was absolutely no sound. On stage or off.

At least thirty seconds of silence elapsed.

A tiny pinpoint of light appeared at center stage. The baby-blue spot caught and framed a delicate blood-red rose in a circular pool of illumination. Slowly the circle of light grew larger. And larger. Until beneath the scarlet rose, a shimmering black evening gown and smooth olive shoulders were visible.

The awed audience made not a sound.

The light continued to pull further back, further back, revealing a beautiful, high-cheekboned face framed with gleaming raven hair.

She stood there in the spotlight, in the silence. Moving not one muscle.

Then suddenly she smiled; a brilliant, blinding smile.

And Laura raised the microphone and said, "Hello, everybody. I'm C.C.'s daughter."